Robert W. Patrick, E. B Williams

Knapsack and Rifle

Life in the Grand Army - war as seen from the ranks. Pen pictures and sketches of

camp, bivouac, marches, battle-fields and battles, commanders, great military

movements, personal reminiscences and narratives of army life

Robert W. Patrick, E. B Williams

Knapsack and Rifle
Life in the Grand Army - war as seen from the ranks. Pen pictures and sketches of camp, bivouac, marches, battle-fields and battles, commanders, great military movements, personal reminiscences and narratives of army life

ISBN/EAN: 9783337220938

Printed in Europe, USA, Canada, Australia, Japan

Cover: Foto ©Andreas Hilbeck / pixelio.de

More available books at **www.hansebooks.com**

KNAPSACK ⚔ RIFLE

-- OR --

LIFE IN THE GRAND ARMY

War as Seen from the Ranks

PEN PICTURES AND SKETCHES

OF CAMP, BIVOUAC, MARCHES, BATTLE-FIELDS AND BATTLES, COM-
MANDERS, GREAT MILITARY MOVEMENTS

PERSONAL REMINISCENCES AND NARRATIVES

OF ARMY LIFE, ADVENTURES, ESCAPES, HUMOROUS INCIDENTS, PATHETIC
INCIDENTS, HEROIC DEEDS, ETC., ETC.

ALSO

A COMPLETE CHRONOLOGY OF THE WAR

AND

A DIGEST OF THE PENSION LAWS OF THE UNITED STATES—STATEMENT
OF CASUALTIES—MONTHLY RATES OF PENSIONS—LATEST
ACTS OF CONGRESS GOVERNING PENSIONS, ETC.

BY

ONE OF THE BOYS

Copiously and Finely Illustrated

BY E. B. WILLIAMS

PORTLAND, OREGON:
J. K. GILL & COMPANY.
1889.

LET ME CLAIM
AS A COMRADE AND BROTHER
EVERY MAN WHO

Fought for the Old Flag.

TO ALL SUCH,
AS WELL AS TO A GRATEFUL PEOPLE,
WHO SUSTAINED OUR BRAVE BOYS
AND CHEERED THEM ON,
THESE PAGES ARE
INSCRIBED

BY ROBERT W. PATRICK.

WILSON'S CAVALRY.

SIGNAL CORPS.

KILPATRICK'S CAV.

SHERIDAN'S CAV.

FIVE FORKS.

ENG. & PONTONIER CORPS.

HANCOCK'S CORPS

CORPS BADGES OF THE UNION ARMY.

PREFACE.

THERE is little field for a general history of the war, but there is always a field for personal narrative and adventure, the recital of patriotic services and sacrifices.

Especially is it desirable for the American people to have a description of the great conflict, as the man saw it who carried the knapsack and rifle, and went into the thickest of the fight. The scenes and records in this book are real; the facts, by reason of their thrilling nature, called for no exaggeration.

The actual names of the persons introduced to the reader are used in only a few instances. Besides rendering the narrative too personal, real names would have made a distinction uncalled for, as thousands not named were as heroic as any celebrated here; but living men and heroes form the characters in the book. Many old army boys will recognize themselves and their acquaintances.

The narrative is followed by Chronological Tables of battles, numbers engaged, commanders, losses and results, the value of which cannot be over-estimated, and a Digest of the Pension Laws, which will be of great service.

CONTENTS.

ILLUSTRATIONS.

KNAPSACK AND RIFLE.

CHAPTER I.

THE CALL TO ARMS.

"I would do all in my power to make our cause win."—General Grant.

ITY of Philadelphia. A mild day in April, 1861.

Stirring news had just come. Flags were flying from ten thousand buildings. The streets were swarming with excited people. Around the bulletin boards of newspaper offices crowds were gathered, and enterprising newsboys were running to and fro, shouting, "Extra! Latest news! Extra!"

A white-haired old man with a sword in his hand was elbowing his way through the crowd toward one of the recruiting stations.

"Where are you going with that sword?" he was asked.

"I am taking it to my son, who expects to be a commissioned officer, and if he is prevented from going to wear it, I shall ask leave to put it on and take his place."

(11)

The old man looked as if seventy winters had bleached his locks. His was a specimen of the spirit that moved the multitude.

Business to a great extent was suspended. It was useless to talk of sales and collections. The stores might as well have lowered their shutters. Banks seemed to have gone into bankruptcy. Factories did not hum with any lively sound, and the thoughts and eyes of their workers were in the street. The excitement had found its way into every home, and the populace, moved by a common impulse and alarm, rushed to the main streets and thoroughfares, to get the latest intelligence. All were talking of the recent events and were earnestly discussing the situation. Groups of men were on the pavements and at the street corners; loud words were spoken, attended by gestures very emphatic, and above all was heard the reiterated cry of hoarse newsboys selling extras with the latest reports.

The flag-staff on Independence Hall, that old historic building where the Revolution was nursed, floated the Stars and Stripes. The faces of the signers of the Declaration of Independence which were hanging on the walls seemed to look more than usually grave, and one could easily have imagined that it would not be a miracle if the old Liberty Bell were to break its silence and with the same tongue that once proclaimed liberty now tell the nation of its peril. This intense feeling in the "Quaker City" was only one ripple on the great wave of the national uprising.

The land had been startled by the fall of Fort Sumter. One little man wearing a major's uniform in the United

States Army, after a spirited defense with his small garrison, had lowered his flag. Civil war was no longer a dream; the reality had come. Major Anderson had received the shot across Charleston harbor, which "was heard round the world." The newsboy's extra was not slow to sell. Men's faces wore a troubled look. The attack had been made, the spark had touched the magazine, the first capture by the Confederates had been announced.

Succeeding days did not allay the excitement. It seemed to grow deeper and more intense. President Lincoln called for 75,000 three months' volunteers. That call waked the nation from the pine forests of Maine to the Golden Gates of the Pacific. Next came the startling report that troops from Pennsylvania and Massachusetts had been attacked in the streets of Baltimore, and Nick Biddle, a colored man from Pottsville, had shed the first blood in the great conflict.

It was known to me that Captain Wall was raising a company of men for the Scots' Legion. I stepped into his recruiting station and said, "Captain, I have come to volunteer. I offer my services."

"I can't take you, Preston; I've more men now than I know what to do with."

"But I'm anxious to go; I shall be disappointed if I do not get the chance."

"Go later," said the captain; "arrange your business affairs and be ready."

I had youth on my side, no family to leave behind, and as for business, concluded my best business was to shoulder a gun. Wall was not the only recruiting officer who had to turn away men.   The ranks filled rapidly, and applications in many instances were made for places that should become vacant.

One thing I could do; I could join the home-guard. People smiled sometimes at the home-guard, but not a few who afterwards became fine soldiers received in its ranks their first drill, and prepared themselves for more active service.   For several weeks I went through the movements, and do not think I was much more awkward than most of the squad to which I belonged.

We sometimes got left for right, attempted to charge when told to halt, shouldered our sticks when ordered to ground arms, faced about in the wrong direction, made a straight line in the form of a letter S, and went through other movements equally astonishing, and which showed our profound disregard of the orders given by our commander.   We could execute a flank movement, each man for himself, and get so indiscriminately mixed that we had to be picked out and assorted.

When ordered to ground arms and were given to understand that it meant placing the end of the weapon on the ground, the noise was not like the sound of a pistol, but more like that of a pack of fire-crackers which wants about three minutes to get through with the business.   Yet practice and patience brought order out of confusion, and people had not much doubt but that we could defend the city triumphantly so long as the enemy was south of the Potomac.   In justice, however, it must be said that the home-guard did not perform deeds of valor for the reason that the occasion was never presented.

Our forces having been defeated at Bull Run, and the President having already called for 500,000 volunteers, I again offered my services, was accepted, and went with Captain Hampton to Suffolk Park, where our regiment awaited marching orders. Being but eight miles out of the city, we received many visits from roughs and desperadoes, who were rendered unusually bold by the excitement of war and the scenes of the camp.

"Halt!" I said to one who was attempting to cross the lines; "you must have a pass!"

"Confound your pass; I want no pass!"

"But you can't cross these lines without one. Stand back!"

"I'm going where I please."

He went where he didn't please, for he went sprawling in the dirt, and the blow that felled him was not from any weapon.

In an instant he drew an ugly-looking knife, and his glaring eye told plainly that he was ready for mischief. One or two of my men seized and disarmed him. This man afterward joined a regiment, and was sent for two years to the Dry Tortugas as a punishment for insubordination. That seemed to cure him, and he made from this time on a good soldier, and a very respectable citizen on his return from the army.

This incident shows the desperate character of many who found their way into the ranks. They were raked out of the slums. And in those ranks could be found the very flower of the land—young men who were college-bred, and had turned aside from lucrative and honorable callings to uphold the old flag. The sons of merchants, bankers, wealthy manufacturers, ministers, lawyers, statesmen, were all there. The home of luxury was left behind. The plow stood still, and the farmer's boy was off to the front. Mothers gave their only sons the last embrace and the blessing that was remembered in the dying hour. Husbands parted with wives and children, and the brave young fellows who had fixed the day when they would stand at the marriage-altar went forth un-wedded to lay their lives upon the altar of their country. Women were no less patriotic than their lovers and brothers. Their busy fingers got ready the lint and bandages for the wounded, and with ardent wishes and hope they followed the fortunes of the war.

We did not have to wait long to get orders from Washington. We went on, although but partially armed and equipped, and there had another experience of life in camp. Washington wore during those days a decidedly military aspect. Troops to the right—troops to the left—troops in front—troops in the rear! One could not escape the omnipresent soldier. Officers galloped hither and yon; the roll of drums filled the air; long trains of supplies came pouring in, and each day added to the number of the regiments arriving from distant points; there was a continual marching and drilling; busy preparations went on night and day, and the Capital, with its wide streets, and the open spaces surrounding it, was one large military encamp-ment. High above all, with majestic dome and imposing proportions, rose the Capitol building, and "our flag was still there."

Our regiment went into camp to complete its outfit and get ready to move. We had no guns as yet, at least not a full supply, but were generously furnished with clubs.

One night one of our men who, for the sake of a name, may be called Brixy, was on guard duty. He looked at his club as if he thought it was a most insignificant weapon for one engaged in the vast undertaking of defending the United States. But he meant to do his best, and he took his place with a seriousness and brave demeanor which indicated that he was ready to defend the Union with the first stick he could get hold of, and no Confederate must attempt to seize Washington so long as Brixy had a drop of blood in his veins.

Brixy paced up and down with the air of a conqueror.

A man attempted to pass, but Brixy shouted, "Hold on, there! Where are you going?"

"Just over here—can't I get through?" And the man stepped forward.

"Hold on," cried Brixy, "or I'll shoot you dead with this ere club afore you know it."

The man did not seem to relish the idea of being shot dead with a hickory stick, and turned back.

Brixy levelled his club, took aim at an imaginary foe, and muttered, "Come on, you ragged scapegraces, I'm just aching to give you the contents of this ere club."

But Brixy's valor soon forsook him. At dead of night he rushed into camp, his hat gone, his hair flying, his eyes a good deal like cannon balls.

He came near rousing the whole camp with the startling announcement, "The Rebs are coming! Sure as

2

you live, they're coming! Wake up, boys! We'll all be catched; there they are!"

"Where, where?" came from a dozen voices all at once.

"Right over there; I heard them. O, there's no mistake about it; I tell you I heard them. Such an awful screeching—there, don't you hear it?"

BRIXY ALARMS THE CAMP AT NIGHT.

Fifty loud roars of laughter, all put into one, waked up the echoes.

"Why, you fool, that's nothing but a screech-owl giving us a serenade!"

Brixy was nervous doing military duty; the sound, it must be confessed, was a most unearthly one; and, expecting that the enemy might appear at any moment, it was not so difficult to imagine that there had been a redoubtable invasion.

The "Confederate yell" became notorious during the war—a wild scream that seemed to come from demons rather than from human beings, and Brixy on more than one occasion found there was something more frightful about it than there was about the harmless hooting of the bird that he mistook for the whole Southern army.

To a veteran who has crawled under his tent, and taken his dry rations and contrasted them with the Thanksgiving dinners he used to get at home, a description of camp life and camp fare will not be of special interest, but the children of the Grand Army veterans, and others of the rising generation, may be curious to know how our men spent their time, and in what way they were occupied from day to day.

It must be understood that our camp was a very busy place. We did not have many idle hours, although there was daily opportunity for something in the way of recreation.

At sunrise came the reveille, the beat of the drum, to let us know it was time to awake and prepare for duty. To most of us, the sun seemed to be a very early riser, got up, in fact, long before there was any real necessity for it. What was wanted, was a sun that could lie abed in the morning, and not get up an hour or two ahead of time and disturb everybody. With the beat of the drum there was an instant stir. The camp took on the appearance of life. Sleepy eyes opened, frowzy heads were thrust out from the tents, toilets were hastily made, or were left unmade, and those who were disposed to forget themselves and enjoy the luxury of a second nap were aroused by their wide-awake comrades.

Immediately after the reveille came the roll-call. Then we repaired to the camp grounds for drill, which lasted

two hours.   This exercise prepared us for breakfast, and
it was no uncommon thing to feel that the preparation
would have been sufficiently complete if we had not been
two hours in making it.

Breakfast consisted of coffee and hard-tack, with
either pork or fresh meat.   We were not in the habit of
having a printed bill of fare; neither did we consider it
necessary to send an order for what we wanted; there
was a singular agreement to the effect that hard-tack and
pork were just the things for breakfast.   Fresh meat
was not apt to be abundant, and required no directions as to
cooking; tenderloin steaks were always rare.   The hard-
tack was the grand stand-by, only the boys thought the
Government ought to furnish hammers and hatchets to
break it up into mouthfuls.   Our men went into hospital
on account of fevers, colds, wounds, overwork and general
debility, but seldom on account of dyspepsia.   We were
not in any special danger by reason of high living.

The doctor's call came at half-past eight.   The sudden
change of the men from citizens to soldiers rendered them
liable to various disorders, and the most stringent pre-
cautions as to health were adopted and enforced.
The sanitary condition of the camp was a matter of dili-
gent concern.

Guard mount came at nine o'clock, and there was drill
again from half-past nine to half-past eleven.   Then we
were ready for dinner.   If the commissary was well
supplied we had bean soup and pork; if not, we had
what we could get.   We contented ourselves with the
thought that soup is always fashionable, and forms the
first course at the " Fifth Avenue," the " Continental,"

and the "Palmer," and if it was not always thick, it was so much the better for softening the hard-tack. A little ingenuity could discover various advantages in thin soup. We were well behaved, took what was given us, and did not cry for more as children sometimes do when treated to only one plate of ice cream.

At two o'clock there was battalion drill, and a re-call at four to prepare for dress parade.

DRILLING RECRUITS.

Then we had supper, which comprised some of the essential ingredients of the meals that had gone before. Preserves and jams not being considered remarkably healthy, we did not indulge in them; and the Government having neglected to furnish us with pound cake, it was surprising to find how many men there were who never ate cake anyway, and did not consider it a proper article of diet. We all agreed that plain food was the best. Truthfully it must be said that there was a disposition on the part of our men to conform to circumstances, make the best of every situation, and prove true to the imperilled cause that had summoned the nation to arms.

After supper the serious duties of the day were relaxed, and some attended the prayer meetings, of which four were held weekly, and others, the large majority, killed time with sports and games, making a specialty of games of cards, until retreat at half-past eight, after which, at nine, the taps sounded, and the lights went out.

The drill was a fine preparation for the marches and battles we afterwards passed through. Some of the men became restless and wanted active service at once. There was a good deal of loud talk. Here and there was one who wanted to cross the Potomac, and march straight down through the Carolinas to Florida. It was useless to wait; things ought to be put in motion.

"I'm sick of this," said one of our men one day. "I came here to fight; I think something ought to be done."

"Well, what would you do, Morse?"

"I'd go ahead. I'm ashamed to belong to such a regiment as this; it is nothing but a home-guard."

Morse flourished his stick, straightened himself up, put on a proud military bearing, and acted as if he would like to lead the combined forces of the United States against the enemy and sweep them into the Gulf of Mexico.

"I'm going home," he said; "there is no use of loafing around here. I tell you what, boys, once give me a chance at them Confederates, and I wouldn't wait to shoot 'em or stick a bayonet into 'em; I'd club them over the head with the butt end of my gun."

"You will have the opportunity probably," quietly remarked one of the boys.

Bye-and-bye the opportunity came. Morse declared he was eager for it. He had already lost a brother and he was thirsting to avenge his death.

The first time he was under fire he started and ran as if death on horseback were after him, and he was not seen again for three days. It looked much as though he had thought more favorably of the home-guard, and had gone back to join it. It was observed that after this incident he talked less about his prowess, and the wonderful feats he would perform if he got a chance. He had enough of active warfare as soon as our gallant regiment was ready to take its place at the front. Morse was not a fair specimen of the spirit that animated our troops, as was fully proved by subsequent events. They went where danger was the greatest, stood like a wall against the terrible onset, swung the old flag through the smoke of battle, braved the hot hail of the bullets, left the trail of blood along their tracks, and rendered a service that cost the weariness of the long march, the sufferings of bleeding wounds, and the very agony of death.

CHAPTER II.

*"Nothing was left us but to make preparation for the
worst "—General George B. McClellan.*

AMP Wilcox—that was the name.
Camp Wilcox was our home, for the
most part, while in Washington.
The companies had their locations
assigned; the streets of our little city
were laid out; the cook and the kitchen
became at once important institutions;
the ground was cleared of all needless
obstructions; the place was made ready not only for
occupancy, but, as far as possible, for comfort. Camp
Wilcox afforded us better quarters than many places we
afterwards found, when a stone was good enough for a
pillow and the sky for a ceiling.

I have recollections of our life at Camp Wilcox which
are not altogether unpleasant, although we were not there
any great length of time.

The first thing to be done was to get accustomed to
our new mode of living, especially the meagreness of our
household possessions in our new home. We were just
about as well off as the "tramp" who carries his entire
stock of worldly goods in a bundle under his arm.

(24)

It is commonly the case that those who are making their first trip to Europe load themselves down with a superfluous lot of baggage. It would hardly be exaggeration to say that they take everything they do not need. The trip consists of an immense quantity of baggage going abroad, and certain persons going along to look after it. One is apt to wonder if there is anything which is not going to Europe.

Just the reverse of this could have been said of our soldier-boys who sprang to arms at the call of President Lincoln. You would not have imagined for a moment that we were making our first trip to a foreign country. The most that we had consisted of ourselves; and we had the appearance of a primitive condition like that of Adam in the Garden of Eden, before the days of leather trunks and hand-bags.

We were not encumbered with dressing-gowns and slippers. We could generally tell in the morning what pair of shoes to put on, and we did not have to spend much time in making selection of a necktie. It was not often that a man was seen with a five-story Saratoga trunk on his way to fight the Confederates. Lucky was the man who was the proud possessor of a coarse-toothed comb, to say nothing of a hair-brush. In charging on a battery it was not considered indispensable that one should present an appearance so genteel as to indicate that he had just come from the barber's.

It is surprising how little one wants for ordinary life when he has to carry it on his back. One thing after another is dispensed with; extra boots, shoes, coats, vests, pantaloons, perfumery, razors and razor-strops, umbrella and silk hat are left behind; and the soldier, hurrying to action, wonders how anyone can find use for the multitudinous articles of dress and furniture he has parted with, but which were thought to be of such vital consequence when he was at home. Each of our men had one trunk—his own body—and that was about all.

The knapsack, however, is worth describing on account of what it contained. Unnoticed hands had been busy with it before the recruit first strapped it to his back. It seemed to contain a hundred corners, and in each there was some little token of love and reminder of those same unnoticed hands. There was the photograph of parent, sister, or friend; perhaps also the letter breathing the warm love of a heart that endured the grief of separation only because the nation's peril was the occasion of it—a letter to be read when far away from the old fireside; and there, nicely packed, was some little book of holy promises, showing the thoughtful affection of one who was sadly wondering whether that knapsack would ever return.

And here it may as well be said that the moral force back of our brave soldiers, and the encouragement expressed by those who had surrendered the ones most dear to them for the conflict, had much to do in keeping up the hope and courage and endurance which distinguished the defenders of the nation. The thought of our men was not more upon themselves than upon those from whom they had been separated.

Camp Wilcox represented hundreds of homes which watched with eagerness the varying fortunes of the heroic souls who had gone out from them.

CARRYING SUPPLIES TO THE SOLDIERS

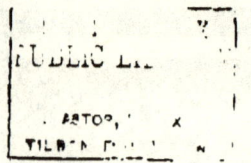

Of course there were certain wise men, oracles of wisdom and prophecy, who knew everything, could explain all the causes of secession, tell just what ought to be done, and what was going to be done, lay out campaigns and forecast military movements: and who seemed to be so gifted in the matter of statesmanship that any position in the cabinet of President Lincoln, with all its responsible duties, would have been mere child's play for the exercise of their conspicuous powers.

One day an ancient darkey, who had been permitted to cross our lines on some business connected with the commissary department, was engaged in conversation by one of our men.

"What do you think we're fighting for?" the old man was asked.

"For Massa Linkum," came the quick response. "You see, Massa Linkum have a big farm: it is Massa Linkum's land; and de Rebs, dey is goin' to build a fence right through de farm, and steal half of it for theirselves."

"Which side are you on?"

"I know which side dat fence Ise on. Some men's on one side; some men's on tother side; and some men's on de fence."

"So you throw up your hat for President Lincoln?"

"Throw up my hat? Lor' bless you, wouldn't I, if dis ole shoulder o' mine wasn't so stiff wid rheumatiz?"

"Don't you think the slaves have some interest in this war? Don't you think it's all on their account?"

"Massa," exclaimed the old darkey, "did you nebber hear 'bout Moses, de man what led de chilen ob Israel to

Canada afore you and I was born? Massa Linkum is Moses, and bime bye he'll upset de Rebs, and de cullud people will go ober dry shod."

Then one of our men, who understood the whole matter, and could expatiate by the hour on the causes of the war, broke in: "Let me tell you: you may never have investigated this profound subject. It isn't every man who can see occult causes with the eye of a philosopher or metaphysician, and trace them to their ultimate consequences."

The eyes of the old darkey rounded out like a pair of full-grown onions.

"Have you never familiarized yourself with that document in our political nomenclature known as the Missouri Compromise?"

"What was dat, Massa? Was it de steamboat dat blew up on de Potomac? Yes, Massa, Ise heard ob dat long ago."

The old darkey was utterly astonished at this new revelation of the causes that led to the war, and in amazement at the startling intelligence, his mouth and eyes appeared to comprise his entire face.

I said to him, "How old are you? You seem to be getting along in life."

As soon as he had recovered from the big words that had impressed him almost to the point of fainting on the spot, he replied, "I think I'm better dan a hundred. I was a lad when I held General Washington's horse."

"So you are one who has seen General Washington?"

"Yes, Massa, I 'members it well. I knows of forty in dis town who says dey held de general's horse, but I doan take no stock in any of dem; dey is a pack ob story tellers."

"Are you personally acquainted with Mr. Lincoln?" asked one who was enjoying the interview with the old man and was willing to continue the sport.

"Yes, Massa, I enjoys de pleasure ob a personal acquaintance wid Massa Linkum. I always touches my hat to de President, and I think he must feel acquainted wid me."

"I WOULD GIB EBERY HAIR OF DIS HEAD FOR DE UNION."

I was anxious to learn how the colored people felt in regard to the war, and so asked the old man if he would be willing to fight on the side of the Union.

He took off his hat and showed a pate as round as a full moon, and equally destitute of hair, and said in the most animated manner, "Massa, I would give ebery hair ob dis ole head for de Union; Ise on Massa Linkum's side ob de fence."

This spirit with part of the colored people took visible shape and organization at a later period, and whether they

could understand "occult causes and their ultimate consequences," or the political "nomenclature" of which the
"Missouri Compromise" formed a part, or not, they did
somehow grasp the fact that the war was crystallizing
around them; and their rude patriotism was stirred in the
cause of their Moses who was conducting them to
liberty.

One of our nights in camp found us comfortably fixed
in tents, with five sergeants in one tent, of which number
I was one. I had been into the city and provided myself
with a bowie-knife, which I knew could be used to advantage in an emergency. That night I had retired before
the others in my tent, and had placed the bowie-knife
under my head in its scabbard. We had been furnished
with straw to lie on, a luxury that did not often fall to
our lot. I was dozing while the others were talking.
One of the number, named Knight, proposed to have some
fun. Any proposition to have fun was sure to find ready
assent, even though the fun was at the expense of some
luckless comrade who had to make himself a martyr for
the sake of the amusement.

I was sufficiently awake and conscious to talk in a
rambling style as one would in his sleep. It was proposed to catch hold of my toe and partly arouse me, asking
at the same time some funny questions.

Just when the sport was at its height I sprang partly
up, seized a wisp of straw, and, as if I were just waking
from a dream or the night-mare, shouted, "Where is my
bowie-knife?"

It seemed to the sergeants as if there were to be an
indiscriminate slaughter by a man who was in a sort of

delirium. Knight was not long in letting go his hold, and the fun began to change and take on a serious aspect.

Again I shouted for my knife and made a lunge for Knight.

"It's me! It's me!" he yelled, at the top of his voice. "It's Knight! It's Knight!"

"I know it's night," I said. "It isn't morning yet!"

On I went as if intent on plunging the knife into the sergeant, who sprang for dear life and darted through the door of the tent.

Incidents of this description which served to break the monotony of our routine life were never forgotten, and afterwards formed a common topic of conversation. When anyone grew nervous, or was frightened by something as harmless as a wisp of straw, the saying would go round, "It's Knight!"

Our first Sunday in camp was a somewhat bustling day, as all Sundays were. Still there was an attempt to make a distinction between this and other days, and treat it with respect. Some of the boys had contrived to find space in their baggage for a book or two, and so, putting all together, the regiment had a very respectable library. The books were passed around from one to another and made to do a large amount of service.

There were those whose ideas appeared to be somewhat confused on moral questions. They did not quite understand what was befitting Sunday. They had been accustomed to reading which was more sensational than religious, and it was not easy for them to see why one kind of books should be set apart for one day, and others for other days.

One of our men wanted a good book to read. and enquired of several who were in a group for a book of that description—a good Sunday book.

He received the offer of a dime novel entitled, " Wild Bill, the Hero of the Western Plains." The book was much more worn than many Bibles are. "Wild Bill " looked rather shabby ; the cover was stained and greasy, and it seemed evident that life on the frontier was damaging. to the personal appearance.

We had many men in our regiment who acted from the highest principle, and were always watching an opportunity to promote the welfare of others. They were good men and true. If any in the hour of danger were more cool and brave than others, they were the men who went into the army, not because of some sudden impulse, nor because they were swept away by the excitement, the clamor, the parade and glory of war, but because of a stern sense of duty, and the feeling that to defend their homes and their country's dishonored flag—dishonored by the hands that were trying to trail it in the dust—was an obligation that must be met even at the risk of life.

Before we received our muskets and other war equipments we scarcely felt that we were soldiers. We had our clubs with which to defend the Constitution and laws of the United States, but not all were as skilful in the use of them as Brixy was who swore he would shoot with his club the first man who crossed the lines without a pass.

And so it was an eventful day when we were marched to the Washington Arsenal and fitted out with arms. The men were in high glee. It looked now as if something was to be done, and every man was loud in his assertion that this was what he wanted.

"How do you feel, Jack, with your gun?" was asked of a short, squatty private, whose rifle and bayonet towered above him like a flag-staff on a one-story building.

Jack humorously replied that as he was not measured for his musket it did not fit.

"I never had any luck yet," he said, "in getting things ready made. What I want is a gun made to order."

"I'll tell you, Jack," came from another, "a horse-pistol would suit your length."

"Ah, boys," retorted Jack, "a bullet that would go over my head would hit you between the eyes. There's some advantage in being short."

"Not in the pocket," quietly remarked another.

We found afterward that one of the most serious misfits in our equipments was the blanket used by the man who was six feet tall and over, which was evidently intended for a man just about the size of Jack.

Within a week from the time of receiving our equipments marching orders came. Soldiers are not expected to ask questions, but we lost sight entirely of this, and wondered and inquired, and thrust inquiries at officers and others as if we expected every movement to be suggested to us and put to vote. We soon learned that our duty was to obey orders, without always attempting to have them explained.

We took up our march towards Bladensburg, where we were placed in the great chain of fortifications that defended Washington between Forts Bunker Hill and Lincoln. We encamped in a beautiful field on the farm of Captain Middleton, one of the nation's true defenders.

3

Our camp was named Camp Graham in honor of our brigade commander.

Here we were destined to remain the whole winter. Military operations were at a stand still, but our time during these months was well employed, for we were thoroughly trained and drilled in the duties of the soldier; and were prepared for the coming struggle. A good part of our attention here was given to picket duty and grand guard, and these exercises were found to be of infinite value when we came face to face with the foe.

We were also employed in throwing up fortifications, and were instructed how to cut down trees and make roads through the forest. These lessons we found in future time to be very profitable. Occasionally we were practised in brigade, division, and corps movements, all of which many considered unnecessary, but which at the right time proved to be of inestimable advantage.

Any one who could have looked in upon us during these winter months would have seen the ingenuity displayed in the attempt to defend ourselves from the cold and secure some degree of comfort. We were experts in making much out of a little. The tents were well staked, the canvas was snugly drawn down at the bottom, the chinks and crevices were closed to keep out the wind, the sleeping places were elevated if possible above the ground, and withal we presented the appearance of a big party who had gone on a picnic and were tenting out for their amusement. We had our daily round of duties, and gradually the regiment was moulded into that kind of living machine which is one of the first requisites of an army in the field. We became inured to hardship.

During the evening the man who could spin a yarn and tell a good story was immensely popular. I will not vouch for the literal truth of all the stories. In fact, it was observed that many of them gave signs of being highly improbable.

" Oh, we have heard that before," I said to Sanderson, who was entertaining with a narrative some men in a tent.

" I know it," replied Sanderson, " but I have not told it since last week, and it has grown since then. I want to give you the enlarged edition. It's a pity if a fellow must always tell a story just as he has told it before. I don't have the kind of stories that are always cut and dried."

The story that Sanderson was narrating related to a thrilling experience which he and some cronies had one night in an old farmer's water-melon patch just outside of Philadelphia.

" What have you got to add to that? " I asked.

" This," said Sanderson : " that we got away that night not only with water-melons but with salt."

" How so? " I inquired.

" Why, the old farmer heard us in our depredations, fired on us with an old musket, and shot us with the salt. Learning, it is said, makes a man smart, but I happen to know that salt makes him smart too."

Thus, with wonderful stories and adventures never written in any book, and which grew in interest the more they were told, together with games, discussions, debates, and occasional prayer meetings we whiled away our evenings.

CHAPTER III.

" And when the love speaks, the voice of all the gods
Makes heaven drowsy with the harmony."

IFE in camp was sometimes monotonous. Our boys were fruitful in resources for their own amusement, yet there was always a general desire to hear from home. When a mail came there was almost as much excitement as when we were ordered to make an advance with the prospect before us of a battle.

It was well understood also that friends at home were always anxious to hear concerning the fortunes of the soldiers in the field, and there were those who kept up a regular correspondence with friends left behind—at least, as regular as circumstances would permit.

Brixy was one of those whose correspondence was somewhat meagre, owing to the fact that his early education in the use of the pen had been seriously neglected. He would not have obtained a situation as bookkeeper with a salary of two thousand a year. He could have made his mark with a hair pin, or the blade of a jack-knife, as well as with a pen. Brixy's fingers

(36)

were not accustomed to those delicate movements which a young man would wish to make in penning a letter to his sweetheart, nor were his brains such as were accustomed to the task of composition and expressing the feelings on paper which agitated his bosom. It was a matter of common report that Brixy had a girl; he had declared that fact very promiscuously until nearly every man in the regiment knew it. And out of the simplicity of his honest heart he had often said he would give certain possessions, such for instance as all his old boots and shoes, and those of every other fellow in camp, if he could just see her again.

Brixy was a youth who took things in earnest. He was honest and awkward. He did not convey the impression that he would ever distinguish himself as a statesman. You would more naturally have expected to see him on a load of hay behind a pair of mules, driving into the city of Philadelphia on a market day, yet, good soul, the tender flame in the heart of Brixy burned with a constancy which was not surpassed by that of the girl to whom he was so deeply devoted, and whom, by the fortunes of war, he had been compelled to leave behind him.

One Sunday Brixy's mind was fully made up to send a letter which should declare his continued affection. If he must die for his country, he wished it to be understood that there was one who would occupy his last thoughts, for she could never be forgotten by her own devoted Brixy. He seemed to feel the responsibility of the undertaking no less than he did when he went on guard duty the first time in Camp Wilcox, and threatened to shoot with a hickory stick the man who had attempted to cross the lines.

Taking one of his comrades aside who was skilful in the use of the pen, and was kind enough to aid those in writing letters who were very awkward at that business, Brixy whispered something very confidentially in his ear, and with pen, ink, and paper they repaired to a tent together, where several others were assembled.

"What shall I say to her?" asked his comrade. "How shall I begin it?"

"I don't know," replied Brixy, "I never writ her a letter. How does a feller gen'rally begin such a thing?"

"I should say, 'My dear so and so:' that is the way I should start it. I would put down first 'My dear.'"

"But she ain't your dear," said Brixy. "She is my dear, and as nice a girl, too, as belongs to any chap in this ere regiment."

"I know she is your dear, but I've got to call her 'my dear' in the letter.

"No, you hain't got to call her any sich thing. I'm not goin' to have you call her your dear when she's mine."

"But that's the way it will have to go in the letter. This letter, you know, Brixy, is to come from you, and she will take it just as if you wrote it."

"But she'll know I did not write it, and some other fellow writ the letter, and is calling her his dear. And do you suppose I'm goin' to have any chap stealin' away the affections of that girl who said she'd love and cherish me, and darn my stockings, to all eternity?"

"Why, Brixy, you don't get the hang of it."

"Yes I do get the hang of it, and you'll get hung too, if you don't stop trying to get ahead of me and cut me out. Gosh blazes, do you think I'm goin' to stand such a thing as that?"

By this time the tent was alive with mirth. The boys took in the comical phase of the situation, laughed heartily, and the more merry they became, the more serious grew the face of Brixy.

"Give her my love," said one.

"Don't you do it," replied Brixy, and started up as if ready to challenge any one who would dare send such a message.

There came another roar of laughter, and Brixy appeared nonplussed.

"Tell her," said one, "I'll get sick if she'll come down and nurse me."

"I'll be sick before you are," answered Brixy; "I've felt bad for two days now." And then with a smile he said, "Don't think you're agoin' to get ahead of me."

"That's right," broke in another, "send for her; send her word you've got the cholera morbus, and if she don't come you'll die of green apples."

"You ain't putting all this down, are you?" asked Brixy of his friend who was attempting to write the letter. "I hain't eat one durned green apple since last year; I don't mind your telling her that; I think she ought to know it. But you mustn't call her your dear, or you won't go home alive."

It required some persuasion to convince Brixy that these messages had not gone into the letter.

"Put in this," said one of the boys: "I'm going to have a furlough, will be home in a few days, and I'll meet her a week from to-night at the front gate."

"No you won't I" shouted Brixy, "the front gate is a rail fence; I've got you there."

"Stop now," said his friend, "and let's get this letter written. How would it do to begin it in this fashion? Let's see, what is her name?"

"Her name is Jane—a good, square name. That's what she's known by everywhere in society. They all calls her Jane, and I'm as proud of it as if 'twas Queen 'Lizabeth or Betsy. I'll never go back on that name."

"Well then, as she is exclusively your girl and you are afraid I will call her mine, how would it do for me to say something like this: 'Jane, I now take my pen to write to you, and wish to say that you are not my dear; I lay no claim to your heart, and you will please not take any love in this as coming from me.'"

"That's it," interrupted Brixy. "Now you've got it; that's what I wanted all the time."

After much tribulation the letter was finished.

"How shall I sign it?" asked the one who had written it.

"Sign it? Why, sign it Joe Brixy; you wouldn't sign any other name to my girl's letter, would you?"

There was another burst of merriment, and Brixy said, somewhat testily, "You seem to be having a mighty good time; you must see something awfully funny."

This did not quiet the merry-making company, who were not averse to continuing the sport.

"Haven't you got her picture?" asked one.

Now, that photograph was what Brixy was especially proud of, and he was not ashamed to exhibit the face which he felt sure was unmatched by any other, and of which he was the proud possessor. He reached his hand down into a side pocket, and drew out a likeness of the girl. Holding it up with an air of conscious pride, he said, "There's Jane! She give me that the day before we broke camp at Suffolk Park; and I'm not afraid to put it alongside any feller's girl; her mother said I needn't be."

BRIXY SHOWS PICTURE OF JANE.

He turned the face of the likeness down and drew it across his coat sleeve, and then remarked again, "There's a speck on her nose, but that's the fault of the picture, not of the girl; just take her nose without that ere speck."

The boys expressed unbounded admiration for Jane. They were all of one opinion, and a loud chorus of praise greeted the sight of the photograph. Each vied with the others in appreciation of the fine points of the picture, while Brixy stood with a broad smile on his face.

Suddenly, while it was being passed around, one exclaimed, "Is that your girl? How did you come by that photograph? That's my girl I'd have you know." And he put on a look of surprise and indignation.

Brixy asked him what he meant.

"I mean that I have a photograph of that very face, and Jane is my girl." And so saying, he took a picture from his pocket and passed it around. The two likenesses were identical, one and the same without any manner of doubt.

Brixy was thunderstruck. "What's the matter, Brixy?" broke in one of the boys. "Is your cholera-morbus worse?"

"I understand it," said another. "She's a gay deceiver; she has been making a fool of you; you thought you had her heart when you only had her photograph with a speck on her nose."

The man who had shown the likeness said nothing, but his face wore a smile which told that there was some joke concealed, which he would not then disclose, but which might be explained at some future time. For that time we will wait, and meanwhile leave Brixy's astounding letter, telling Jane she is not his dear, to convey to that young lady the startling intelligence.

CHAPTER IV.

"Push things."—President Lincoln.

HE country was restless. The silver-tongued orator of Boston had said that we had a Quaker general on the Potomac, and Quaker guns at Manassas.

The feeling that some forward movement should be made with the opening of spring was general throughout the land, and expressed itself in newspapers, public meetings, and conversation upon the street.

Suddenly orders came to us to prepare for an advance.

"I'm willing," said one of our officers.

"Just what I've wanted," remarked half a dozen others, or words to that effect.

There was a spirit which was eager to try conclusions with the Confederates. In the beginning of the struggle Mr. Seward, Secretary of State, had predicted that thirty days would end it. Yet now for months our forces had been defending Washington, haunted by the unpleasant memories of Bull Run.

It would be impossible to describe the confusion and excitement which attended our preparations for the march. Many things which had hitherto been considered indispensable were found to be cumbersome, and were abandoned for the bare necessaries required for the movement. There was a look of eagerness upon faces, and a hurrying to and fro. Such condensing and packing and strapping and shouldering as was witnessed that morning would not, I am sure, be found outside of army life. We were well drilled, understood every order that could possibly be given, knew what was expected of us, were in good health and spirits, and much as we had enjoyed our sojourn upon the land of Captain Middleton, that fine old gentleman whose genial face I shall never forget, we were glad to turn our backs upon the quarters where we had undergone so much of hard training, and where withal we had spent so many happy hours.

Over the chain bridge we took our line of march, and the first day we made about ten miles. Night coming on, we went into camp and by that time we were having a very damp experience. The rain poured down in torrents, and the soft ground was easily converted into mire, and we were in a predicament.

"Hello, Bill!" shouted Sanderson, "don't you think it would be well to change your clothing? You may catch cold."

Bill North, poor fellow, looked the picture of despair. His Sunday suit, like that of all the rest of us, was left at home. He turned to me and said, "Preston, this is worse than that last night on guard duty at Camp Wilcox."

"Yes," I said, "and I am sorry for you, but you must take the chances."

"I'll do it," he said, "so long as I've got a breath in my body." Poor fellow! That was not long.

Bill North was more plucky than strong. Sanderson was equal to almost any emergency, and could march all day and then snore all night on the moist ground, as efficiently as he could tell a story, adding an additional story every time he told it, until it threatened to reach the altitude of the Washington Monument.

For a day we remained and did not attempt to make further progress. Word came from the advance of our army that we were not seriously menaced by the Confederate legions. The terrible fortifications around Mannassas Junction had been abandoned. Earthworks had been thrown up, and preparations for an extended siege had been made, but the enemy had suddenly disappeared. The awful guns which were mounted, and pointed toward our lines, proved to be logs of wood with their ends painted black, each in the distance, as seen through our field glasses, affording a very good representation of a cannon. These were the Quaker guns which Wendell Phillips, the Boston orator, made so much fun of, affirming that they were quite in keeping with the character of McClellan, and the only guns he had sufficient military genius to capture. Our movement was only a feint while preparations were going on to transport the Army of the Potomac to the Peninsula, by which route we were to move on to Richmond. On the third day after leaving our old camp-ground we were back again; which reminded us of the redoubtable French king who triumphantly marched up the hill and then marched down again. We had not been under fire, but had been under water. It would have been nearly as appropriate to call us the naval force as the land force.

Orders soon came again to break camp and proceed in another direction. This time we marched through Washington, over the famous old long bridge, and thence to Alexandria. Here we went aboard the steamer "Nellie Baker," bound for Hampton Roads.

Here there seemed to be two difficulties not easily overcome: our regiment was too large, and the steamboat was too small. It did not appear to be easy to diminish the regiment, nor to enlarge the boat. The hundreds of men who had been spread out for some months over Captain Middleton's farm were now collected and packed together like sardines. They seemed to bulge out over the boat as a mess of greens would from a market basket.

Very soon the men laid themselves down to sleep, being completely tired out, and there was no room left for the guards to march, who must, of course, be changed at the appointed time. Every deck and inch of floor was covered with human flesh. Of course the sleepers could not be stepped on, and so the only way for changing guard was for those who were to go on duty to lie down and roll over their comrades. This at any other time might have created merriment; but, as I recollect the scene and the utterances, those who had sensitive olfactories might have smelt brimstone and heard oaths that were never thought of before the war.

The passage was rather rough; at least it seemed so to most of us, for we were not much accustomed to travelling by water. If any one felt bad, he comforted himself with the reflection that to "feel bad" was a pretty general complaint, and was only to be expected of those who were not old sailors. The only thing about the boat we liked was the name: there was a suggestion of romance about "Nellie Baker," and that was the only romance afforded by the boat or the trip. The scenery along the shore would not rival that of the Rhine. There was a dull and uninteresting appearance, for the most part, which was relieved by an occasional battery or clump of half-starved trees. The chief thing to be said for our voyage is that it was perhaps a trifle less tedious and disagreeable than an overland trip would have been, with feet sore and limbs stiff from long marches over hard roads.

A sight of Fortress Monroe assured us that our brief voyage was ended, and we must part with "Nellie Baker," just as many of our boys had parted with those who bore other feminine names considerably more interesting.

If it had not been a harbor and water instead of land, I would say that we were on historic ground—at least a locality destined to become historic. A strange-looking object fell upon the sight as we glanced out over the water.

"What do you think that is?" I said to Brixy.

"It looks like an old cheese-box," said Brixy. "I wonder what on airth it is."

"You have heard of the man," said Sanderson, "who went to sea in a tub, haven't you?"

The thing seemed to puzzle Brixy. "What would a man want to go to sea in a tub for?" he said. "Didn't they have boats in them days?"

I answered Brixy's question as well as I could, and was helped out by one of the men, who said it really did not seem more strange that a man should attempt to make a voyage in a tub than that the United States should choose for its naval defence such a cast-iron cheese-box as that.

But that odd-looking vessel was not a thing to be ridiculed. What we saw was the turret of the Monitor —the little boat whose fame about that time filled the world, and which was victorious in the memorable contest with the Merrimac. Putting the glass to the eye we could discover that the larger part of the boat was under water, and that the turret was made of heavy iron plates securely bolted together. Two portholes were to be seen, or, more strictly speaking, openings through which the guns were fired. This turret was a kind of revolving drum, so constructed that the guns could be pointed in one direction or another without changing the position of the hull.

The Confederates had built high hopes upon the Merrimac, which, it was claimed, would sink the entire United States navy, and so expose Washington that it would not be a difficult undertaking to land a force and capture the Capital. The Monitor was an experiment. She went into the battle without any data upon which a prediction could be based as to what she would do. She proved equal to the emergency, and so crippled her antagonist that little was left of her except a worthless hulk.

THE BATTLE BETWEEN THE MONITOR AND THE MERRIMAC.

And now that I have ventured upon even a brief description of this celebrated conflict between the two vessels, let me introduce a brief quotation from the narrative of one who was a participant in the struggle :—

"Like gladiators in the arena, the antagonists would repeatedly rush at each other, retreat, double, and close in again. During these evolutions, in which the Monitor had the advantage of light draught, the Merrimac ran aground. After much delay and difficulty she was floated off. Finding that her shot made no impression whatever upon the Monitor, the Merrimac, seizing a favorable chance, succeeded in striking her foe with her stem. Soon afterward they ceased firing and separated, as if by common consent. The Monitor steamed away toward Old Point. Captain Van Brunt, commander of the Minnesota, states in his official report that when he saw the Monitor disappear he lost all hope of saving his ship. But, fortunately for him, the Merrimac steamed slowly toward Norfolk, evidently disabled in her motive power. The Monitor, accompanied by several tugs, returned late in the afternoon, and they succeeded in floating off the Minnesota and conveying her to Old Point."

This was the victory of the strange craft whose appearance was described by the exclamation of a sailor when first seeing her: "A tin can on a shingle."

The same writer continues: "A fierce artillery duel raged between the vessels without perceptible effect, although the entire fight was within close range—from half a mile, at the farthest. down to a few yards. For four hours, from eight to twelve, which seemed three

4

times as long, the cannonading continued with hardly a moment's intermission. During the battle the Merrimac lost two killed and nineteen wounded. Her starboard anchor, all her boats, her smokestack, and the muzzles of two of her guns were shot away."

The effect of this victory of our little ship was electric. The whole North was ablaze with excitement and joy. A revolution had come in naval warfare, and henceforth iron-clads were destined to come into use among the great marine armaments of Europe.

Having given a hearty cheer for the odd-looking cheese-box, we landed at Hampton, and were not unwilling to bid adieu to the "Nellie Baker." On we marched toward Newport News, where we went into camp to await the arrival of General Couch's division to which we belonged. Here we remained but a few days and then were again on the march.

Our next halt was made near Warwick Court House. I had read of the dilapidated condition of many of the old towns in Virginia, where the labor of the whites principally consisted in overseeing the labor of the blacks. This was anything but favorable to the thrift and appearance of villages and plantations. Warwick Court House did not give any remarkable sign of ever becoming the metropolis of the country. Wooden buildings, which might have been painted at some primitive period, were scattered along the streets, and if a more substantial structure was to be found, it carried a look of decay suggesting that the end of all things had come. One could have imagined that the people had been asleep like Rip Van Winkle, and had just opened their eyes and were astonished at the fact that war had come.

In the good old times, Virginia lawyers at Warwick Court House could prove the guilt or innocence of those who paid them large fees for little labor.

We were on the sacred soil of Virginia, the old State which claimed herself to be the mother of Presidents, but now, after some division of sentiment among her people, had passed the ordinance of secession, and had waked up suddenly to find that she was to be one of the great battle grounds of the Republic. It looked to us as if her soil was anything but sacred and was more fit for the tramp of armies than for the arts of husbandry.

"How would you like a plantation down here?" I asked one of my comrades.

"What do they raise here, anyway?" he said.

"I don't know what they raise just here," broke in another, "but I have been informed that in some parts of the South they raise cane."

"I can see that," I replied. "You mean sugar-cane."

"I guess we are here, boys," he answered, "to raise another kind of Cain."

"I wonder if dey raise shickens down here," queried Herr Blinn, a sturdy German, built much upon the plan of those Dutch ships which you may have seen in pictures, whose breadth of beam suggests the idea that they were intended for sailing sidewise as well as forward. "Der shicken is my favorite bird. Geese, ducks, swans, bullfrogs," exclaimed Herr Blinn, "der shicken is de pest bird ob dem all."

Herr Blinn found many to agree with that opinion, and there seemed to be a quiet understanding among the boys

that at no distant time they would test the quality of the
surrounding poultry, and would ascertain whether it was
of a tender age, or ancient as the village near whose antiquated streets we were quartered.

Herr Blinn was just the man who could carry a hen-
roost by storm. His strategy was superb. His plan of
capture was laid as elaborately as if he were attempting
to surround General Johnston's army. There was no
opportunity for failure, no provision for retreat. The
charge was conducted with the dash and heroism that our
regiment was wont to display in taking a battery. Un-
conditional surrender was the stern demand of Herr Blinn
when he bore down, horse, foot and dragoons on a chicken
coop. If Herr Blinn could have received promotion on
his merits in making captures and bringing in prisoners
of this description, he would have been made Major
General, and decorated with a special medal unanimously
ordered by Congress.

These lighter sketches of what happened in ordinary
army life, cannot be omitted without failing to convey a
correct impression of what went on from day to day.
We shall arrive at more serious incidents and events,
alas, all too soon.

CHAPTER V.

SEVERAL HAPPENINGS.

"We must stand our ground, let what will happen."—
General W. T. Sherman.

 E knew we would soon smell fire; we were getting upon the enemy's ground.

"Good morning, sergeant," I heard some one saying, and turned to see who it was.

"Corporal Vail," I replied. "Good morning. Are you ready to take a battery?"

The corporal braced up, as if eager for the fray, and said, "I think I might do something toward taking a battery, but there is one part of the service that I'm sure I would never be fit for."

"What is that?"

"I don't think I could ever make a sharp-shooter. Do you know, when I used to go out gunning, I sighted the game, shut my eyes, and banged away."

"That was about the way a girl would shoot a pistol. Did you ever kill anything?"

"Not as I remember, but I used to frighten crows and wild pigeons terribly."

(53)

"No damage done, eh?"

"None, except when the gun kicked. No, Preston, I never could make a sharp-shooter."

We drifted off into a discussion of the question whether our men would stand up well the first time they were brought under fire. We hardly thought they would.

We knew that the first time a soldier goes into a fight he instinctively winces and dodges. He may be brave, but coolness will have to come from experience. When missiles are hissing within six inches of his head, he is sorry that he cannot execute a forward movement by retreating. He is apt to wonder why he ever joined the army. He would prefer to be a spectator, rather than an actor. He would be more willing to look on, and give his whole attention to it, than to bare his breast to the murderous fire of the enemy. It is a common remark of commanding officers that men are of no great account until they have seen actual service in the field, and have become seasoned. Conflict teaches them how conflict should be faced and endured.

At Warwick Court House our regiment performed picket duty, and details of men were sent out to keep close watch of the surrounding country.

We had halted on the north side of the Warwick Creek, a stream neither sufficiently wide nor deep to protect us from an opposing force. Opposite to us, on the other side of the creek, the Confederates were gathered, as if intending to dispute our advance. Hitherto we had not been brought into close quarters with the enemy, and had not had an experience of shot and shell. We were not to remain there undisturbed. A nervous feeling crept over us in view of the fact that we were within reach and range of Confederate guns.

A light battery was brought into service, and the shells began to fall around us, if not in a shower, yet one at a time, and with such effect as to cause us to wish that we could either return the attention we were receiving, or place ourselves in a position of safety. Our men started as if shaken up by an earthquake; and while there were those who boasted that they were not afraid of the little battery playing upon us, it was noticed that they kept a very keen lookout for the shots that came from it.

The first shock and tremor being passed, a call ran along the line for Herr Blinn. Herr Blinn, it must be known, was possessed of extraordinary strength. His weight, if I may be considered good at guessing, was about three hundred and ninety pounds. He was in the habit of playing with cannon balls somewhat as a boy would with marbles, tossing them up, catching them, flinging them over his head, scattering a crowd of men by throwing them into the air, and then telling the men to stand from under, and performing various other antics suited to a circus ring.

Herr Blinn had conveyed the impression that he was afraid of nothing, and that nothing would give him greater pleasure than to catch a flying cannon ball in his hands, provided he could get a fair chance at it.

"Herr Blinn! Herr Blinn! Where are you?" the men shouted.

Now, our circus man, whose favorite bird was the chicken, had just captured several and was on his return to camp.

"Come on, Blinn, and catch these cannon balls!"

We noticed him standing behind a large tree several feet in diameter, as if fearing that any ball fired in the direction of our camp would be sure to strike a man of his dimensions; still a considerable part of Herr Blinn spread out beyond the gigantic tree on each side, and was exposed to the enemy's fire.

Whizz came a cannon ball, and Blinn, with a look of astonishment upon the broad expanse of his face, exclaimed, "Mine Gott, but dot vas close!"

Bang came another, and Blinn, with an appearance of grave alarm, again exclaimed as he clung to his feathered fowls, "Blixen, put I vas afraid dot dese shickens will be spoiled!"

Time passed, and in a few days the boys in gray tried the battery again. We had taken up our position on the top of a hill, at the foot of which flowed a beautiful stream towards the York River. On the face of this hill we prepared our meals, when we could find anything to prepare. Our circus man who was more fond of cannon balls belonging to ourselves than of those fired at us by the Confederates, again entertained us with a pleasing adventure. This time he had captured a young pig, weighing, perhaps, twenty or twenty five pounds, and a fire having been built on the brow of the hill, and the pig having been cut in two, he was industriously engaged in roasting one part, which anyone would have judged from Herr Blinn's dimensions, would afford him just about a square meal. Quick as a flash of lightning out of a clear sky, the battery on the other side of the creek opened, and a ball, grazing the ground, tearing it up, and making general havoc, struck not many yards away.

Blinn started as if it had been imbeded in his own corporation, and shouted, "Mine Gott!" then suddenly rolled over, frightened almost out of his senses, and went down the hill like a beer-barrel, amidst the bursting shells and din of laughter, still holding on for dear life to his pig. It was hog up, and then man up, and so on alternately until both rolled into the creek.

BLINN MEETS WITH AN UPSET.

We remained here several days waiting for provisions, but under the spring thaws and the dripping rains, the roads had become impassable. It was evident that under these circumstances we could not move forward. Richmond was quite as secure as if half a million men had not been placed in the field; and all military operations, the plans of the most brilliant generals, the valor and courage of troops, all sieges, marches, bombardments, were dependant on the weather. In thinking of the situation, I am confirmed in the opinion that the weather just about rules the world, that it can upset the shrewdest plans, stop the boldest operations, and even decide battles, as it did at Waterloo.

Our men were detailed, and occupied in making corduroy roads, for which the natives of Virginia may thank us to this day. Trees from six inches to a foot in diameter were felled, cut into lengths of eight or ten feet, laid side by side across the road, which, in some instances, had to be made solid with stone so that the timbers might not disappear, and over this kind of a track men marched, and supply trains made their way. We were not able to do all of this kind of work which needed to be done.

A wagon train had to be sent to Newport News to bring up provisions for the men who had not been so successful in foraging as Herr Blinn had been, and who knew the taste of chicken and the savory odor of young pig, only by distant recollection. Our regiment was detailed to guard the train. The teamsters informed us that the roads were improving and that already the ears of the mules were appearing above the mud. They assured us that animals supposed to have been hopelessly lost in the mire had been seen just rising above the surface. They felt confident from this that there was a bottom somewhere—a thing of which they had entertained grave doubts.

My own recollection is that in some instances when a dozen mules had been hitched to a wagon, they floundered in the mud, and it required a whole company of men to draw out the mules. But with a long pull, and a pull as strong as we could make it, after we had been several days on one-fourth fare, we reached Newport News, where Uncle Sam, bless his dear big heart, had provisions stored in ample quantities. On our return we found the roads repaired and everybody happy.

Constant annoyances from the Confederate force opposite made our men uneasy, and even our chaplain, supposed to be a man of peace, was seized with a frenzy of retaliation. The first Sunday we spent at this place I strolled down to the creek to see what was happening along our picket line. I had heard the crack of rifles, and knew that the two sides were exchanging shots. Minie-balls were occasionally whistling through the air.

"What, chaplain, are you taking a hand in this kind of business?" I said.

"I don't want to be idle, you know, Preston."

"Well, if you fire at the Confederates with your gun as skilfully as you do at our men with your sermons, I guess you will be reckoned a sharp-shooter."

He had captured a carbine, and with some fifty rounds of cartridge was defending his country with pious enthusiasm.

"You see, Preston," he remarked, "I have always found gunning an exciting amusement, and it is none the less so when you can draw the bead on one of the enemy instead of a wild duck or a squirrel."

"At the best," I said, "war is a scourge, is attended with infinite suffering; and blood and destruction always follow in its path. But now that I am in, and have gone in from a sense of duty, I commend the cause to God; and my own life, too, I offer if called for."

"Preston," he answered, "this is not your war nor mine. It has been forced upon us, but I am firm in the conviction that some great good is to come out of it. The blast will clear the air and purify the nation."

Sentiments of this description were entertained by the vast majority of those who had hurried away from their peaceful pursuits to maintain the Union, and hold up with their strong hands the flag-staff from which waved the Stars and Stripes. No armies composed so largely of citizens, educated men, sturdy yeomen, and men from the various learned professions, ever had gone into the field before. Both in the North and South the material of the army was the finest that the nation afforded. It is said that Napoleon once remarked that France is the only country which fights for an idea; we felt that ours was fighting for a principle.

It was no disadvantage to our gallant regiment to be held as we were face to face with the foe, although there was no general engagement at this point between the contending forces. It placed the men upon their guard, convinced them that we were not engaged in a holiday pastime, nerved them up to a sense of duty in the midst of danger, produced upon them a certain moral effect, and developed the highest qualities and characteristics of the soldier.

We knew that important operations were just ahead. Months of inactivity were to be redeemed. Those who were left at home and were supplying the sinews of war would not be satisfied with a Quaker general and Quaker guns." "On to Richmond" was the cry that rang through the North. But with us it was a serious ques-

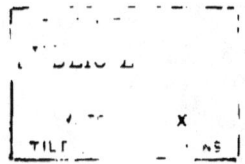

ON TO RICHMOND.

tion how we should ever get to Richmond through the
sacred mud of Old Virginia, and whether, after we
arrived there, we would find any Richmond above ground.
It seemed to us as if the mud were deep enough to imbed
any ordinary town; but the sun was doing his work and
the frost was slowly yielding, and we joined as heartily
as any in the cry, " On to Richmond! "

Our men were eager and restless. We did not fully
understand how large was the undertaking which the
Northern army had on hand.

One morning one of the subordinate officers was seen
very carefully putting on and adjusting a vest. It was
new, seemed to have something peculiar about it, and
was the object of a good deal of curiosity.

" What do you think, sergeant," said Sanderson, " that
vest is iron plated."

" Where did it come from? " I asked.

" Don't know; suppose his father sent it to him."

The ingenuity of home had been taxed to get some
defence for the young officer, and the vest, plated in iron
and covered with cloth, was the result.

" Hello! " shouted Sanderson, " has that thing got iron
plates behind. There's where you'll want them."

The crowd laughed with the exception of the officer.

" Wouldn't it be a good thing," remarked Corporal
Vail, "if the Government would furnish us all with
breast-plates? "

" I think it would," said Brixy, "and I'd like 'em on my
legs, too."

Brixy's idea of having breast-plates on his legs produced a smile, but Brixy's serious look led to the

impression that he could not quite understand what the humor was all about.

Sanderson interrupted by saying the whole regiment had breastworks.

"What breastworks?" inquired Vail.

"Herr Blinn," said Sanderson, amidst the amusement of the boys. "Put him in front, as General Jackson put the cotton bales at New Orleans; that's all you need to do."

"Here he is!" shouted one; and at that moment the identical Blinn, of comprehensive proportions, came near.

"Blinn," I said, "we propose to put you in front of our regiment for breastworks."

"Vat you do? You put me in der vront? I dond obshecks to dat ven we goes to forage. Den I gets der virst shicken." A self-satisfied smile crept slowly over the forty-acre face of Herr Blinn.

"You see, Blinn," I said, "you are an important man. Your size can never be lost to view; if they would make you color-bearer our men would know where they are whether they saw any colors or not."

Sanderson's mind was dwelling on the vest which the young officer had received. "I'll tell you, boys," he exclaimed, with enthusiasm, "I can make a breast-plate of something better than iron; and I've got the stuff to do it with."

"What's that?"

"Hard-tack!" shouted Sanderson. "Just carry a piece under your vest; cover your stomach with it, and the whole Confederate army couldn't get in."

"I know," said Vail, "the whole Confederate army couldn't get into my stomach; there isn't enough stomach, but of course you wouldn't say that of Herr Blinn."

"Shentlemens," remarked Blinn, "you makes fun of dis stomach, but it is der very pest kind of stomach."

"Why?" I said; "because it holds so much?"

"Because dis stomach was so thick. If der comes von bullet and I gets hit, dot bullet stops before it gets into vere I lives."

We saw the point, and all congratulated Herr Blinn on a thickness which might prove to be Providential in an engagement.

We also envied our stout comrade, the soft mattress he always carried with him, enabling him to lie down on the hardest ground with ease and comfort. Nature had furnished him with husks and hair, and he was in no danger, as I was, of having his bones stick through when he camped down at night on stones or frozen ground.

"Preston," said our chaplain, "why is Blinn like a sermon?"

"Because he's heavy," I said.

"Very good, but that's not it; because he's padded."

"Rather hard on you, chaplain."

"Why is he not like some of your sermons?" asked Sanderson of the chaplain.

"I don't know; tell me."

"Because he's short."

The chaplain took it good-naturedly, and remarked that hereafter he would throw grapeshot, and not carry on a protracted siege.

"Did you say you could make a breast-plate of hard-tack?" he asked of Sanderson.

Sanderson intimated that he could iron-plate the whole regiment with that material, and it would be the surest kind of a defense.

"I guess you have done it already," said the chaplain.

"How so?"

"The sermons seem to glance off, anyhow."

It was about this time that our men began to realize the cost of war. They learned that sacrifices were to be made. They had smelt fire. They understood that a good soldier was one who could suffer and endure. The spirit of heroism had fully taken possession of the men.

I judge that I was not alone, however, in occasionally turning my thoughts backward to the scenes of by-gone days, and the faces of friends whom I might never meet again. There was much in our active service and the various devices of fun and amusement to occupy the mind, yet there were moments when we pictured our return and the greetings that awaited us; and I am confident that the one who peruses these lines will consider it pardonable, that we did not forget the homes we were defending, and the sacred interests which had been so largely sacrificed in the higher interest and duty of patriotism.

CHAPTER VI.

"TRAMP! TRAMP! THE BOYS ARE MARCHING ON."

"I believe we are equal to our work."—General Winfield S. Hancock.

 ERE is a live contraband," said our captain, who had captured a young darkey soon after we struck the Peninsula. "He is about six feet and six inches tall, and you can see, boys, that the darkey is beginning to look up in the world."

"Yes," said Juniper Jackson, "I looks down on lots o' folks."

Juniper straightened himself up, and the breadth of the grin on his face was proportioned to the length of his body. He was about seventeen years old, and had wasted no time in growing.

"Vat dey gives you to live on?" asked Herr Blinn, with a look of eager inquisitiveness.

"Corn cake," replied Juniper.

"And it makes you grow shust like von cornstalk."

"Take him for a flag-staff, captain," said Sanderson. "You might go through all the swamps of 'Ole Virginny' and not find such a pole as he **is**."

5   (65)

"Where did you come from, Juniper?" I asked him.

"Don't know, Massa, I was just picked up."

"You've got an aristocratic name; how did you come by it? Who was your father?"

"General Jackson," responded Juniper, with a look of unbounded pride.

"And how did you get the name of Juniper?"

"Dat, Massa, is a Bible name."

Juniper had no shoes, probably for the reason that no pair was ever made capacious enough for his pedal extremities, each of which must have measured fully sixteen inches in length. The few clothes he wore were of the coarsest kind, and fluttered around him like a shirt on a bean-pole. General Butler, with the sagacity of a lawyer, had announced that as negroes in slavery were the property of their masters, such of them as were captured by our forces were "contrabands of war," and we were under no obligation to return them. Hence came the name of "contraband."

Every morning Juniper appeared to wake up taller than he was the day before. He had grown through his shirt at the top and his trousers at the bottom. Bare neck, bare legs and feet, indicated that he was bent on getting completely out of his garments, as a caterpillar turns itself into a butterfly—a colored butterfly in his case.

The scenes in camp greatly interested Juniper, although he seemed to have a constant sense of danger, and a feeling that at any moment he was liable to get hurt. His large eyes rolled about in a restless way, but it may be questioned whether, if he had been frightened out of

his wits, his hair ever would have stood up straight.
We thought we would keep him with us, make him useful, and that he would soon become accustomed to the
smell of gunpowder and the noise of bursting shells.

I shall never forget the terror expressed by his countenance when the battery opened upon us from the other
side of the creek. The moment the shells began to
explode, Juniper exploded too, and in the most original
negro dialect exclaimed, "Hold on dar!"

MARVELLOUS FLIGHT OF JUNIPER JACKSON.

But the enemy did not "hold on"; they fired away
with the best aim they could take.

"What in de world dem fellers mean," shouted
Juniper, "frowing dem tings ober year whar dere so
many men? Why, the fust ting dey know dey hurt
somebody, and den dey'll be sorry fur it!"

"Don't get excited, Juniper," said the captain, who
claimed a special interest in the young contraband on
account of having captured him.

"I didn't specs dis, Massa," exclaimed Juniper. "It's no place yere for dis nigger; Ise goin' to make myse'f scarce!"

Off he started at the rate of about fifteen miles an hour, his long legs serving him better than the four legs of any mule on the ground would have done. Soon he was beyond the reach of bombshells, and that was the last we ever saw of Juniper Jackson. Where he stopped, or whether he ever stopped, must remain an unsettled question.

"If we ever come to a retreat," said Sanderson, "I would like that fellow's legs."

"Your legs are long enough as they are now," remarked Corporal Vail, "when going into an engagement."

"I wouldn't be surprised, corporal," retorted Sanderson, "if your legs should prove to be full short at such a time."

While lying near Warwick Court House we had no opportunity to put up tents. as we expected marching orders every hour. We contrived to make a shelter by taking rails, putting one end on the fence and the other on the ground. and spreading our rubber coats over them. We crawled under, and congratulated ourselves that we had something beside the sky for a covering. Herr Blinn had one whole fence-corner to himself, and then stuck out on all sides.

The first evening we were here a good many wondered how long we were to remain, why we did not advance, and why a thousand other things did not happen, which President Lincoln himself could not have answered. It was not easy to understand that if our superior officer wished to keep us in the corners of a rail fence it was our business to get into the corners, say nothing, and accept the situation.

"Sergeant," inquired Corporal Vail, "what are we here for?"

"To do our duty," I replied, "and obey orders."

"How long will we remain here?"

"That depends on circumstances. When General McClellan is ready and Yorktown is captured, we shall probably go forward."

"I hope that will be soon," said Vail.

"So do I, but you know it would never do to move on and leave an army in our rear."

"That's so," chimed in Brixy. "I did not come down here to be shot in the back. I don't want a Reb tagging me. Get 'em ahead of you, boys."

"Get ahead of them, you mean, Brixy," I said, "and win. That is what we mean to do."

The Confederate General Magruder was intrenched at Yorktown with 11,000 men. Our force vastly outnumbered this, but we began elaborate preparations for a siege. There was no real intention on the part of the Confederates to make a protracted stand at this point. We performed picket duty while operations were going on for capturing the town.

On the day Yorktown was evacuated we received marching orders. Tents, knapsacks, every possible incumbrance was to be left behind, and we were to press on without delay. We marched about seven miles, went into bivouac, and sent a detail of men to bring up our

baggage, which we did not receive until some hours after
we needed it.

All night the rain poured down in torrents, and we
were completely exposed to the storm.   We made a raid
on rail fences, and carried them, if not at the point of the
bayonet, yet by the force of arms, made up rousing fires,
and in the absence of tents and blankets managed to
keep pretty comfortable   The rails were about as dry as
Uncle Sam's hard-tack, and they had need to be in order
to burn in a pouring rain   If anyone slept, it must have
been with eyes open and standing.   By daybreak the
knapsacks, tents, and blankets had arrived, and we were
again on the march.   Magruder had withdrawn his
troops, together with the 50,000 or more that had been
brought to his aid under General Joe Johnston.   They
had retreated twelve miles, to Williamsburg, and had
there made a stand to dispute our advance to Richmond.

As we pressed on in the gray light of that early dawn
we heard the sound of battle.   It grew more and more
distinct.   The fight had begun at Williamsburg.   We
hurried forward.   The rain came down with great violence
and drenched us.   The very elements were impeding our
onward progress.   We marched in mud over a foot deep;
I frequently found it over the tops of my boots.   Slow
and labored were our movements.

"If we were attacked now," said Sanderson, "I think
we could make a stand."

"Yes," said Vail, "I doubt if we could get away.
Nobody would accuse us of not sticking."

"Well," exclaimed Herr Blinn, "I'm stuck."

Poor Blinn, with his heavy weight!   He was puffing

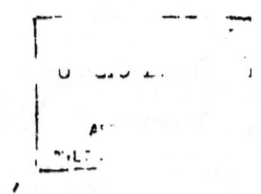

HANCOCK'S ASSAULT AT WILLIAMSBURG.

like a porpoise; only porpoises usually puff in the water, but Blinn was puffing in the mud.

We reached the scene of conflict before sundown, and were immediately assigned a position in a plain over which the cavalry and artillery had been manœuvreing. Here the mud was as bad as that through which we had marched, and some of our men, myself among the number, walked out of our boots, and had to institute a search to find them. Some facetious Northern war journal might have contained such an advertisement as this: "Lost, strayed, or stolen, the Army of the Potomac! Last seen in the mud near Williamsburg!"

The firing ceased, and we bivouacked in a strip of woodland. The night was long, the ground was wet; we were sufficiently exhausted to sleep anywhere, but our rest was disturbed by the discomforts of the situation. Lo! in the morning the Stars and Stripes were floating from the formidable entrenchments in front of us. Our men had carried every position held by the enemy.

First-class engineering skill had been displayed in constructing these fortifications, and our men remarked that if we had been intrenched at this point we could have held our position against the whole Confederate army. The works had been well planned, and slaves had been employed, with pick and shovel, to prepare for our advance. There were five or six of these strong earthworks, and so arranged that any attempt to take one of them could be resisted from others. In front of these fortifications there was a swamp, over which we made a corduroy road of muskets captured from the enemy, in all perhaps three or four thousand. We wanted some-

thing to prevent our wagon trains from sinking in the
mire, and as we had arms of our own, and could not take
those captured along with us, we put them to use in
another way, and made sure that they would never do
service again against the United States.

This movement left the quaint old town of Williamsburg in our possession. At one time it was considered
quite a smart, aristocratic place, being the county town,
with court-house, jail for white people, something worse
than a jail for colored people, and what might have been
in the good old times a pretty fair hotel.

Here is located the famous William and Mary College,
from which the sons of many of the "first families of
Virginia" have graduated. Thomas Jefferson, James
Monroe, John Tyler, Chief Justice Marshall, Peyton
Randolph, president of the first American Congress, John
Randolph, of Roanoke, and General Winfield Scott
were all graduates of this college. In the September
following our capture of the town, the college building
was burned while the place was occupied by the Union
forces, but it was used as a hospital for the Confederate
wounded during the engagement I have just briefly
described. We found it crowded with poor fellows,
many of whom had fought their last battle.

My attention was called to a bright young man who
was apparently dying. He was lying in one of the long
halls on the floor, with a little straw for a couch, and all
around him were others who were wounded, and some who
had been released from their sufferings by death.

Taking him by the hand, I said, "I am a Union man,
and yet I feel as if I would like to do something for you.

You have been fighting under the other flag, nut if I can be of any service to you, I will render it cheerfully."

He gave me a look of gratitude, and said, " I'm so glad you have come; I was asking one of your men if there was not some one who could comfort a dying man, and he said he would send you."

THE DYING CONFEDERATE.

"You seem to be seriously hurt."

"Yes," he gasped, "I am wounded badly. Oh, war is a terrible thing!"

"Do you think there is any chance for your life to be saved?" I asked.

"No," he replied, "I'm wounded unto death."

"Who are you?" I inquired. "Where do you come from?"

There was an air of gentleness and refinement about him that attracted my attention. I knew he was from some good family, and was a young man of more than ordinary education and attainments.

He clung to my hand and said, "I am a son of Rev. Dr. M——, of North Carolina. I'm so glad I've found a friend; I can't last long."

The look of death was on him. "What a strange experience this is," I thought, "that two men can draw swords against each other, and then can forget their hatred, and wash it away in blood." If he had not been wounded and dying, it is safe to say we never would have mingled our prayers and tears together as we did. My very heart went out for the poor fellow, who, far away from home, in a soldier's hospital, lying on a thin couch of straw, was cut down in the very bloom of youth, and was breathing his last with no one but a stranger, and he an enemy, to cheer his closing life.

"Will you make me one promise?" he said.

"I will do anything for you, Heaven knows," I answered. "What is it you wish?"

With earnest look, and still holding my hand, he said, "If you can ever get a chance, won't you send word to my father that you met me here, and tell him all about it?"

"I certainly will. You can die with the assurance that I will get the news to your home just as soon as any communication is opened with the South."

"I know it will be sad for them," he continued, "but tell them I died at peace with God and men, and that you were with me. Tell them, too, that the Friend who sticketh closer than a brother was with me, and all is well."

A smile rested on his lips. He was happy at the thought of being able to send a message home. That message, let me here say, was sent at a subsequent period, and several letters, expressing gratitude that the dying boy found a friend, were received.

I did not wish to see him die. It was enough to look at his pale face, and know that the end was near. I made him as comfortable as I could, obtained some tea, toast, and a little butter for him, which he seemed to enjoy, and then bade him good-bye.

One thing he said which I shall not forget. We were speaking of his being on one side in the conflict, and I on the other.

"Believe me," he said, with as much energy as he could command in his weak condition, "I love the old Stars and Stripes still."

It was a frank confession to make. He had been swept on in the great secession movement, as thousands of others were, and had gone into the war without a great deal of thought, and, perhaps, as much from youthful enthusiasm and the love of adventure as from any other motive.

Those years of army life were stormy. As memory looks backward I can recall many thrilling scenes. There are pictures whose colors do not fade. One of the most vivid is that scene at Williamsburg, the captured town, the retreating enemy, the suffering wounded, and, chief among the many wan faces, that of this brave youth, gasping out his young life. He was but one of thousands who went out in the freshness and hope of opening manhood, and fell upon the crimson field. I have always had a sweet satisfaction in the thought of having done for his relief and comfort all I could. Suddenly we had met; we were strangers to each other, and fighting on opposite sides ; we parted as true friends, I believe, as any in either army.

Tramp! Tramp! We were on the march again. Our army was pushing forward toward Richmond. The weather was beginning to be warm. Overcoats were an encumbrance; blankets were too thick and heavy.

"I'm hot," remarked Brixy. His red, honest, country face gave evidence that Brixy had told the truth.

"You'll be hotter," said Sanderson, "before we get through with this business. When you get in front of a thousand muskets or a blazing battery, there is something about it that thaws you out and takes the rheumatism out of you."

"I hain't got any rheumatiz," answered Brixy," but I've got an awful cold in my head."

"That's because you are out too late at night; you don't get in early enough."

"What has a feller got to get into?" queried Brixy. "We didn't bring any houses with us, and some of the time we've had nary a tent; how is a feller to get in early?"

"I heard of one of the boys," said Sanderson, "who had a cold in his head and lost it."

"How did he do it?" Brixy asked.

"Lost his head!"

"I don't want to lose my cold in that way," remarked Corporal Vail, whose red eyes and hoarse voice showed that he too was a sufferer from being out late at night.

"Well," answered Sanderson, "if that remedy doesn't suit you, shall I give you another?"

"Let's have it," replied the corporal.

Sanderson put on one of those serious looks peculiar to him, when about to tell one of his improbable stories, and began: "Get one peck of boneset, boil it down, and drink two quarts at night. Take a few sticks of black licorice to moisten your throat and loosen things in that quarter. Smoke four ounces of cubebs and blow the smoke through your nose. Soak your feet in hot water; a handful of mustard thrown into the water will be a great help; if it takes the skin off, it will grow again. Take a good dose of brimstone, molasses and butter: this is a remedy of long standing, and in connection with other things will prove beneficial. Half a tumbler of syrup of wild cherry will be good; and you should add to this five tablespoonsful of Jayne's Expectorant. Put a mustard plaster on your chest and another on the small of your back. Get two ounces of ipecac and take it in two doses, fifteen minutes apart. Heat a brick as hot as you can bear it, and put it to your feet; when it gets cold heat it again. Put four gallons of boiling water in an iron kettle, and sit over it thirty minutes; be careful after this that you don't get more cold. Take three teaspoonsful of paragoric every twenty minutes: this has a tendency to dry up a cough, and should be used early. If you feel worse after this treatment, take a sweat by wrapping up in six blankets and having hot water poured over you. One thing you certainly must not omit; you must make a free use of cayenne pepper; it is very warming, and I have heard many old women say is excellent in a case of cold. In fact, the treatment I have mentioned, corporal, is very highly recommended, and not one iota of it should be omitted. Try it—all at once. mind you—and see if it doesn't take hold."

This, as nearly as I can remember, was Sanderson's remedy for a cold. If he ever gave it to another, I am certain it was enlarged and improved, and numerous valuable items were added.

The weather by this time was getting settled and warmer. Still there were heavy rains to come, as we subsequently found to our great discomfort. The first day of our march from Williamsburg was an expensive one for Uncle Sam. The boys had more of this world's goods than they could use or enjoy, and the road was strewn with abundant clothing. If anyone felt the need of making preparation for a cold night by adding to his stock of blankets, he had facilities for doing it. Some of our men looked like retail venders of old clothes. They had the appearance of peddlers with packs.

"What are you going to do with that big load of stuff?" was asked of Brixy.

"I don't like to see things wasted," replied Brixy. "There's an awful lot of good things spoiled on this 'ere trip; I think they ought to be saved, and I'm goin' to do what I can toward it."

"Do you suppose you will want all you've picked up?" said Vail.

"No, but I hate to leave anything behind. I don't need it, but it's too bad to see such a pile of duds thrown away."

"You're like an old woman I know," said the corporal, "who found half a box of physicing pills in the cupboard, and although she was perfectly well, she took the pills sooner than have them spoiled."

"Did they help her?" asked Brixy.

"Well, no, not exactly, but she saved the pills."

CHAPTER VII.

THE STORM OF BATTLE.

"I quake not at the thunder's crack,
I tremble not at noise of war."

"WHAT do you think of this for soldiering?" asked Sanderson, with a shiver, as the rain came drizzling down on our marching columns. "It's ten times as cold as charity."

"We'll be lucky if it isn't ten times as warm as charity before we're through with this job," answered Corporal Vail, with a shrug.

"What do you mean, Vail?"

"I don't like it, that's all. Here we are miles south of the Chickahominy, and all the rest of the army on the other side. We may at any minute pop into a hornet's nest of the Johnnies."

"And get more stings than honey for our rations," rejoined Sanderson. "What do you say to that, Herr Blinn? You're likely to have fire from the other side to cook your bacon."

"Dat's goot," replied Herr Blinn, with a broad grin. "But if the Cornfeds try to gook my bacon I'm goin' to roast dere lamb chops, dat's shure." (79)

The line of march lay through Savage Station, of the York River Railroad. On we went, step by step, towards Richmond, which now lay not many miles to the south. Vail's remark was not without reason. We were far in advance of the main body of our army, which lay beyond the sluggish and poorly bridged stream which we had lately crossed. Our small division of 4000 or 5000 men was marching into the lair of the whole Southern army, and might be gobbled up as easily as Herr Blinn had gobbled up the porker on his last foraging trip.

Luckily most of our men did not know of this, and most of the balance did not care. The column was as light hearted and reckless as if it were a carnival to which they had been invited. No one dreamed that within twenty-four hours many of those brave souls would be stretched silent in death, or tortured with painful wounds.

After advancing some distance further we were sent out on the extreme right to strengthen the picket guard. There we encamped for the night, only a few hundred yards distant from the Confederate outposts. Fortunately for our peace of mind we did not know how dangerously exposed was the position we occupied, as the enemy was under cover of the woods, and hidden from our view, and we passed the night in comparative comfort, despite the continued rain.

Yet there were indications of stirring events in store. At intervals during the night and morning a sharp fire broke out between the picket lines, sometimes rising to quite a fusillade. It was good discipline for the men, as they grew accustomed, through these false alarms, to fall briskly into line, without waiting for orders.

The memorable 31st of May dawned at length on that dreary and dripping region. As the men stood at ease, after their breakfast, a Confederate officer, who had been captured by the pickets, was marched past the regiment, very much crestfallen at the thought that he had been made prisoner without a shot. It was the first close look most of us had had at an officer of the enemy, and the men gazed at him as at some strange animal.

Yet he was a brave fellow, despite his ill luck, and bore himself soldierly, as he was marched past the staring line.

"Take a good look, boys," he remarked, defiantly. "One Reb, with empty hands, isn't much to be scared at. Look out if you don't see enough to take the starch out of you before you are much older."

Some of the men answered this boastful remark with a laugh of derision, which was sternly checked by our commander.

"It is not manly, lads, to laugh at the helpless," he said. "You had better heed him than deride him, for if I am not mistaken his words will come true before night."

This rather sobered the reckless spirits of the regiment, and brought a shade of pallor to the faces of some. The frequent rattle of guns from the picket lines was not reassuring, and it was impossible to guess what hosts of foes might crouch under the shelter of those swampy pine woods that stretched far to the right and left in our front.

"Goin' der send out a voraging barty dis morning?" asked Herr Blinn, anxiously of the captain.

6

"That's not a bad idea," answered the captain, with a wink to the others. "You are good on the forage, Herr. You might take a half-dozen men and see what you can do in the way of feathers or bristles."

"Dat's bery goot," remarked the fat man, with infinite satisfaction. "Dere vas a gentleman hen talking off here to der right, dis morning."

"No, no, I want you to forage in the piece of woods, here in our front."

"Mine gracious, in dere!" cried Herr Blinn, with eyes like saucers. "Why dem woods is just vull of Cornfeds."

"There will be one less, when you bring me out a nice fat corn-fed Reb by way of rations."

"Mine gootness, no! Dere might be von vight, captain, unt you couldn't spare me from der ranks."

A laugh at Herr Blinn's sudden desire to fight passed through the lines, and there came a succession of jibes from the light-hearted fellows, in which I took no part. I was too anxious just then to learn what was in store for us to feel any interest in this frivolity. That the reader may better understand the situation of affairs, I will briefly describe the position of our troops.

The advance of the army comprised two divisions, under General Keyes. Of these the division commanded by General Casey lay at Fair Oaks, a station on the York River Railroad, some three and a half miles from Richmond. Couch's division, of which our brigade formed part, occupied a position on the Williamsburg road, one mile to the southeast of Casey's ground. Our regiment formed the extreme right of the line, the four other regiments of the brigade extended to the left, though there was a gap between them and Casey's right. The brigade was under the command of General Abercrombie.

We occupied a space of open ground near the railroad, with a long line of woodland to the southward, our picket line being advanced only three or four hundred yards to the edge of the swampy ground in front. There had been no time to prepare any breastworks, and we had but our stout hearts and good guns to defend us against the overwhelming force which might lay within the deep shadows of that pine forest.

Yet the day passed on until noon, and all remained quiet. Even the spiteful fire from the picket lines ceased, and it seemed as if the Confederates had withdrawn their advance.

We took our dinner quietly and coolly, there being much laughter and joking at the expense of those who had shown dread of an attack.

"Didn't stop any cannon balls, Herr Blinn, hey?"

"Nor capture any fat Johnnies?"

"How about that fun you promised us last night, Vail?" asked Sanderson.

"Wait," answered the corporal, grimly. "A day begun isn't a day ended."

"Don't see how it could be," rejoined Brixy, in perplexity. "Not till the sun goes down anyhow."

"I don't set up for a prophet," replied Vail. "But if —"

His speech did not end. Nor did the morsel of bacon in his fingers reach his mouth. For at that instant the silence suddenly ended in a terrific outbreak of noise far to the left. It sounded like a wild yell from ten thousand voices, hardly softened by distance. This was immediately followed by a startling burst of musketry, mingled with the roar of far-off cannon.

" By the Lord. Casey has got it !" cried our captain, springing to his feet, and standing with his hand to his ear in a listening attitude.

The uproar redoubled. Though a mile distant it seemed to be scarce a hundred yards away. The storm of battle had burst. The ambushed Confederates had sprung like wildcats from the shelter of the woods, and were pouring in overwhelming numbers on Casey's surprised and dismayed troops.

The surprise was almost as startling to us as to the troops attacked, and without a moment's hesitation we sprang impulsively to our feet and fell into line. No brigade or division commander could be seen, and our regiment, with the one adjoining on the left, waited impatiently for orders. Yet the fierce and incessant firing on our left showed where duty called us, and Colonel Wilcox led us at a double quick towards the scene of conflict, hoping to find some higher officer.

Guided by the roar of battle we struck off from the main road towards the right. Here a scattering volley met our ranks, and the men began to fire at the point from which the attack came. At this moment a flag was displayed by the assailing party.

" Cease firing !" commanded Colonel Wilcox. " It is the Stars and Stripes ! They are our own men !"

The attacking force drew back under cover of the

woods, and only then did we discover that we had been deceived. The Confederates had unfurled the Union flag, and withdrawn under cover of its sheltering folds! Some of our men had been slightly wounded, but fortunately no one was seriously the worse for this cowardly trick.

"Sergeant Preston!" cried Colonel Wilcox to me, as the regiment came to a halt.

I saluted and waited his command.

"I want you to select five men and make all haste to the left. You must find one of our generals, either Abercrombie or Couch, and report the position of the regiments. Say to whomever you find that we are anxiously awaiting orders. Be quick about it. There is not a second to lose."

Hastily selecting a squad from the nearest men I led them rapidly forward, towards where the incessant flash and roar told of a terrific battle.

"Keep a sharp lookout," I commanded. "There is a regular slaughter-pen ahead of us. Take care we fall into no trap."

I had scarcely spoken when I saw something that gave me a start. We were now about 200 yards from the regiment, and near some bushes, under which I had caught sight of a man's figure. He was creeping stealthily along and dragging his rifle.

Turning, I commanded my men in a low tone to lie down, and stepped behind a tree myself, with one eye fixed on the lurking figure. The next moment he reached the edge of the bushes and rose to his feet. There was revealed a tall, lank Confederate, more than six feet in height.

The gentleman was destined to a disagreeable surprise. In an instant I had stepped from my cover and levelled my musket at his head.

"Surrender!" I cried, sternly.

Never in my life have I seen a more surprised or a more scared personage. The rifle fell from his hands, his teeth chattered, and his knees bent as if hardly able to bear his weight.

"HOLD! I SURRENDER!"

"Do—don't shoot!" he faltered. "I surrender."

"You had better," I remarked, grimly. "Come on here, lads. We have got a prize. What are you doing here, fellow?"

"Takin' a look after you Yanks. Wish I hadn't."

"Found more than you bargained for, did you? Now see here, my man, I want you to tell me the truth and I will see that you are taken care of. How many men have you in those woods?"

"Reckon 'bout thirty thousand," he replied, with more

show of confidence as he became assured tnat we did not intend to eat him on the spot.

" Who commands them ?"

" General Johnston's the head boss, and General Longstreet's thar, too, I reckon."

" Where are the troops located ? Are any of them in our front ?"

"They're just scattered round ginerally," he answered, drawing up his long figure. ' Likely you-uns 'll smell powder if you hang round yere much longer. Our boys are back there thick as bees in a hive. They've busted your lines yonder a'ready."

This was evidently true. Casey was plainly giving way at all points, and falling back in disorder before the overpowering assault.

After a few more questions I gave the captive in charge of two of my men, directing them to take him back to a small shed near by and wait for our return. We then hastened forward. At every step the uproar increased in violence, and the evidence grew stronger that Casey was being whirled back in disorder.

At this moment I observed a party of three horsemen, rapidly approaching. We waited under cover of the fence until they came near enough to make evident the features of General Couch. He was attended by a single aid and an orderly. As I stepped out into the road he started and drew up hastily, as if in doubt of my intentions.

" Who are you ? " he shouted, laying his hand on his pistol.

" A friend, general. I have been sent by Colonel

Wilcox to look for you. Our regiment is at a loss for orders."

"Ah!" he cried, with a look of relief. "That is to the point. What are those men doing back there? Have they a prisoner?"

"It is a 'Butternut' scout, whom we just captured. He has given us some useful information about their forces."

"Very good. Wait for me here."

He rode briskly towards the men with the prisoner. I could see that he was closely questioning him. After a few minutes he rode back to where we were waiting.

"You have done a good day's work, sergeant," he briefly said. I will not forget your service. What is your name, regiment and company?"

He wrote these down in a note book as I gave them.

"Now hasten back to your regiment with all speed. Tell Colonel Wilcox to march by the left flank, double quick, and report to me at Fair Oaks Station. Lose no time. Just now delays are dangerous."

Scarcely stopping to salute, I dashed away across the open field, followed closely by my men. The general sat motionless for a minute, surveying us. He then wheeled his horse and galloped rapidly away.

Colonel Wilcox rode anxiously from the line as we approached. Receiving the order, he at once put the line in march. Breaking into double quick the regiment hurried onward, the ardor of battle burning in the faces of the men. They were in the mood to give a good account of themselves in the coming battle.

Reaching the location indicated, we found the Sixty-fifth New York and two companies of the Sixty-first Pennsylvania, with three guns of Captain Brady's battery. the whole force numbering about twelve hundred men.

The noise of battle had died away somewhat to the left. There was an ominous stillness in the woods on our front.

" How goes it with Casey ? " was the general cry, as we marched into line with the preceding regiments.

" Swept away like chaff," answered a sergeant of the Sixty-fifth. " They were ten to his one, and took him by surprise at that. The rest of our brigade have gone with him."

"And we're left here as a forlorn hope," cried Vail, discontentedly, as he looked around him. " What the blazes is to cover our flanks I don't see, if the enemy turns on us."

" We might build up a breastwork of hard tack," answered Sanderson, with a laugh.

"Or put Herr Blinn forward to catch the bullets."

"Not mooch," rejoined the big German. "Vat you call pullets mit too legs, unt fedders in dere tail, dem's der kind I catches."

The storm of the battle had now sunk to a low refrain. We lay in our exposed position for nearly an hour without an attack and scarcely sight of the foe.

At the end of this time General Couch rode hastily up. A few words in a low tone passed between him and the colonels of the regiments. Then the order came for us to fall back and take up ground to the rear.

This seeming retreat was received with some grumbling, though it was welcome to the older and cooler heads, who had been shrewd enough to perceive the danger of our former position.

The retrograde march continued for half a mile, when we were again ordered to halt and join line of battle. The position we now occupied was evidently far superior to that we had left. In front of us was a fence, and just beyond that a ridge of earth, that formed a highly convenient natural breastwork. Just beyond this again, was the line of the woodland. And looking at this it was apparent that we had no time to lose in occupying our new position. For through an opening in the woods we could see the long lines of the Confederate troops, marching upon us in serried battalions.

Battle was at hand—our first real conflict since we had enlisted for the war. I cannot speak for the feelings of the others, but for myself a shudder of terror passed through me, and it needed all my energy to nerve myself to the conflict.

As we fell into line the second section of Captain Brady's battery thundered up and took position, one section being stationed at each end of the brigade. The guns at once opened on the foe with grape and canister, cutting long swathes through the advancing ranks, and retarding their movement. But the position of our advance corps was a perilous one. To the left the retreat of Casey seemed to have been checked, and he was holding his own in the bushes against the hordes of the enemy. In our front the woods swarmed with infantry, whose numbers it was impossible to estimate. It was certain that we were frightfully outnumbered, and the nearest supporting corps was fully three miles in the rear.

"Ride back with all speed," cried Couch to an aid, and hurry up reinforcements. The roar of the guns must have been heard to the river, and our troops may be on the road. Tell them we will hold our own till they come."

Away went the aid at a brisk gallop, while a shout of defiant courage came from the men who had heard the general's promise. The Confederate forces were evidently massing in the woods, and there was momentary danger of an assault in force. We nerved our hearts for the impending struggle, many a silent prayer passing up from firm-closed lips at that critical moment.

"Be ready, men," cried Lieutenant Colonel Shaler. "Color and general guides on the line!"

"To h— with color and general guides!" broke out Colonel Cochrane in a passion. "Men, lie down!"

This order was hastily obeyed, and not an instant too soon, for as the line sank to the ground there came from the woods in our front a terrific volley of musketry —the first we had ever experienced. The storm of bullets hurtled over our heads, or buried themselves in the ridge of earth that protected us. That fortunate command saved the lives of scores of our gallant troops.

A fierce and rapid fusillade followed, the battery playing actively upon the woods, while we emptied our muskets at long range in the direction of the ambushed foe.

This continued for some time, the enemy keeping under shelter, and not venturing upon the ground that was swept by our bullets. There now came a cheering shout, that rippled along the line.

"It is Sumner! It is the gray-haired hero himself! All is right now, lads!"

These cries were called forth by the appearance of a soldierly figure, who galloped furiously up, followed by the aid whom General Couch had sent out. It was Sumner, in hot advance of his corps, which as we afterwards learned, had marched without waiting for orders on hearing the distant sounds of battle, waded the Chickahominy breast high, and hastened at all speed to our relief.

Along the road came flying up the famous Ricket's battery, which had in some unaccountable manner crossed the stream. The horses were white with foam as they tore onward, the guns springing like things without weight behind them. In a moment more they took position on a knoll to the left, and in less time than I can tell it, the guns were sending their death-dealing shot into the bushes, discoursing the sweetest music that ever came to my ears.

Up came the brave Sumner, his hoary locks waving in the air, his face full of warlike fervor. He appeared to me at that moment the perfection of valor and soldierly dignity.

He at once took command, and after a few words with Couch, the latter rode out towards the woods, and as coolly as if he had been on dress parade, inspected the half-hidden masses of the foe.

"They are forming divisions in close column for the charge," he called out to Sumner, as he rode back.

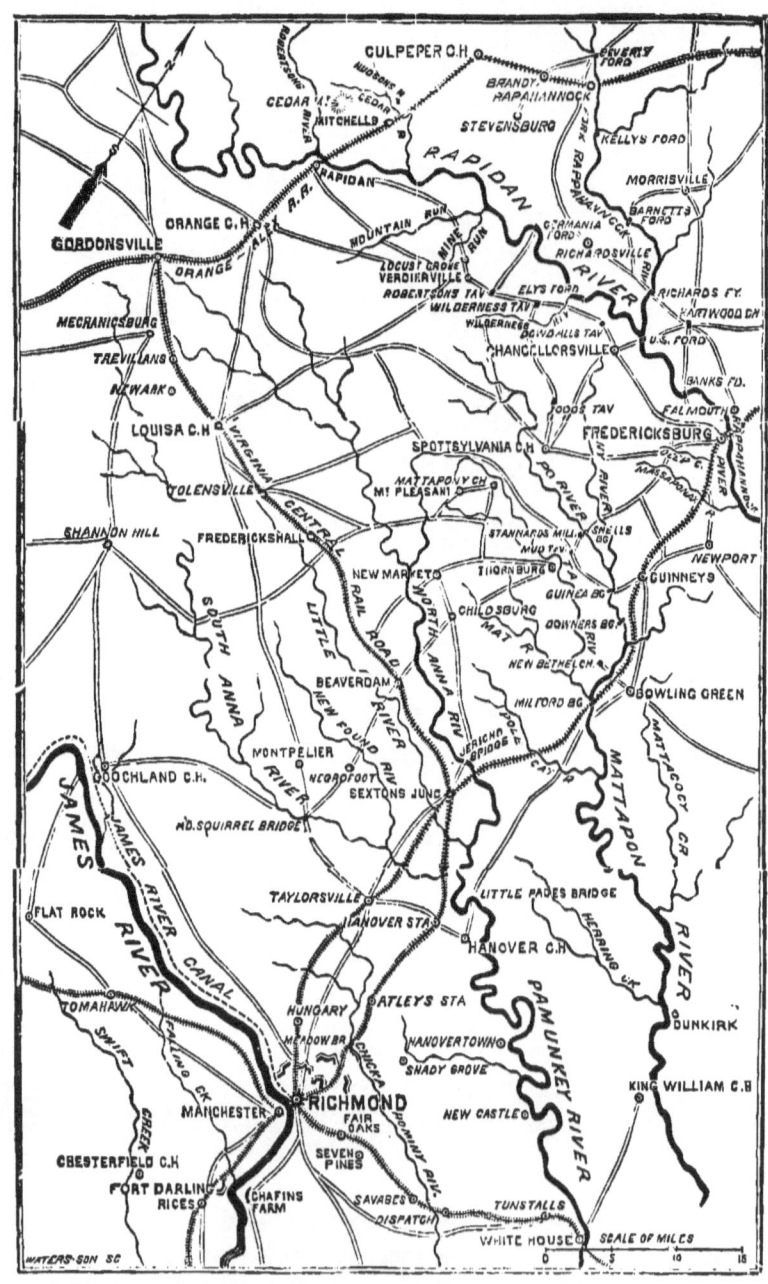

MAP OF VIRGINIA, SHOWING FAIR OAKS, THE WILDERNESS, ETC.

"All right," rejoined the veteran. "Let them come. They will find us ready. Captain Rickets, double shot your guns with grape and canister, and hold your fire for the word of command. General Abercombie, see that your men do not fire a shot till they get the word."

Several minutes passed, during which we waited with compressed lips and gleaming eyes for the coming onslaught. Then with a terrific yell the thickly massed line of the foe burst from the woods, and charged all along the line.

"Give it to them! Left oblique!" came the welcome order, and in a moment a torrent of balls tore through the ranks of the charging enemy, while left and right the batteries poured forth their flood of deadly missiles.

The advancing lines reeled like wheat before the wind, yet on they came, steadily and bravely, only to meet a yet more destructive volley. It was more than flesh and blood could bear. They reeled back to the cover of the woods, falling like autumn leaves before our deadly fire as they went.

Yet the fight was by no means taken out of them. They had scarcely time to form ere they again advanced, and charged this time to within ten feet of the fence which sheltered us. Seven times in succession within the next two hours the desperate charge was repeated, and each time with the same result. The position which had been so skilfully chosen for us seemed impregnable. The ground was already thickly strewn with the dead and wounded of our foe, while scarce a name had been lost from the roll-call of our regiment.

It is said that this charge was led by General

Magruder in person, who cried to his troops as he led them forward:

"Boys, that is my old battery—the one I formerly commanded, and by the gods I'll capture it, if it costs me a thousand men!"

He meant it too, for after a lull the Confederate hordes again formed, under cover of the woods, and dashed forward with the same impetuosity as before. Again they were torn and rent with close volleys of musketry, grape and canister, and reeled back to the cover of the woods with terrible loss.

Yet, this could not go on forever. They outnumbered us greatly, and fresh troops could be seen hurrying up to the scene of conflict. If once our line of shelter was broken hardly a man of us would be left to tell the tale.

But now, mellowed by distance, there came to our ears the inspiring rattle of the drum, beating a quick march, and as we anxiously turned we beheld the welcome infantry columns of General Sumner, hastening to our relief, and deploying to the right and left about 700 yards in our rear. Hope sprang into our hearts at the cheering vision. For now we felt that our flanks, which until now had been in serious danger, were secure.

"Your men must be exhausted with their brave defence," said Sumner. "What say you, Abercrombie, shall I relieve them with fresh troops?"

"No, no," answered our heroic commander. "They have faced the foe for two hours. They will face them to the end. They are as immovable as a stone wall. Every man had his hundred rounds dealt out this morning, and they have bullets enough left for the enemy."

These stirring remarks, which were made in our hearing, were answered with wild cheers by the men, whose blood was up to full fighting heat.

Their cheers were echoed by a savage yell from the woods in front, and the columns of gray again emerged from the forest, and dashed over the blood-stained field in close order. With indomitable courage they rushed upon our line, which met them with the same death-dealing reception as before. To the left they charged upon the battery, their impetuous rush not ceasing until they were scarcely twenty yards distant from the deadly guns.

It was the fiercest and most obstinately contested movement of the day, but our position was impregnable, and after advancing until almost within touching distance of our line the ranks of the foe wavered, bent, broke, and went reeling back, stubbornly firing, while we poured withering volleys in quick succession into their faces.

The repulse was completed by the regiments of Sumner's command that had formed on our left, and at this moment poured in a terrific volley and charged in their turn on the retreating foe.

Back they went, torn by thousands of balls, their regiments broken into scattered squads, and every man flying for life to the forest which so long had sheltered them, while at each moment scores fell before our hot and unceasing fire.

" They will not come again." said Corporal Vail, as he wiped the dust and sweat from his heated brow.

" And we can sleep on the bed we have made," I replied, pointing to the trampled grass beneath our feet.

We were right. That desperate charge was the last they had the courage to make. The battle was ended, and we had held our ground. For hours a battalion of raw troops, that had never before faced a hostile volley, had held its own against fearful odds, and sustained itself until relieved by reinforcements.

That a thousand congratulations passed through the ranks need not be told. Every man of us felt that he had won a badge of honor, and that terrible bath of fire went far towards making veterans of the gallant troops, who had so long held their own against heavy odds in the well-fought and well-won fray.

The battle was ended, and victory won, so far as our section of the fighting corps was concerned.

CHAPTER VIII.

THE LULL AFTER THE STORM.

"The musket stills its rattling sound,
The soldier rests on honored ground."

HE sentiment of pride and satisfaction which remained to us after the bitterly contested battle of Fair Oaks was needed to brace us against the discomforts of the succeeding night.

With the coming of evening it again began to rain. Yet very few of the men had either tents or blankets. The many false alarms of the few previous days had made them careless, and when the heavy firing began most of them sprang to their arms and fell into line without a thought of creature comforts. I, however, suspecting that this was more than a feint, had taken care to secure my knapsack and haversack, and to fill my canteen with cold coffee, before joining the ranks. I was heartily laughed at for my precaution, but just now the laugh was on my side, and that of the five other men of the company who had followed my judicious example.

However, it was no time for selfishness, and we divided

our treasures as far as they would go among our luckless comrades.

"What is your opinion of war now, my poor Sanderson?" I sarcastically queried.

"You're an old bird, sergeant," he replied. "But the rascally Confederate that secured the dinner I left by the fire is welcome to it. Likely enough it is the last he will ever eat. I would give a dollar though, just now, for the fried liver and onions I was green enough to leave behind."

"I say, Brixy," cried Vail, "what has become of your dinner?"

"Gobbled by some Johnny Reb," answered Brixy. "I left it cooking on the fire on purpose."

"You did? What for?"

"Just to amuse the Rebs with the fun of eating it till old Sumner could come up and give them particular Jesse. I'd sooner they gobble my blankets and bacon than gobble up the whole regiment, and march our brave boys back through Richmond as a Confederate circus."

"Good for you, Brixy," came in a chorus of responses.

"Hello, Thompson, what has become of Morse?" I demanded. "I have not seen him eating Rebels for lunch, as he promised."

"Drowned in a bog of his own brag, I fancy," replied Thompson, with a snrug. "I saw him with a handful of canteens running off for water as we fell into line this afternoon, and he has not yet come back. I tell you that you might as well try to swallow an elephant as get Morse into a battle. If talk could drive back the enemy he would soon end the war, but when it comes to fighting, our brave blowhard begs to be excused."

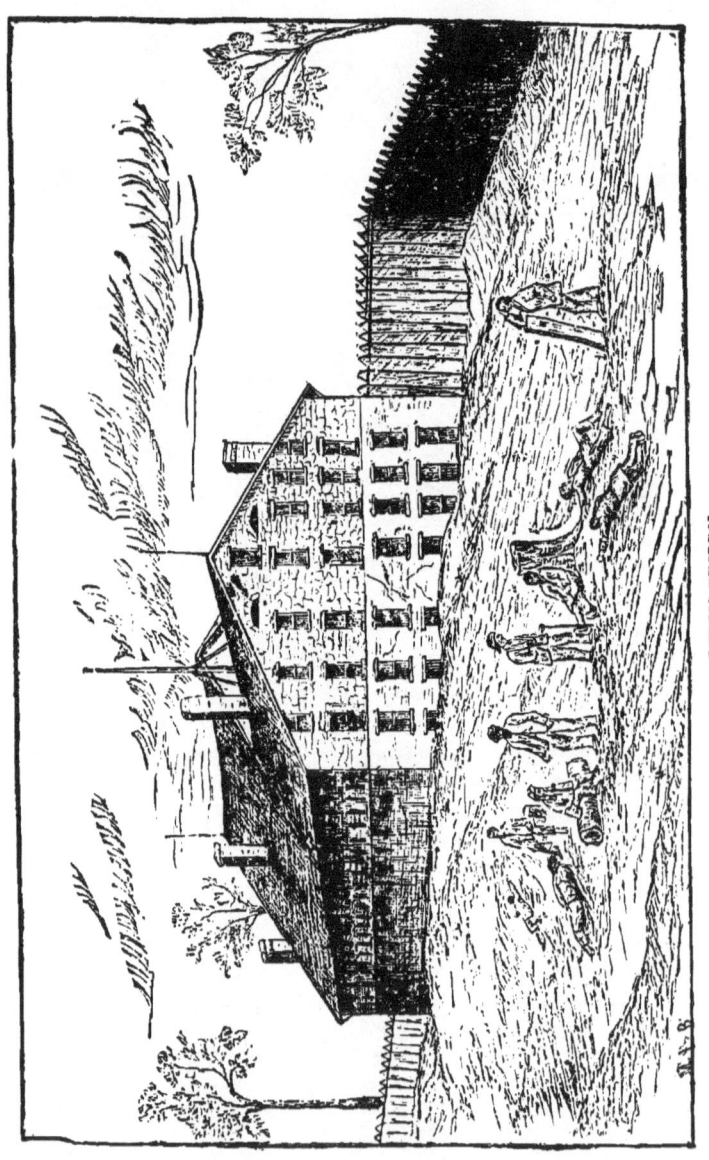

LIBBY PRISON

Captain Brady walked up to where we were chatting at this moment.

"This has been a stiff bout, my lads," he said. "How many of our poor fellows are down, sergeant?"

"Not more than thirty or forty out of the regiment, I think, in killed and wounded together. And I doubt if that many would have fallen if the men had obeyed orders to keep under cover. I do not believe we could have improved our position by a week's work at intrenching."

"You are right there," replied Lieutenant Charles; "nature has worked here for our preservation. That ridge of earth holds a weight of bullets which, but for its Providential aid, might have swept our regiment from the earth."

The discomfort of the night ended with the dawn of the next morning, in the gleam of a bright June sun that quickly dried our soaked clothing. Provisions had also been forwarded by the commissary, in response to Sumner's order that those who had done the fighting should be fed.

The night had been spent in succoring the wounded of both armies. By dawn of day new troops were on the field, and the brigades of Kearney and Meagher charged through the woods in our front, to unmask any lurking troops. But they only met with dead and wounded enemies.

All that night could be heard the ringing of bells and the shrill shriek of the locomotive as the trains from Richmond busily carried off the dead and wounded of their army.

I shall never forget the ghastly sight that met my eyes on the afternoon of the next day; when our line, with replenished haversacks, was advanced to the near locality of our old camp.

It was my first realizing experience of the horrors of war, and it was with a shudder that I gazed on the field over which our foes had made their desperate charges of the previous day.

Long lines of dead bodies showed with what precision they had charged, the torn and shattered corpses in some places lying two or three deep. The grape and shells of the batteries had here made fearful havoc in their ranks. their bodies being rent by ghastly wounds of every conceivable kind.

Here and there a body stood, supported by a tree, as if still on guard. Others were sitting, supported in like manner. some of them of such life-like appearance that we involuntarily questioned them, not dreaming that they were dead until we failed to get an answer from the lifeless lips.

Among them we found Champ Davis, a cousin of the president of the seceding States, who had commanded a brigade in the army. We knew him by finding his name printed upon the linen shirt he wore.

There was one point at which the more reckless of our men broke into jeering laughter, despite the depressing influence of the scene. On reaching our old camp we found a barrel of whiskey, which had been ordered to supply spirit rations to our men the day before, but not issued by the quartermaster. Fully thirty dead bodies lay in the immediate vicinity of the barrel, which had evidently served as a central point of attraction.

"It is thirty-pace whiskey," declared Sanderson, "and has brought them down lively. It is lucky we did not drink it, boys."

"You are right there," said Captain Brady, walking up to the group. "You see now the bad effects of too much liquor, my lads. I have done my best to teach you, but you can observe it there for yourselves."

"It's only Union whiskey in Confederate stomachs that hurts," answered Sanderson, with a laugh. "I calculate their applejack would bring us down at shorter range yet. But I reckon our lads can stand their share of the right stuff in the right place."

"What has been the actual result of the battle, captain?" I asked, curiously. "I know what our brigade has done. There are over a thousand men in gray dead on the field, and fifteen hundred prisoners in our hands, while our total loss is not over a hundred and fifty. But how about Casey? He must have caught it hard."

"He has lost terribly," answered the captain; "the assault on his lines was simply fearful. Thank God for Sumner, I say, or we would all have gone under. By the way, I heard a good thing just now about old Heintzelmann. While we were at it yesterday, tooth and nail, a New York colonel who had been on picket duty, hurried up with two companies, and asked the general, anxiously, where he could find his brigade. 'I can't tell you that, colonel,' said the old man, with his odd look, 'but if it is fighting you want, just go in, colonel; there is plenty of good fighting all along the line.'"

The laugh that followed was checked by the sound of musketry far off to the left. It was a skirmish fire, though it seemed growing heavier as the minutes passed on.

While we were listening, orders came to throw up breastworks, and make our position as secure as possible. This we hastened to do, not knowing at what moment we might be treated to some of the previous day's experience. The knoll we occupied had woodland behind it, and swamp in front, the latter being masked by a bushy growth that might serve as a cover to the enemy.

The sounds of battle had long lulled, and I was out at some distance on our left, with a squad of men, seeking suitable material for our breastwork, when a one-armed officer, with the shoulder straps of a general, rode up, and saluted Captain Brady, who was standing at a short distance from us.

"What was the firing we heard awhile ago to the left?" asked the captain, after a few words had passed.

"The Confederates were gathering in force again," answered the general. "They drove in our picket line, but they have been whirled back into the swamps. Old Sumner and Heintzelmann went for them double quick, and set them running like deer through the woods."

He was silent for a moment, and then remarked, with a lowering brow :

"I'd give the last dollar I have in the world for ten thousand of the troops that are lying idle on the other side of that ditch. If I had them I'd lead them into Richmond before night, or lay down my sword. By Jupiter, there's a coward or a fool somewhere near the head of this army ! See here, captain, have you a trusty man you could depend on to make a scout through those woods? It might prove a dangerous service, but—"

He fixed his eyes on me as he spoke.

"What say you, Preston?" asked Brady. "Here is some livelier duty than building breastworks. Are you willing to undertake the service that General Kearney desires?"

So it was the brave Kearney before me. I had never seen him before. My heart beat high with hope and excitement as I answered:

"What are your commands, general?"

"Take these men—can you depend upon them?"

"They are all trusty fellows."

"Then scout through the bushes and woods in front as far as you can in safety. Get as near Richmond as you dare venture. I fancy you will find the ground deserted. If you can do so bring me back a prisoner, or any useful information about the foe. But be cautious. The service is a dangerous one."

"I will do my best," I answered, as I turned back to the men, and acquainted them with what was in prospect.

A cry of satisfaction broke from their lips. They dropped their tools and ran eagerly for their arms, quite willing to exchange their severe labor for stirring even though dangerous adventure.

In a few minutes we were ready. The swamp in our front was passable by stepping on the grass hummocks that thickly dotted its surface. A short time brought us under cover of the bushes, and very soon we found ourselves in the woodland beyond, quite out of sight and hearing of our lines.

The caution to which we had been charged did not

seem here needed. The pine forest was open and we could see for a considerable distance into its depths. But no living being besides ourselves seemed to occupy it. Where the previous day thousands of troops had massed, now only some broken munitions and limbs of trees, rent by cannon balls, told of the fiery struggle. The wounded had been removed, the dead buried, and the forest shades deserted.

Spreading my men out in a scouting line to the right and left, and directing them to keep a sharp lookout, I led the way cautiously forward, watching every movement in the shadowy depths before me. The wood grew thicker as we advanced, though the undergrowth had been cut or trodden down by the Confederate forces.

In this manner we kept on until we had progressed considerably more than a mile. An utter silence reigned around us. Even the feathered and furred inhabitants of the forest seemed to have vanished. It was the most absolute solitude I had ever trodden.

Here and there we came across clearings and open spaces of considerable extent, with an occasional dilapidated house. But these were all deserted. Every living thing had left that desolate region.

"There has been a clean skedaddle," cried Thompson, one of the squad. "They have gone back in a panic. See here, sergeant, where they have flung away their muskets. By all that's good, I believe we could have rattled them clean through Richmond, if we had kept up the chase."

"You may be right," I replied, looking at the evidences of hasty flight in the muskets and haversacks that here strewed the ground. "It looks like a stampede."

"There is a wide reach of open ground ahead," said another of the men, coming towards me. "Is it safe to venture further? We are not two miles from Richmond."

"Stay here," I replied, briefly. "I will go forward and reconnoitre. Be ready to come to my aid if you hear my whistle."

Leaving them I moved cautiously towards the line of open daylight, which could now be plainly seen in advance. A hundred yards or two brought me near the edge of the woodland. Through the thinning trees I could see a considerable stretch of open ground, dotted here and there with buildings.

It was risky work to go forward alone, but I was bent on discovering something of more value than we had yet learned. Fortunately at this spot a stream, well covered in with bushes, ran towards the edge of the woods. Stepping into its bed I made my way under cover of the thick leaves, until the point at which the water broke out into the open ground was reached.

Looking out from my covert, I found that I was on the edge of a road, that ran past in a southwesterly direction. Beyond it was a stretch of level country, thinly wooded, and in the distance the flash of a river. It was the James! And those spires visible above the clump of pines to the right could be nothing less than the spires of Richmond, the capital of the Confederacy! I was as close to it as any of our army were likely to be for years to come, except as prisoners.

I seated myself on a stone in the bed of the stream and fell into a deep reflection, the circumstances through which I had passed, the situation in which I now was, the probabilities of that uncertain future which yet lay blank before me, flowing in succession through my mind. With my eyes fixed on those far-off spires I sank into a deep reverie, forgetting my mission and the danger to which I was exposed in the flow of vagrant thought.

A sound to my left called me suddenly back to my senses, and put me at once on the *qui vive.* Evidently mounted persons were advancing along the road. I could hear the clank of harness and the sound of voices.

I drew back into the deeper shadows, and crouched down under the bushes, with my piece in readiness for action.

It was a moment of intense excitement as the sounds came nearer. The next minute three horsemen, in the Confederate uniform, rode into full view. They were evidently officers, and were riding slowly forward, conversing as they did so.

Sorry now that I had left my men behind me, I listened intently, hoping to gain some information from their talk, since there was no hope to take any of them prisoner.

"It is lucky for us the Yanks did not advance this morning," said one of them. "You never saw such a panic as those flying cowards made when they came rushing back into the city. A determined push would have lost us our capital."

"And it is not safe yet."

"Not if the Yanks knew."

"Is it true," asked a third, "that Johnston was badly wounded yesterday? I have just come up from below, and am not posted in the news."

"Yes, the general got it badly. He will not lead an army for months to come, if ever."

"But who replaces him? The army is not safe for a minute without a leader in this emergency."

"It has a leader and a good one. General Robert E. Lee, the best soldier in the Confederate States, was appointed commander-in-chief this morning. You can take my word for it he will give a good account of himself before many days."

I had heard these words during the interval in which they reined up by the stream to give their horses a drink.

GEN. ROBERT E. LEE.

They now rode on, their conversation dying away in the distance. But I had heard enough. The information I gained was of the utmost value. Waiting till they were beyond hearing I withdrew from my lurking place, and made haste back to where I had left my men. Briefly acquainting them with my discovery, I led the way over the ground which we had before traversed, and in a half hour more we were again in the Union lines.

As we emerged from the bushes the first person upon whom my eyes fell was the one-armed hero under whose orders I had been acting. He stood some distance to the right of the line, conversing with General Abercrombie. A flash lit up his bronzed face as he hastened forward to meet us.

"Welcome back, my brave lads!" he cried. "You bring me no prisoners. Have you learned anything?"

"Plenty," I responded. "I have had the best of good

fortune. The Confederates seem to have retreated in a panic. The ground for a mile or two in front is deserted, and it is strewn with muskets and knapsacks. But that is not all. The Confederate commander, General Johnston, is badly wounded. A new commander-in-chief of the Confederate army was chosen this morning."

"Ha!" cried Kearney. "Do you know his name?"

"Yes, sir. It is General Robert E. Lee."

Kearney started back as if he had been shot.

"Lee!" he exclaimed. "By Jupiter, that's mighty news! I know him well! There is not his superior in the regular army. McClellan must know this at once. But are you sure of this? How did you learn it?"

I briefly related to him the circumstances of the scout, his bronzed face lighting up with satisfaction as he listened.

"You have done nobly, sergeant," he answered. "Don't forget that you have made General Kearney your friend. Good day."

Waving his hand to Abercrombie he rode rapidly away, too interested in the information I had brought him to waste an instant in useless words.

CHAPTER IX.

A CHANGE OF BASE.

"The thwarted host is forced to lose the day,
    Then gathers courage for a fiercer fray."

ATE in June, after two or three weeks inaction which succeeded the battle of Fair Oaks, the regiment was detailed for picket duty, and marched off, in the bright June sunshine, to the point selected in the front of our lines, very glad to exchange idleness for action.

On our way we passed a most heartrending spectacle. It was a Confederate intrenchment, which an infantry charge had heaped with dead, many of whom had been so hastily buried that the rain had washed off their slight covering of earth. From a single point more than fifty half-buried corpses could be counted—here an arm projecting, there a leg, yonder part of a man's head. It was a revelation of the horrors of war that brought tears from the eyes of many who were utterly unaccustomed to weep. Although we believed that these men were mistaken in the views they held, yet we knew that they were honest in their convictions, and as brave as ourselves, and that they were being mourned in Southern

(109)

homes by friends as dear as those we had left behind us in the North.

"For Heaven's sake lead us on?" cried Corporal Vail, turning away with a shudder. "This sickening sight is enough to make me vow to never pull trigger again."

"Thank God, I did not take part in this charge," I replied. "If I thought that I had killed any of these poor fellows I am afraid the terrible sight would haunt me for the rest of my life."

"Oh, come, come," cried Sanderson, with affected indifference; "don't be getting sentimental. They've only got what they bargained for, and words are wasted. Do you think the Rebs will moralize over us when they find us in the same situation?"

"God forbid that any of us should meet that dreadful fate," I answered, as we resumed our march. "You are talking like a heartless idiot, Sanderson. You don't mean it, but that doesn't excuse such a remark."

Sanderson was silent, and seemed thinking as we left the frightful scene behind us. My reproof had evidently touched him deeply.

Our picket line was posted so near that of the Confederates that the men could converse together. And this they did not hesitate to do when there were no officers present, despite the strict orders that no communication should be held with the opposing forces. It is impossible to prevent soldiers from establishing a temporary truce under such circumstances, and entering into friendly relations with those whom they may do their best to kill within an hour afterwards. War is not a matter of personal enmity, and it needs a certain degree of heartlessness to seek the life of an individual antagonist, even where one may fire with an easy conscience at an opposing line.

It was not long ere an active trade was set up between our men and the Johnnies (the title which we usually gave them in exchange for their Yanks), and penknives, tobacco, tea and coffee, of which commodities they seemed particularly fond, were freely smuggled over the line of the picket guard in exchange for Confederate goods of various kinds.

Towards three o'clock in the afternoon, while this contraband trade was briskly going on, and highly friendly relations existed between the opposite pickets, our ears were saluted by the sound of heavy cannonading from our extreme right, in the neighborhood of Mechanicsville.

A sudden start took place among the men, with a tendency to withdraw to their posts, and resume their hostile attitude.

"Oh, come now, Yanks," cried one of the Confederates, "what's the odds o' that to us? Let 'em bust away over yunder if they want ter. Them ain't us."

"Best get back now, Butternut," I replied; "the fair weather is about over. We're going to have squalls, and it may not be safe to stay out in them."

"Shoost wait, sergeant," cried Herr Blinn, puffing out like a walking hogshead between the two army lines. "We've got von liddle drade, me unt dis Cornfed." He pointed to a thin-jawed fellow, about one third his size.

"It's a regular David and Goliath business, cried Vail, with a lo d laugh. "Look out, Herr, he don't fetch you with a sling."

"It wasn't eggs that David slung at the giant," rejoined Sanderson, pointing to the two traders.

Herr Blinn was exchanging an old tin tobacco-box for a half dozen eggs, which the Confederate had somewhere procured.

"Take care of them, Herr," I cried. "Maybe they are charged with powder. They might go off."

"Dey'll go off in von vrying pan, dat's how," replied the fat man, with great dignity, as he carefully deposited the eggs in his haversack.

"Sure as shooting there comes Captain Brady," cried Sanderson, with a wink to the others. "Hadn't we best shut up this shop?"

"Tumble back, Herr," shouted the lads; "here comes the captain. My, won't you get particular rats if he catches you dickering with the Johnnies!"

At this alarm the fat Dutchman turned and waddled back at his best speed towards his post. It was an unlucky haste. His foot tripped in a root, and down he came with a sound as if a base drum had been suddenly exploded.

But that was not the worst of it. When he scrambled to his feet, mid the laughter of both picket lines, there was a double stream of white and yellow slowly trickling down his leg, from which there came a highly unpleasant odor.

Herr Blinn stood the picture of dismay and despair, while loud shouts of laughter rose from both sides.

"I've shoost busted dem eggs," he said, piteously, thrusting his hand into his haversack, from which he withdrew it with the juicy contents trickling from every finger.

"They're bad eggs, anyhow," roared Sanderson. "Bless us, how the man smells! Take him down, somebody, and dip him in the Chickahominy, before the provost guard smells him out."

HERR BLINN AND HIS SMASHED EGGS.

"Smell him out! They would run from him now quicker then from a battery of the enemy."

"Shoost show me der man as wants to put me in der Chickenhominy," cried Herr, angrily. "I'll bunch his head, now you bets! Ain't dis chicken-hominy enough?" He held up his fingers with their dripping contents. "Dem eggs vas pad, you Cornfed, and I vants mine box back."

"All right, Fatty," cried the laughing trader. "Give me my eggs back then. Isn't that fair, boys?"

8

"Yes," screamed everybody. "Can't go back on that, Herr."

Herr Blinn looked unutterable wrath on the laughing crowd, and particularly on his thin-jawed antagonist, while his cheeks puffed out with spleen. ,

"You know vats I do?" he said, as he thrust his fingers again into the ill-smelling mixture in the haversack, and drew them out streaming. "Dem's pad eggs, Johnny. Shoost you waits till der first pattle, and I shoots you mit my gun, by blitzen, I does!"

With this parting shot, Herr Blinn waddled back to his post in the picket line, swelling bigger than ever with indignation, while roars of laughter and a thousand jibes, followed him in his retreat.

By this time the noise of battle to the right had waxed louder, and it was evident that something serious was in operation. Little did we dream then that it was the first act in that disastrous affair, since known as the Seven Days Fight, during which the Union army was to be driven back from its advanced post to a new position on the James River, with terrible loss in men, stores and prestige.

By evening the roll of musketry and roar of cannon rendered it evident that a fierce battle was in progress. All communication between the picket lines was now broken off, both sides held themselves on the alert, and if there were any further exchange it was likely to be of bullets instead of knick-knacks.

The next few days were active ones. About sundown, of the succeeding day, being supplied with forty extra rounds of cartridges, we were ordered to march to the support of the right wing of the army. This march continued all night long, over dusty roads, with water seemingly as scarce as in the desert, while rumors of indefinite disaster were everywhere in the air. Our men had been borne back by overwhelming numbers. Danger, perhaps death, awaited us. We were marching as a forlorn hope, to cover the retreat of the army. All this was anything but encouraging to the weary men, so resolutely tramping onward through that hot and dusty night.

It was dark and dismal. No one could conjecture into what pit of death we were going. On we hurried, hour by hour, weary, parched with thirst, choked by dust, hastening on to where an occasional roar seemed to say that the battle had lulled only, not ceased.

Daylight found us in a position on the left of our columns, which were retreating in every direction. Word reached us that McClellan was simply changing his base from the York and Pamunky Rivers to the James, but the long lines of troops that marched for hours past us to the rear looked far more like defeat than change of base.

They were the troops that had borne the brunt of the preceding day's battle at Glendale and Frazier's Farm, though little indication of so fierce a struggle was visible in their present appearance.

As our corps marched past we wheeled into line with it, our position being occupied by other troops. The march continued to Savage Station, then the main base of supply of the army. Here had been collected vast stores of provisions and ammunition, while a great hospital here established made the post still more important.

Cries of indignation rose from the troops when it was found that not only were these stores to be abandoned, but that the sick and wounded in the hospital were to be left as prisoners in the hands of the enemy.

"A change of base!" roared Thompson. "A base change, I should call it! And our regiment has not fired a shot! Good Heavens, boys, it is enough to make a man's blood boil!"

"Why don't they lead us against the foe?" yelled Morse. "I'll engage to lay out a dozen of the Confederates for my part of the business."

"Like you did at Fair Oaks, I suppose," retorted Vail. "You ran off with the canteens that day to put up canned Rebels in, I calculate."

Morse shrunk back at this shrewd shot, and we heard no more from him about eating Rebels for that day.

On the next day it became evident that the stores and the hospital were to be abandoned. We were ordered to load all the wagons that could be spared with provisions and ammunition, and to destroy the remainder, after leaving a bountiful supply for the use of the sick and wounded.

The destruction of this material was one of the most impressive sights I ever witnessed. It commenced about noon of June 29th. Hundreds of barrels of flour, rice, sugar, molasses, salt, coffee, etc., with a long line of boxes of crackers, fifteen feet high, were hurled into the flames, the men working with a savage joy to destroy that which there was no longer hope of saving. Barrels of whiskey and turpentine, and even boxes of ammunition, were thrown indiscriminately into the seething fire, until the flames shot up higher than the tops of the loftiest trees, while explosion after explosion hurled blazing fragments in all directions through the air.

Yet heedless of danger the men worked on like madmen, determined that not an ounce of this valuab'e material should fall into the hands of the triumphant foe.

The most striking scene of all was that which now took place. A long train of cars stood waiting on the track, with the engine fired up, ready to fly forward at a touch.

Into these cars were heaped shells, kegs of powder, and other stores of ammunition which could not be safely flung into the flames. This done, a fire was built under each car. When the flames caught to the wood-work and began to spitefully creep and curl outward and upward the engine was set in motion. Away went the blazing train like a huge fiery serpent. The road-bed was here down grade, and the engine gathered speed at every moment, until it rushed onward with frightful velocity, dragging its serpent of flame behind it.

Soon a crashing roar of explosions began, hurling blazing fragments high into the heavens. Powder-kegs went off by wholesale, great bombs were hurled bursting into the air, shells dashed upward with wild shrieks, until the atmosphere seemed alive with hurtling, crashing, blazing monsters, tearing like gigantic fireworks through the trees, or flinging the waters of the river up in flashing jets.

The last scene of this terribly sublime vision was when the train reached the Chickahominy, the railroad bridge over which was destroyed. So great was the impulse of the train that the engine with the first car leaped out fully forty feet from the shore, and sprang over the first piers of the bridge, where it remained suspended in mid air, a striking monument of war's destruction.

The spectacle was one such as has seldom been seen on earth, and all the troops within view stood gazing at it spellbound until the last shell had exploded, unable to remove their eyes from a luridly impressive vision of ruin, such as they could never hope to behold again.

The store of provisions alone destroyed in this awful holocaust was estimated as sufficient to supply a full month's food for our army.

I cannot describe in detail the disastrous Seven Days retreat, of whose most striking scenes I saw but little, our regiment having been fortunate enough to escape in great part the bath of fire through which so many others passed.

The only pitched battle of the retreat in which we took part was the desperate engagement of Malvern Hill, which I may briefly describe.

Shortly before that engagement I was approached by one of the bravest and most intelligent of my comrades, who wore, just then, a very shadowy aspect of countenance.

"Sergeant," he said, "can I trust you to do me a special favor?"

"Certainly, Lewis," I replied. "But come, my poor fellow, why these gloomy looks?"

"Will you promise to convey this to my darling mother?" he asked, handing me a letter which he took from his wallet.

BURNING TRAIN RUSHING INTO THE CHICKAHOMINY.

"With pleasure, my dear boy. But you have quite as much chance as myself to give it to her."

"Not so," he replied, sadly. "I have a strong presentiment that the next engagement in which I take part will be my last. Do not imagine I regret taking up arms in the defence of my country. I would give a hundred lives. if I had them, to save my beloved father-land from ruin. The one life I have to give I feel is already doomed."

"Come, come, Lewis," I cried, cheeringly. " Let me hear no more of these dark forebodings. You have had bad dreams, my good friend. Of course, I will take charge of your letter. But I do not apprehend that I will have any need to send it to its destination."

Lewis smiled sadly, as he turned away, as if too full of emotion to trust himself to further words.

I may close this brief record by saying that within forty-eight hours the brave fellow was laid in a hero's grave by comrades who felt that they had lost in him one of the noblest souls in the regiment.

The battle of Malvern Hill was the most desperately contested conflict of that week of battles, and really the turning point between defeat and victory, had not the plans of our general intervened; for the Confederate forces suffered a disastrous repulse.

Our regiment formed part of the centre, the army stretching out far to the right and left, in a highly advantageous position, upon which the host of the enemy exhausted its strength in vain.

It is but justice to the Confederate forces to say that their assault was made with skill and determination, though with a little too much self-confidence, to which much of their heavy loss was due.

They came on as if expecting to meet a dismayed and disheartened army, which would yield like water before their assault. On the contrary, they found themselves beating like yielding waves on a wall of rock, from which they were hurled back baffled and beaten.

Charge after charge was made with furious energy; now on our right, now on our left, now on our centre, yet not an inch did the bulwark of Union breasts and Union guns give way. Again and again their leaders urged them on to the fray. Again and again they were hurled back in defeat and disorder.

The fierce and deadly contest ended in an advance in force of our right, at sight of which the enemy quickly withdrew behind the shelter of his hastily built intrenchments, leaving the hotly contested field densely strewn with hosts of dead and dying. At least three fell on their side to one on ours in that memorable engagement.

The event that followed this battle was, in fact, a surprise to all parties, even more so to our antagonists than to ourselves. They naturally expected that the victory we had won would be followed by an advance in force, and they nerved themselves during that night of dismay to defend Richmond against our expected triumphant advance.

To their utter astonishment, therefore, with the dawn of the next morning they found the post we had so desperately defended vacant, and the whole army of the Union vanished as if it had been a phantom of the night.

Our astonishment was no less than theirs when we

received orders for a night retreat. It need not be said that there was abundant grumbling within the Union ranks, as they marched wearily away from the scene of their victory during the hours of that night. The feeling was general that "some one had blundered," and that, had we been led by a man of nerve and daring, we would have made our next night's bivouac in the streets of Richmond, instead of behind the intrenchments at Harrison's Landing, where our week's retreat ended.

All the satisfaction that remained to us was that we at least occupied a position of safety, behind the impregnable fortifications that defended our new position, and that the flowing waters of the James, which ran in liquid lines past our new camp, assured us abundant supplies, in place of those that had been consigned to the flames during our retreat.

Yet, it was not safety that the army demanded, but victory and advance, and it flung itself down in baffled rage behind its new intrenchments, with much of the snarling fury of the bulldog that has been torn away from the throat of its foe.

We were sure, as history has since proved, that a portion of the Confederate forces reached Richmond in their retreat, where they lay, in nervous dread, behind their fortifications, in expectation of that Union advance that never came.

CHAPTER X.

OFF DUTY.

"Hands strengthen, and nerves turn to strings of steel,
While listening ears await the bugle's peal."

HE terrible week of battle through which the Army of the Potomac had passed, in its disastrous retreat from the swamps of the Chickahominy, was succeeded by a month of much needed rest and recreation in the well-guarded camp at Harrison's Landing.

Here, with the broad stretch of the James River on one side and a line of impregnable intrenchments on the other, we were as safe from danger or annoyance as if we had been at home, and the soldiers, with characteristic carelessness, seemed to forget that there was such a thing as war, and to fancy that there was nothing in life but enjoyment.

Some brief description of camp-life and camp-pastimes may not be here amiss, as a foil to the scenes of war and bloodshed, of terror and tumult, through which we have recently led the reader.

It was not all recreation, it is true. The discipline of the army needed to be kept up. There was picket duty

ARMY OF THE POTOMAC IN THE SWAMPS OF THE CHICKAHOMINY.

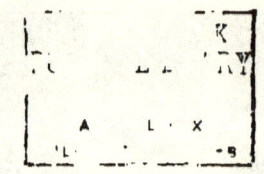

to perform, and camp guard, together with a bountiful allowance of drill and parade. Yet there was abundant time for recreation, into which the men entered with a zest as deep as if there had not been a care in the world.

It was now the midsummer month, the weather of tropical fervor, and outdoor life seemed the natural way of living. In this sultry season the river that flowed by the camp was a sanitary agent of the utmost value, and it was no uncommon sight to see thousands at once bathing in the clear waters of the placid stream, disporting themselves as if the army had suddenly become amphibious, and was seeking its foe at the bottom of the flowing river.

These exercises in the water were paralleled by as active physical exercises on the land, pitching quoits—or horse shoes, where the classic instrument could not be obtained—running, jumping, wrestling, and all possible methods of getting rid of superabundant muscular vitality.

It must not be said, however, that all the men of the army occupied themselves in these rude physical sports. A walk around the camp at any time would reveal numbers otherwise engaged. Hundreds might be seen, seated in the shadows of their tents, engaged in reading, or in studies of various kinds in accordance with their tastes and opportunities. Others seemed to spend a great portion of their time in correspondence, shedding ink as profusely as they had recently shed blood; while many others seemed satisfied with the mere enjoyment of life, lying for hours on their backs in the warm bath of the sunshine, in a delightful "*dolce far niente*" which no Italian lazzaroni could surpass.

Among these devotees of sheer laziness may be particularly named the contraband hangers-on of the camp, the charcoal-tinted patriots who had ventured within the circle of tents, and many of whom were employed by the officers in light duties, among which basking in the sunshine seemed one of the most necessary.

It is astonishing with what zest your genuine African enjoys the summer sun. Sons of the tropics, born under the dog-star, and only truly happy in a midsummer temperature, with all the chores done up, and nothing left but to lie in listless idleness under the blazing beams of a nice day, their shining black faces could be seen here and there about the camp, the very picture of greasy content and happiness.

Yet it was not all a contraband paradise, as some of the ebony gentlemen found to their discontent. One evening, about eight o'clock, we were startled by the vision of a stream of light, like that of a shooting star, darting across the river, while at the same time the flash of a cannon was seen beyond the James. It was quickly followed by the plunge of a shell across the camp, causing hundreds to involuntarily make it a polite bow as it passed. It was generally admitted that it was not quite the thing to try to stop any such whizzing visitor. This first shell was quickly followed by others, succeeding each other like horizontal rockets.

"Well, as I'm a living man, if the rascals haven't planted a battery of Whitworth's on the hills back yonder!" exclaimed Captain Brady, who formed one of a small group who were enjoying the spectacle. "I wonder what harm they expect to do us at that distance?"

"Maybe they have some old shells they want to get rid of," I replied. ' A chap could count fifty while that stream of light is crossing the river. The man who don't slide quietly out of its path must want to commit suicide"

But everybody did not seem of this opinion. A queer-looking contraband, who had made his first appearance in the camp the day before, and had amused some of the lads by a display of ready negro wit, came hustling up to the group at this minute, his eyes starting from his head till they looked like the optical organs of a lobster.

"'Fore de Laud, what's dem?" he demanded, nervously "What's gwine on ober dar, gemmen? Dis nig nebber been in camp afore, an don't un'stan sich contraptions. 'Tain't dat way you git yer rations, be it?"

" I'm afraid you'll find those dumplings hard to swallow Pomp," answered Corporal Vail. "You'd best stick to bacon and hard-tack, and leave these chaps for fellows that have better stomachs."

" Oh, de marcy!" cried Pomp, as one of the shells swished over our heads and exploded beyond the camp limits in the rear. "Dat ain't de sort of ting I comed yere fur. If de're gwine to fling dem things round permiscuous dis nig's gwine to absquatalate, mighty spry."

"I thought you were a braver fellow than that, Pomp," I replied. "You're not going to fly the colors because the chaps yonder are flinging over a few empty cocoanut shells?"

"Don't call dem em'ty? Seems ter dis nig dat dere bustin' full o' fire. Dere's enough in one of 'em to burn down a meetin' house. It's all bery well talkin', gemmen, but I am gwine to advance to de rear. Got mustered into dis yere camp yisterday. Gittin' peppered ter day. An dat kind o' pepper an' mustard is altogether too spicy for dis darkey's bacon."

"Come, come, Pomp," cried Captain Brady, who had been listening with amusement to this conversation. "I thought you came here to win glory. Now, any soldier will tell you that there is no glory in a retreat."

"Dat mout be de case," answered Pomp, seriously. "I won't disputate dat. But if der ain't glory in de rear, dar's solid satisfaction. An some how or uder dat fits better in dis nigger's craw."

"See here, Pomp. Suppose you were out in the woods on a possum hunt, and the dogs had just got a big possum treed, and were dancing and barking like wild round the tree. I suppose you'd be afraid to go forward then, for fear the possum might bite you. I calculate you'd advance to the rear, and wait by the camp fire for your share of possum fat."

"Oh, hush!" cried Pomp, with his eyes shining like two diamonds, "jist drap dat dar. Ain't no use makin' de nig's mouf water. Dem two cases ain't parallel nohow."

"I don't see any difference," answered Brady, with a laugh of amusement.

"Anyhow, I guess de possum fat by de fire's de best part of de game, arter all. On'y you can't git de fat till you've cotched de possum. But de chap as cotches one o' dem whizzers 'll git more fire dan fat."

"I hope they don't call that sleepy business shelling," said Sanderson, who had just sauntered up. "Why, they don't know the first principles of the art. It's enough to give a fellow the blues, to have to wait five minutes between shells. There's nothing lively or interesting about it."

"'Fore de marcy! you don't want it wuss dan dat?" demanded Pomp. "Like ter know what you call lively."

"I'll tell you," answered Sanderson, with a wink to the others, that told he was primed for one of his hard stories. "I don't know whether any of you folks were along with old Scott when he shelled Vera Cruz, in the Mexican war. If you'd been there you'd have found out what shelling means. That was what I call lively work on both sides. Why, gentlemen, while it lasted there was a perfect arch of iron in the air. A fellow might have walked under the flying shells in the shade, and not know the sun was shining. If it had rained then there could not a drop of water have got through. The rain would have run off that arch of shells just as it runs off a roof."

"You raly don't mean it?" cried Pomp.

"Solid gospel," answered Sanderson, without a smile. "I'm afraid we'd all have been blown to kingdom come only for a little stratagem. We had some thoroughbred terrier dogs aboard that we had trained to pull the fuses out of the shells before they could explode. You know how lively terriers are when they get after rats. Well, between you and me, they were so spry that they had some of the fuses out before the shells reached the deck. Fact; we put in new fuses, and rattled their own shells back at the Mexican rascals. There was one curious incident which I must relate, and you can believe it or not, as you please. We had an old rooster aboard our craft who kind of got envious of the dogs. I'll vow if the two-legged reprobate didn't go for the next shell, and snatch the fuse out as clean as a whistle. But the confounded old rascal had to stop and crow over his job, and while he was doing it another shell exploded and cut him up into stewing meat. We had chicken stew at our mess that night, out of the remains of that defunct rooster."

"Shoh, now! you don't 'spect us to b'lieve dat, anyhow? Ain't der too much gravy about dat rooster stew?"

"I only wish you had been there," replied the narrator, with an offended air. "I would have given you the wing to gnaw. It was tough enough to last you till now."

"If it was as tough as your story it might have lasted till doomsday," rejoined the captain, with a laugh that was echoed by the whole party.

But we cannot dwell too long over those fugitive conversations, with which we helped to relieve the dullness of camp life. Yet I may be permitted to relate one other incident of an amusing character, before proceeding to the more serious affairs of a soldier's life.

Among the amusements of camp life that of card playing must not be forgotten, since it serves to while away many an hour which might otherwise have been heavy on the hands of our comrades. Nor were these games entirely innocent. The greater part of them, indeed, were gambling enterprises, and many a poor fellow lost the pay he had risked his life to earn, and which was often sadly needed by those he had left at home.

For my part I never touched a card, carefully avoiding any indulgence in the alluring and dangerous sport. The incident to which I refer happened at another camp, and after I had been promoted to a higher position than that of sergeant, but it may be related as an illustration of camp sports.

I still adhered to my resolution to indulge in no games of chance, and a party of fun-loving officers laid their heads together to play a joke on me, which unfortunately for their plans turned rather awkwardly on themselves.

They had but a single pack of cards, which it was impossible to duplicate, as we were at the time cut off from all communication with Washington. After finishing their evening's game, a group of the lively fellows visited my tent, and while some of them held me in conversation on a trifling subject, one of the others slipped the cards under the pillow of my cot.

Suspecting that they were up to some trick, I made an investigation after their departure, found the cards, and quietly transferred them to a small stove I had in my tent. This done I turned in to peaceful slumbers.

Early the next morning they were back again.

" Come, friend Preston," cried one. " This is a sweet business I hear about you."

"What do you mean?"

" Professing to be so highly virtuous that you can't touch a card, and yet keeping a pack in your tent, with which you play solitaire every night."

9

" I fancy not," I coolly replied. " If I were a betting man I would lay you a wager you will find no cards in my tent."

" No use trying to get a bet out of you. You are too confoundedly strait-laced for that. But at any rate we will expose the hypocrite. Go for him, Wilson. You know where he keeps his private pack."

One of the officers at this thrust his hand under my straw pillow; but he quickly withdrew it, with a very shame-faced look.

" The rascal !" he muttered. " He has stolen a countermarch on us. Look at his quizzical face, gentlemen."

" Perhaps this is what you are looking for," I replied, opening the stove door, and pointing to the ashes of the cards.

" Oh ! you abominable villain, you have spoiled all our fun !" roared Wilson. " That was the last pack in the camp, and not another to be had for love or money. What under heaven shall we do now for amusement ? I vote we fling the fellow into the stove after the cards."

" I am sorry to have spoiled your fun, gentlemen," I replied, " but you know the old proverb that they who go for wool are apt to come back shorn. However, you have not fared as badly as another innocent individual I know of. Sit down. So long as I have ruined your little game with the cards, let me see if I cannot amuse you with an apropos story."

Crestfallen at their discomfiture, yet always ready for a good story, the group of officers disposed themselves to listen to my narrative.

" I do not know if any of you knew old Friend Slo-

comb, of Delaware county," I began. "I can only say
that he was as stiff-jointed a Quaker as ever spoke out
loud in meeting, and that he had a daughter who was as
wild a piece of feminine flesh and blood as ever wore a
bonnet. She was the one thorn in the old man's flesh,
which no amount of energy could pull out. Fortunately
for him he did not know of a tithe of her wild pranks, or
he could not have lived under the load. In fact, she was
not quite wanting in goodness of heart, despite her wild-
ness, and she knew too much of the old gentleman's
sledge-hammer ideas of propriety to care to come into
any direct conflict with him. Yet, Sally Slocomb had
no dread of being on the edge of a precipice, since she
trusted to her wits to keep her from falling over.

"On one occasion she had gone so far as to invite a
card party to her home, trusting to the old gentleman's
absence to give them a free field. Unfortunately for their
sport, in the very midst of the game, the front door was
heard to open, and a solid step sounded in the hall.

"'Bless us,' cried Sally, 'there's the governor now.
What in the world is to be done?'

"But she was never long put to it for an expedient.
The old gentleman's Sunday overcoat hung by the window, and quick as a flash she had snatched up the cards,
and deposited them in the capacious pocket of this gar-
ment. When Mr. Slocomb entered, his worthy daughter
and her friends were engaged in a demure and pious
conversation of the most edifying character.

"It had been Sally's intention to rescue the cards from
their hiding place at the first convenient opportunity.
But unluckily all thought of the affair slipped out of her

giddy head, and when **Mr.** Slocomb put on his **overcoat**
to attend meeting the next Sunday morning, the pictured
devices of Satan still snugly reposed in its right-hand
pocket. Yet utterly oblivious of this he made his way up
the broad uncarpeted aisle with his usual stately gravity
and air of pious meditation. He had reached the head of
the aisle, in full view of the assembled congregation,
when Satan put the idea into his head that his **nose**
needed blowing.

FRIEND SLOCOMB ASTONISHES THE BRETHREN
AND SISTERS.

"Unfortunately for him, the same mischief-loving
Satan had directed the cards when they fell into his
pocket, into the folds of his capacious handkerchief.
And when he flirted this square of linen about in the air,
preliminary to blowing his nasal trumpet, the cards were
sent flying over the aisle and pews, to the utter horror
of the congregation. As for the old gentleman himself
he stood as frozen with horror as if he had pulled the

devil, instead of the devil's bible, out of the depths of his overcoat pocket.

"It was a situation worthy the pencil of a great historical painter. The groan of dismay to which the old fellow gave vent seemed to have come up from his boots. And the exclamations which rose from the congregation were fully as deep and dismal. There was no escape from the fact. There lay the dreadful evidence that brother Slocomb had fallen from grace, and sold himself into the hands of the enemy of mankind.

"What followed is something of a long story, but I will cut it short. It will suffice to say that the old fellow was severely handled for his delinquency. He could not explain the mystery of the cards, except on the theory that old Nick himself had slipped them into his pocket, for the purpose of disgracing him. As his devout brethren were not quite ready to accept this theory, friend Slocomb was on the point of being formally read out of the church. But at the last minute Sally came to the rescue of her worthy and down-trodden daddy, and told the true story of the dreadful business. That she was duly contrite over her work I cannot affirm. She seemed to view it as a royal joke, rather than as a mortal sin to be repented in sackcloth and ashes."

A burst of laughter from my audience marked their appreciation of my story, and served to cover their discomfiture in the matter of the cards. But I was not forgiven for my part in the affair until the opening of communication with Washington gave them an opportunity to replace the lost pack. Their vexation was the greater because the story got out in the camp, and it was long before they heard the last of it.

Our era of idleness at Harrison's Landing came to an end one fine morning, in the promulgation of orders to pack up and break camp immediately. At once bustle and confusion succeeded the former restlessness. Where we were to go no one knew. The air was full of rumors. Yet the only positive feature in the matter was the striking of tents, the loading of wagons, and the multitudinous duties necessary to the moving of an army from a fixed encampment.

To our surprise the line of march was taken up, not for Richmond, but for Yorktown. It was a decided retrograde movement. And now the rumors began to take more definite shape. The fact came out that the Confederates had stolen a march on us, and were menacing Washington, with only General Pope's army between them and the capital.

On the day we reached Alexandria the stir of the battle was in the air. A hard conflict was in progress on the old Bull Run ground. We were hurried through and took post with other troops as an advance line to protect Washington from the peril of capture.

Defeat had come to the Union forces. Pope had been beaten and driven back from his position. It was a moment of need and danger. But for the opportune arrival of the tried troops from the Peninsula the capital of the Republic would have lain at the mercy of its mortal foes.

CHAPTER XI.

"Who heard the thu der of the fray
Break o'er the fi d beneath,
Knew well the wat..uword of that day
Was, ' victory or death !' "

"EE is in Maryland with his whole army!
Have you heard that news?" I said to
Vail.

"That is not all," replied the corporal.
"It is reported that McClellan has been
placed in command again."

"I wonder what will be done now,"
came from one of the men, and instantly
a group was gathered, all eagerly discussing the situation.

"If Lee is in Maryland," I said, "that means danger
to Baltimore, and probably to Washington, too."

"If Lee is in Maryland," said Vail, "there is but one
thing to be done ; our army must meet him, and he must
be driven back."

All agreed in that conclusion, yet there was some difference of opinion concerning the military genius and
efficiency of our commander-in-chief.

We had marched nearly parallel with the Baltimore and Ohio Canal until we were not far from Clear Spring. Here our division received orders to move with all haste to Harper's Ferry. We were ready to march anywhere and meet the invaders. There was a general feeling that the Confederates were carrying their operations pretty far north. This bold advance of Lee seemed to rouse the spirit and determination of our men, and although a good deal worn and wearied by the previous campaign, we were ready for a forward movement. It was also felt that Harper's Ferry was a strong point and ought not to be lost without a determined effort to save it.

It was reported that the place was threatened by overwhelming numbers, and General Miles and his entire command were in danger of being captured.

This September day on which we received our orders, was hot and dusty, but there was not a moment to be lost, and no account could be taken of roads or weather. We had our own willing legs to carry us, and we pressed on with all possible speed. There was nothing to be gained by our advance. Harper's Ferry had already succumbed to the Confederates; and comment upon this surrender was afterward loud and bitter throughout the army and the North. Some of our men declared that an investigation of the transaction ought to be made. The commander disappeared, and having lost his life, as was reported, there could be no military inquiry. He was apprised of our coming, and must have known that re-enforcements were on the way. When we arrived on the bluffs where we could overlook the place, we found it already occupied by Confederate troops; and as our commander, General Couch, was preparing to make an attack, in the hope of regaining the lost position, we received orders from McClellan to hasten to Antietam.

On our way thither, as we were passing down through a valley and over a little stream, we came to a negro cabin, a forlorn shanty standing in the edge of the wood. The inmates knew they had nothing to fear from us, and one old patriarch ventured out to help our men to a drink of water from the sparkling rivulet.

"Here, Brown, will you have some?" was asked by one of the boys.

The old man started as if a flash of electricity had been shot through his frame. The rude wooden bowl, with which he had been dipping up the water, dropped to his side, and he evidently had something to say.

"What is it, old man?" some one asked.

Brown had stepped forward to quench his thirst, and was drinking from a cup that his friend had handed him.

"Excuse me, gemmen," said the old darkey. "Did somebody speak de name o' Brown?"

"Yes, this is Brown, this man here that's drinking," said the other.

The old darkey bowed his head, gave as good a salute as he could, and seemed to be profoundly impressed.

"What are you bowing and scraping to him for? He doesn't know you; do you think he's one of your relations?"

"Ha, ha, Brown, I didn't know we were going to find any of your friends or relations down here," broke in one of the men.

The old man stood with a look of profoundest respect,

while Brown was manifestly an object to him of great interest.

"What are you bowing. to him for?" he was asked again.

"Gemmen," said the ancient negro, "'cause his name is Brown. Excuse me," he continued, "but be you de son o' John Brown?"

"MASSA" BROWN TAKES- THE CORN CAKE.

"No, I have not the honor to be the son of John Brown. I suppose you mean the John Brown of Harper's Ferry, whose soul is marching on?"

"Dat's him, Massa; dat's de one. And you ain't his son?"

"No; there are a good many Browns, you know, and my father was not John," was the reply.

"Mebbe you're his nephew?" continued the old man.

"Not that either," said Brown.

"Gemmen," exclaimed the old darkey, "he don't belong

to John, but it's de best name dis side o' Massa Linkum. If Adam had two names, I beliebs one on 'em was Adam, and de udder on 'em was Brown."

The boys were amused, and broke out into a kind of spontaneous cheer for the antiquated admirer of the "hero of Harper's Ferry."

The old man's wife meanwhile had come out of the cabin with something wrapped up in her dress, which was partially gathered up in front. She was greatly pleased to see our soldiers, and seemed to be anxious to express her satisfaction.

"What ye got dar?" inquired her husband.

"I brought de corn cake," she responded; "it's hot, and right out ob de ashes."

"Gib it to dis gemmen! Gib it to Massa Brown! Massa Brown's de man must have de corn cake—de whole on it, 'cause he's one ob de Browns, and dat's his name."

Brown was the lucky one that day, and having accepted the humble gift, and as politely thanked the old woman as if she had been a queen, we were again on our way and hurrying forward.

We finally reached the point where we could hear the distant boom of cannon. The roar of thunder came to us, and every man's blood ran faster. Over the plains, hills, valleys, came the awful sound, and there was something about it that inspired and nerved our men and made them forget their weariness. There is nothing like the noise and shock of actual conflict to rouse an army-man and get him ready for the fray. As we drew nearer we could hear the rattle of musketry. We knew the two great armies were engaged, and it would be a battle of Titans. Boom, boom, went the artillery, and sharp and severe was the fusillade of small arms. The very air seemed to quiver, as if made nervous by the struggle, and hearts beat high, and feet seemed to scarcely touch the ground as we pressed on to join the combatants. There was something which said more plainly than words could have done that our brave boys were ready to stay the hands of their comrades and conquer, or fall upon the field.

About five o'clock we reached the scene of conflict, and were immediately sent to a position on the right wing of the army. Although we had marched that hot summer day about twenty-seven miles, yet at actual roll-call there were not more than twenty absentees in our whole regiment. The men seemed to be made of iron, and they were proud to get back from Harper's Ferry and have a hand in what proved to be one of the most desperate conflicts of the war.

General Pope's command had been compelled to fall back within the intrenchments around Washington Banks succeeded Pope who was ordered West. The capital was menaced. This rendered the contest at Antietam more critical. There was a crisis in military affairs. The country was quivering with anxiety. We felt the responsibility that rested on our arms, as our forces were brought face to face with the troops of General Lee, already flushed with success.

As we pressed on farther into the line of battle, we knew our brave boys were steadily gaining ground, and driving the stubborn foe. The woods and fields prevented us from learning this by actual sight, but as we paused to await the order for action, we discovered that the sound of the musketry was moving farther and farther away. The strains of martial music could not have excited our division as did the rattle of guns which was gradually growing fainter and fainter. There was more music in that fierce fusillade, diminishing in force and moving onward every moment, than in "Yankee Doodle" or the "Star-spangled Banner." It told that splendid work for our forces was going on, and we were probably masters of the situation.

We could also hear the rousing cheers of the boys in blue. These were loud and hearty, and were altogether different from the wild shouts that came bursting from Confederate throats like balls screeching from the brazen mouths of a battery.

"Hear that!" shouted Sanderson, in a state of evident excitement. "Is that what they call the 'Confederate yell?'"

"If noise would win the day," remarked Vail, "we would be routed and captured, every mother's son of us. I would think all the demons of the infernal pit had been turned loose."

There came another terrific yell. It died away for a moment, and then was taken up and renewed with ten-fold vigor.

"I wonder if those fellows get double pay for screeching like that," continued Sanderson. "They can beat us, boys, when it comes to yelling; it is enough to frighten a wild hyena."

"Are you frightened, Sanderson?" some one asked.

"I shall never take the noise of a screech owl again for the 'Confederate yell,'" said Brixy. "I guess I can tell the difference now."

"There ain't screech-owls enough in all creation to set up such an infernal hooting as that," remarked another.

I will not attempt here to give any idea of that unearthly yell, but, once heard, it could never be forgotten. Ask any old soldier his opinion, and he will honestly say that it was peculiar to the Southern army.

As we marched upon the field of action we relieved the troops who had borne the brunt of the day's fighting at that particular point. When the opposing force saw fresh men confronting them they immediately opened the conflict anew. Briskly we responded, and soon had the satisfaction of perceiving a disposition on the part of the enemy to retire. Our officers and men were anxious to make a rapid, forward movement, and despatched a courier for permission to do so. Especially were we anxious to capture a battery that had been annoying us, and had proved even more destructive to our predecessors than to us, but we were directed to hold our position and await further orders. General Couch, however, commanded us to throw out a couple of regiments as skirmishers, and establish our picket-line considerably in advance, thus securing a better position. In this we were completely successful.

Then fell the shades of night. It did not take us long, after the fatigue of the day's marching and fighting to refresh ourselves with coffee and other rations, and then drop down upon our arms to sleep—some to dream of the delights of home, and those they were destined, as the event proved, never to meet again.

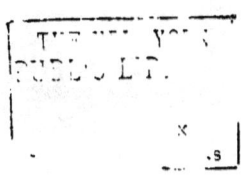

DASHING ACROSS THE BRIDGE AT ANTIETAM.

During the night the messages from our picket-line were frequently received at head-quarters, which, in turn, were reported to the officers high in command, all indicating that some remarkable movement was going on among the enemy's forces in front of us. Either they were receiving large re-enforcements, or were moving their artillery toward the rear, as if intending to recross the Potomac in the darkness. The day had been a bloody one. The valor of both sides had been fully displayed. The loss in the ranks and among the officers showed the desperate character of the struggle. Each army stood like a granite rock, and was determined not to yield an inch; and it was still doubtful which side would prove to be the victor.

Morning with rosy light dawned over the embattled hosts, and a stir ran through our ranks which indicated preparation for the deadly onset.

The history of our operations has been written, and I need do nothing more than narrate the transactions that came under my immediate notice.

The gallant Sumner advanced until his position was not far from the Dunker church on the Sharpsburg pike. Our troops there performed deeds that covered them with glory. Charge after charge was made by the enemy with a desperation almost unparalleled, but brave Sumner and his hardy men stubbornly held their ground against the legions hurled upon them by Longstreet and Lee. Here was witnessed some of the fiercest fighting in the whole engagement.

At this point Franklin's corps, of which we formed a part, reached the field. It seemed as if we could feel the effect of our coming before we joined in the battle. We were there none too soon. I was told afterward that one officer on another part of the field, who had been stunned by the din of cannon and clatter of musketry, and had seen the Confederates, like an avalanche, sweeping everything before them, whispered to a comrade, "That's Franklin. Hear him!" It was life or death to our battered forces, and we plunged forward as if every man were a regiment in himself and equal to a thousand. If there can be anything sublime in the fury of battle, that day saw it.

We were ordered to fill up a gap between General Hooker and General Sumner. The Confederates had noticed the gap, and were ignorant of the arrival of our troops. They had massed their forces under cover of the woods behind the Dunker church. Suddenly we saw their solid columns advancing on a double-quick run with arms at will. It seemed to be a Niagara sweeping the field. That same old demoniacal yell rent the air, and the onset was so terrible that for a moment our men wavered. Smoke and dust made the air thick, and the roar of cannon shook the earth. The recoil of Sumner's troops was only for an instant. Immediately they reformed on our right, and met the charge by a counter charge. Great masses of men were hurled against each other with a force that resulted in terrible havoc and slaughter. It was like two locomotives, at full speed, meeting each other in frightful collision. The contest was hand to hand. The enemy were frantic, apparently, and their raggedness and lean, worn, haggard look only made them seem the more wild and desperate.

Just then Richardson's division came up like a whirl-wind, and adding their forces to ours, we drove the daring foe like chaff before us. The Confederate commanders tried to rally their men in a hollow through which ran a road, and there again there was bloody work. Three and four deep the men and horses were afterward found to be lying, and in some places eight and ten deep, as if a breastwork of the dead had been made for the living.

Our men named the place "Bloody Lane," and Bloody Lane, let me say, is one of the historic localities, of which our country has so many. I never saw so many horses, dead or wounded, on one field as I saw that day. One especially was noticed whose head was erect as though he snuffed the battle afar, and one foot was extended as if he were ready to spring with a bound to his feet. In that position he had died after being struck by a cannon ball, and there he remained, stiffened and ghastly, for many days. Dead bodies of the enemy were also scat-tered in the adjacent corn-fields, and in places were corded up like piles of wood thrown down with one piece above another. Rank after rank had fallen, and the ground was about as completely covered as if a whole division of men had been ordered to lie down side by side for sleep. It has been said, and probably truly, that no spot on any of our crimsoned fields contained so many dead within the same space as this I am describing.

The Confederate charges were all made by close columns in mass. We could easily trace their line of battle by the gray coats left upon the field, the men who, in the attempt to rush to victory, rushed to a soldier's grave. The woods around the Dunker church were

10

piled with the slain, and several thousand abandoned rifles and muskets showed that the enemy was a good deal demoralized. It was reported that for a number of days subsequently the valley below us in Virginia was filled with unarmed stragglers who had broken away and were escaping to some more congenial locality.

Before active operations could begin next morning, we discovered a flag of truce in front of us, and the officer in command was instructed to inquire what it meant. A request had come from the Confederate commander that both armies should bury their dead. There was to be no passing beyond the lines by the forces on either side, and neither army was to change its position during the hours of truce. We acceded to the request, and for the moment forgot the sanguinary strife in the attempt to pay respect to the brave men who had fallen, and give them a decent burial on the field where their valor had cost them their lives.

I doubt if any reader of these lines who is not an army man can fully realize the strange incongruity of this truce. It afforded a direct contrast to the scenes of strife and carnage. The men who had fought one another so desperately the day before were now exchanging cordial greetings, and were hobnobbing together as if they were old friends.

One could hear such an off-hand salutation as, "Hello, Yank!" and then the response, "Hello, Reb!"

"Give us a shake," said a rough-looking Confederate to Herr Blinn, and held out his scrawny hand. "Let's shake while we can; none of you fellows will have a chance to shake anybody's hand by the time we get through with you."

Herr Blinn took the hand of his new acquaintance, and compressed it with his own capacious paw until the man winced, and cried, "Hold on!"

"Dot vas shust what I vas doing," answered Blinn, amidst the merriment of the crowd. "You see I vas so glad to meet you."

"Don't be so glad again," said the other, shaking his fingers.

"Not unless I meets you dead," responded Blinn, who would not abate his loyalty, nor soften down the bluntness of his expressions.

While this was going on, a number were striking up bargains and making all manner of trades. Some wanted tobacco for coffee; others would exchange a jack-knife for a pen-knife; and others wrangled in the attempt to trade an old stub lead pencil for a pair of shoe-strings. The battle-field was converted into a market, and men were as eager to make bargains as if they were buying a farm instead of dickering over an old corn-cob pipe.

"Let's trade shoes," said a strapping Confederate to Herr Blinn. I can't get a pair in the whole army big enough for me."

Off came Blinn's shoes and the other got into them. "Here, Jake," he cried to a comrade, "come on; I can take you right in with me."

"Yes," said the other, "you could put our whole company into them shoes; they would make good bridges for our men to cross the Potomac on."

Blinn had succeeded in getting his toes into the shoes of the other man's, and could go no farther. "I makes

no drade mit you," he remarked, "dere's too much small-
ness to dem shoes ; you dinks I give you vat's so pig for
vat's so leedle ?   I does no such ding."

Blinn could not have traded shoes with many men
without being taken at a disadvantage, if size had been
the main thing to be considered.

"Hello, Reb," exclaimed Sanderson to one of the
enemy ; "got anything you want to trade ?"

"Don't know ; what you got you want to get rid of ?"

"Hard-tack," said Sanderson, "and lots of it."

"Hard enough, Yank, I guess," said the other.   "I
like it pretty well, though ; I just found some pieces on
the field, and I managed to eat them."

"How did it come to be in pieces ?"

"Got run over by the wheel of a gun-carriage."

"I'll tell you, boys," said Sanderson, "how we can
break up hard-tack ; just let a battery run over it ; that's
a new way of doing it."

"Don't put down too much at once," interrupted
Vail, "it might break the wheels and disable the
battery."

Sanderson managed to trade off some of his hard-tack
for pancakes, or slap-jacks, as they were commonly
called, and turned to leave.

"Hold on !" shouted the Confederate, who had contrived to break off a piece and was attempting to chew
it, "this is the grittiest thing I ever tried to eat ; it's got
stones in it."

"Let's see," replied Sanderson.

The Confederate took something out of his mouth,
examined it, and exclaimed, "Danged if it ain't a piece
of one of my teeth."

"You may be thankful that it didn't break your jaw," replied Sanderson. "It's hard to satisfy some fellows, anyway."

The man lifted the butt of his gun and made a motion which indicated that Sanderson's days were numbered. He grabbed a piece of hard-tack, held it out at arms' length, and said, "Don't strike me; just hit that; I would like to see your old gun smashed to flinders."

There was a hearty laugh all round, and the friendly dickering went on at a brisk rate. This was a phase of army life so new and unusual that all seemed to enjoy it.

The Confederates playfully boasted that they were going to whip us, and we resented with spirit all such talk.

Meanwhile the burial of the dead went on. We had an opportunity to see what carnage had been wrought by the conflict of the previous day. There were charges of infantry, and counter charges; and the blue and gray were stretched side by side in the calm embrace of death. Horses were lying here and there among the men who had fallen, and the ground was reddened with blood. Dismounted cannon and exploded caissons were scat - tered about in confusion. The field had been trampled until there was little sign of vegetation; it had been beaten to dust under the feet of the contending forces. The heaps of slain told where the battle was the fiercest, and the brave men wept as they lifted the mangled forms of their comrades and carried them away to their shallow graves. Fine young fellows who, a little time before, were dashing over the disputed field, men beloved by all who knew them, had met their death like heroes, and the ranks where they stood were to be closed up, and their names were henceforth to be spoken with praise for their valor, and regret for their fate. There was little said at the roll-call; there was a silence that was pathetic.

Another sight, and that a sad one, must not be overlooked. I noticed several houses that had been demolished; nothing was left but heaps of ruins; homes had been emptied, and the inmates had fled from their own firesides to seek a shelter and place of safety elsewhere. If the buildings had been allowed to stand they would have afforded a cover for squads of infantry who, being protected, could have inflicted incalculable damage on the opposing forces. I judged that it would be easier and cheaper to build new houses than to attempt to repair those that had been wrecked by the grim necessities of war. Those homes which had cost long and patient labor, and perhaps an economy that had been exercised for years, were swept away as in a moment. All private interests and comforts were ruthlessly destroyed by the blast of battle. We could not consult the convenience of families whose homes were in the path of the advancing army. But ruined houses and barns did not present so ghastly a sight as did the men who had been slain, or were mangled by wounds that made it necessary to place them in hospitals.

The bugle sounded the end of the truce, and the men of both armies sprang to their positions, as eager for the next trial of strength as if no friendly intercourse had been going on between them.

The Confederate legions could not recover from the blow already received. Lee was more anxious to secure the safety of his army than to make fresh conquests, or measure swords with his antagonist. The Federals were grimly set on holding the advantage gained. Our troops half forgot the terrible cost of the battle in the excitement and joy of success.

The invasion of Maryland had been repelled. The South found that in counting upon the enthusiasm and co-operation of the people of Maryland she made a huge mistake. The bombastic proclamation of General Lee, seeking by flattery and an appeal to sentiment to win the populace to his cause, had failed. It was treated almost as indifferently as if it had been a scrap of old newspaper blown upon the wind.

Lee's bold army was rolled back, and with the skill of a master he made good his retreat.

CHAPTER XII.

HOST AGAINST HOST.

"The soldiers of the great West have added new laurels to those already won on numerous fields "—*General H. W. Halleck.*

ENERAL GRANT had been placed in command of our armies in the West. Already he was coming forward as one of the principal figures among our gallant commanders. The men were convinced of his pluck and tenacity, and there was a general conviction that Grant "meant business."

I was speaking of him one morning to some of my men as we were discussing the situation throughout the country. Major Beckstein joined eagerly in the conversation, which was all the more animated for the reason that so much uneasiness was felt respecting the unsettled policy at Washington as to the command of the Army of the Potomac.

"Three cheers for Grant!" exclaimed the major; and then without waiting to have them given, he continued, "they say Grant is a hammerer; he sticks like a good fellow, makes up his mind to do a thing, and bye and bye it's done."

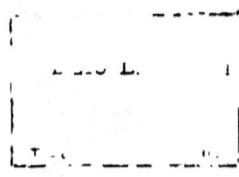

NAVAL BATTLE AT MEMPHIS, TENN.

" Let him be a hammerer," I replied; "there are some things that ought to be hammered, and nothing but hammering will serve the purpose."

" I don't care how he wins," broke in the major again, "if he only does it; and I don't believe the South will ever be subdued by a military parade and the music of a brass band."

" I think Grant is a fighter," I said, " and if he shall prove to be the best fighter, he will be the most popular man in the country. Don't you know, major, the newspapers are trying to manage every campaign, and are all the time clamoring to have something done?"

" Yes," replied the major, " there are many men who show their patriotism and valor by staying home and expressing their opinion as to how the war ought to be carried on."

" That reminds me," said Sanderson, " of the man who was giving advice to a friend that had quarreled with his wife. He would make her do better and behave herself. 'No, you wouldn't,' said the other. ' Why wouldn't I?' 'Because you haven't got her for a wife; you don't know the woman.' And so its always easy," continued Sanderson, " to tell what other people ought to do; let them try it "

" Talk is cheap," said the major, " and any man who shows a capacity to act is the one the country is going to believe in."

" I think Beckstein," I answered, "that every man of us is convinced that bombs and cartridges and bayonets will have to end the struggle, and I shall be surprised if we don't see some hot work before our army is ready to give up the contest. I think, as you do, that we can't blow a bugle, and beat a drum, and march in uniform, and wave a flag, and win the contest by doing nothing more; there's got to be fighting."

This I said with the feeling which was shared by nearly all our men, that on several occasions our troops had not been allowed to take advantage of their successes and opportunities, and the conflict had not been made as vigorous as the exigencies demanded. Of one thing I am confident: our gallant heroes were ready for any danger and sacrifice that promised any advantage or success.

We were not altogether pleased with the fact that our garrison at Harper's Ferry had surrendered the place, and that "Stonewall" Jackson had captured that stronghold at so trifling an expense.

Bragg had been operating in the West. His advance on Cincinnati had failed, and he tried then to deliver over Kentucky to the Confederacy. The battle of Corinth had been fought, and in Tenessee the Union lines had been extended south by the capture of Memphis.

Fresh troops were wanted after the losses sustained by sickness and in our recent campaigns. The call came, and again the North responded. Those who did not wish to undergo a personal experience in the army adopted the bounty system, and sent others to fill the gaps, and replete our diminished forces.

After Antietam our army was a good deal disorganized. We had lost a good many men by malaria and fever among the swamps of Virginia, and about every regiment had ample material for starting a hospital, even after we escaped from the sickly region where our operations had been carried on.

Along the Potomac our troops were distributed after Lee had been foiled at Antietam and had found to his great mortification that the people of Maryland were by no means friendly to his advance.

MRS. PETERS WELCOMES OUR TROOPS WITH HER GINGHAM APRON.

We learned many little incidents that showed the spirit of the population along the line of Lee's march.

"How did you treat them?" I said to an old woman who, as she had no Union flag to welcome us with, was waving her gingham apron from the front door of her cottage with an enthusiasm which led me to fear that the apron would be spoiled beyond redemption.

"How did I treat them? As they deserved," she exclaimed, with an emphasis such as a woman knows how to give.

"Did you get a call from them?" I asked.

"Lor, yes; and I hope you'll return it for me."

"You were not pleased to see them, I take it."

"Not much; they stole pork out of my cellar, and then they added insult to injury by calling me 'granny,' I wonder what they took me to be. And as sure as you live, 'twas the first time I was ever called 'granny.' O they're a rough set. No, Mr. Officer, my neighbors always have respect for me, and they know my name is Mrs. Peters; believe me, it was the first time I ever had my feelin's hurt by being called ' granny.'"

"I guess they thought you were not giving them a very warm reception," I remarked.

"I wanted to give them a reception they would remember," spoke up the old lady, still holding on to her apron and waving it occasionally as if she were driving chickens away from the door. "They wanted water, and I told 'em I'd give it to them hot if they didn't clear out. Lor, Mr. Officer, they all looked as if they wanted washing. It would have just done me good to pour hot water on the whole gang."

" You wanted to baptize them, I suppose, with a hot tea-kettle," I replied.

"Well, not exactly that, 'cause you see I'm a Babtist, thorough-going, a 'hard shell,' as some calls 'em, and I did want to put them under, and have the water bilin', too!"

"Pretty vigorous treatment," said Vail.

"I know it," broke in the old lady, "but it does some things a mighty heap o' good to cook 'em. I just told 'em I'd like to fight 'em with hot water."

Mrs. Peters emphasized her remarks with her apron,

holding it up, and flourishing it vigorously, and bringing it down with a force that suggested death and destruction to General Lee's whole army if she had the management of the campaign.

"And there's that pork," she continued; "they took the best of it, but, gentlemen, what's left, and such as it is, you're welcome to it."

" Egscuse me," interrupted the familiar voice of Herr Blinn; "if dot pork is scarce, I don't obshecks to poultry."

I should do injustice to the loyal people of Maryland if I did not here make grateful mention of their kindness to our troops. The very poorest were willing to lend aid, and, with the exception of a few sympathizers with the Confederate cause, we received from the populace evidences of joy and satisfaction at our coming. Water which was fit to drink, was one of the greatest blessings they conferred; for we had been farther south among the swamps where water was more like a poison than a healthful beverage. Little acts of kindness made us all feel as if we were not far from home. Bandages and plasters for sore feet, liniment for stiff joints and limbs, needles and thread for sewing the rents in our worn clothing, fruit to eat, and more substantial fare when it could be afforded, all contributed to show the spirit of the people and to make us forget our fatigues and sufferings.

Our division was ordered to Williamsport, and thence to Hancock, where we remained but a few days. The next move found us resting on the Sharpsburg pike, and doing picket duty along the banks of the Potomac We had an opportunity to recuperate somewhat our wasted energies. The change to a less wearing and taxing service was of immense advantage, and our men improved in health and spirits every day. If we had remained much longer in the swamps of the Chickahominy, we would have lost more from our ranks by disease than we did in actual engagement on the field. The climate and surroundings put new life into our tried veterans. Brixy's country color came back to him, and Sanderson facetiously remarked that Herr Blinn did not look so pale and thin as he did a little time before, and that there was no longer any danger that Blinn would go into an early decline. Sanderson himself did not have the appearance of being very delicate.

Still the people at home were fighting the war out, and newspaper generals were asking, "Why doesn't the army move?" Many thought General McClellan should have pushed on like a cataract beyond Antietam, after Lee had been worsted and escaped south of the Potomac; but it was understood that McClellan had no clothing nor supplies for a forward movement.

One of our men who talked a good deal, and made as much noise with his tongue as he ever did with his musket, broke out indignantly, "Why doesn't McClellan push on, and follow up and get through, and let us go home?"

"No supplies," some one replied.

"Confound it," said the other, "McClellan is always getting out of something. If it isn't hard-tack, or blankets, or clothing, it is something else. He'd stop the whole army a month to get plasters for the fellers' corns."

It must be admitted that there were delays which even to this day are unaccountable, not only on the part of our commander-in-chief, but on the part of others, some of them in very high position.

The command came in October to move, and we recrossed the Potomac at Berlin. We marched by the way of New Baltimore, remaining there a few days. Here the news reached us that General McClellan had again been suspended, and ordered to report at his home at Trenton, New Jersey. This was the last of his military life, and he never afterward was placed in command. This action of the Government caused a vast amount of comment among our soldiers, some approving it, and others condemning it in unmeasured terms. General Halleck came in for a full share of blame, many declaring he would rather see the Army of the Potomac shattered and disbanded, than to see it successful under any other general than himself or one of his favorites.

General Burnside, having been appointed commander, there was an expectation at once that vigorous measures would be enacted, and in this the country was not disappointed.

Lee was intrenched at Fredericksburg. The shattered ranks had been closed up, the stragglers had been called in, the strength had been husbanded and increased, and at this point, a natural fortification in itself, he resolved to make a stand. There was no Richmond for us so long as there was a Fredericksburg for the Confederates. I will not discuss here the wisdom or folly of the resolve to capture this place at that particular time. Nothing save a bold push would satisfy the war spirits at home. On we pressed.

General Burnside had received the promise that pontoon bridges should be sent without dely that he might throw his army across the Rappahannock. How the

failure is to be accounted for, or whether it can be accounted for at all, is a question of a puzzling character; but days passed, and pontoons came not. Our army had arrived, after vigorous marching, at Falmouth on the north bank of the river. Hooker, Sumner and Franklin were in command of the various divisions. "Fighting Joe Hooker" had the name of using speech as hot as the shot from a Union battery, and was reported to have made it a little extra hot through impatience to act against the enemy.

"FIGHTING JOE HOOKER."

About the 10th of December the bridges arrived, and by this time Lee had made the most of his position, and every hour of our delay had been to him an advantage.

At once our men began to get the bridges ready for crossing. This was a perilous undertaking. The Confederate pickets were prepared for sharp and effective resistance, and some of their batteries began to play with a liveliness that, to us, was not altogether agreeable. We had no cover, but were compelled to work in a position that was fully exposed. The most our men could do was to exchange shots with the enemy, and fight across the river. Along a stretch of several miles this desultory conflict went on, while the troops detailed to lay the pontoons were suffering severely, many having been

PONTOON BRIDGE

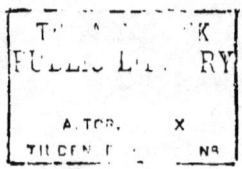

killed, and others wounded. Under a damaging fire the brave boys worked away, the sound of the axe and hammer mingling with the rattle of the enemy's rifles.

I noticed one arm drop after the tool had been lifted; the blow was never given; a bullet had arrested the falling stroke. The man was hastily carried to the shore, and another instantly stepped forward to take his place. Blood ran over the boards and timbers of the bridges and reddened the river beneath. Still the undertaking was pressed steadily forward until probably half the space to the opposite shore had been covered, when the firing became so sharp and deadly that it was madness to attempt to face it.

Instantly our artillery began to rain its iron hail upon the city of Fredericksburg in front of us. Shot went screaming through the air, over the river, and fell upon the doomed town in a frightful storm of devastation.

Orders were given for some of our troops to cross in boats above and below the bridge, and this movement was speedily executed. The regiments at once formed, checked the enemy's infantry column that was advancing toward the river, and in a brief space of time changed the situation. Again came the sound of axes and hammers; our men had sprung to the work of pontoon laying with fresh resolve, and soon there was a pathway for our army from bank to bank. Our spirited forces went over with quick step and high courage; whether all felt that it was an advance into the jaws of death, and so joked and frolicked through a spirit of bravado, or were really ignorant of the dangerous and desperate nature of the contest, at all events there was hilarity among our advancing

11

veterans, which, alas, was soon subdued and changed to a more serious feeling.

Probably General Lee could have held his position with ten thousand men. It is not likely that more than a small part of his command was actively engaged at any

PONTOON BRIDGE AT FREDERICKSBURG.

one time. His line of defence was well chosen, and by working night and day during our vexatious waiting for pontoons, he had intrenched himself strongly back of the town in an elevated position, simply defying any attempt to dislodge him. Up to these blazing heights, amidst the terrible baptism of fire, bullets and shells falling like rain upon the fatal field, our gallant boys charged, and paid most dearly for their bravery. The slaughter was shocking, beyond all power of description. Long rows of ambulances moved away to the rear, and the groans of the wounded and dying rose through the din of battle, and the fiery storm that swept down from the impregnable intrenchments of the foe.

The town of Fredericksburg was battered by a hundred guns. The frightened inhabitants had fled as our army approached; the streets were abandoned save by marching infantry and unlimbering batteries; the houses looked like deserted prisons, while on all sides was the havoc of battle, buildings riddled and torn, chimneys overturned, roofs blazing from hot shot, debris of every sort scattered about in wild confusion.

The result of this unequal contest is well known. The Union forces went to their doom as if going to a jubilee. Never was valor more conspicuous than on that dreadful day. To carry the heights along which the foe had planted all the munitions of defense, was an impossibility, and yet that impossibility was attempted over and over again with a courage and daring that amounted to absolute recklessness.

Intrepid Sumner led our centre, and as darkness drew on, bodies of infantry were shifted in order to strengthen his command. But the day's carnage was not to be repeated. Soon after the thick night settled down over us, I could hear the tramp of infantry withdrawing over the bridge to the opposite side of the Rappahannock.

"Are we going to retire from the contest, colonel?" I asked.

"Yes," he answered, "and for the reason that our men cannot perform a miracle. I tell you, Preston, to take that stronghold would be a superhuman thing."

"I know it, but all the same I would like to see it done."

"The cost would be too great," he continued, "and we shall be lucky if we get off without being broken up and thoroughly thrashed."

And here let me say that had it not been for the stubborn determination of as brave an army as ever drew a sword, the day would have ended in an inglorious rout; but our forces moved and acted like a living machine, and by their courage and endurance saved the North from what otherwise would have been an overwhelming disaster. General Meade distinguished himself by penetrating the enemy's lines, and if he had been promptly and ably supported the fortunes of the day might have been rescued. With such aid as we felt might have been rendered by troops not engaged, Meade could probably have held the ground gained when he turned Lee's flank. The morning saw our army saved, although our loss in the engagement was heavy.

Discipline helped us splendidly and we came back without the loss, so far as I know, of artillery or wagon-train. One or two caissons had been blown up during the battle, but we left very few equipments, and very little material of any description that could be of any value to the enemy.

In the afternoon, while the battle was raging in fury, it became necessary to send a message to Stafford Heights on the north side of the Rappahannock, a point which overlooked the town of Fredericksburg, and in fact the whole field of the engagement. I volunteered to deliver the order. Major Beckstein grasped my hand as I prepared to render this service, and wished me success and a safe return.

My message was to be delivered to our chief of artillery who at the time was superintending a battery of twenty-pound Parrot guns that was actively engaged in shelling the Confederate lines over the heads of the boys in blue. The spot where the battery was planted was not only a fine point of observation, but also a capital place for getting a good aim at General Lee's intrenchments.

"What are you doing here?" I said to one of the artillerymen.

"Just firing at a mark, sergeant," he answered. "Do you know," he continued, "we can shoot a gun like one of these as if it was a rifle. It carries straight as an arrow."

"Better than the guns they used to make in old times, then," I replied. "We have got weapons of all sorts just about perfect now"

"I don't see how they did any damage in the Revolution with their old muskets," said the man. "Why, my father had one that had been through the war, and you couldn't hit a barn door with it at a distance of ten paces. I've used it many times, and the only thing I ever hit was a dog, and I hit him with the butt end of the musket."

At this moment two generals were in conversation with the chief of the ordinance. They had their glasses to their eyes and were looking across to the formidable works on the other side of the river.

The chief also lifted his glass, paused a moment as he

surveyed the lines of the enemy, and then said, "Do you see that officer riding a white horse inside Lee's fortifications?"

We all saw the horse and his rider distinctly.

"You won't see that horse long," exclaimed the artilleryman, whose acquaintance I had just made. "Anyhow, I'll try him."

"You don't think you can hit that target at such a distance, do you?" I inquired. "I don't believe it can be done. How far is it, chief?"

He thought the distance was not much less than three miles.

The gunner took aim, and then said, "Now look! I'll be ready in a moment."

The horse and rider were in motion. The gunner made his calculation, pointed his gun, and in a moment the ball went as straight through the air as though it had been a beam of light. Quick as a flash the white horse with his rider fell. I have never seen or known a finer piece of cannonading than that.

"By Jove!" shouted one of the officers, "you have dropped him."

The other officer broke in, "It's the most expert piece of marksmanship I ever witnessed."

We all agreed that it was a feat seldom equalled, as we broke out with three hearty cheers for the gunner.

My order having been delivered, my next concern was to rejoin my regiment. The whole surrounding locality wore a feverish look, and a tremor seemed to run through the very ground under foot. The loud report of bombs and the sharp continuous roll of musketry rose upon the air, while here and there aids were seen galloping from point to point with hurried orders, or bringing news of the fortunes of the day.

As I sprang out from a clump of underbrush, intending to leap across an unfrequented road and shorten the distance I had to go, suddenly I came into collision with a horseman. He was going at full speed, and had no time to draw in his reins and save me from the danger of being trampled to jelly by his horse's hoofs.

"Hold!" I shouted, as I almost fell headlong down the bank into the road.

The rider gave a sudden jerk, rose in his stirrups, instantly drew a revolver, and as his horse sprang by me he turned and fired. One fore leg of the animal had struck me on one side, though fortunately not with any great force, and I turned over just as the ball grazed past my head and buried itself in the ground beneath.

The man halted a little farther on and came galloping back.

"What do you mean?" I demanded, with an anger which must have been evident.

"And I would like to know what you mean," he answered back. "What in all creation are you doing there, and who are you?"

"Doing here? I'm not here to be shot, thank you," I responded.

"'Pon my word," the aide de-camp replied, "I took you to be a highwayman, or some one of the enemy who meant to capture me."

"Couldn't you tell by my uniform," I asked, "that I am a Union man?"

"I had no time to think," he replied. "You came on me so quick that I fired almost as by instinct. Beg your pardon, I hope you are not hurt."

"Not hurt," I said, "but mighty near it."

Away he sped again, and when I arrived back the boys wondered what mishap had befallen me. My appearance was against me, and my clothes were stained with the sacred soil of Virginia.

"See here, fellows," exclaimed Sanderson, "Preston's wounded!"

"Where?" shouted half a dozen.

"In his pants," jocosely answered Sanderson. "Those breeches will have to go to the hospital."

"I'm thankful that I'm not wounded worse than that," I responded.

Later events gave me an experience of rents and wounds in the flesh instead of clothing.

While in camp one morning not long after this, I received word from our colonel that he wished to see me on important business.

"Sergeant," he said, "I have forwarded your name to Governor Curtin for promotion as second lieutenant."

I pleasantly answered, "You seem to be taking liberties with your men."

"That is only what they must expect, if they are the kind of men who are worth taking the liberty with."

"Colonel," I replied, "I can only say I have not avoided any service, and have tried to do my duty."

"Sergeant," he continued, "one of our companies is at present without a commanding officer. You will immediately report for duty and take command."

1 thanked him cordially, and assured him I would strive to prove worthy of the trust.

Heavy rains had fallen; the weather was wet and chilly, and the camp-fire at night was a comfort and a necessity. Rails taken from the fences in the neighborhood were used for fuel and our orders were to take only the top rail. Each fellow obeyed the orders, carried off the top rail, and soon the bottom rail became the top one.

Not long after this other changes and promotions in our corps were made, and I received my commission as captain, retaining the company that had been previously placed under my command.

One serious drawback about this time to the efficiency of our troops arose from petty jealousies. There was a struggle for place and promotion. Men wished to make capital out of their service in the army. My commission was all the more gratifying to me because it came in the natural order of things, and was attended by the confidence and best wishes of my men.

CHAPTER XIII.

"What concentrated joy or woe, in blessed or blighted
love!"

"RIXY has heard from Jane!"
These were the words that were
whispered about among the men one
morning while we were lying in camp.

Some of the men were of the number
who were present when Brixy, by the
aid of a comrade had prepared that
astounding epistle described in a pre-
vious chapter. It had been received in due time by the
captivating young lady to whom it was addressed.

A glance at Brixy was enough to convince any one
that at last he had heard from Jane. There could be no
doubt about it. The heart of Jane had been beating
true to the gallant soldier boy who was "off" to the war."
Every look and motion of Brixy seemed to say, "Three
cheers for Jane!"

If the letter had come from Vanderbilt announcing
that he had given a handsome legacy to Joe Brixy, it
could not have been any more welcome, and Joe Brixy
could not have been any more happy.

"I hope there is something in that letter for me," said one of the boys. "Did she send her love?"

"Has it got a lock of her hair in it?" chimed in another. "I don't care if it is tow hair, if she has tied it with a blue ribbon."

"Jane ain't no tow-head, let me tell you," Brixy indignantly replied. "Her hair is a little colored, I know, and grows rather straight, but she makes it kind o' crooked sometimes by doing it up in papers, and then you ought to see it."

"Ask her to send me one of the papers," broke in Sanderson, still maintaining his reputation for being a wag. "Of course, Brixy, I would like one of her curls, but if I can't get that, I'll take the other. Anything, you know, just for a keepsake."

"Look here, captain," said Brixy, "these fellers who ain't got any girl, and can't get none, are trying to steal away Jane's affections. She's got hair enough, and curl papers too. but none for them. She's true to Joe Brixy; that's the kind o' girl Jane is."

"I congratulate you," I replied.

"Yes," he went on, "she don't raise curls for other fellers. If she was bald as a singed cat and had to wear a wig, she'd give every hair of it to Joe Brixy. No, captain, she don't raise hair nor curl papers for any chap except Joe Brixy."

Brixy's honest, brown face was beaming with satisfaction, and the simple hearted fellow seemed to be happy as a king. I had noticed that he was always in a state of unusual excitement when letters were brought into our ranks. It was so, in fact, with all the men. The arrival of the mail was a great occasion. Words cannot describe the anxiety we always had to hear from home. I have seen the eager look of expectation change to one akin to despair when the orderly had called over all the names superscribed on the batch of letters, and the one who had been waiting so anxiously for news was again disappointed. And I have known men actually to be made sick and unfitted for duty for the reason that no tidings had been received from loved ones left behind. I am happy to record a fact so creditable to our men. Let no one call it weakness on their part. It showed that the heart which beat high with patriotism and courage was also possessed of the finer feelings of human nature, and the gentle emotions of a true and noble manhood. These could not be weakened by the bitterness of deadly strife, nor trampled out by the iron hoof of war.

It was a great occasion for Brixy when he received his letter. It was in answer to the one he sent, in which, as he was not writing it himself, he had directed the one who did write it to assure Jane that he did not consider her as his girl and the expressions of love were not for her; and then had insisted that it should be be signed with the name of Joe Brixy, a thing which had to be done for him, as he was a good deal deficient in the matter of penmanship.

I almost thought we would have to take Brixy to the guard house for insubordination when the letter was placed in his hand. He held it up, waved it over his head, and began hopping about like an Indian in a war-dance, ‑breaking in upon the conversation already described.

"Give us the double shuffle." called out Sanderson.

Brixy's boots were of a comprehensive kind. and his stiff limbs were not sufficiently nimble to make a success of such an undertaking, but as he was in a lively mood he made the attempt.

"Do your best, now," said Brown; "here, let me hold your hat."

"Let me hold the letter," said Sanderson. "Perhaps you'll let me keep it?"

"Not much; a letter from Jane wouldn't come home to you as it does to me."

Brixy planted his left foot on the ground, and limbering up his right leg as well as he could, began shuffling in genuine school-boy fashion.

"You're only a one-horse dancer," exclaimed Sanderson. "Why don't you let fly with your other foot?"

"If Jane was here," responded Brixy, "she could do it. One horse? I tell you, boys, Jane is a whole team at it. You see, Sanderson, I'm not very graceful with that left leg, and that's the reason why I do all my dancing with the tother. As Jane says, I like them that's graceful. Now, she can do it with both feet, and is just as nat'ral on one as the other. Lor, boys, I wish you could see her."

The boys gave various expressions which indicated that it would afford them no little pleasure to see Jane in a lively double shuffle.

"Yes," continued Brixy, she handles one foot just as well as tother. The only time I ever knew her when she didn't, was when we had one of them donation parties at Parson Kirk's and the young folks got out into the kitchen; then Jane didn't do her best, 'cause she said, as 'twas the Parson's house, and a sort o' pious place, she'd dance with only one foot."

During these proceedings, which interested and rather amused a number of the men, Brixy's letter had remained unopened. It was a question how he was to get at the contents. The writing inside was all Greek to Brixy. Jane's simple heart might have overflowed, and gushed like a freshet, but he would have been none the wiser unless some one had read the tender missive and conveyed to him the meaning of the precious lines.

"Let me take it," said Corporal Vail. "I'll tell you what is in it."

Brixy could trust Vail, as everybody could, and rely upon his kind spirit and honesty.

Vail took the letter, broke the seal, looked at the coarse scrawl, and managed to make out the hand-writing, although it was not an easy thing to do. He read as follows:

"Joe Brixy,

"If you aint dead, you ought ter be. I don't care if this finds you buried ten foot deep. What did you mean, Joe Brixy, by writin' sich a letter as I got from you? If you're alive, I want you to answer If you're dead, I'll egscuse you. You're a big villin, and Marm says to tell you so. Do you think—?"

"Hold up!" shouted Brixy, that ain't from Jane."

His eyes had been bulging out more and more during the reading of the few sentences, his face took on an expression of utter astonishment, and he stood with his capacious mouth wide open.

The corporal read on : "Do you think I'm goin' to stand that kind o' tretement? Didn't you say you'd never forget your Jane, and no girl that ever seen stars was so dear to you as your own sweet Jane? Then to tell me I ain't your dear—I ask agin what you mean, Joe Brixy ? "

"Gosh blazes !" shouted Brixy, "do you s'pose I'm goin' to believe Jane writ that ? No sir ! I tell you, Corporal Vail, you're just makin' that up. 'Tisn't in the letter at all, I know it ain't." And Brixy looked angry and confused, red and white, silly and thunder-struck, all at once.

The boys were wild with the fun, and told the corporal to read on. Brixy, with great vehemence, maintained that Vail was playing a joke on him ; and a girl as true as Jane was never could have sent such a letter to the one she loved above all others.

"It's all here," protested the corporal; "every word of it. I'm not deceiving you, nor making up anything."

"That sounds just like a red-head !" exclaimed one. "O, she's got some other fellow in her eye."

"Hello, Brixy ! " called out another, ' didn't I tell you I'd cut you out ? Don't you remember, I'm the one that sent my love to her in that letter she got from you ? I would't read you what she wrote to me ; it would make you feel bad."

" Boys," said another, "do you want to see a picture of Jane? I showed it to some of you when Brixy showed you his. Here it is, and no speck on her nose either."

Brixy was puzzled. "Tell me now for sure, corporal," he said, "is all that in the letter you read just now ? "

"Every word of it."

"Then I swear she's gone back on me; Jane's not the girl I took her to be. Why, corporal, I didn't tell her she wasn't my dear; it was the other fellow what writ the letter."

"But," said the corporal, "it came from you."

"No, it didn't come from me; I never writ her a letter in my life. What makes her think she ain't Joe Brixy's dear when the other fellow said she wasn't his dear, and I never said it to her at all?"

"Let's hear the rest of the letter," said Brown, and the corporal read on:

"What did you tell me, you black-hearted retch, when you left me? Think of all the nights we've sot up together, and walked up and down the road, and leaned over the fence. I thought you was somebody, but you ain't fit to be shot at. Don't come home alive, Joe Brixy; come dead, if you're comin' at all."

Brixy looked wilted, and that was remarked by Brown.

"Wilted because jilted," said Sanderson. "Have we had all the letter?"

"Not quite," replied Vail; "there's some poetry here. I think it was put in as a finishing touch."

"Read it," broke in a dozen voices.

The corporal read:

> "My pen is poor, my ink is pale,
> They ought to ride you on a rail."

"Is that all?" inquired Brixy, with a look of anxiety. "I don't want any more letters, boys. She's been and got mad over nothin'. She don't know how to take things. Why, when we parted that day at Suffolk Park she was just as sweet and nice; now see what she's done; just see how she treats a feller."

"They're all alike," said one.

"O, no," said Sanderson; "they can't all dance as Jane can, and write poetry of that sort. Shall we carry out her wishes and ride you on a rail, Brixy?"

"Shentlemens," exclaimed Herr Blinn, his immense size indicating that his weight might be computed by the ton, "if dot Brixy is to be rode on von rail, I volunteers to dake his blace and ride der rail."

HERR BLINN'S CONVEYANCE BREAKS DOWN.

A shout went up at the idea of riding a man of Blinn's ponderous proportions on any such conveyance, and none were displeased at the mark of sympathy shown by him for Brixy. Of course the rail broke, and when Blinn came down there was a shock like an earthquake.

It may seem singular that two letters should have brought about such a misunderstanding; but it must be remembered that one was not penned by the lover who sent it.

The mystery of that second photograph yet remains. How another should have a picture of Jane, and be boasting that she was his girl, is something that cannot be solved here and now.

I have felt compelled to state the truth in this falling out between one of our boys and his adorable sweetheart, although I am aware it may leave some actors in the scene open to the suspicion of playing off certain practical jokes.

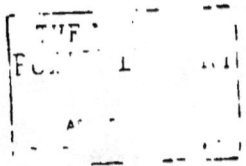

WINTER CAMP AFTER A SNOW-STORM.

CHAPTER XIV.

" Chilled Nature takes a vail of snow
To hide her withered face."

URING the winter we remained in camp not far from Falmouth. Military operations, to a great extent, had to be suspended. Wind and snow were not friendly to the advance of infantry or artillery.

Very little duty was required of our men except on guard and picket ; this was something that never could be dispensed with. We had enough to do, however, to secure fire-wood. Although we were encamped in a piece of woods of some extent, the trees very soon disappeared and scarcely a vestige of fuel remained. Then we pushed out to places some distance away, and before spring arrived we were compelled to carry our fuel two miles or more. This was a species of exercise somewhat subduing to the boys, and not well calculated to improve their temper. The green wood was heavy, the roads were not in the best condition, and Sanderson facetiously remarked that he would prefer to be at home with his wife to bring up the coal.

"Would you allow her to do that?" said one of the men.   (179)

"I always had an accommodating disposition," remarked Sanderson.

"Besides," broke in Brown, "probably she wouldn't care to have the fire go out."

This hit at Sanderson's lazy habits was relished by the group.

It was cause for surprise and congratulation that we had so few cases of colds or coughs, although our men did not enter a house of any kind for a year or more, and only shelter tents were provided for them. With that invention which comes from necessity, we adapted ourselves to circumstances and made the most out of a little. Each man was allowed one piece of tent-cloth, four feet by six in size, but in order to make the best of this scant allowance the boys divided themselves into fours. I do not mean to affirm that they quartered themselves; the enemy was ready to do that when occasion offered. The men grouped themselves in fours, and, securing logs of convenient length, framed them together, and built a foundation three or four feet high, and on this set up the tent, reserving two pieces for the ends, to keep out the cold and rain. The joints of the logs were stuffed with genuine Virginia mud, which was thick enough, in all conscience, to keep out the frost or anything else. With no little ingenuity a fire-place was constructed, with a barrel outside for a chimney. If a puff of wind sometimes filled the tent with smoke, and brought tears to the eyes of the inmates, they had at least coat sleeves, if not pocket handkerchiefs, to wipe away these little ebullitions of feeling. Many were the scenes which indicated that our soldiers were very tender hearted, and could weep on the shortest notice.

"Brixy," said Corporal Vail, one day, " what makes
your eyes so red?"

"Thinking of Jane, I guess," said Sanderson.

"Come over to our tent;" said Brixy, "and I reckon
you could cry without thinking of any girl. You see,
the wind has blown the old barrel off from the chimney,
and the fellers all feel bad enough about it to cry."

It must be said, however, that our camp was a pretty
comfortable place. Uncle Sam made every possible effort
to provide us with fresh meat, and such vegetables as
could be obtained. One of the dainties of which we had
a good supply was onions. The boys in blue looked
upon these as one of the most desirable dishes that could
be obtained, and men who would have spurned them at
home took their onions as an old toper would his glass
of grog, often shedding tears of gratitude, or if not of
gratitude, still shedding tears for some reason or other.
Our men discovered that onions were sometimes stolen
as fast as boys would rob an orchard, and were eaten raw
with as much relish as if they had been strawberries and
cream.

"Three cheers for onions!" shouted Brixy; "I always
did like 'em. They don't improve a feller's breath much,
but in the army one can't always be thinking of his
breath."

"That's so," interrupted Vail, "you are mighty lucky
to have any breath at all."

When the weather permitted, and the ground was in
proper condition, we had battalion and brigade drill, as
we needed to be thoroughly posted in these movements.
Occasionally we improved ourselves in the skirmish drill,

thus preparing for exigencies which might overtake us
when called again into active service.

It was found that many of our soldiers were inclined
at times to be superstitious, and frequently little occur-
ences were thought to foreshadow coming events. One
night I dreamed that eight or ten of our officers were
standing in a particular part of the camp. We formed a
squad which enjoyed the company of one another, and
were naturally drawn together. In my dream I thought
we were looking towards the camp of one of the New
York regiments, and watching their battalion movements.
I dreamed I saw a turkey-buzzard flying over their camp
towards ours. "Now," said Captain Knox, "just mark
whose tent that bird lights on, and it will prove a sure
precursor of death." It swooped over our heads, fluttered
downward, and alighted on the tent of Captain Dolby.
"Boys," said Knox, "I'm glad it did not light on my
tent." At that moment I awoke.

By way of amusement I told my dream to the very
men who, as I supposed, were standing with me at the
time.

"A singular dream," remarked Knox. "I hope it
does not mean any disaster to any of us."

"I don't think it does," exclaimed Sanderson. "I
once dreamed that an old uncle of mine died and left me
a big fortune."

"Did he die?" asked one of the men.

"Yes, but he didn't leave me the fortune. In fact, he
never had any."

"I had a dream once, too," said another. "I dreamed
that I was married to a certain young lady, a nice one,

too, and I was about the happiest fellow that ever lived."

"Did that come true?" I asked.

"Partly," said the other. "The girl got married, but I was left out. Yes, boys, I've often thought of that dream, and it makes me rather doubt that such things ever come true. It was all her own fault though."

"You ought to have told her the dream," remarked one. "Perhaps she would have made it good."

"I did tell her," the other replied, "and what do you think she said? She asked me what I had for supper. I have never taken much stock in dreaming from that time to this."

Still it was evident that the men were somewhat uneasy. They seemed to think that the old saying of dreams always going by contraries was not always to be relied upon. We agreed that we would say nothing to Captain Dolby, lest he should exhibit the same superstitious feeling which marked so many of our men. We were not willing to say or do anything that would cause him any anxiety; and at the same time there was a manifest feeling of relief among the group that the turkey-buzzard had not alighted on their particular tent.

To finish this part of the story, let me say that when we entered upon the next campaign, and were charging the enemy's entrenchments, the brave Captain Dolby was mortally wounded, and fell within three feet of where I stood. Perhaps I would never have thought of the co-incidence had not Captain Knox and the others reminded me of it, and begged that if I ever happened to dream again I would mention it to no one, a thing which I faithfully promised to do.

Of course our camp had within itself varied sources of entertainment. The long hours were whiled away in harmless amusements, and frequently these were well worth an admittance fee. The stories lasted pretty well, one suggesting another, while an effort was made by each man to improve upon the one who had gone before. Some of the yarns were of the most improbable character. This, however, did not detract from their interest, and they were always relished by the listeners.

We had also material for good male choirs, and some of the old songs, brought from homes far away, were sung many times over. And these were sometimes sung, too, by voices which would not have made a success as bass or tenor in a first-class opera.

Herr Blinn was always ready to take a hand in the amusement, and seemed to enjoy the sport according to the size and weight of his body. When he laughed he shook from head to foot, and his loud guffaw was heard for tents away.

"Give us a song now," said Sanderson one evening as a number of boys were assembled in a tent, about half of whose space was filled by the ponderous Blinn.

"Yes," chimed in another, "I've never heard you sing 'Mary had a little Lamb.' That's a favorite ditty of mine; I always did like the characters in that song."

"Which do you mean?" said Sanderson, "Mary, or the lamb?"

"Shentlemens," remarked Herr Blinn, "I likes both. I likes Mary and I likes der lamb. I likes 'em roasted."

"Which?" inquired Sanderson, "Mary or the lamb?"

There was some merriment over the conversation, and

especially at Herr Blinn's characteristic hankering for something that was roasted and good to eat.

"Well, are we going to have the song?" some one asked.

"Shentlemens," said Blinn, " I dinks you never heard me vistle."

"Oh, no," broke in a dozen, " that's something you never have done. Come, now, whistle for us."

"Don't take in a full breath and whistle as hard as you can," said Vail, " you might blow the top of the tent off. Just give it to us mildly; anyhow, I'm going to hold my hat on," and Vail clasped his hat with both hands as if afraid of losing it.

Blinn threw back his shoulders, took in a full breath, puckered up his lips, and made the attempt. If either Mary or her lamb had been present, I imagine they would have been frightened. The noise was something between a whistle and a screech.

" I begs pardon, shentlemens, I can't vistle; dot vas von break down."

" Why can't you vistle?" interrogated Sanderson.

" Cos I vas so hoarse."

" Well," said Vail, " you're the first man I ever saw whose lips got hoarse instead of his throat."

" Dot makes me feel pad," replied Blinn : " it vas not doing shustice to Mary and de lamb. Ven I gets petter, and my vistle gets no more squeaks, den I vill make it go shust like von bugle."

" Well," broke in Sanderson, " as you can't entertain us with music, suppose we get up a wrestling match."

" Shust de ting," responded Blinn.

" We don't want the match to be unequal," continued Sanderson, "and I suggest that we match four men against Blinn, one on each side, one in front, and one behind."

There was an audible smile at this suggestion.

"That will hardly do," I remarked, "for how would the man in front know the movements of the man in the rear? Some one would have to act as courier, and tell him what was going on."

The wrestling match was all in favor of Herr Blinn. The four men might have joined hands and surrounded him, but once planted on his broad feet, it was impossible to upset him.

With such pastimes and playful doings we passed the months in camp, and managed to break the monotony. We were patiently waiting for the kind of weather which would permit the army to move. That there should be home-sickness, more or less, was only to be expected, but our men kept it mostly to themselves, and were slow to admit it. We had all that could reasonably be demanded for our health and comfort. The organized bands of helpers at home were looking after our wants, and there was really so much enjoyment in our camp life that not all were ready to end it when the time came for the next campaign.

CHAPTER XV.

"On ye brave,
Who rush to glory or the grave!"

ITH the arrival of open spring we were again on the move.

General Burnside had retired, and General Hooker had been placed in command of the army. Burnside afterwards led the Ninth Corps, and was always the man to give a good account of himself.

Hooker made some changes in the army, infusing fresh vigor, and especially raised the cavalry corps to a higher standard than it had before attained.

Up to this time the Confederate cavalry had shown great efficiency, having things pretty much its own way, and had been successful in raids which might have been prevented if we had not been defective in this branch of service. More and more it became plain that our cavalry were not unequal to their foe.

I witnessed an encounter which will confirm the truth of the foregoing statement. The contest occured on an immense plain, and I was so placed as to obtain a good view of the entire field. The Confederate General J. E.

(187)

B. Stuart had won renown by his daring exploits. Our Union commander was, I think, General Gregg. The

conflict took place at Rappahannock Station, and was nothing less than a charge, swift and desperate, on the part of each body of horsemen. It appeared at first to be a sham battle. The troopers of each side plunged headlong into the encounter, meeting with terrific force. Here and there we could distinguish the blue and gray.

GEN. KILPATRICK.

Horses and riders rolled over each other in wild confusion, and in much less time than it requires to describe the scene we could see them re-mounting their steeds, preparing for the next onset, while those who kept their saddles would wheel with the speed of the wind, and with close ranks would renew the attack, with unslung carbines, and then with sword crossing sword. Although it was in the light of day the flash of the fiery weapons was brighter than the beams of the sun. The dust and smoke of the battle soon hid the combatants from our view. A momemt later the cloud broke, and we saw the Confederate cavalry in retreat, and our spirited troopers preparing to follow up their advantage. As far as I could judge, the forces were about equal in number.

"That's healthy business," remarked an officer standing near.

"What is?" I enquired.

"Why, horseback riding."

" Healthy enough," I said, "unless you get a bullet put through you, or get ventilated with a sword. To tell the truth, I had about as soon take my horseback riding in a safer place."

" There wouldn't be so much excitement about that," the other replied.

" That would depend," broke in a third, " upon the kind of animal you were riding. I tried a mule once, and I don't want anything more exciting than that. The mule was excited behind, and I was excited all over."

" Did he throw you ? " I asked.

" Well, yes ; if you had seen me strike, you might have called it that ; I prefer to call it a rapid method of dismounting."

Great preparations were now going on for the grand movement which we all knew was coming. The country wanted the army to move ; the soldiers were impatient to be led on to Richmond. The last attempt had proved to be a failure. Rains had been pouring down ; the mud was deep ; the roads were in shocking condition, yet Burnside made an effort to go forward. It was a hopeless task. No body of men with wagon trains and artillery could wade through such mire. The plan had to be abandoned, and to this day is known as the " Burnside stick in the mud." Burnside could not dry the roads by issuing an order.

Hooker had laid his plans, and boasted that nothing in earth or heaven could thwart him. It would have been better to save the boasting until the time for taking off the harness.

We broke camp near Falmouth and marched toward

Fredericksburg, to the same place where we had crossed the Rappahannock before. General Sedgwick was in command of our Sixth Corps. We found the First Corps on our left, and a part of the Second Corps, commanded by General Couch, on our right.

The First Corps made a feint of crossing, while the balance of the army marched to Banks' Ford, and there crossed the river after a stubborn resistance, the Sixth remaining in front of Fredericksburg during the afternoon and night. The First, under General Reynolds, and the Second moved in the night, and followed the main army toward Chancellorsville.

The next morning's reveille aroused us at four o'clock, and after a hasty toilet, and cup of coffee with hard-tack and pork, we immediately crossed the Rappahannock, and took up a strong position in an orchard that had already formed a valley of death, having been fought over three or four times at the first battle of Fredericksburg.

We occupied it this time without firing a musket.

" How is this ?" asked some of the men.

" Because the Confederates have a much stronger position, and one more easily defended, on the heights behind the city," was answered.

We threw out a line of pickets and skirmishers a sufficient distance to prevent anything like a surprise, and laid down to rest, knowing that we had better husband our strength for the coming struggle.

We spent a quiet Saturday evening and part of the night in the same place, but about one o'clock were noiselessly called into line of battle and marched toward

THE MORNING REVEILLE.

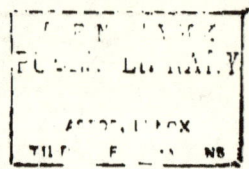

Fredericksburg, about a mile away. We moved forward until we could hear the conversation of the videttes of the opposing force. We had prepared ourselves for a charge, having laid aside every unnecessary article ; even our haversacks were left behind. Each man was provided with only canteen of water, rifle, and cartridge-box filled to overflowing, and twenty extra rounds of ammunition in his pockets. Officers had sword and pistol. We had advanced under what were called light marching orders.

No resistance was made to us although we were within 200 hundred yards of the enemy's entrenchments. Nearly their whole force had been withdrawn to oppose General Hooker's advance toward Chancellorsville. Probably they expected nothing more than a feint to be made by our corps. At break of day we were again in motion.

The inhabitants of Fredericksburg seemed terribly alarmed at our appearance in their quaint old town, which had already tasted the horrors of war, and now again was placed between two contending forces.

As soon as daylight fully set in, General Sedgwick prepared to carry their works by storm. Two or three batteries were placed in the most advantageous positions, and our artillerymen were not long in silencing the guns that had been saluting us with grape and canister. We could see that other batteries were being hurried up to reinforce those that had been disabled. General Sedgwick was not slow in opposing force to force, meeting battery with battery.

To our entire division was given the desperate work of storming the entrenchments. The **Fourth** and **Fifth**

Maine regiments, with the Twenty-third Pennsylvania, were ordered to charge by front line of battle, supported by the Sixth Maine and Sixty-seventh New York. The Sixty-first Pennsylvania, commanded by Colonel Speer, the Forty-fourth New York and the Eighty-second Pennsylvania, commanded by Major Bassett, together with the Sixty-fifth New York, under Colonel Hamlin, were formed to attack by the left flank. All these regiments were under the command of General Alexander Shaler. Other gallant officers might be named. In the meantime the opposing forces were not slumbering, but were bringing up all the reinforcements they could command, and were strengthening their already strong position, so as to repel the assault they were sure was coming.

"We shall not all come back alive," said Beckstein, as his keen eye anxiously glanced toward the strong works in front of us.

Just then I heard Brixy's well-known voice requesting some comrade to take good care of him if he were wounded, or bury him decently if he should be killed.

"Suppose I was wounded myself," said the other; "how could I take care of you then?"

"In that case," answered Brixy, "I should have to look after you."

There was something pathetic in such conversations among our men, as we stood there facing probable death.

The command came, "Forward! double quick! charge!" The men started as if electrified. As if with one step, and moved by one will, on we dashed. Confederate batteries had been so placed as to sweep the street up which we were charging. Hot volleys of grape and canister were poured into our devoted ranks, and were so terribly effective that our troops were completely swept from the road. The Sixty-first Pennsylvania, which had the post of honor in this flank movement, suffered tremendous loss, as did all the regiments, especially at the raised causeway, and bridge over a small creek which they were compelled to cross, the creek running between Mayre's Heights and the town of Frederickburg. On those Heights was done some of the warmest work of the whole war.

DESPERATE CHARGE AT THE SECOND BATTLE
OF FREDERICKSBURG. .

At this point the most terrible slaughter occurred, as the enemy had complete knowledge of the range. Hotter and hotter grew the storm of fiery hail that beat upon our heroic troops. Balls whistled through the air

13

like the tempest in a forest. There was something grim and awful in that deadly reception which our men met from those blazing heights, and something magnificently daring in their onward rush and furious charge. Wave after wave of deadly hail beat against their brave breasts, as if they were destined to annihilation. Thick and fast the heroes fell, and the road was strewn with the wounded and the dead. Yet every one of the gallant fellows who fell, if he could have been called to his feet again by resurrection, would have fixed his eye again upon those stormy heights, and would have leaped forward to plant there the Stars and Stripes.

Orders came to fall back, but we were not in a mood for that. We had no idea of losing the ground we had soaked with blood. Just at this crisis, Major Bassett called for the colors of the Eighty-second.

There was a moment's delay, and Captain Marsdale seized the colors, and, hurrying to the front, handed them to the impetuous leader.

He turned, waved the flag in the face of the regiment, and shouted, " Boys, follow me! Forward, the Eighty-second!"

He sprang ahead. His face was toward the foe, and his feet seemed hardly to touch the ground. Undismayed by the pelting blast of deadly hail, he dashed across the bridge. Less than one company in number dared to make the desperate plunge, or else the men were halting under the supposition that we were to retreat. Bassett succeeded in getting partly under shelter of a building.

Turning to me with a look on his flushed face that

told of anger and disappointment, he shouted, "Preston, where are our men?"

We glanced back beyond the deadly path over which we had come, and saw the regiment standing as if dazed, and undecided what to do.

"Captain!" cried the intrepid Basset, "go back and rally the men!"

It was a command to run a fearful risk. I took no time to canvass the situation, nor to think of chances.

As I started to run the murderous gauntlet, our brave leader shouted again, "Rally the boys! Bring them over!"

Then pointing to the rugged intrenchments, he exclaimed, "Those heights have got to be taken, and we'll do it if the heavens fall!"

I leaped away on my errand, and succeeded in reaching the other end of the bridge in safety. About a hundred and fifty men responded to the call, and were willing to charge the enemy's works. At this instant brigade commander General Shaler rode up. Turning to me, he shouted, with an oath, "What do you mean? Don't you know the orders are to fall back?"

"General," I responded, "we can't fall back; our colors are yonder across the bridge!"

I pointed to our fiery major who was waving the flag, and anxiously waiting for the remainder of the regiment to advance. General Shaler took in the situation in a moment, shouted to the men, "Forward!" and dashed across the bridge at a breakneck speed.

It was not long before our flag was planted where the Stars and Bars had floated so defiantly.

The work of death was terrible. The brave Colonel Speer fell within ten feet of the enemy's lines; I stepped over his dead body as I was about to mount the intrenchments. Probably a dozen of our troops were within the enemy's breastworks when I leaped down from the top and joined them. My foot caught as I jumped, and I nearly fell headlong, while balls were whizzing over me. The man who leaped down behind me was shot through the heart just as his feet struck the ground.

"There they go!" shouted Vail, as he pointed to a number of Confederates who were making good their retreat.

"Hurrah!" cried Sanderson, with as much enthusiasm as if he were cheering for the whole regiment. "It's worth coming through that chasm of death to see those fellows running; they jeer at the Yanks, but they're willing enough to keep out of our clutches."

Sanderson gave another hurrah on his own private account, and then struck Brixy's cap down over his face, saying to the honest boy, as he stood and tried to take in the situation, "Why don't you hooray? Don't you know we've whipped 'em? Why don't you yell?"

"Wait till I get a good ready," remonstrated Brixy.

"Now!" cried Sanderson, and a cheer went up that was heard far and near.

"You didn't come in on time," exclaimed Sanderson, "you're too slow."

"Hurrah!" cried Brixy, and turning to Sanderson, said, "You didn't come in at all."

There was no lack of cheering and rejoicing, yet our work was too serious and pressing to admit of much time being spent in congratulations.

"Have you seen Marsdale?" I inquired of one of the regiment. He told me the spirited captain was hurt and had been compelled to go to the rear. As soon as the lull came, and I could reach the spot where he was lying, I learned the particulars from his own lips.

"You see I was in that narrow cut," he went on to say, "and a piece of a shell struck my musket barrel and knocked it out of my hand. I found then that I had been wounded in the shoulder, although in the rush and excitement of the charge I didn't know when I was struck."

The news of our success cheered him, and he made no complaint about his wound.

"The odds were all against us," he said.

"Yes," I replied, "and our victory is all the more memorable on that account."

Three men of our regiment distinguished themselves by capturing two cannons and a caisson, with three horses attached to each, each man bringing off one trophy. These belonged to the Washington Light Battery, of New Orleans, and were brought to the north side of the Rappahannock, and were safely conveyed to the Capital.

By this charge the loss of troops was heavy, among them the gallant captain who was the subject of a dream already related.

We captured here about 700 prisoners; all the enemy's wounded fell into our hands, and a vast number of small arms. All the troops engaged in this terrible charge vied with each other in acts of daring, and it would be invidious to single out any regiment or regiments for special praise. I wish to do injustice to none.

All bore their part in planting our colors upon the enemy's defenses, and it was glory enough to work the miracle that day which it had been said no human power could perform.

At Salem Church the retreating column of Confederates halted, threw up some hasty intrenchments, and awaited the onset, which was not long delayed.

Unfortunately for us matters at Chancellorsville had proved disastrous to our forces, and General Hooker, it seems, was standing on the defensive, if indeed a retreat had not been already commenced.

This enabled General Lee to dispatch heavy reinforcements to aid his men who had been driven back from Fredericksburg. The engagement at Salem Church was very stubborn, both sides contending with great spirit and courage, the losses being very heavy, as the fighting was at short range. The first brigade of the first division made repeated charges, determined to carry the position at all hazards, but our antagonist was just as determined. Lee's deep-laid plan seems to have been to surround General Sedgwick and capture his entire command, but we had no intention of falling into any trap, or of trying the hospitalities of any Confederate prison.

Up to this Sunday evening we had heard no news from General Hooker. There was an ominous silence which many of our officers supposed to indicate a retreat by one side or the other. Our men remained under arms and ready at a moment's notice to fight or march. General Sedgwick displayed great courage and coolness, showing a strong front, manœuvring up to three o'clock on Monday afternoon for the very strongest position that could possibly be selected, so that if matters came to the worst we could give a good account of ourselves.

At this critical juncture I glanced down the road and suddenly saw a body of horsemen rapidly approaching. "What can that be, corporal," I said to Vail, "and what does it mean?"

"Good!" shouted Vail, "a reinforcement, I guess. I reckon we shall need all the help we can get."

"It is a brigade of Union cavalry," I said, as the troopers, on full gallop, came nearer.

"Where is your general," hurriedly inquired the officer in command; "I have an important message for him."

The news of what had taken place spread rapidly among our ranks.

"Just as I told you," interrupted Major Beckstein, "Hooker is falling back; Lee means to capture our entire force, and has set his whole army in motion to do it."

We waited for the shades of evening, that we might cut our way through all opposing forces towards Banks' Ford, and so join General Hooker on the north bank of the Rappahannock. The information brought to us by General Averill saved us from disaster. We effected the recrossing of the river about nine o'clock Tuesday evening. The advance guard of the enemy commenced shelling us while we were passing over the pontoon bridge, over which a part of General Hooker's force crossed the day before.

Having encamped that night in the woods not far from the Ford, the next day found us back "in the old camp ground" near Falmouth. We selected a much pleasanter location than the one we had occupied all winter, and afterward spent considerable time in making it look attractive, some of the men constructing flower beds, which were filled with the choicest varieties of plants the woods of Virginia afforded. And here, let me say, that some of these are well worth cultivating.

We called our new temporary home "Camp Shaler," in honor of our worthy commander, General Alexander Shaler, whose skill and bravery had been tested, and whom we had learned to respect and obey, believing he possessed the ability to lead us on to deeds of renown.

One morning not long after this I remember feeling pleased at the arrival of a stranger in our camp, whose coming had been anxiously awaited for some time.

"Hello, captain," came from the cheery voice of Sanderson, "you are looking happy; what good luck has befallen you now?"

"You'll be happy, too," I answered, "when you get the news."

"Don't keep me in suspense; has the paymaster come?"

"Major Morse is really here," I said, "and our camp never looked so happy as it does this morning."

"Ha! ha!" ejaculated Brown, "it was lucky for me that my credit wasn't good; I shall have fewer debts to pay."

"I guess you might have borrowed," I replied, "if any of the boys had had any money; they were all in your fix—no credit because there was no money."

Just then the unmelodious voice of Brixy was heard singing, "Who wouldn't be a soldier boy?" Major Morse with all his gravity could not help smiling at the honest delight of Brixy.

"How are you, major?" exclaimed Brixy. "Glad to see you; been looking for you this long time; come again, major; durned if you come any too often."

"It is pleasant to have a hearty welcome," responded the major.

"Well, major, you'll always get it from Brixy; jist remember that. I don't care how often you come, there's one feller here you can count on as always glad to see you."

Brixy expressed the sentiment of the whole camp; the redoubtable major was a general favorite.

"Now," said Sanderson, "Halleck will send us South right away."

"How so?" I inquired.

"Because he'll want the Johnnies to get some of these greenbacks. Oh you can depend upon it, there'll be a forward movement right away."

Some one was wanted to poke fun at, and Sanderson made his own selection. The major furnished us with three months' pay. We were at no loss to dispose of our wages. Some of the men had left families behind who were in need of their earnings. Others were in want of various comforts for their daily service, which could be procured from the quartermaster upon payment of army prices.

"After all," remarked Corporal Vail, "it is cheap to be in the army. You don't have to buy any Sunday clothes. I get along very well with only one suit, and I find I don't really require broad-cloth. And then, too, I can wear shoes that are not French calf. A fellow can save blacking, too, and if he hasn't any hair brush, he can comb his hair with his fingers."

"Yes," said Sanderson, "it's a saving in silk hats, and diamond studs."

"Ice cream, too," chimed in Beckstein. "You don't have to take your girl out, and find that when you ask her to have a second dish she thinks you mean it."

"Soda, too, and ginger pop," said Brixy. "Lor, boys, hain't I spent a lot for them things afore now? I don't regret it though; it's many a good time I've had." And Brixy's face evinced the liveliest interest in the conversation.

It was agreed on all hands that it was very economical to be in the army, that the chance to save compensated for the toils and dangers, and so with pleasantries as to the advantages of being in Uncle Sam's service the boys amused themselves, while it was more than probable that within one week's time every one of them would be as impecunious, and hard-up for money, as if our paymaster had made no disbursements.

CHAPTER XVI.

" Erect they stand, a valiant band,
The strong defenders of the land."

"B E READY for the inspection officer at four o'clock!" was the order given by our colonel.

It was a bright morning, although it had rained during the night, and the drops of water were still dripping from the trees.

"Look your best now," said Major Beckstein, involuntarily surveying himself from head to foot, as if intending to observe his own order.

"We can't all be handsome as you are, major," I remarked, "but if it were put to vote in our company, which is the best looking lot of men in the regiment, I know which company would get the vote."

" And if the question were as to the best looking man, every man would get one vote," replied the major.

Our commanding officer, overhearing the conversation, broke in, "I will tell you who are the handsome ones when we go into the next engagement; let me see how you look then !"

Our company began to prepare for the inspection. Even Brixy combed his hair. Blinn went around inquiring for soap, and Sanderson joked him by telling him he should get a whole box, as it would take that amount to go round—not around the company, but Blinn.

"Polish up all the brass!" said Beckstein.

"Give me your cheek!" exclaimed Sanderson, as he seized a rag and some polishing powder; "I'll make you shine so you'll be seen clear across the field."

A moment later I saw Herr Blinn trying to engage a contraband to wash his shirt.

"You vants to earn somedings?" asked Blinn.

"I don't mind, Massa, but I doan want no more o' your shoes to shine; it spiled a hull box o' blackin' tother day, and I lost money on de job."

"Dot vas not der size of der shoes, but der size of der pox," said Blinn. "I vants to-day a shentleman to put my shirt in order—a laundry shentleman: you understan's me?"

"Yes, Massa, and I'd do it if I could git a pardner, but it jist wants two or free of us for dat job."

"Blixen," cried Blinn, "you organize von companie to vash a shirt? I vashed dot shirt alone der last time, two or dree veeks ago."

"Boss," said the darkey, "you'd better let out de contrack to some udder party; I hain't got no mule to haul dat shirt to de ribber, and do de bizness as it oughter be' done."

The contraband was not anxious for so large an undertaking, and Blinn had to be his own "laundry shentleman."

Our muskets, which were liable to get rusty, or at least to lose their bright appearance by constant use, were soon in first-class condition, looking as if they had just came from the armory. Straps were rubbed, buckles were polished up, rents in clothes were mended, seams that had ripped were sewn up with such a doubling of thread that it was certain a rip would never come in the same place again, caps were brushed, and shoes were carefully dug out of the mud in which they had been encased. There was a general scrubbing and dusting.

"Do you belong to this regiment?" asked Sanderson. The words were addressed to Brixy. who had so fixed up his personal appearance and transformed himself that his comrade professed not to know him.

"Now you see me," said Brixy, "as I used to look when I went a courtin', only I had more grease for my hair then, and my boots weren't nothin' like so easy."

"No wonder," said Sanderson, "that there's a girl at home who is breaking her heart over you."

"How does my hair look, anyway?" inquired Brixy; "you see I combed it, but it seems to stick up; I think bear's grease ain't no great accomplishment, but it sort o' plasters down a feller's hair, and makes him look rather trimmer; you hain't got none, have you, Sanderson?"

"No bear's grease," said Sanderson, "but something a great deal better."

Of all fellows to enjoy an opportunity for a practical joke, Sanderson was about the chief. He repaired to his tent, took a bottle of mucilage, scratched off the label which told what it was, and, bringing it to Brixy, assured him that it was hair-oil of a superior quality.

"I don't want to take it all," remarked Brixy, as he poured out a quantity into his hand.

" O don't mind about that; take all you want."

"My hair is like bristles," said Brixy.

"That will be just the thing for it," said Sanderson. Others were looking on, and contriving in one way and another to conceal their smiles.

The inspector came at four o'clock.

As the men were forming in line Brixy said to Sanderson, " Wasn't that hair-ile you gave me to-day rather sticky? I tried to comb my hair afterwards, and I thought I'd pull it all out, and then I put my cap on, and now I can't get the durned thing off"

"Just a peculiarity of the oil," said Sanderson; "best quality, sticks like glue, lasts a good while; you don't have to comb your hair for a fortnight; it all lies down and stays right there."

There was a blank look on Brixy's face which seemed to express the hope that he might be able to appreciate the merits of the hair preparation.

It so happened that Sanderson had been out the previous night foraging. The rain and darkness were favorable for a midnight predatory excursion, but the clothes of those who were engaged in it were a good deal soiled, and their personal appearance was not improved.

Sanderson had not been able to get himself into the most presentable condition for the inspection. He had partly polished his musket, got the thickest of the mud off his shoes, righted up his collar, and drawn his belt one hole tighter. And he had carefully brushed the mud, contracted in his foraging raid, from the front of his clothes, so that one-half of him looked tolerably well, but there were shocking omissions behind. The mud was plastered upon his clothes in the rear, and a thorough cleaning was badly needed. There was little evidence that the brush had touched one half of his clothing, although the other part was in fair condition.

The inspector was bent on doing his work thoroughly. He was not going to give a surface glance at the men, and then pass them. He was there to inspect, and inspection with him meant neither haste nor negligence.

He surveyed the company in front, looked at all the men in turn, made such criticisms as he thought were required and then passed to the rear of the men.

Sanderson stood in an attitude of self-complacency, erect and apparently confident that there would be no trouble about his passing muster. He supposed only the front side of his dress would be inspected, and that the part would escape which, in his haste or carelessness, he had neglected to put in order.

"You should look well on both sides," remarked the inspector as he walked past the men who were in dress parade. "What would you think of a coal-carrier who went home at night and washed only one side of his face?"

"Should think his wife would kiss him on the clean side," whispered Sanderson.

"Just then a hand was laid on Sanderson's shoulder, and the inspector said, "Here is one man I notice who has brushed himself up and looks pretty tidy in front, but is all splashed with mud and dirt in the rear!"

Instantly Sanderson responded, "A good soldier, captain, never looks behind!"

The inspector could no more conceal his sense of the humor in the reply than could the men in the ranks, and he ventured upon no more criticisms concerning the dress of the company.

After various movements, various attitudes and performances, all of which seemed to give satisfaction to the inspector, he wished to get the men in line.

It is the perfection of military drill that a hundred men can be made to step, wheel, charge, go through the motions with arms, all as one man, and can so form a line that, looking from the end, there shall appear to be only one man, or the thickness of one. And the men should so stand that a straight line drawn from end to end would touch each man's breast. We wished it understood that there was nothing required of a soldier which we could not perform, and we fancied we were up in good shape on this particular occasion.

"That's no line," savagely remarked the inspector, as he was standing near me.

"What's the matter?" I ventured to ask.

"Why, it sticks out, and bulges, and wabbles about; I tell you the front side of some of those men wants hewing off with a broad-axe, and then smoothing down with a jack-plane."

"The men can't help their shape," I remonstrated, "and I'm of the opinion that they are constructed about as other men are."

The inspector was vexed and in a very unpleasant mood. He would attempt to get the line straight, and some luckless fellow would step a few inches too far forward, and when told to stand back, would get a foot too far in the rear.

The attempt to form line, however, would have been attended with success but for one obstacle, and that was one of gigantic dimensions.

"Now," shouted the inspector, "I want no more fooling! Do as I tell you; obey orders as to eye and shoulder, and get straightened out there."

He held his sword out horizontally and motioned to several parts of the line to stand back. There was a stir among the men, and an effort to meet the requirements of the officer.

HERR BLINN THROWS THE COMPANY OUT OF LINE.

Any one who could have stood and sighted our men would have discovered one protuberance standing there like a hogshead in a line of fence-posts.

"Get back there! Get back!" came in loud tones from the inspector, and he motioned to the spot where Herr Blinn was standing.

"I know what the trouble is," shouted the inspector, "it's that fellow's stomach!"

14

Blinn, meanwhile had stepped back until his front boundry was on a line with that of the others.

"Now, it's all right!" exclaimed the officer, "it's queer I didn't see that before."

The men on each side of our good-natured Dutchman glanced towards his place as if trying to see him, but were only able to discover that part of his pussy corporation which was in line.

The inspector having satisfied himself as to the front, stepped back to look at the line on the rear.

"Forward there, you big fellow," he shouted "Forward two or three paces, and get straightened there!"

Poor Blinn! He put the company out of line first in front, and then in the rear, while the officer's orders that he must step forward or back two or three paces made the jolly Dutchman laugh with all the rest.

The inspector said pleasantly to Herr after the mirthfulness of the situation was comprehended by him, "You are a hard man to make a soldier of; you ought to be put in a company by yourself.

"Dot," replied Blinn, "vas pecause you don't know how. You vants to know how you gets me into line?"

"Yes, I would esteem it a great favor to be told that very thing."

"Vell den, you put dem Yankee shads, dot was so thin as a spade, about three deep; stand dem up, captain, one in vront of de udders, and see if dot vas not de vay I gets into line mit dem on de fore side and de hind side."

The inspector, with a laugh, said, "Oh, yes, if I should make the line deep enough I could bring it even with you in front and rear, but I wasn't trying to mass the troops."

When Brixy retired that night it was noticed that he had his cap on. He was in his natural condition for the night with that exception. All his efforts to get his hat free from the adhesive qualities of the hair-oil had proved unavailing, and with some warmth he was heard remarking to the comrade who had generously donated the hair preparation, that "he could not see as that ile was so much better than any other, and if there was any left it need not be saved on his account."

When asked by one of the boys why he wore his cap to bed, he replied that he had some cold anyhow, and did not wish to get any more.

CHAPTER XVII.

A CRISIS APPROACHING.

*"Now muttering wrath comes floating
on the wind."*

ITHIN one day from the time we had been made happy by our paymaster we were on the march again to the Rappahannock. We crossed with some difficulty.

The next day was one of quiet, and the men enjoyed their opportunity for rest. We could lie down on the hardest ground; we could take a stone for a pillow and make believe it was soft; we could go to sleep as if resting on a bed of down. Towards morning I was awakened by Sanderson calling out to Herr Blinn, "For Heaven's sake don't snore so loud; you will let the whole Confederate army know where we are, and we shall all be captured."

Herr Blinn rolled over and exclaimed, "Mine Gott! you dinks I snore? Dot ish von pig mistake, cos I am avake, and how can wan man shnore ven he ish avake?"

"But you did snore," said Sanderson, "and there isn't a brass band in the army that could be heard so far."

(212)

"If I shmores, vy not I hears him mineself? No man vas nearer to dot shmore dan mineself."

"I heard you," said Sanderson, "anyhow, and I hope you won't blow your trumpet any more to-night."

"Blixen!" exclaimed Herr Blinn, "if mine drumpet vas go off by himself, how can I shtop him?"

On the second morning we were wide awake at four o'clock, and at six were on the march for the front line. Some old copies of a rhyme I composed to chronicle our movements are still in existence, and part of these I insert, as they embody a scrap of our history.

This morning, just at break of day,
  We were called into line,
To go and watch the enemy,
  Upon the picket line.

We ate our breakfast in great haste,
  Prepared to march away,
Our gallant major leading us,
  We looked for active play.

When in the field, drawn up in line,
  The Rebs began their pranks,
And sent a flying shot or two
  To thin our Union ranks.

Our men deployed right steadily,
  Responsive to the word,
And to our posts marched readily,
  Though booming guns were heard.

No picket, by the rules of war,
  Should be shot down at sight,
But this is what the foe has tried
  Upon our daring right.

Yet at this game we, too, can play,
  And murder them in turn;
We'll prove to them this very day
  We've powder, too, to burn.

"Long-range black rifles" need not fear
Sharp-shooters in the front;
And when it comes to shorter range,
We'll bear the battle's brunt.

Our volunteers, beneath the flag,
Are always ready found
To take their stand where duty calls,
Though dangers gather round.

The rhyme circulated through my company, and the men obtained copies as mementoes of the day's transactions.

Our men had been very much puzzled to understand the movements of our division. We seemed to be groping in the dark; if the high and mighty powers in command knew what was expected of us they certainly had the faculty of keeping it to themselves.

Just at this time the mystery of our movements was cleared away. The resources of the South were sadly depleted; General Lee was getting into straits, and was driven to a bold move by the exigencies of his position. Already he was on the march toward Maryland and Pennsylvania to replenish his commissary, exchange his worn-out stock of horses for better ones, and gain an advantage by capturing some of the Northern towns. It seemed likely that both Baltimore and Philadelphia were objective points for his army. The movement of his troops explained the movements of ours.

Still there was an enemy in front of us. We were furnished with picks, spades, and shovels, and ordered to throw up a substantial line of breastworks all along our front, to convey the impression that we were to remain permanently, or at least meant to be prepared for any

TROOPS CROSSING THE RAPPAHANNOCK.

emergency. Soon the dirt was flying in all directions.

"Brixy," shouted one of the men, "keep your spade at home; you are too free with it."

"I've used a spade before," replied Brixy. "I used a spade once in this way; let me show you."

Brixy gave the man a broadside with so much force that the blow was resented. There seemed likely to be trouble, and some of the men stepped up to interfere.

"Brixy," I said, "don't you know that that spade was made to use on dirt?"

"Yes," said Brixy, "that's why I used it on him."

It was agreed that Brixy's wits were getting sharpened.

News came to us that our troops had marched towards Washington, and that Lee's whole command had crossed into Maryland and was pushing on towards Pennsylvania, only enough troops being left behind to watch our movements in the fortifications around Fredericksburg, consisting of General A. P. Hill's Corps, and part of General Ewell's. It was reported that Lee's cavalry had already reached Chambersburg. Now we began to surmise why the Sixth Corps had been ordered to recross the Rappahannock. Our men appeared to comprehend the situation, and gave up the idea that there would be a third battle of Fredericksburg. Just before evening set in on the day that brought us this information, we made a feint to deceive the Confederates. We appeared to be preparing for an attack all along the line, and moved our regiments back and forth as if fresh reinforcements had come to our assistance. In the meantime every man was furnished with five days' rations, and forty extra rounds of ammunition. This proved to us that we were to follow the army of the Potomac, and that possibly long marches would be required of us.

We were ordered to march with all haste toward Acquia Creek, taking the main road to Dumphries. We found our division at the Creek, where they had halted for breakfast. While my servant was preparing a cup of coffee I enjoyed the luxury of a bath in the Creek, which was here about five feet deep, and clear and cool.

As we pressed on the hot sun beat upon us most unmercifully; the roads were very dry and dusty, and, to add to all the other discomforts, we had to march about two miles through a forest over a road flanked on each side by a brush fence, which by accident or other-wise had been set on fire. The heat and smoke increased our suffering, and we were a good deal like Blinn's pig which he roasted at Warwick Creek.

Herr Blinn with his ponderous weight labored at a great disadvantage. The perspiration in streams was flowing down his spacious face.

"Has any shentleman ~von pocket handkerchief to lend?" he inquired.

"Give him an army blanket," remarked Sanderson, showing his same old disposition to get a laugh upon somebody.

We finally reached a clearing, and here I became so affected by the heat that I was almost blind, and fell over unconscious. General Shaler observing this had an ambulance at once provided, and for a few miles I was treated to a free ride. That night I slept soundly and was able to take up the line of march next day toward

Fairfax Court House. We passed within two or three miles of Mount Vernon, Washington's old homestead. Time did not permit of our paying a visit to the spot associated with the "father of his country," yet we seemed to be treading on sacred ground. Having encamped for the night within a mile of Fairfax Court House, and having rested quietly for the day following, we again fell into line, moving on towards Centerville, using the old pike that General Washington had often travelled over after his retirement to Mount Vernon. I could not help contrasting in my mind the changes that war had wrought since Washington's family coach rolled along the ground now trodden by the feet of his country's defenders. Then there was an appearance of thrift and prosperity; now, as far as the eye could reach there were signs of desolation. Houses looked forsaken; fences had been removed; fields were neglected, and a storm of ruin seemed to have swept over the country.

Here and there we met some of the inhabitants, who were genuine Virginians, although not in every instance belonging to the "first families."

Among others we fell in with one Sambo, whose face was very black, and who was a typical darkey of the full-blooded sort. He had picked up an old army mule somewhere, and being of a speculative turn of mind, he wished to strike a bargain, sell his mule, and secure some ready cash, or provender, of which he seemed to be in sore need.

"Ise got a mule over yere," said Sambo, "and I wants to sell him. De ole woman wants to keep him for a family hoss, but I don't."

"Is he a good mule?" asked one of our officers.

"Yes, Massa, and steady. He don't kick out behind wid his fore feet."

"Probably not," replied the officer. "How old is he?"

"Can't tell, Massa."

"He's a female mule," broke in Sanderson, "and the age don't appear."

"But I dink he's young," continued Sambo; "his teef ain't all gone yet; and he seems kind o' hungry like."

"Can you see his ribs?" inquired the officer.

"Dat's all right, Massa; you wants to see his ribs, and den you knows he's well put togedder. I wants no mule what hain't got ribs nuff. Yes, Massa, Ise happy to say I kin satisfy you 'bout de ribs."

"Has he got any tricks?" the officer inquired.

"Nary a trick," rejoined Sambo; "leastways I neber knowed him to run away. Some mules and hosses gets fiery, and jumps an' runs; dis mule ain't no sich mule as dat; he's well broke"

"Fetch him round, and let's see him," said the officer.

Presently Sambo appeared approaching our wagon-train, leading an old dilapidated mule, which, so far as any modern appearance belonged to him, might have been owned and used by George Washington in the last century. His head drooped, his long ears hung down, his joints were stiff, and he was far gone with decay. It was plain that he was not deficient in ribs, as Sambo had said.

"He neber runs away, Massa," exclaimed Sambo.

"I believe you," said the officer.

"Dere ain't no great style 'bout him," continued the darkey, "but for all dat he's a pop'lar mule. When I had him over to der camp-meetin' I came near losin' him; one ob de breddren tried to steal 'im."

Sambo's mule created a vast amount of amusement. He certainly was a reliable beast. He hadn't life enough to play any tricks, and whenever he was left, there he could be found when wanted.

"I think you had better let the old woman have him for a family hoss," said the officer, and Sambo, disappointed at not disposing of his piece of property, shambled off. The mule looked as if he had been through the war, and Sambo looked as if he had kept the mule company.

Things generally in Virginia were much like this ancient animal and his owner, sadly in need of renovation.

CHAPTER XVIII.

HURRYING TO THE FRAY.

"My men, we must be there."—General Alexander Shaler.

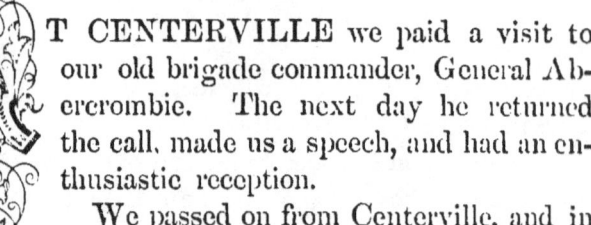

T CENTERVILLE we paid a visit to our old brigade commander, General Abercrombie. The next day he returned the call, made us a speech, and had an enthusiastic reception.

We passed on from Centerville, and in the evening of our first day's march received the news that General Hooker had been removed from the Army of the Potomac, and General Meade had been placed in command.

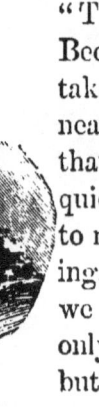

"That suits me," shouted Major Beckstein. His statement was taken up and echoed far and near. Amidst all the changes that had followed one another in quick succession, this appeared to many to be the most gratifying. It aroused enthusiasm, for we all looked upon Meade not only as a man of sound loyalty, but also as a very able commanding officer.

GENERAL MEADE.

(220)

By noon of the next day we were on the banks of the Potomac, in the vicinity of Edward's Ferry. Our army by this time found pontoon bridges a necessity, and carried them along as an Indian would carry a bark canoe upon his back. We did not need to seek shallow places in rivers, nor build solid bridges; we could send on the materials, put down the floating structure in a few hours, and then go over dry shod. The greater part of our corps had passed on several days before; it was behind the main portion of Meade's army.

"Just as I thought," exclaimed Brown, "General Lee's troops have crossed the Potomac ahead of us."

"Yes," I responded, "that's the news, and it is also rumored that the advance guard of the Confederates has already entered Pennsylvania."

"That is a desperate move," Brown remarked, "and I think it shows, not the strength of Lee, but his weakness. He must do something to replenish his stores, and keep up the spirit and hope of the South.

"We're going to have hot work," exclaimed Knox; "it will be the hardest battle yet fought."

"Very likely," I answered, "and it will prove the turning point of the war."

"I'm ready," shouted Sanderson, as he threw his cap in the air. All along the line hats were thrown up, and a wave of enthusiasm was sweeping over the men. An aid, riding up at this moment, inquired what the excitement was about.

"Don't know," shouted Brixy, as his hat went up again.

"Just blowing off steam, I guess," said the aid.

The impression was universal that a decisive struggle was at hand, and the courage and determination of our troops rose accordingly. As soon as the advance of our brigade reached the north bank of the Potomac the colors of all the regiments were unfurled, and the bands struck up patriotic airs; a favorite among them was "Maryland, my Maryland." The people turned out along our line of march, and gave us many expressions of their good-will.

The daughters of Maryland looked on us with bright eyes, and our boys were not slow in returning all the attention they received.

One fair-faced Miss, while waving a handkerchief from a window, accidently dropped it. That was the last she saw of the handkerchief. It was caught up and retained as a keepsake. Later in the day Brown was seen fumbling about his pockets as if looking for something he had lost. The handkerchief was gone, having been taken without leave or license by some light-fingered comrade.

"Somebody stole that," Brown remarked, petulently.

"You stole it to begin with," said Knox.

"Here's a pretty contest," I said, "as to which shall have a Maryland girl's handkerchief."

Just then Brown saw another fair-faced young lady waving a handkerchief from a window by the roadside. "Couldn't you drop that by accident?" he asked.

"No," she briskly responded, "but I could do it purposely," and down came the handkerchief.

Brown caught it, folded it up, fumbled about in his breast, tucked it away, and said, "There, the fellow that gets that will have to strip me to do it."

These incidents show that our men appreciated every

loyal demonstration on the part of the people whom they met. I never liked to think I was surrounded by foes, and I am sure there was a feeling of relief among our troops whenever we stepped on loyal soil.

Occasionally we received a frown instead of a smile, and had glances thrown at us that were sharp as Confederate bayonets.

All the night of July 1st, we were crowding on towards Gettysburg. The storm of battle had been raging throughout the day, and among other disasters we had lost General Reynolds, who sealed his valor with his blood. We marched hurriedly in the direction of Emmetsburg, the coolness of night being preferable to the heat of the day, and enabling our hardy troops to travel with comparative comfort. We were eager for Gettysburg. We did not want the great battle decided without having a hand in the struggle.

Rumors of a terrible conflict began to reach us. I tried to satisfy myself of the truth or falsity of these, and especially was I concerned to ascertain whether the Union losses were as great as reported. Every man I met and questioned had a different story to tell. The preponderance of rumor was against the success of our arms, but this did not damp my ardor nor that of my men for a moment. The hearts beat faster and the march grew swifter.

One thing gave me some encouragement: every evil report seemed to come from those who treated us coldly, and gave no cheer to the boys in blue. I guessed that the rumors were exaggerated, and believed that Meade was holding his own.

Although we missed our way, had to retrace our steps, and lost a couple of hours of precious time, we crossed at daybreak the Pennsylvania line. I felt my step grow lighter. Our bands struck up the "Star-spangled Banner," the men fell into close marching order taking the correct step from the music, and up went three cheers and "a tiger" that made the air ring. It was a scene of enthusiasm, and I could hardly believe we had been all night upon a forced march, and that this had been · preceded by several days of marching through midsummer heat and over dusty, wearying roads.

The old farmers, the countrymen who had backbone and sinew, gave us a cordial welcome. They and their families stood at their gates as we came up, and supplied us with milk and various eatables until their stores were exhausted. I do not think the old farmers had reason to imagine we were suffering from any sickness, or loss of appetite. We gave every evidence of being healthy.

There was not in every instance such generous treatment. I remember seeing in one village through which we passed a woman who had just taken several loaves of bread from the oven.

" Will you sell me one of those ? " I asked.

" I had rather sell you poison," she snarled out.

"Pardon me, Madam, I won't rob you of that, and I hope you'll take all you've got."

A little farther on, five or six men were standing, and were making fun of our troops who were footsore and lame. We were always ready for a little sport, and never objected to having jokes cracked in a harmless way, but when the fun was accompanied with a sneer from

HALT ON THE MARCH.

strangers which plainly meant a lack of sympathy with our cause, every man bristled up with resentment.

"Look at that Yank!" cried one of the bystanders, "he's playing that he's lame, and is trying to drop out."

The poor fellow spoken of was one of the best men in my company, and was putting forth almost superhuman efforts to keep up with our column. He was not really fit to be on the road, but his courage and energy urged him on. I felt indignant that this limping sufferer should be made a subject of sport and contempt, and turning to the group of scoffers, I said, "Instead of jeering at our boys, it would look much better if such able-bodied men as you are would shoulder musket, and help drive the invaders from the soil of Pennsylvania."

There came an oath from one of them, with the insolent words, "You are paid to fight."

I drew my sword in an instant. I was sufficiently indignant to render the braggart a fit subject for a surgeon or an undertaker. With the flat side of the weapon I dealt him a blow which sent him sprawling in the dirt.

His remarks suddenly came to a close.

"Yes," I said, "I'm paid to fight, but this I'll throw in, and won't charge anything for it."

Our brigade commander who had noticed the man, and heard his insulting talk, cried, "Well done, captain; why didn't you use the edge?"

It is needless to say that the rough element in the village was cowed, and we had no further trouble.

I found we were within sound of the great battle. We were getting nearer. Lee's thunder, answered by

15

Meade's, was borne upon the gentle winds. Across the open country came the ominous boom which told that the conflict was hot and desperate. We halted for dinner, and a short rest, which was much needed by our worn troops. Springing to our feet again, we pressed forward. The constant rumble of our artillery and wagon-trains, with the sound of excited voices and the inspiring strains of martial music, nearly drowned the noise of battle.

About four o'clock we arrived within a mile and a half of Gettysburg. Here we deployed to the left, and halted in a piece of woods to rest. I took off my boots for a moment, turned them down, and the blood dripped out.

"Captain, I see you're wounded," remarked Sanderson; "frightfully lacerated in the heel by a tight boot."

"So am I. So am I," shouted twenty others.

Off came the shoes, and streams of blood poured out, which attested the severity of our march of nearly forty miles since the evening before.

"If you come out all right, boys," continued the jocose Sanderson, "you will have a chance to draw a pension for getting a sore heel."

"Some of us," I replied, "will have deeper scars than that to draw pensions on, and if asked to show the wound, we may not be able to produce the heel. We may have to go home on crutches."

We were not allowed a long time for rest. The order came to fall into line, and go with all haste to reinforce General Sykes' Corps at the base of Round Top.

It was easy to tell from the incessant roll of musketry that hot work was going on, and we could also perceive

that our men were falling back step by step from the
approaching storm of shot and shell. As we drew nearer
the scene of carnage, our ranks had to open wide to let
the wounded pass through. The brave fellows, with
dying breath in some instances, cheered us on.

I noticed one who was trying to speak, and I leaned
over to catch his words, scarcely audible in the turmoil
of battle.

"Captain," he gasped, "it's awful hot in there—but
go on!" He gasped again, and, waving his trembling
hand, said, "Give it to them—God bless you—let me
hear that you've won the day!"

There was but a moment to pause, and I hurried on,
my men following into what seemed to be a burning pit
of death. Sykes' Regulars were making a last stand.

Suddenly a wild cheer rent the air, and rose loud and
clear above the confusion of the field. In calmer hours
that thrilling cheer will now come back to my memory, and
my impulse is to spring to my feet, as if again plunging
into the fight, swept onward by the fury of the charge.
That cheer was more than the brazen peal of a bugle or
the strains of martial music.

What did it mean? The Pennsylvania Reserves had
started up like a lion springing upon his prey. They
went in with a determination that amounted to desperation, and the waning sun that day looked upon a scene
of heroism scarcely surpassed in the annals of war.
With the utmost bravery they carried the point, checked
the advancing columns of gray, and sent them in their
turn up the mountain, and over the crest, sweeping them
far beyond where their advance had held their line of
battle, before they desisted from the terrific onset.

I doubt if our troops ever appeared to much better advantage than during some of those awful hours at Gettysburg. The discipline, the courage, the enthusiasm, the leadership, all came out in a way that makes language poor in any attempt at description.

Round Top, that historic spot at far-famed Gettysburg, was now in possession of the Union troops.

In the dusk of the evening a group of officers approached our position. One of them accosted me. I saluted him, and awaited his communication.

"Captain," he said, "your men must be pretty well used up."

"We had a long march," I answered, "before we reached the field."

"The boys have done nobly," he exclaimed; "I'm proud to command such troops."

"And we are proud of our commanders," I said; "that's half the battle."

"Let your men know," he said, "that their superior officers appreciate their sacrifices and valor."

"That's Sykes," whispered some one, as the group disappeared; "he's a stormy old regular, and there's nothing green, boys, about him."

A wave of the old veteran's hand acknowledged our outbreak of enthusiasm as he vanished across the dim and smoky field.

GENERAL REYNOLDS,
Fell at Gettysburg, July 1, 1863.

CHAPTER XIX.

THE FOE HURLED BACK.

"Though the mighty come forth in their pride,
And legions be swept from the land,
Forever the names of our patriot band
In the volume of fame shall abide."

T WAS a night of suspense. About nine o'clock we laid down upon our arms, the trodden battle-field under us, and the arched sky above us.

The morrow was sure to bring great events. The country was awaiting the issue with nervous dread, but here at the scene of the fiery conflict confidence rested upon the Federal troops, and the final conclusion was impatiently looked for. We were lying on the field already plowed by the struggles of contending hosts, and were trying to rest between two days of battle.

Just as I was yielding to the fatigue caused by the long and rapid marching and field service of the last twenty-four hours, Thompson, who was lying near me, turned over, then raised himself up, and looked around.

"You seem to be restless," I remarked; "not sick, I hope."

"Only thinking," responded the brave fellow; "just thinking of home, and of what may possibly happen to me here."

"You've gone through safe so far," I said, "and I would hope for the best."

"I tell you, captain," he replied, "if I were to fall, my chief concern and regret would be for those I should leave behind, and who are to-night in the dear old home, thinking of me, and anxiously wondering what is my fate."

He spoke with great feeling and earnestness, and while my heart was moved I could not help thinking how many in their dreams that night would have visions of a similar home, and a family group who would not close their eyes in sleep.

My friend then recalled the parting scene when he bade good-bye to father and mother, and other members of the household.

"Yes," he continued, "I know a mother's blessing rests upon me—and, captain, she's a good mother too, God bless her—and I've felt a kind of security all along, and have hoped her dear old eyes would see me coming home sometime."

He brushed a tear away, and then crawled over nearer to where I was lying, and spoke low, with tremulous voice. "If anything happens to me, I would like the folks at home to know I thought of them as I laid down to my last sleep."

We were silent then. Our thoughts were a long way from the crimson field of Gettysburg.

Human strength has its limits; ours had been taxed

to the utmost, and sleep soon settled down upon the long rows of men stretched upon the ground.

About four o'clock in the morning we were quietly aroused, spent half an hour in getting a cup of coffee and a needed breakfast, and then were on the march toward Culp's Hill, almost the extreme right of our position. A little rest had put fresh life and vigor into our hard-wrought men, and we moved on with high hope and daring step.

We were not a moment too soon, as a portion of our brigade was actively engaged before six o'clock. We went to support the second division of the Twelfth Corps, commanded by General Geary. His troops had been assailed by overpowering numbers the evening before. The Twelfth had been compelled to send large reinforcements to the left and centre of our line, leaving the division of General Geary to occupy the position formerly held by a much larger body of troops.

This gap in our lines the Confederate General Ewell was not slow to observe, and determined to make the most of his advantage. He ordered a general charge. Our brave Geary and his fighting division were compelled to shorten their lines, and of necessity to fall back, which they did with their faces to the foe. Their ammunition having been expended, their only defense was cold steel.

Geary was dressed in an old blouse, with few of the outward appearances of a general. Hat or no hat, it was all the same to him. He bore evidences of the "wear and tear." His hair was uncombed, his face was brown and rusty, his garments were shockingly soiled, and he might have been taken for a "tramp" who had suddenly appeared upon the field, ready to lead where any would dare to follow.

A teamster was a little distance away, driving a pair of very deliberate mules, attached to an ammunition wagon.

Geary approached him, and cried, "Hurry up!"

By this time the wagon was standing still, and the mules acted as if they intended to spend the day there.

"Hurry up! Come on!" exclaimed the general, his eye flashing with rage.

"I'm in no hurry!" provokingly retorted the teamster. "I won't hurry up for you."

"Do you know who I am?" shouted the general.

"No, and I don't care to!"

"I'm General Geary," he thundered out, and drawing his sword he rushed toward the sluggish driver, and shouted, "Move on, and mighty quick, or I'll run this through your lazy carcass!"

The man started as if shot, and, frightened half out of his senses, cried, "I will! I will!"

The mules suddenly grew spry, and it was not many minutes before the ammunition was served out.

Just at this juncture the advanced regiments of our brigade came up, and, falling in beside Geary's veterans, the position was regained that had been held during the night.

Soon after a furious cannonade was commenced, and for a time we were led to suppose that our own batteries on Cemetery Ridge had mistaken us for the Confederates, or that the enemy had secured that important point from our men. Quickly we unfurled our colors to show who we were. Soon we discovered that the firing came from Confederate guns on Seminary Hill. We seemed for a moment to be entirely surrounded, but happily this was a mistake.

The cannonade was but a prelude to the vigorous assault made by General Ewell after receiving strong reinforcements.

At this instant we went in with a will, and after firing one volley we charged all along the line. It was steel to steel, foe to foe. The sound of clashing weapons rose upon the morning air; men fell like leaves from wind-shaken trees, and others leaped over their prostrate bodies, and plunged furiously into the fray.

The enemy was driven back with slaughter, and our troops regained the advanced line they had occupied the day before. The breastworks thrown up by our men had been improved by the Confederates, to be used in case of need, but they were so hotly assailed they did not stop there, and left us in complete possession.

This was the last effort to turn our right during this memorable battle.

"What next, captain?" inquired Vail, as he wiped the perspiration and dust from his flushed face.

Major Beckstein overhead the question, and broke in, "Boys, Meade is going to act on the defensive; so it is reported."

"Lee can't stay here unless he sweeps the field," said Vail. "If de doesn't drive us, we shall drive him."

"They're a hard looking crowd, ain't they?" remarked one of our boys, referring to the Confederates. The one

who made the remark did not look as if he were dressed
for a state occasion. His hat had disappeared, one shoe
was gone, his shirt was the color of the Gettysburg soil,
his nether garments were rent as if he had been raked
fore and aft by a Gatling gun, and he was sadly in need
of repairs.

"You think they're a rough-looking crowd?" said
Sanderson: "I wonder what they thought of you."

"Thought he'd make a good 'butternut,' I guess,"
chimed in another.

"Fellows," interrupted Sanderson, "you are all brave,
but do you want to know who is the coolest man in our
whole division?"

The one whose clothing was in such a dilapidated state
was standing near bearing patiently the fun created by
his tattered garments.

"Here's the coolest man," continued Sanderson, pointing to him; "there's scarcely a rag on him!"

"You're the coolest, I think," remarked the man, as
the conversation ended.

It is a matter of history that the first part of this day
at Gettysburg passed without exciting incidents. Each
army appeared to be waiting for the other. Major
Beckstein's report that General Meade had resolved to act
upon the defensive proved to be correct. The hours
passed slowly. It was the lull of the storm that was
gathering force for deadlier work. The comparative
silence was but the tempest holding its breath until the
dreadful moment for action should come.

I could see the position held by the Union army, and
I felt confident that it could not be dislodged. Our men

were placed with the care and skill of a military master. The line extended from Round Top along Cemetery Ridge, approached near the village of Gettysburg, and then bent backward towards Culp's Hill, the whole forming the shape of a long-handled hook, thereby enabling us to take every advantage the ground afforded. It was a solid array of living men, a long, close breastwork of tried heroes, fully alive to the great crisis which was at hand.

Toward midday we could see that some important movement was going on among the Confederates massed in the woodland opposite our lines. They were bringing their artillery into position for one grand onslaught. Battery after battery was hurried into place, until the whole field in front of a large part of our lines was bristling with open-mouthed cannon.

There was a stir all along our ranks, for we knew what was coming. Thousands of living men were to face a fierce bombardment from more than a hundred bellowing guns. We were not sheltered in any fort, interposing thick and solid walls of stone or earth between us and the shot and shell soon to pour in merciless fashion into our serried battalions. Calmly we surveyed the preparations for the wholesale slaughter, and awaited the beginning of the conflict.

General Meade's army was well supplied with artillery, and it was unlimbered for action. The batteries were made ready, and the men took their places, eager for the battle. Galloping aids hurried to and fro conveying orders. Our hundred guns were shotted. Meade, and Warren, and Sedgwick, and Hancock, and Shaler, and

Geary, in short all the commanding officers, were awake
to the situation. Field-glasses scanned the operations
of the foe, and orders flew thick and fast along our
ranks.

One battery of the enemy opened, and then another,
and another. The thunder had broken loose. Our
artillery answered back, and the aim was no less deadly
than that of the exasperated foe. The earth shook, and
the crash of more than two hundred guns rent the air, an
awful, prolonged, and deafening sound.

Soon the enemy was shut in by a murky, sulphurous
bank of smoke, through which gleamed bright flashes of
vengeful fire.

While this terrific artillery duel was in progress, my
division was ordered to change position and reinforce the
Second Corps. I had heard and witnessed some heavy
cannonading previous to this, at Fair Oaks, at Malvern
Hill, at Antietam, at the first battle of Fredericksburg,
but this roar of cannon surpassed by far everything of
the kind that had gone before. It was the very sublimity
of mortal combat.

A portion of our march was through woodland. The
iron tempest shattered the trees, tore off branches large
and small, strewed the ground with fragments, and placed
us in great danger even from the falling limbs. To all
appearance a cyclone was sweeping through the woods,
levelling everything before it. The deadly storm did not
stop our advancing troops.

As batteries on both sides were shattered and disabled,
others came up to take their places. The moments
lengthened into minutes, and the minutes into hours, as

the raging combat went on. The cannonading so long continued grew wearisome, and every man of us was ready to welcome its cessation.

Our Union batteries gradually withheld their firing, finding that the Confederate guns were not after all going to annihilate us, and it would be well, as far as possible, to save our ammunition, and be ready for the next emergency. Our batteries awaited the command for action.

BATTERY GOING INTO ACTION.

It was under cover of this artillery warfare that the Confederate General Longstreet massed his forces for what was, perhaps, the most desperate charge of the whole war. Everything was staked upon that bold move. It was a trial of strength and heroism between two armies that had often crossed swords before, and its issue was sure to have a decisive effect upon the great struggle which had so long been going on.

General Lee attempted the tactics of Napoleon at Waterloo, gathering the flower of his army to retrieve his declining fortunes. The die was to be cast, and it would be glorious victory or irretrievable defeat. History would date from that hour. It cannot be doubted that every man in the Confederate army, from the illustrious commander down to the lowest private in the ranks, was alive to the crisis, and was possessed with an enthusiasm for triumph which did not reckon the value of life.

Longstreet and Pickett formed their men in two lines,

one in advance of the other. The gallant Pickett, who had won fame as a reckless, daring leader, the man beyond all others for such a deadly charge as this, was to make the assault, and if possible, rout our sturdy forces. His men were not accustomed to defeat or repulse. They formed the picked division of

GEN. LONGSTREET. the Confederate army. They were to General Lee what the Old Guard was to Napoleon, men for a crisis, who could carry the flag wherever it was possible for human valor to win. They were proud of Virginia, the State from which they were recruited, and never did men of better metal go into a fight.

The attack was made on our centre on Cemetery Ridge. Lee supposed the silence of our batteries indicated that they had been disabled by his own guns, and at once the command was given to charge.

There was something magnificently grand in this last, desperate effort to carry the day. Thirteen thousand gleaming bayonets flashed from the advancing column. It was a forest of steel, and the reflection of the light added splendor to the scene. Pickett's gallant troops, flushed with past victories, were supported by the fine divisions of Wilcox and Pettigrew, and the whole plan of attack, both as to the men selected and the attempted execution, gave evidence of the highest military genius.

Across a field for a distance of some thirteen hundred yards the Confederate column had to advance. Suddenly the Federal batteries on Cemetery Ridge were endowed with new life. Step by step, with a proud military bearing and an enthusiasm that showed itself in every motion, the foe pressed on. It was a charge into the jaws of destruction and death. Our infantry remained quiet in position, calmly awaiting the headlong onset, while the Union batteries opened a galling fire.

Pickett's two lines merged into one, and his ranks were torn by the balls and shells hurled with deadly precision. His supports on the right and left halted, staggered like drunken men, tried to regain themselves and close the ranks through which great chasms had been made, but finally reeled back, unable to face the fiery tempest.

But Pickett's own division did not falter. The men seemed to be made of the same stuff as their bayonets. They swayed to and fro as tall grass waves in the wind, and finally veered to the left of the point at which they were aiming. With the most desperate courage they held their ground, resolved at all hazards to penetrate the Union lines.

When within two hundred yards of our waiting ranks, two Federal divisions opened upon them a hot fire of musketry. They returned it, and attempted to dash forward.

This was the critical moment. They could not withstand the pitiless storm of lead and iron, the hot hail that beat upon them. Their brave column stood for an instant, then a part of it broke in wild disorder, and Meade's army was the victor of Gettysburg.

Our ranks were willing enough to open and let the foe come in, for we knew we could capture all that should penetrate our lines. The troops adjoining the Philadelphia brigade on the left made a quick move by a right wheel, outflanking the charging column, and a similar move being made on the right, the foe was completely entrapped, and two or three thousand prisoners fell into our hands.

A part of Pickett's force rallied, and took possession of a stone wall not far from our line of earth-works. Here they planted the blue flag of Virginia. At once they became a target for our rapid fire, front, right, and left, and, as by one impulse, they dropped their guns, and fell flat upon the ground to escape the terrible storm that was sweeping the field.

Nearly thirty stand of colors were captured by our troops, and a large part of the assaulting division was made prisoners. The ground over which the Confederates had charged so valorously was strewn with the dead and wounded, and soaked with blood.

General Lee at once set about the task of gathering and saving the remnants of his shattered army. Nothing was left to him but to retreat. The invasion of Pennsylvania, from which so much was expected, had ended in disaster. The superb battalions on which he had built his hopes, having done all that even Southern courage and heroism could accomplish, had been flung back in disorder and defeat. Our intrepid boys had covered themselves with glory. The wall of stone where the gallant Virginians planted for a moment their riddled flag, was not more solid than the Union ranks that faced the onslaught and decided the fortunes of the day.

The Confederates—those not captured or placed *hors de combat*—fell back in a disordered mob, while our batteries continued to pelt them, raking the ground over which they were retreating, and also Seminary Hill which was in their possession.

It is reported that General Lee turned to an English officer who was present, and said, "This has been a sad day for us, Colonel—a sad day—but we can't always hope to gain victories."

From what is known and believed now, if General Meade had ordered a charge all along our lines the victory would have been even more decisive, and Lee would not have escaped south of the Potomac with as considerable body of troops as he did. But Meade was unable to obtain the desired information as to the number and disposition of the Confederate forces, and judged that "prudence was the better part of valor." Or, had our troops that were held by General Halleck around Washington been ordered to occupy the south side

16

of the Potomac, as was reported to have been requested by General Meade, Lee's army might have been nearly, if not quite, wiped out of existence.

Gettysburg is a historic spot. The veterans love to go back and live over again the vivid scenes of those three days of conflict. The day following the close of the great battle was the Fourth of July, the Nation's anniversary, and henceforth the third of July will be a fit companion of the patriotic day that comes after it.

Our men forgot their dangers and wounds in the shout of victory that went up from the hard-fought field where their valor was so illustriously displayed.

I saw smiles of congratulation upon the very faces of the dying.

CHAPTER XX.

"Fair hands have sent the bandages and lint,
That tender pity wraps o'er bleeding wounds."

 EGORRA, captain, we've had an illegant foight, haven't we?"

I recognized the voice as that of Barney Roach. Barney Roach, a true-born son of the Emerald Isle, a frank, whole-souled fellow, was a favorite among all who knew him.

"That's the kind of shindy, captain, that just suits Barney Roach; I never had so foine a time in my life."

The blood was trickling down Barney's face, and I asked if he was wounded.

"Just hit in the scalp, captain, and got a hard knock on me pate. I didn't know what I was about for a while; it's the best bit of fun I've had out of the whole scrimmage."

"You seem to enjoy a fight more than most of us," I said.

"Aye, captain, but begorra I was sorry to see the Rebs retreat; it stopped the proceedings and inded the sport." (243)

"We've won the battle, Barney," I replied, "and for my part I'm glad the fighting is over."

"Och, captain, your'e one o' thim fellers that are always spoiling things; sure it's a pity the row broke up so soon—ah, mon, 'twas an illegant row!"

A smile spread over the face of Herr Blinn which was proportioned to the size of Pennsylvania, whose sacred soil we had been defending. Blinn, ponderous as he was when we left Virginia, seemed to have been growing larger on the march, and looked as if fighting agreed with him no less than it did with Barney.

"Did you get hurt?" I said to the huge Dutchman, as he waddled along to the place where I was standing.

"Only von or two leedle scratches," he answered.

"Where?" I inquired.

"On his face, of course," broke in Sanderson, as he glanced at Blinn; "if he was wounded behind he'd never know it in front."

Blinn had learned to take good-naturedly all the jocular allusions to his immense size, and sometimes was ready with a reply.

"Ov coorse dot scratches vas on my vront side, but, shentlemens, shust look at Sanderson and you vinds de scratches pehind."

This implied statement that Sanderson would turn his back to the foe got the laugh on that notorious wag, which, it must be admitted, he appeared to enjoy as much as anyone in the group.

Barney, who had been out of sight for a few moments, was now seen returning with something in his hand, which he was flourishing in a most defiant fashion.

"Hello," shouted one of the men, "what do you call that?"

"That, begorra, that I call me weapon. Give me that, byes, and I wouldn't be afraid of all the Rebs that's now skedaddling to the Potomac. Indade an' I wouldn't."

"A queer weapon that is," said Captain Knox, who had just joined the company.

"Och, mon. there's nothing quare about it: it was good luck to me that I picked it up as we were marching through the open woods this afternoon.'

Barney flourished a stick about four feet long, whirled it over his head, drew back with it and put on a pugnacious look, as if nothing would suit him better than to try his shillalah on the head that was nearest.

"Begorra, byes, it's good sarvice this did to-day."

"You didn't fight with that, did you?" asked Knox.

"Bless me soule if I didn't; I fired me musket, and then held it in me lift hand—it was in the way all the toime—and then I went in with this splendid stick. Ah, byes, what's one of thim spluttering muskets beside such an illegant club as that is? 'Pon my word, I didn't enjoy the scrimmage at all, at all, until I got a chance with me shillaly."

We stood talking over the events of the day, and it was not long before we were reminded that night was drawing on. Great numbers of men on both sides had been wounded, not as slightly as Barney and Blinn were, but so seriously that all our surgical forces were taxed to the utmost, and all who were willing to volunteer as nurses were gladly assigned to that duty.

Every farm-house, barn, and shed in the vicinity had

been improvised into a hospital. There was need of all
the shelter and attention we could get. Our men in doing
hospital duty and taking care of the wounded did not
pass by the enemy. The plea of humanity rose above
political opinion and hostility to the old flag. We could

THE CHAPLAIN IN A HOSPITAL TENT.

not turn away from the groan of a poor dying man, even
though an enemy. Blue and gray were all alike when it
came to the staunching of blood and pillowing of the
head of the dying.

Some of the Confederates were greatly surprised at the

kind treatment they received, and said, "We uns can't understand you uns; you fight us like devils, and treat us like friends."

Hospital tents were in use, but were insufficient to accommodate all the sufferers.

At one farm-house there were gathered not less than fifty wounded men. Some came hobbling on disabled limbs; others were carried tenderly by strong and willing hands; others were laid on stretchers and borne hastily to the temporary hospital, where ebbing life might possibly be saved.

I took my frugal supper, as did many others, of hardtack and pork, and gave all the coffee and tea to the wounded. Only a few could be laid on beds; the number in the house would not afford such a luxury to many. Down on the rough floors, hard, and, for the most part uncovered, the poor sufferers were stretched, each face wearing its mute, appealing look for help.

Some were laid upon the turf in the yard, under the open sky, and there had to await their turn to receive the attention of the busy surgeons.

Nor was this all. Here and there might be seen one whose face was strangely pale. I touched a man who had been bolstered up with his back against the walls of the house, and he stared at me without a motion. His stony look chilled me. He was dead.

I approached another, upon whose white face a dim light was flickering. He had managed with great effort to raise himself on his elbow, and was looking at something he held in his hand as I came near.

He was not known to me, but he wore the blue, or

rather the crimson, and my heart was moved as I looked at him."

"Can I help you?" I said. "Let me brace you up;" and I put my hand back of him to prevent his falling backward on the floor.

He was looking at a photograph, and for a long time held it, gazed at it, and repeatedly kissed it, without saying a word. His shattered frame was trembling with emotion.

"There's blood on it," he slowly said, as if his strength were nearly gone, and he could hardly speak.

"That's no disgrace, my lad," I answered.

"I know it," he responded, "but it blurs her face." He paused a moment, and then said, " But I shan't forget her face; no, captain, I couldn't forget that face if this picture was all blotted out with blood."

He kissed it again, and the red stain was on his lips.

"She's very dear to me," he gasped; "she hoped I wouldn't get shot down so quick I couldn't take this picture from my pocket before I breathed my last, and she has her wish."

I could hardly speak, for I was so moved by this tragical, romantic incident that I hardly felt like uttering a word.

"Let me down," the wounded man said; "it tires me to lie on my elbow."

I laid him back as gently as I could, and was going to ask him if there was anything he wanted; if so, I would try and get it for him. An orderly had just passed him before I came, and had taken his name, and such other particulars as were required, and had also noted his wishes, and made record of his messages to be sent to friends.

No sooner had he touched the floor and settled down in his weakness than he motioned to me. I knelt down and bent over him.

"The light! The light!" he faintly whispered, and motioned to have the lamp, which was dim, brought to him.

I granted his wishes and held the light down over his upturned face. He raised his hand, still holding the precious photograph, and gazed at it again. It seemed to hold his spirit spell-bound. He could not get his glazed eye away from it.

"It's blurred," he gasped again, "but, captain, I don't care; I've got her face in my heart; I know she's thinking of me now."

"Surgeon," I said to Doctor Emmons, who was not far away, "can you do nothing for this man?"

He gave me a look which was not reassuring, waved his hand to indicate that he wished me to be silent, and made no verbal reply. I knew that the case was hopeless, and nothing could be done to save the life that was trembling in the balance.

"Don't leave me, captain," faintly whispered the dying man;" it won't be long now."

"You have the satisfaction of having done your duty," I remarked, trying to comfort him.

"My only regret is that friends will look for my return, and I shall not see them again," he replied.

I leaned over the pale face, and watched the spasmodic breath growing shorter.

"Put your hand under my head," he whispered.

I did so, and shortly after, holding still the stained photograph, he passed beyond the echoes of battle and the groans of wounded patriots. A calm peace rested upon his face, and the blood-stained uniform he wore was his dress for a soldier's burial.

I took the photograph, which I could see, through the marks of blood, was the picture of a fair young face, opened the breast of his coat, and laid it over his heart. He gave one more gasp as if the picture had thrilled him with a new touch of life. That was the last. A brighter light had dawned.

As I rose to turn away I felt a hand laid upon my shoulder. A low voice said, "Captain, do you know that Brown is wounded?"

The question startled me. "Not seriously hurt, I hope?"

"I think not," responded the one who had informed me, "but he would like to see you."

In the yard of the farm-house stood a shed, open wholly on the front side, and some half dozen men had been laid there on couches of straw. Brown was among the number, and as I entered the place I recognized him by the flickering light of a candle not far from the head of his bed. Union men and Confederates were lying there side by side, and no distinction was made in the kind and faithful attentions bestowed by our surgeons and helpers.

I saw one of our boys hand a drink of cool water to a "Butternut" just as I entered, and turn and give a drink from the same cup to one of the Union men. They were drinking together from a common cup of suffering, and also from a common cup of refreshing. The blood of conflict obliterated the colors of blue and gray; only the gaping wounds were thought of, not the side of the contest in which they were received.

"Is that you, Brown?" I asked, as I came near the spot where he was lying.

He reached out his hand and grasped mine firmly.

"You haven't lost all your strength," I remarked; "I trust you are not badly wounded."

"A flesh wound," he responded; "the surgeon has just dressed it, and says it might be much worse; I don't think it's anything serious, yet it is beginning to be painful."

The Confederate soldier, who was receiving the cup of water as I entered, seemed much interested in the conversation.

Presently he said, "Friend, won't you come here a moment?"

I was soon by his side, expressing my regret at his misfortune.

"Did you call that man Brown?" he inquired.

"Yes," I replied, "that is his name; I know him well, and am glad to learn that he is not very badly hurt."

"Well," said the boy in gray, "I've been trying to watch his face, and get a good look at him."

"Why?" I inquired; "do you think you met him in the fight?"

"I think I may have met him somewhere," he answered; "anyhow it seems to me that his face is sort o'familiar, and I've been studying for some time and trying to place it."

"Perhaps so," I remarked; "there have been many instances of men meeting as enemies, who found out that they were old friends."

Brown seemed to be overhearing the conversation, and raised himself partly up, turning his face toward the couch of the Confederate prisoner.

"Does he think he knows me?" asked Brown, as he tried to get a look at the man. "Not by my name, I guess, for the woods are full of Browns."

The man quickly said, "I used to know Hackett Brown; the name is familiar to me; I thought your face was like—"

Brown interrupted him by eagerly asking, "Who are you, and where did you ever know Hackett Brown?"

"That's his name, surely," I said to the man. "Really, you are not mistaken."

"I thought I could not be mistaken in that face, and when I heard the name I felt more sure than ever."

"What is your name?" quickly came from Brown; "I wonder if I remember you."

"You ought to," said the other, "for we went to school together twenty years ago, sat side by side, have been in many a scrape together, and were good friends until I got uneasy and went away from home to seek my fortune."

"Are you Billy Weston?" exclaimed Brown, evidently much excited.

"I am Billy Weston, Hackett," cried the other, "and I never have forgotten you. Heavens, I never thought I should meet you here!"

Weak as they were from loss of blood and fatigue, both men leaped to their feet.

At that moment a surgeon entered, and was at a loss to explain these strange actions.

" What are you doing?" he shouted. "Going to have another fight? Come, we don't want any duels here!"

"No fight!" ejaculated Brown. But the two men sprang for each other. The surgeon stepped in between them to separate them.

"Go back!" he shouted; " lie down: you're crazy!"

"Anything but that," I said. "It's just two old friends meeting unexpectedly."

"I'll give you the only hand I've got," ejaculated Brown, as he reached out his left hand toward Weston.

" I can't give you either hand," broke in Weston, who was badly wounded in one arm and slightly in the other, " but I can give you a foot!"

He held up one of his feet as he laid one arm on my shoulder, and in a most amusing way Brown caught hold of it, crying, " Let's shake, Billy!"

A smile lighted up the faces of the other men as they witnessed this singular greeting, which was one of the little pleasant incidents, relieving for a moment the grim severities of war.

The men soon had to return to their couches, and Weston was a good deal exhausted.

"Would you have known me?" he inquired, after a short rest.

"Never," replied Brown; "you've changed; and, besides, I never expected to see you in such a place as this. What would you have done, Weston, if you had met me in the charge, and had known me?"

"I don't know. I might have called you a cussed

Yank, and run my bayonet through you. Thank God, Hackett, I didn't meet you!"

The two men agreed that it was not best to talk on the question of right and wrong in the contest; and so began to narrate the experiences through which they had passed since they separated so many years before.

"I wouldn't fight you boys, now," exclaimed Weston, finally.

"So I've brought you over to the Union side," said Brown.

"After such generous treatment as this," continued Weston, "I haul down my colors. You might have left me on the field, and perhaps I would have died, but I have been cared for as if I were a friend and not an enemy. You've treated me better than I deserved."

While this conversation was in progress; I noticed that two surgeons with instruments, bandages, and lint, were making preparations to perform an operation. A poor fellow was lying in one corner of the shed, and was suffering great pain. His right arm below the elbow had been badly shattered by a fragment of a shell.

" We shall have to take that hand off," said Surgeon Emmons, as he approached the man in a manner that indicated business.

"Don't do it!" remonstrated the sufferer. "I can't lose that hand; why, doctor, that's my right hand, and I can't live without it."

"You can't live with it, as it is now," said the doctor; "there's but one thing to be done: it will have to come off."

The man raised his arm in the dim light, looked at the

terrible wounds, and burst into tears. A thrill of sympathy ran through the place, and I almost wished I could give my own right arm and let him keep his. He plead long and earnestly to have his hand saved, and only after he was assured that his life would be in danger if the amputation did not take place would he give his consent.

The bandage was soon adjusted, and the surgeons were not long in doing their ghastly, yet merciful, work.

As the man came to his senses, he exclaimed, "My hand! My hand! Is it gone? Where is it?"

He felt all about for it with his other hand, trying to find it.

"What do you want of it?" said Emmons.

"Want to bid it good-bye!" sobbed the poor fellow.

The hand, frightfully lacerated and bloody, was held up before him. He gazed at it with a kind of despairing expression, turned his head away, and then giving it another and last look, said, "Good-bye; I shan't see you any more! Oh, it's hard! It's hard!"

As I passed out from the sickening spectacle of wounded men, torn and maimed, another spectacle more appalling caught my eye. Lying in the yard not far from the shed was a pile of human limbs that had been amputated—hands, arms, feet, legs, thrown together, a frightful heap, waiting for burial, and telling as nothing else could have done the desperate nature of the battle.

The men on both sides had been hacked and hewn mercilessly, and while I realized that Gettysburg was a triumph I also knew that Gettysburg was a carnage, and a costly offering on the altar of the Nation.

Just then I heard a voice that was giving vent to numerous enthusiastic expressions. It was the well-known voice of Barney Roach.

"Are you here, Barney?" I began.

"Begorra, captain," shouted Barney, "it's worth coming for; do you see that pile o' stumps that's been cut off?"

"It's a sorry looking mass," I said, as I turned my head away. "As a lot of torn and shattered limbs, it is a great success."

"You're roight, captain, it's been a very successful scrimmage; the war is going on illegantly. It's too bad some of the byes lost a hand, and have only one left. You see, captain, with two hands a lad can carry a musket and a shillaly."

"How would it be, Barney," I said, "if you were to lose a hand?"

"Bad luck to the musket, but I'd stick to me stick!"

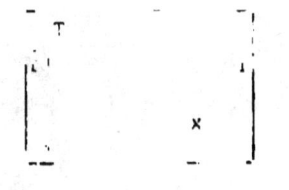

SURRENDER AT VICKSBURG.

CHAPTER XXI.

"Dark fortune drives their squadrons back ;
'Away !' they cry ; 'the foe is on the track !'"

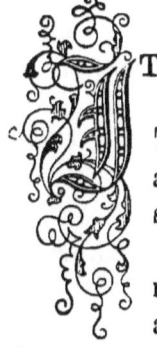T WAS the Fourth of July.
"Grant has captured Vicksburg!"
This was the news that flew along our ranks
as we held that day the field of Gettysburg,
so hotly contested and so valorously won.

Major Beckstein hurried away to our
regiment with the exciting intelligence, and
as the men sprang to their feet a prolonged
shout went up and mingled with loud hurrahs that were
heard on right and left.

The official report of Grant's renowned achievement
was read out at orders that evening, and our flags waved
proudly.

Faces that were worn and haggard by the fiery ordeal
through which we had passed, were lighted up with
smiles of joy, and spontaneous congratulations were
exchanged between officers and the rank and file.

A group of men struck up the "Star-spangled
Banner," and our redoubtable major, who vowed he
never sang a note in his life, roared and bellowed with

17

all his might, sometimes in tune, more frequently out of tune, sometimes getting the words of the song, and sometimes the words of some other song, and occasionally no words at all. Still he sang, and as no one else could understand him he probably understood himself.

Rain had fallen, and the mud was the only bed most of the men had to sleep in the night before. While at the field hospital, helping the wounded, I found a board about six feet in length by fourteen inches in width. I held on to my prize, and resolved to have something between me and the wet ground when I attempted to sleep. I tried to determine which was the soft side of it, and concluded that whichever side I took I would think the other must be the softer; but on that hard board I laid myself, and there, surrounded by the dead and dying, where the battle had raged the fiercest and the carnage was the most terrible, I slept as if I had underneath me a bed of down.

It soon became known that our officers had displayed a valor worthy of being emulated by their troops. Sincere regret was expressed at the casualties that had taken place.

We had to mourn the death of Major-General John F. Reynolds, and Brigadier-Generals Zook, Kosciusko, S. H. Weed, and E. J. Farnsworth. These fell before the storm of death, and their names are embalmed in the nation's annals.

GENERAL HANCOCK.

General Hancock commanded the Union centre, against which Pickett's tremendous charge was aimed, penetrating our lines in several places. We heard with deep sorrow that Hancock had been wounded.

He was not alone in his misfortunes. Major-General D. E. Sickels, and Brigadier-Generals Paul, J. Gibbons, who succeeded Hancock, T. A. Rowley, and F. C. Barlow, of the United States Regulars, were all carried bleeding from the field. Our rejoicing had in it a minor strain.

No less deep was the grief over those who had stood at our sides, and in the strength and glow of valiant manhood had gone into the conflict, and would not answer again to the roll-call. During the day we were ministering to the wounded and burying the dead.

But there was work ahead. Lee had retreated, yet his army was not destroyed. He was a master of military tactics, and knew how "to save the pieces." He was determined to get out of our way, and make ready to continue the fight.

"Four days' rations!" exclaimed our colonel; "boys, I suppose you know what that means."

"It means hard-tack and pork for breakfast, and pork and hard-tack for supper," growled Sanderson.

"It means more than that," I ventured to suggest, "Is it not so, colonel?"

"You are right, captain; we shall be on the march before many hours."

As the rations were being served, Sanderson humorously suggested that Blinn should be left behind, and that double rations could then be served to the men in the next campaign.

"Here's your pork, Blinn," cried Sanderson.

"Dot pork, shentlemens," said Herr Blinn, "vas dry; der pest pork is vat comes mit fedders. I likes dot kind vat crows more dan it squeals."

"Just like him," said several of the boys, for by this time Herr Blinn's tastes and peculiarities were well known.

Sanderson was busy with his pencil and paper. In a moment he looked up and said, "Here's an outline for one of the great historic pictures of the war."

A dozen men crowded around, and a number asked, "What is it?"

"Herr Blinn planting the Stars and Stripes on a hen-roost!"

There was a burst of merriment as Sanderson held up his comical drawing.

"Blixen!" shouted Blinn, "dot vos no goot; I sees no shickens."

"Oh, the chickens," said Sanderson, "are all inside."

"Inside of what," promptly asked Vail, "the coop, or Blinn?"

The next day we were on the road, and reached Emmittsburg. Our advance guard had struck the rear part of the Confederate force, and exchanged shots with the flying foe. A portion of our cavalry were hanging on Lee's rear, worrying the Confederates, and picking up stragglers.

The rain continued, the roads were heavy, and the progress of both armies was slow.

Next day we were detailed to guard a wagon-train, a kind of service that none of our troops liked. The wheels would sink, the mules would jerk, and flounder in the mire, and the men would have to come to the rescue, and by sheer strength get the team started again.

A teamster's old straw hat was seen lying in the road. "Take it up carefully," said Sanderson, " you may find the fellow under it. One of our wagons has been lost, anyhow, but we can't stop to dig for it." .

Several days' march brought us to the Baltimore and Wheeling pike. Taking this we passed through Funkstown. Here the Confederates had made a stand, and seemed determined to dispute our advance. We could see them in strong force moving about behind their breastworks.

"Byes, there's a lively time coming," shouted Barney Roach; "it's been moighty dull and uninterestin' the last few days."

"You said you'd stick to your stick, Barney; have you done it?" I asked.

He held up his club with a look that seemed to say, "Do you think I would be such a fool as to leave this behind?"

"Will we foight 'em, captain?" eagerly asked Barney.

"It looks as if we would."

" Begorra, captain, I've had the blues, for it looked as if the foighting was about over; hurrah for the shindy! It's just that, captain, that will keep up me spirits."

"So you are going in with that stick, are you?" queried Sanderson. "I'll tell you, Barney, these war correspondents will get hold of what you are doing, and in a day or two it will all be out in the newspapers."

" Will it?" exclaimed Barney, his face glowing like the sun. " What will the newspapers say?"

"Something like this, in big letters," resumed Sanderson, "'Barney Roach charging on the Confederacy with a shillalah!'"

Our conversation was soon interrupted. Four companies from my regiment, with detachments from three New York regiments were thrown forward as skirmishers. Being placed in command, I ordered an advance to relieve the troops belonging to the Third Corps. Here we were to await orders, and within half an hour orders that were not altogether pleasant reached us. We were to capture the first line of breastworks, which was in a commanding situation, and would make an excellent position for our batteries in case of a general engagement, which now seemed imminent.

When everything was ready, we sprang forward to make the assault and take the parapets in front of us. We soon came to a seven-rail fence. Over it we went with a bound.

At this moment there came a volley of musketry. Captain Knox staggered as if wounded, but rushed forward the next instant. Some eight or ten of my men had been struck, and we knew at once that we were not engaged in any boys' play; it was a hot place.

We charged through a corn-field where the corn was high enough to prevent the Confederates from taking deliberate aim, thus rendering our loss comparatively small. Coming nearer the enemy's works, we dropped down under cover of the hill for the troops on our right and left to get into line with us. Presently a few shots on our left told us that our men had not been so successful in their advance, and were suffering from sharpshooters who were there in force.

" Look!" exclaimed Vail, "they are in the tree-tops."
"That's coming pretty close!" said one of the men as
a bullet grazed his head, notching his hair.

I had crept up pretty well in front, and was partly
sheltered by a projecting knoll, telling the men to keep a
little back and protect themselves as well as they could.
The whistling music of bullets was more exciting than
that of brass instruments.

Suddenly Vail dropped his head as a sharp-shooter
took aim, and cried again, " Don't you see him there in
the top of that tree, the impudent rascal? He is picking
off our men as coolly as if he was shooting squirrels."

Flashes of fire and puffs of smoke broke out from the
trees, which showed plainly where the riflemen were. I
knew they must be dislodged before making our charge,
or many of our men would get hit by their deadly aim.

I could see one cool fellow quietly seated in the crotch
of a tree, loading and firing away as deliberately as if in
no danger himself. He probably thought he was protected from view by the leaves and branches, but the
puff of smoke every time he fired, told plainly enough
where he was.

Turning to one of the men I asked for his rifle. He
handed it to me loaded. Just as I fired in the direction
of the tree another bullet grazed my head.

"Give me another rifle!" I cried; "pass them up fast
as you can!"

I sent another shot, and another. It was evident that
I was a mark, for the bullets struck on all sides of me.
I fired again.

"There he goes!" shouted one of the men; "you hit
him that time!"

We saw the man tumble from the tree.

Just then there was a sound on each side of us of men advancing.

Those of us who had been waiting for our comrades sprang to our feet, gave one tremendous cheer, and charged up the hill, our whole line, which must have been nearly a mile in length, rushing on the Confederate breastworks. When within twenty yards we fired one volley, and then with bayonets fixed mounted the works. So enthusiastic and determined was the charge that we carried everything before us.

The larger part of the enemy had fallen back to avoid capture. Their rout was complete, and we sent about two hundred prisoners to our division headquarters.

We expected a charge of our whole force would be ordered, for we believed such a move would result in capturing the rear guard of Lee's army, but we did not see an officer above the rank of captain from the time General Bartlett gave us the order to take the works until nine o'clock the next morning.

"Now for Williamsport!" shouted Major Beckstein. We were soon on the march again, and all hands were ready to express the opinion that if forced marches would capture the Confederate legions we were in a fair way of doing it.

Our capacity for going ahead and catching Lee's army, was equalled only by the capacity of his army for going ahead too, and not getting caught. We made a considerable capture of the last brigade of his retreating forces, and would have taken more had they not plunged into the Potomac, swimming to the other side.

CHAPTER XXII.

ADVENTURES OF THE PURSUIT—*Continued.*

"It is better to chase than to be chased."—*General Sedgwick.*

E WERE again on the south side of the Potomac, having crossed on our pontoon bridge. Lee was doing his best to escape.

His army had already met with serious losses, so great, in fact, that its power for coping with the Army of the Potomac was broken. Gettysburg was a fatal blow to Lee, who had built his hope of the final success of the Confederate cause on his northern invasion.

It was said, and doubtless truthfully, that from the time Lee left Virginia until he re-entered the State, he lost in battle, by disease and desertion, eighty thousand men.

We were almost constantly on the march after crossing the Potomac.

A fine landscape view greeted us near Front Royal, a place often referred to in army despatches during the war. The beetling hills, the outspread fields, and shadowy groves stood out upon our vision, and exclamations of admiration burst from the ranks as the men gazed upon the scene of beauty. It seemed sacrilege that a region so romantic and lovely should be trodden and wasted by the hoof of war. The fair valley and romantic uplands were marred by the havoc which always attends the march of an invading army.

We had halted one day for a short rest, and as blackberries were plentiful in the adjacent fields and bushes, the men soon scattered in all directions, and were foraging.

Presently a squad came rushing in at a headlong rate, and I was startled by this sudden retreat. They were flying as if they had been put to rout by a bayonet charge of the enemy.

"Halt!" I cried. "What does this mean? Are we attacked?"

"Yes!" exclaimed Sanderson, "and driven back; couldn't stand our ground in that thicket."

"We ran," shouted Brixy, "and never stopped to fire; I'm glad I'm out of it!"

"Then we had better form, and charge, and drive them out," I said.

"You can do it if you like," said Sanderson, "but I won't go in there again."

"You will obey orders," I replied, sternly.

"Shoot me for a deserter," said another, "but you won't get me into that place again."

There was a comical look on the faces of the men which indicated that there was something queer going on. Just then Corporal Vail came in on a run, his hat gone, and his whole appearance showing that he had beat a hasty retreat.

"It's worse than a Confederate battery," he exclaimed. "I'd rather face a charge by Pickett's whole division."

"What is it?" I asked, my curiosity a good deal excited.

"It's a durned skunk!" shouted Brixy, and then a shout of laughter burst simultaneously from the whole group.

"Well," I said, "you're a brave set of fellows to be driven away pell-mell by an animal no bigger than a cat. You ought to be ashamed of yourselves."

"That animal," said Sanderson, "is considerably bigger than he looks; I don't estimate him according to his size, but according to his ability; he's a good deal like a Gatling gun—more in him than there looks to be."

"If what's in him would only stay in him," said Vail, "I wouldn't care, but it won't. Try him yourself, captain."

I had no desire to make any such trial, and congratulated my men upon escaping without being hit by the enemy.

"I don't want any more blackberries from that patch," broke in Sanderson; "they are green and not fit to eat."

While this amusing scene was going on other men were scattered about in other parts of the bushes, and were gathering and eating the berries with a hearty relish. There was another incident which came near being a tragedy, and costing one of our boys his life. As he was filling his tin cup with berries he disturbed a venomous adder which stung him in the palm of the hand before he could take the alarm and escape.

He gave a shriek which could not have been more startling if a shell had exploded at his feet and blown him over. It was a sharp cry that I shall never forget, and I wondered what it meant. I was a short distance away. and ran to him at once. In less than half a minute the terrible blow had begun to show its effects; death would soon result unless something was done.

The poor fellow, white as a ghost, glared at me, and for a moment appeared to be stunned beyond the power of speech. Suddenly he recovered himself and cried, "Captain, I'm a dead man! What shall I do? It's all up with me!"

There was no time to be lost. Every instant the hot poison was doing its deadly work. One might have seen the hand swell and the wound grow purple, so rapidly was the venom taking effect.

"Give me your arm," I shouted, "and be quick about it!"

In an instant his coat was stripped off and his sleeve rolled up. I took my handkerchief and tied it around his arm below the elbow to prevent the poison from reaching the body. Thrusting in the bayonet from his musket, I twisted the handkerchief with all my might to stop every particle of circulation.

"Find a surgeon!" I cried. "Bring him instantly!"

Two or three men started at once to obey the order. Luckily there was one close at hand. He saw the danger, and exclaimed, "That arm must come off in two seconds!"

He went about it immediately, and in fifteen minutes had amputated the arm at the elbow; but before this time the arm had swollen to twice its natural size. The surgeon declared that the twisted handkerchief saved the man's life.

Somehow the berries had lost their flavor, and the men were not anxious to gather any more from that particular spot.

Another march of a couple of days brought us to Warrenton Junction, near which we encamped. We knew Lee's shattered army was in full retreat, yet could not be far away. We had struck its rear guard once or twice already, but we were to halt until we received further orders to advance.

We were near the summer residence of the Lee family. The third day or so after we arrived a detachment from each regiment in our brigade was placed under my command for picket duty. Our lines extended around the Lee mansion. They were established so as to join the pickets of the Second Corps on our right, and those of the Third Corps on our left.

This was "carrying the war into China;" in other words, into one locality of the "first families in Virginia." The Lee mansion was not an object of veneration among the Union troops, and they did not have the fear of that particular family before their eyes.

They hinted that nothing would give them greater pleasure than to burn down that mansion, so closely associated with one of the renowned commanders of the Confederacy.

I received word that Mrs. Lee wished to see the officer in command. I repaired to the house and found her very nervous and excited, but for all this her demeanor was dignified, and every look and word showed that she was a lady of the highest culture and breeding.

After a salutation, I immediately said, " I am here, I believe, by your request, and would be pleased to learn your wishes." .

" We are safe, I trust," she said, " and shall receive no harm from the Federal troops."

I assured her that we had no intention of committing any depredations. She informed me that some of the men we had relieved treated her servants and some of the members of the family rather uncivilly.

" Can you give me an assurance that this will not be repeated ? " she asked.

"I can, Madam. It is no part of a soldier's duty to make war on defenseless women ; while my men remain, both your household and your property will be respected."

" I am grateful," she replied, " for your promise of protection."

It was evident that other members of the family were pleased to know that they were quite safe, notwithstanding the Union forces were at the very door. The servants who were near whispered to one another, and seemed to be relieved from all apprehension.

As I was about to leave, Mrs. Lee, in a very polite manner, said, " Captain, our dinner is ready, and we would be delighted to have you join us."

"With great pleasure," I replied, thinking of the pork and hard-tack which had formed the staple of my diet for so long a time. I began to wonder whether I would not forget myself and eat with my fingers instead of with knife and fork, and whether I would not be caught trying to break a piece of bread on my knee as if it were a piece of Uncle Sam's hard-tack, dry as one of our chaplain's sermons.

We sat down to an ample dinner which was served in true Virginia style, and with an air of princely hospitality. It seemed to me an event worth noting that a Union officer should be so handsomely treated by a family of such prominence in the cause against which I was fighting. I was not at all abashed at the table, and Mrs. Lee and her family must have concluded that if our army were all like me as to capacity it could swallow easily the whole united South. Uncomfortable as I had been from hunger, I am not sure but I arose from the table feeling a good deal worse than when I sat down. I felt that I had a reputation to sustain, and would do well to show myself as efficient at the hospitable board of Mrs. Lee as our soldiers had in driving the Confederates back to the ancient commonwealth of Virginia.

At all events that table was soon like the field of Gettysburg after it had been swept clean by Meade's invincible host. The good lady had reason to believe Union men could take everything before them.

After dinner we arose and adjourned to the drawing-room. I assured the young ladies that I was fond of music, and asked one of them to favor me.

"Perhaps you sing yourself," she remarked.

I replied, "I have already given you my word of honor that nothing shall be done to frighten you, or cause you any alarm. and I must, therefore, beg to be excused."

She smiled, and seating herself at the piano she rendered in excellent style the "Bonnie Blue Flag," and "Away down South in Dixie."

Jumping up she turned to me and said, "You are the first Yankee officer for whom I ever performed."

I playfully said, "Thank you, Miss; I see it has not broken your instrument, nor cracked your voice."

After bidding the family good day, and repeating my promise to prevent any annoyance of them, or rude treatment, I hurried away to my headquarters.

"Vas it von square dinner?" queried Herr Blinn, with a voracious look upon his expansive face. "Dot vas pad luck."

"What was bad luck?" I asked.

"I vas not dere to get dot dinner."

"Bad luck for me," I said; "if you had been there, the Lee family would have been reduced to famine besides."

"You go pack to-morrow?" inquired the rotund Dutchman. "I speaks for de position of aid."

That afternoon I made a complete tour of the picket line, and as the woods seemed cool and pleasant I thought I would pass through and take a look at the open country, which I believed was not far distant. I sauntered on in a kind of careless way, not thinking how far I was going, nor surmising for the moment that I was likely to get into any danger. At length I was a considerable distance beyond our picket line. I discovered my mistake, but thought I would survey the locality, become a scout, and see what there was to be seen.

On one side of me was a peach orchard which had some fine fruit growing on the thrifty trees. An old homestead was not far away, which appeared to be deserted. I concluded that the family had fled before the approach of our troops. The peaches were tempting to look at, and, being thirsty, I made up my mind I would try their quality.

As soon as I jumped over the fence I observed a movement that aroused my suspicions and convinced me I was on dangerous territory. I knew I was alone, and a sudden wish came over me that I had not strayed quite so far away from my men. What was I to do if I should suddenly encounter any of the enemy? I resolved myself into a council of war, and held a consultation with myself as to the best method of procedure. I was ready for any ordinary emergency, but had no special desire to meet a whole division of "Butternuts." I feared that in that case I would lose the benefits of Mrs. Lee's bountiful dinner which I had eaten a few hours before.

My council of war, the decisions of which were remarkably unanimous, was scarcely concluded, when I discovered a squad of ten or fifteen guerillas. I began to think I might have an opportunity of visiting Richmond before I could help carry our flag into that celebrated town, which the Union troops had been so long trying to reach. If I were going there I preferred to choose my company.

Here was a dilemma. Some of the guerillas were already preparing to mount their fleet steeds, and it looked to me as if they meant to make me a prisoner. I knew there was no hope of my escape except by stratagem.

Instantly I put my fingers to my mouth and gave three loud whistles, and cried as if to an orderly in my rear, "Bring forward my horse! Forward! Company A,

18

First Cavalry! Double quick, march! Here they are, here they are! Surround them!"

As if in a great hurry to find my horse, I cleared the fence, and then turning upon the marauders fired three shots in quick succession.

By this time they were all mounted, and a more frightened set of troopers never sat in the saddle. They seemed to think the whole force of Union cavalry was at hand. Away they went like the wind, putting spurs to their horses, and not even stopping to look back.

I lost no time in retracing my steps to my headquarters, determining then and there to avoid making such unpleasant acquaintances in the future.

It is a well-known fact that the majority of those who professed to be farmers did more to reinforce the bands of guerrillas than any other class of citizens, and were the most dangerous of all the enemies we met.

CAPTAIN R. W. PATRICK.

Our men found this a very desirable camping ground, with plenty of water, abundance of good shade, and excellent roads in all directions. Provisions were plentiful, and were largely drawn from the surrounding country.

A striking scene occurred at this camp one Sunday evening. A chaplain of one of the Pennsylvania regiments announced that he would hold a religious service, and invited all to attend who felt like doing so. A large congregation assembled at the appointed time.

Of course the service was in the open air, and as the

day was departing and the soft shadows of evening were just beginning to fall, everything conspired to render the service peculiarly impressive. Around us were the symbols of savage war. Officers, guards, stacked muskets, men in the blue uniform of the Union, long rows of shelter tents, troopers and horses in the background, all helped to throw over the scene a strange solemnity. Could it be that the brave spirits of our departed comrades who had fallen in the great fight were hovering around us?

One of my men, Thompson, who, as already related, had opened his heart in confidence to me as we were lying on the field of Gettysburg awaiting the last onset, came near, evidently overcome with emotion.

"Thompson," I said, "does this make you think of home?"

His only reply was to brush away the tears from his bronzed cheeks. When he had subdued his feelings so as to be able to speak, he said, "Captain, what a host of prayers and good wishes are following our gallant boys! I still feel a strange sense of security, and in the hottest charge I am as calm and undismayed as I am standing here at this moment."

I had read of the British General Havelock and Captain Hedley Vickars, those heroes of the Crimea, and I at once thought of them, and their upward look of faith and trust in every hour of danger. The men stood thick around me, most of them with heads bowed and in a thoughtful mood. Visions of distant homes and friends were floating before their eyes.

The service progressed, and the singing had one of our

best brass bands for an accompaniment. The strains, clear, loud, and prolonged, rose on the still air of that beautiful evening, and, floating far away, gently died out in silence. Invisible powers were resting down upon our camp.

A fine chorus of male voices took up the songs, and, as every part was well represented, the harmony was complete. It was the sound of many waters, and as captivating, it seemed to me, as the noise of "harpers harping with their harps."

The chaplain announced the well-known hymn:

" My days are gliding swiftly by,
    And I, a pilgrim stranger,
    Would not detain them as they fly,
    Those hours of toil and danger.

CHORUS:—" For Oh, we stand on Jordan's strand,
    Our friends are passing over,
    And just before, the shining shore,
    We may almost discover."

The men took up the words and sang them with a heartiness which showed they were in full sympathy with the occasion.

Suddenly I discovered that the remainder of our regiment not far away were joining in the singing. It was a unanimous and spontaneous lifting up of voices, the echoes of which came back to us as if an invisible chorus were responding in sweetest melody.

Then our whole brigade joined in; then regiment after regiment, and brigade after brigade, until it appeared that the whole army right and left of us had united in the resounding song. The hills and valleys were suddenly awakened from their deep repose, were made vocal, and were ringing with the far-sounding refrain. All that imagination ever dreamed of the power of music was here realized, and in the intervals our men stood in hush of spirit to catch the lingering strains.

The sermon was in keeping with the hour, and prepared the way for the closing act. When the last hymn was given out, beginning with the verse:

"In the Christian's home in glory,
There remains a land of rest,"

thousands of voices took it up with unabated enthusiasm, and the effect was repeated, only with greater intensity, if that were possible.

Having remained here about four weeks, we broke camp, passed Warrenton Junction, at this time the depot of supplies for our army, and in less than a day were in the neighborhood of White Sulphur Springs.

"This is a watering place, I hear," remarked Sanderson, "for the first families of 'Ole Virginny;' they must like the smell of the infernal pit."

"Begorra, they think it best to get used to the smell," came from a Hibernian voice, with a strong brogue.

"Barney," I said, "wouldn't you like to test the quality of the water?"

"Aye, captain," responded Barney, "but what is the water good for?"

"Good for health," broke in Sanderson; "you should drink a quart at a time to get the full benefit of it."

"It's a quare counthry," said Barney. "It raises petaties, cabbages, Rebels, and sulphur. I belave if one o' them springs was set on fire it would burn with the brimstun. Whew, byes, there's a smell of divils round here."

By this time a group had assembled. and were much amused at Barney's characteristic remarks. Sanderson handed him a quart pail full of the strongest water, and said, "There, Barney, drink that; it will do you good."

"I'll take it for the corn on me foot," responded Barney. And then lifting the pail toward his lips, he exclaimed, "It's many a man's health I've drunk with jolly old Bourbon, but, byes, I'll drink your health with a quart of brimstun!"

"Down with it," shouted Sanderson.

Barney took one swallow, scowled and puckered up his mouth, while a shiver shook him from head to foot, and then he threw the pail on the ground, and swung his stick at Sanderson as if anxious to fracture his cranium.

"What are you doing?" asked Sanderson, in his most tantalizing way.

"Didn't ye say, 'down with it?'" Barney shouted. "I've done as ye said; I'd sooner drink the rinsings from me ould musket. Och, man, this water is spiled; the smell of it came near knocking me shillaly out o' me hand!"

"Does fellers ever come here on their weddin' trip?" asked Brixy.

"Yes, I replied, "why do you want to know?"

"'Cause I'm not comin'," answered Brixy.

There were ruins all about us. The immense hotel, where so many brilliant scenes had been enacted by the aristocratic families of Virginia, and the surrounding cottages, had been burned in the retreat of Pope and McDowell during the preceding year; but we could imagine the festive gayety of the town in the old days when it was renowned as a fashionable watering-place.

As the men repaired to their posts to get ready for another march I heard the redoubtable Barney exclaiming, "Is it health they get by drinking that water? Faith, byes, such health would be the death o' me!"

We pressed on in our march toward Brandy Station. In one part of the route we were overtaken by a rainstorm, could make but slow progress through the mud, and were very uncomfortable. The boys hit upon the expedient of lighting fires at intervals of a mile or two. One detachment would get warm and partly dry at a fire, put on more wood, and then move forward to the next fire.

Our hardy general was a great favorite with his troops. I used to hear men saying, "Here comes Sedgwick; it's all right now."

The general was always on good terms with his men, was not averse to accepting a good cigar, or telling a pithy story, and was popular, although severe when occasion required it, and every inch a soldier.

Toward evening of that wet day Sedgwick was standing by one of the fires which was completely surrounded by men. He was out of harness, was taking the march as easily as possible, and did not preserve a style in keeping with his rank as one of the great commanders. His nether extremities were widely separated as he stood warming himself by the crackling fire.

A soldier came along who was looking for a place to

boil his tea-kettle. He could not break through the cordon of men surrounding the fire.

"There are more ways than one," he remarked, and slipped his kettle over the end of a long stick, thrust it between Sedgwick's legs, not knowing the man was his general, and held it over the flames.

There was a smile on the men's faces, and they wondered whether the general would feel that his dignity was offended. He stood perfectly still until the kettle boiled, then seized the stick, took off the kettle, and, handing it to the man, said, "You had better get back to your place or Sedgwick will be after you!"

"I'd douse the hot water on him," said the man.

The men could not help laughing at the soldier's mistake, and Sedgwick seemed to enjoy the fun as heartily as any. He was strongly endeared to his soldiers, and by little attentions and acts of kindness, such as making frequent inquiries in regard to their health and rations, he showed that he was awake to their best interests.

GENERAL SEDGWICK. Brandy Station at this time was in the hands of the Confederates. Our division, commanded by General Newton, advanced across the plain and struck the north-west angle of the fortifications. The Second Division of the Sixth Corps, marching under cover of the woods, made an attack on the south-east angle, while another detachment crossed the Rappahannock further down the river, so as to make

an onset in the rear, and prevent, if possible, the escape
of those within the intrenchments.

The attention of the enemy was naturally drawn
toward our division which was advancing across the
plain. Gallantly the men went forward, and when we
were within rifle range the other troops made a determined charge on the enemy's flank and rear. The Confederates fought desperately, and were favored by their
breastworks, but the attack was so well planned and so
resolutely executed that there was nothing left for them
but to surrender as prisoners of war.

Some of the Maine and New Jersey troops exhibited
the finest bravery, holding their fire until within a few
yards· of the enemy's lines, and then with cold steel
cleared the intrenchments, capturing every man within
the works. We also secured a pontoon bridge by which
our division crossed the river and advanced to occupy
the heights beyond.

During our stay here I was again detailed on brigade
picket duty, having detachments under my command
from each regiment of our brigade. We were ordered to
relieve the cavalry pickets who had done duty on the
outposts until this time. Our headquarters were established at a farm-house, beautifully situated, with the
appearance of having been a home of wealth and refinement, but now deserted and partly ruined.

While at this mansion we received a number of distinguished visitors. The guard fell in and presented
arms to no less than four general officers.

One morning our colonel came galloping up, and bringing his horse to a sudden stop, shouted, "Lads, the

President is here. Prepare to receive him; he will soon
be at your headquarters!"

During this announcement a contraband, who went by
the name of Cuff, and was excessively black, had started
up as if a shell had exploded under him, and stood with
his mouth suggestive of the Mammoth Cave, and his
eyes bulging out as if they were balls ready to be shot
from a mortar.

"What's dat?" he shouted. "Massa Linkum comin?"

"Yes, Cuffy," said one of the men; "he'll be here
pretty soon."

"Lor, Massa, I wants to get down on dese bare bones
afore Massa Linkum."

"What do you wish to do that for?"

"Kaze Massa Linkum pitched ole Pharoah into de
Potomac, and is goin' to set all de cullud people free.
Yes, sure as de day of judgment, we is all bound for de
land o' Canaan."

Cuff was very religious, and I asked him if he always
prayed for the President.

"Lor, yes, I prays dat when he gets to hebben he may
have de true color of de Lord's people, and be black as
I am. Captain, Ise sorry you're white; it's a great
misfortin."

This was said with an expression of profound sympathy for the trial I was enduring on account of my color.

"What else do you ask for when you pray for Mr.
Lincoln?"

"Why, Massa, I asks dat when he dies he may not hab
to go to hebben in an ole army-wagon wid a pair o'
spavined mules, but may hab a chariot and hosses o' fire
like Elijah had!"

Cuff had to cut short his eloquent harrangue, for President Lincoln at that moment rode up, attended by General Meade and a number of other officers.

At the request of the President I pointed out our picket lines, and also the line of the enemy, about a mile away. Inside our lines we could also show the residence of John Minor Botts, a man worthy of a place in history for his fidelity among the faithless.

"Thank you," said President Lincoln, as he turned to leave; "I am pleased with the appearance of the men and the work already accomplished."

We uncovered as he passed us, and Cuff was so anxious to honor the President that I doubt if he put on his dilapidated hat for the rest of the day.

CHAPTER XXIII.

CONFEDERATE PRISONERS.

"These bonds that fetter hand and foo*
Are not the masters of the soul."

"**C**APTURED! captured!" shouted Major Beckstein, as he opened a newspaper just received by mail, and looked at the large heading on the first page.

Instantly a crowd of men gathered around, all eager to hear the news. Whether Washington had been captured, or some important victory had been gained by one army or the other in the West, we could not guess. The major looked so grave that it was easy to conclude some important event had taken place which would have a decided bearing on the fortunes of the war.

A dozen questions were thrust at the major, all at once.

"Captured!" he exclaimed; "too bad, boys, but it can't be helped; that's the greatest news we have had lately!"

The major was not inclined to give any of us a look at the paper, and while he withheld the intelligence our

(284)

curiosity was growing more and more intense. All we could learn at the moment was that there had been an important capture of some sort.

It should be remarked here that our gallant Captain Knox had disappeared a few days before we broke camp at Warrenton Junction. It was generally understood that he had been placed on furlough by reason of sickness. There was a good deal of mystery about his sudden departure, and all inquiries elicited no satisfactory answer. All we knew was that a brave and handsome officer had suddenly left us. He might have been detailed for special duty, or to attempt some daring exploit.

The patriotism, the daring, the dash and heroism of Southern women all through the great struggle are well known. They acted an important part from first to last.

"Boys," exclaimed the major, "if our men are ever vanquished it will be by the formidable women of the South; there isn't a man of us that could stand before their assaults."

"What have they been doing?" asked one who was standing near. "Have they been getting up a secret expedition to strike a blow at our army?"

The major interrupted by crying, "Captured! Our valiant Captain Knox has been captured by a Warrenton belle!"

A shout of mingled exclamation went up, and the group of men was rapidly augmented.

"Yes, here it is," said the major; "a correspondent has told the whole story, and you can see it is headed in large letters, 'Captured!'"

"I know what will end the war," exclaimed Sanderson; "we have only to make love to all the pretty girls and marry them; then there'll be no more war."

"None in the field," I said, "but perhaps a hotter war in the camp."

"Not while the honey-moon lasts," said Sanderson.

"Three cheers for Knox!" shouted one of the men. They were given in rousing style.

"Three cheers and a 'tiger' for Mrs. Knox!" exclaimed another, and the shouting continued.

"If I am ever captured," said Vail, "I want it to be in that way; I think I would prefer it to Libby Prison."

"Experience would determine that," I ventured to remark.

The news of Captain Knox's successful adventure formed the topic of conversation for the whole day.

"Hundreds of Confederate officers are held by us," I said to the men, "and they were not captured in any way so pleasant as that; and I understand many are to be sent North and put under guard."

"The best place for them," said Brown, who had recovered from his wound and was again on duty.

We were near Brandy Station on the Alexandria and Richmond Railroad. The season being well advanced, we surmised that we would spend the winter at this place. Communication was open direct to Washington, and supplies could easily be forwarded to the army.

"There is something very commonplace about this town," remarked Sanderson; "in the name, I mean."

"How is that?" I asked.

" Why, at home there is a ' Brandy Station ' on nearly
every corner of the street; and now we have actually
fetched up at the place that has that very name."

"Hi, mon." shouted Barney Roach; "it's a foine
place! It's I that could be contiuted to spend here the
rest of me days!"

But we were not destined to remain long. Soon after
our arrival, orders were read to each regiment offering a
furlough of thirty days and a large bounty to all who
would enlist for three years from that date, the Government cancelling the remainder of the time due by the
men, who, upon re-enlistment, would thereafter be known
as veteran volunteers. About sixty per cent. of our
regiment availed themselves of this liberal offer, and in
less than a week the muster-rolls were prepared. and the
men ready for the homeward journey. They were in
high spirits, and acted like a parcel of colts who had
slipped their bridles.

The day before the detachment from our regiment
started for home I received orders from our corps-head-
quarters to accompany the men to Philadelphia, for
which duty I immediately prepared myself. We passed
through Washington on our way North.

Sanderson facetiously remarked that he would stop
and select his seat in the Senate chamber, as he expected
to be elected to that honorable body as a reward for
brilliant services in the field.

" Conspicuous ability in retreat," said one of the men.

" I resent that," replied Sanderson; " my front is not
behind."

Our regiment being finally complete again, the ensuing

winter found us guarding Confederate prisoners at
Sandusky, Ohio. As field officer of the day, my duty
was to number these men, and my first receipt was for
3780, all commissioned officers. We tried to treat them
well, and mitigate the pains and privations they had to
endure, but with home and family and friends far away,
they were objects of pity.

One day I saw a sad-looking prisoner sitting with his
face buried in his hands, and his form bent over as if a
mountainous weight were on his shoulders. Just then
a company of visitors was passing through the prison.
He looked up through his tears, and then began again to
sob convulsively.

"You are feeling sad," I said, in a tone that was
intended to comfort him.

"Have you a family?" he asked.

"No, my lad," I replied; "I am free from all cares of
that sort.

"Then you don't know how I feel; you 'uns are very
kind to us, but would to God you could send us home."

My heart was touched, and I believe I would have
liberated the poor fellow if it had been in my power, and
would have turned his grief to joy. Just then he saw
the group of visitors, among them a bright little boy
about half a dozen years old.

"Is that your child?" he cried to a lady who seemed
to be the mother.

"That is my boy," she answered.

Tears came in a fresh outburst to the prisoner's eyes.
He brushed them away, sprang to his feet, reached out
his long bony arms, and, rushing toward the boy,

caught him up, and convulsively hugged him to his heart, and kissed him over and over again.

"Pardon me, Madam," he exclaimed, "but he's like my boy—at least the boy I left long ago, and God only knows whether he's alive or dead."

A thrill of feeling ran through the group, and we stood in a silence, which was broken only by sobs.

THE CONFEDERATE PRISONER AND THE LITTLE BOY.

With a voice that betrayed emotion the lady said, "I'm very sorry for you; your lot is a hard one."

"Madam," he answered, "I could bear the marches and dangers, the hardships and wounds; I ain't takin' on because I'm a prisoner, but to be separated from—"

He could not speak; emotion sealed his lips. And he was only one of hundreds whose chief trial was not that they were held in prison by our forces, but had neither home nor wife, nor sweet-faced children, save in memory.

I wrote to friends in Philadelphia for contributions such as would make the prisoners comfortable, and such

19

a response in the way of preserves and jellies, canned fruits, clothing, and even Bibles, deserves to be mentioned here, and placed to the credit of the kind-hearted givers. These were contributions outside of those furnished by the Christian and Sanitary Commissions, which the people of the North sustained so generously in their noble work.

With the opening spring of 1864 we were ordered on to Washington to report to General Meade. Then away we went to Spottsylvania, one of the points well known in the annals of the war.

The Union troops had a large number of prisoners on hand, and we were to convey them by steamer to Point Lookout. It so happened that I had on one steamer eleven hundred Confederates, and only fifteen men to guard them. Arrived at Point Lookout, the spirited sons of the South were a good deal mortified to find that the troops on guard at the prison were colored.

One of the officers that we marched to the prison met one of his own slaves, clad in the livery of Uncle Sam. It was a strange incident, showing how matters were reversed as the conflict went on.

A look of surprise, and then of disgust, was visible on the face of the Southerner as he saw that one of his former slaves was now his master. "Hello, Cuffee, you there?"

"Yes, Ise yere. Stand back dar!" and Cuffee presented his bayonet. "Stand back dar, or I'll run dis frough you."

The prisoner had to obey, for Cuff was on his dignity.

"I members well de time when you whipped me in de swamp, and I wasn't guilty nudder. You'll neber lick dis nig_er again; back wid you!"

There was fire in the colored soldier's eye, and his order was law.

CHAPTER XXIV.

"Who runs away
"Will live to fight another day."

T was a warm mid-summer morning. The sun had risen in a haze, but it had now dispersed the mists, and was pouring its light in a broad flood over the fertile Virginian valley. In the distance the mountains lifted their blue peaks into the transparent atmosphere. Near by lay a level expanse of soft greensward. Here a farm house and there a piece of woodland added variety to the landscape. Not far away a sluggish stream flowed on in winding curves. Still nearer a dusty road ran straight southward.

Such was the general character of the scene on which we gazed that sultry morning, though it is not easy to put into words its total effect, the soft shading of the green into the blue, the flood of light which filled the atmosphere, the flash of the waters, the glimpses of more distant landscapes through the mountain openings, all these peaceful and charming influences of nature which were in such marked contrast to the thunder-cloud of war which filled the valley, and threatened to break out at

(292)

any moment in the lightnings and thunder of battle, and the hail of death and ruin.

We were at a considerable distance in advance of the main body of the army. I had been directed the evening before to take a squad of men and push through the night down the valley, to take a Confederate prisoner if possible, and to pick up all the information I could as to the actual and projected movements of the enemy.

Our generals, in fact, were just then considerably in the dark as to the state of affairs in front of us, and more than one scouting party was out on the same general errand as our own.

It was now about ten o'clock in the morning. From where we were no sign of the army was visible. All was, indeed, so quiet and peaceful that no one would have dreamed that war and terror lay so near. Except for a flying bird the scene appeared deserted. Not a human form was anywhere in sight. Not even an animal was visible. All life seemed to have deserted that smiling plain.

I had with me several of our old acquaintances, Sanderson, Vail, Brixy, Thompson, and others. Herr Blinn, however, had been left behind, as one of the heavy weights, though the hope of some free foraging had made him beg hard to join our party.

Just in advance of where we now were the road curved, and led by a low bridge across the stream. There were indications that it joined another road, masked from us by trees and bushes, on the opposite side.

At this point Brixy, who had made a reconnoisance on his own account to the creek side, came hurrying back, with a scared face.

"They're over there in force! Rebs! sure as you live!" he ejaculated. "Cavalry, now you bet. I heard the clank of harness. And enough of 'em, from their noise, to gobble us all up."

This alarming communication was not altogether agreeable, though there were some of the party who put but little faith in Brixy's war news.

"Scared by bull-frogs again, I'll bet a cow!" cried Sanderson, "He don't know the difference between a big frog's voice and a bugle call."

"I reckon I do, then," replied Brixy, with great seriousness. "They ain't a bit alike; any fool ought to know that. And I didn't hear no bugle. It was the rattle of harness and voices."

"Maybe we had better retreat; or seek cover," said Vail, cautiously. "We'd make a sorry show before a troop of cavalry."

"We must first make sure that we are not running from a shadow," I declared, positively. "If there are any horsemen so near our army they must be on a flying scout. We have been directed to bring back a prisoner, or some information, and I am not inclined to return empty-handed and empty-headed. Follow me. We will make a cautious advance. There is good cover on the other side if we find a force too strong for us."

"Don't you want to send despatches to head-quarters?" asked Brixy. "I'd sooner advance to the rear, just now."

"Come on," I commanded, sternly; "and keep a still tongue, if you know how."

I led the way to the bridge, the men following me. We did not move without caution, however. Every point was inspected, every sound listened to. Yet we reached the opposite side of the stream without hearing or seeing anything to justify Brixy's alarm.

"You thundering cowboy!" cried Vail, angrily. "What do you mean by that cock and bull story? I believe Sanderson is right. You were scared by a frog."

"It was a frog that wore a saddle, then: and had a bit in its mouth," muttered Brixy. "You better tell me at once I'm a fool."

"I've told you that often enough to convince any reasonable creature," grinned Sanderson. "But it don't seem to have the proper effect on you. If I should say now—Jupiter! there is something!"

"Who's the fool now?" demanded Brixy.

These last words had been called forth by a rattle of harness and the sound of wheels from behind the screen of trees that lined the road side. Voices were audible too, though little could be made of them at that distance.

"Silence!" I commanded. "Lie down, or get under cover. Come, Vail, let us find out what this means."

Carrying our pieces at a ready we cautiously advanced, while the men sought the shelter of the trees which partly filled the field in which we stood.

A few minutes brought us to the road side. It was banked up here, and we were below the level.

The sound of wheels was now near and loud. There seemed to be some heavy vehicle moving along the road just in front of us. The voices we had heard were here quite distinct. We crouched down and listened.

"De Bressed Laud, nobody neber seen de like!" came in the voice and idiom of an old darkey. "Golly, Mass

Joe, but I was a'most skeered white. Dar's more ob 'em dan dar were o' de Israelites dat got drowned in de Red Sea."

"There were no Israelites drowned," came the answer, in a laughing, girlish voice. "It was the Egyptians."

"I disremember," muttered the old darkey. "Don't b'lieb it reads dat way in my varsion. Howsomever, dar dey am, millions and millions ob 'em."

"Marcy on us, why don't ye stir up the horses?" cried the cracked voice of an old woman, in a tone of general alarm. "Lay on the whip, Joe. I'm desperate afeared of the Yanks. The Laus knows what they'll do if they catch us."

"I've a notion old Sip's been scared by his shadow," answered the man addressed. "But they can't be far back there, and we must get on."

The loud crack of his whip followed, with cries to the horses. The increased jingle and rattle showed that it had not been without effect.

Vail and I looked at one another, while a low laugh broke from our lips

"So this is Brixy's cavalry," I remarked.

"Refugees. And scared out of their wits," said Vail. "I vote we give them a worse scare."

"Bring up the lads," I answered.

Vail whistled in response, and in a minute or two our men came running up.

A few hasty words, in a low tone, told the lads what was in the wind. I had laid my plan on the spur of the moment, and quickly communicated it. I was in the humor to give the refugees as severe a scare as possible.

Meanwhile Vail's whistle seemed to have alarmed them already. Their voices ceased, but the crack of the whip showed that the horses were being urged forward at all the speed possible.

Half our small troop darted across the road to the other side, and we ran swiftly along under shelter of the bank until the sounds told us that we were again in advance of the party of refugees.

At this point I climbed to the level of the road and took a peep through the screen of bushes. What I saw may be told in a few words.

Ploughing through the deep dust of the road came a long, heavily-built, white covered wagon, sagging down in the middle, and drawn by two shaggy but sturdy horses, that moved along at a slow jog trot.

Inside the wagon, which seemed well filled with sundries, two faces were visible. One of these was that of a wrinkled old woman, in a white cap, and looking as scared as if she had seen a legion of ghosts.

The other face was drawn back into the shadows of the wagon. I could just make out that it was that of a young girl, that seemed to me very pretty, and rather amused than alarmed.

Trudging along beside the animals, just now in a half run, were the two men whose voices we had heard. One of them was a tall, thin-faced Virginian, dressed in the rough garb of a farmer, and glancing anxiously from side to side, as he strove to hurry his slow moving horses.

The other was an old negro, black as midnight, his grizzled hair and the shining white of his eyes, the only contrast to his ebony skin. He was driving before him a young cow, which did not seem to approve of the pace. But old Sip held her by the tail, and at every other step brought down on her tawny hide a resounding smack from a long and slender switch, to which she seemed to pay very little attention.

" I vow to marcy dar neber was sich a lazy cretter ! " he ejaculated, as he wiped the dust and sweat from his face. " On'y as I's a church member, and a shinin' zample to de young folkses, I's sadly afeared I'd swar right out. Dis yere cow don't mine de switch no more nor if it were a cat's whisker. If dis ting goes on I'll clare cut a club, an bust her tarnal hide, dar now."

I could hold in no longer at the old fellow's predicament, but burst into a loud laugh, that sounded clearly through the still morning air.

It produced a striking effect. The old woman drew back with a cry of fright. The driver started, and shouldered his whip as if it had been a rifle. Old Sip let go the cow's tail, and stood with uplifted hands, his eyes rolling wildly in his head.

" Fore de marcy, what dat? " he ejaculated.

At this moment, without waiting for me to give the signal, someone of the party whistled. In an instant there was a sound of feet, a crashing of bushes, and a general rush from both sides of the road.

In less time than I can take to tell it a dozen stalwart fellows occupied the road, both in front and in the rear of the fugitives, with.levelled muskets, and looks of fierce determination.

" Halt ! " I cried, sternly, springing after the men through the bushes.

The order was not needed. The horses came to a standstill as suddenly as if they had been drilled in the ranks. The fugitives were differentiy affected.

"Oh Laus, the Yanks has got us!" cried the old woman, flinging herself back with a scream. "We're all goin' to be murdered!"

Of the two men the white driver staggered back against the nearest horse, trembling with dismay, and pallid of face.

Old Sip seemed nearly scared white. He dropped on his knees in the middle of the road, with clasped hands, and teeth that rattled like castanets.

"Oh, de land o' glory!" he ejaculated. "Dey's yere, an' it's all up wid us! Jiss popped up outer the ground, like de witch of Endor! De bressed marcy, won't ye drop dem shootin' tings? We surrenders. Tell 'em we surrenders, Mass Joe. De old nig ain't no Secesh. He neber was dat, Mister Yanks."

A general laugh broke from the men at the old fellow's ludicrous terror. At my command they grounded their levelled muskets, and stood at ease. The only one of the fugitive party who seemed indifferent to the alarm was the cow. She quickly strayed to the road side and began munching at the grass as coolly as if she were in her own pastures at home.

There was another member of the party of whom I have not spoken. This was the young lady, of whom we had yet caught but a shadowy glimpse, from her position well back in the wagon.

She now sprang forward and bounded agilely into the road, facing our line of bearded soldiers without a show of fear in her glittering black eyes. She was dressed in the rough homespun of the country, but was of a shapely, graceful form, and had a very pretty face, that now blazed with anger.

"How dare you stop us in the high road!" she demanded. "We are on our own soil, where you are base intruders! Out of our way, you Yankee mud-sills! Back to your kennels, and don't dare to interfere with a Virginian gentleman and his family."

She looked like a young fury as she spoke, doubly handsome in her indignation and burning hatred of the Northern invaders.

I waved my hand in warning to the men, some of whom looked angry at this tirade. I then walked up to the furious little beauty.

"That will do, Miss," I remarked. "If you take my advice you will find shelter again in the wagon. Your railing don't affect me, but I cannot answer for all my men."

The Virginian, who had recovered somewhat from his pallor, now laid his hand on the shoulder of the girl, and sternly checked the truculent answer upon her lips.

"Back with you into the wagon," he commanded, decisively. "Leave me to deal with these gentlemen."

"Gentlemen!"

I never heard more concentrated bitterness than the tone in which this was spoken. But the girl's mood seemed suddenly to change as she recognized the helplessness of their situation. Her face reddened. Her eyes grew suffused. Covering her face with her hands, to hide these evidences of emotion from those whom she regarded as mortal foes, she hurried back into the wagon, where the old lady was rocking herself and moaning as if she expected nothing less than murder.

By this time old Sip had scrambled to his feet. Too much scared to know just what he was about, he hurried to the cow, caught her by the tail, and began to belabor her lustily with his limber switch.

"Dat all you got to do, you good for nothin', young fool!" he ejaculated. "Reckon you want to get gobbled up by de Yanks, and turned into beef steaks and roast chops. Don't make no sort o' dif'rence to you, I reckon."

"Keep away from there," I ordered, noticing that Brixy was suspiciously near to the rear of the wagon. "Now, my good sir, we don't mean you any harm, but you will do well to answer my questions. You seem to be running away."

"From the Yankee army. That is so. And you will not find many people and much stock waiting for you in the valley."

"Then I have only to tell you that you are a set of idiots. The Yankee army does not get all its rations by foraging on the inhabitants. Where are you going to?"

"I don't know," he helplessly replied. "We'll fetch up somewhere, I reckon. If I had my way I'd stayed at home, but they were all too scared."

"Not the young lady, I fancy."

"Wal, no. She's got pluck enough for the whole of us."

"You talk of the Yankees foraging. I see you have a fine heifer there. How did you keep it from the Confederate foragers?"

"They wouldn't touch the property of a loyal Southerner," he answered, proudly.

"We jiss locked the critter up in the milk house, an'

lost de key," broke out Sip, as he brought down another whack on her tawny hide.

"So, I see the tender mercy of the chivalrous Johnnies," I replied, with a laugh. "How long ago was that?"

"It were yesterday mornin' when de rear guard passed," answered Sip. "As soon as we heard dat de Yanks were comin' we up and follered."

"Ah, you want them to have the heifer, then? You are driving it into the way of their foragers."

"I jiss don't calkerate so," answered Sip, with a look of cunning. "We're gwine for de pass of de mountains yonder, and de army's off down Winchester way. If you could climb to de top ob dat church steeple you might see 'em all—de hull army of Southern salvation jiss runnin' way from de Yanks."

"Hold your tongue, you old ninny," cried the young lady, suddenly flashing out again. "Don't you see he is pumping you to learn the position and movements of our army?"

" You are quite right there, Miss," I answered, taking off my hat to her. "And it is as well for you all that the old man has spoken out so plainly, or I would have had to take one of you back prisoner, to get just this information. You can go on now. But if you take my advice, you will turn back to where you came from. You will lose more from this crazy flight than from what little foraging might be done."

"Thank you," muttered the girl. "That is just what I said myself."

"It is good advice, at any rate. Good bye. You may live to learn that a Yankee may be a gentleman, and that we are here for other purposes than to rob quiet farmers. Shoulder arms!—March!"

The men closed up and walked away with a soldierly step, leaving the fugitives to take our advice or not, as they deemed best. What they did I do not know to this day. The last glimpse we caught of them, on looking back, the wagon was standing still in the road, while the Virginian and the young lady of Southern sympathies were in deep conference. Opposite them old Sip was still whacking away at the obstinate cow, which minded him no more than if his whacks were finger taps.

A laugh of amusement from the boys marked their appreciation of this final view.

"What have you got there, Brixy?" I demanded, noticing that he had flung a rubber cape over his shoulders, and had grown suddenly fat beneath it.

"Nothing," he answered, hastily. "Only a watermelon I found in the field by the creek side."

"A watermelon! It's a queer shaped one then," I answered, as I caught the cape and flung it aside.

To my surprise and anger I saw that there depended from the rascal's shoulders a brace of hams, one on each side.

"So that's what took you smelling about the wagon! And after all my boasting of Yankee honesty. I have a strong notion to march you back and make you return the plunder."

But this proposition brought such a host of objections from the men that I was reluctantly forced to give in, and let Brixy keep his plunder.

About noon that day we rejoined our brigade, with what small information we had obtained.

CHAPTER XXV.

NEW WAR MOVEMENTS.

" The battered drum resounds again,
And makes fresh life in valiant men."

T the beginning of March, 1864, General Grant,* having been nominated by President Lincoln for Lieutenant-General of the Union armies, a grade that had been extinct since the retirement of General Scott, was confirmed by the Senate, and he entered at once upon his duties.

At the White House, Mr. Lincoln in the presence of his cabinet and General Halleck, presented him with his commission, expressing in a few words his own confidence in the great commander, and then adding, "As the country here trusts you, so, under God, it will sustain you."

The General, after paying a compliment to the "noble Union armies," ended by saying, "I feel the full weight of the responsibility devolving upon me, and I know if it

---

*The accompanying likeness of General Grant, pronounced the best ever issued, is from the last photograph ever taken of him for a steel plate engraving.

(304)

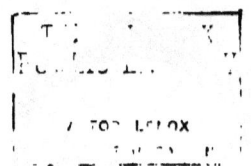

is met it will be due to those armies, and, above all to the favor of that Providence which leads both nations and men."

Grant immediately held a consultation with Meade, and then left for the West, meeting Sherman by appointment at Nashville to confer with him.

Aside from the scattered troops of the Confederacy at this time, there were two main armies. Lee was moving toward Richmond, and concentrating there all the forces he could command. He knew that with the fall of Richmond his cause would be lost, and he prepared with all haste for his last, stubborn resistance. There was less hope in his ranks when it became known that the hero of Donelson, Vicksburg, and many other struggles already renowned in the annals of the war, had assumed supreme command.

Atlanta was the most important strategic point held by the Confederates in the extreme South, and Johnston was looking after that, with the military skill for which he had become famous. The field of operations was getting narrowed down. There was more fighting to be done, and hard fighting too, and each side dreaded the final throes. Grant believed that only heavy blows would end the contest, and he prepared to give them where they would tell to the best advantage.

Our corps was on the march towards Mechanicsville, and having disposed of our prisoners, we made haste to re-join our division. We crossed the North Anna River, and, failing to get supplies, we pressed on with great difficulty, hungry, tired, as vexed as we dared to be in a service where we had staked everything, and finally

20

passed Chesterfield Station on the Fredericksburg and Richmond Railroad.

Not far from Mechanicsville I had an exciting experience when on picket duty. I had been appointed field officer, and had to look after our lines, which extended for several miles. I placed my men so as to guard every part of our army lying back of us, and during the day passed along the line three times to make sure that everything was right.

We held our position until ten or eleven o'clock that night, when I received orders to gather all the men I could, without causing any alarm to our watchful enemy; and where there was the least danger of doing so, the pickets were to be left on their posts, so that the enemy should not be made conscious of any movement. Whatever was to be done must be done quietly. I was here informed that our troops had marched at sundown, and were now about seven or eight miles distant.

I immediately determined to save all the men, and commenced at the left of our line, ordering them to report at a given point, a farm-house about the centre of our line. The men had been changed somewhat after dark by the corps officer of the day, and no information of this change reached me. I lost my way while passing through the thick woods, the darkness being so intense that I could not see my hand as I held it up before my face, but taking my bearings as best I could, the stars being now hidden from my view, I made an attempt to find the men who had been so faithful in discharging their duty. I at last heard the challenge from a Confederate soldier, who was probably like our own men on

the outpost, "Who goes there?" and discovered by his
accent that he was a Southerner.

I dropped down in the long grass that happily grew
there, and, pulling out my revolver, soliloquized that
either he or I should fall a victim if he desired to become
too intimate with me. I presume, as he could hear
nothing, or see nothing, he came to the conclusion that it
might have been a rabbit, or some other animal that
caused the noise. He turned, and I beat a hasty retreat
in the opposite direction ; and soon in the darkne s of
the woods I was lost to his hearing.

But where to go, or how to go, was now the mystery
I was compelled to solve. Looking up, I saw the north
star through the rift of a cloud, and guiding my steps
as best I could, I pressed on with all my energy, hoping
soon to find the men I was looking for.

Just here was another dilemma ; while running with
all my might amidst the darkness, I plunged down a
precipice, how deep I cannot tell for I had no means of
measuring the distance, nor indeed had I the desire; I
was more concerned how to get out. Finding myself
stuck in the swamp, which it proved to be, I tried
unsuccessfully a number of times to extricate myself,
and instead of getting out, seemed to be deeper in the
mire than ever, and I now began to think what would
become of me. I dared not call for help, as I would be
more likely to find foes than friends. Making a desperate
effort, I got one foot extricated, and placing that upon a
branch of the tree that grew out of the bank down
which I had fallen, got the other foot out, and then found
I had lost my sword in the descent. I would about as soon

have parted with my life as with my sword, but after a long search I stumbled against it. During all this time I failed to discover that in falling I had received a dangerous cut over my right eye, from which the blood was flowing freely.

In a few minutes more I found our line, and Vail, now Sergeant Vail, who passed the word along for the men to report with the greatest secrecy at the appointed place.

All our men escaped, and after an all night's march, at almost double quick, we overtook our division at daybreak.

As I think of that night's adventure, I realize that I came unpleasantly near missing the opportunity of narrating it in these pages. The mire was soft to get into, though hard to get out of, and it was the softness that saved my life, after falling so many feet.

There was an eagerness at this time in the Union ranks for vigorous operations, and it soon became evident that "the silent man," our new commander, was perfecting his plans, and getting ready to satisfy the army which only demanded that he should lead the way to conquest.

CHAPTER XXVI.

FORAGING AND FIGHTING.

"Whoever knows must keep the secret well ;
A curse for him who's mean enough to tell !"

NE morning, while on our way to Cold Harbor, an old colored woman came within our lines, and began doing a promiscuous business in the sale of eatables.

"Pies yere!" she sung out. "Nice fresh pies, ten cents a piece, two for a quarter!"

"That's an enterprising Dinah," remarked Sanderson, "selling two ten-cent pies for a quarter: it beats us Yanks."

I called her to me and said, "You don't mean that, do you?"

"Yah, I mean dese lubly pies is ten cents apiece, but if you'll take two you habs 'em for a quarter; dat's cheap nuff."

"But you sell them higher by twos than you do singly."

"I sells 'em for no more'n they're worth ; dem's nice pies; one on 'em is worth ten cents, and two is worth a quarter."

"Well, here are ten cents for one," and I took one of Aunt Dinah's pies.

"Dat's right; dey's good and cheap."

"Now, I'll take another; here are ten cents more," and I laid hold of another pie. "Now, don't you see you've sold them at ten cents apiece, and you have got twenty cents."

"Dat ain't fair," cried the old woman, "gib me dat udder five cents!"

I explained that I bought them at ten cents apiece, gave her all she asked, and did not owe her any more.

"You're cheatin'," the old woman exclaimed; "yer thinks yer can get ahead o' dis ole cullud woman, but de Laud will smite yer as he did ole Pharaoh, and you'll hab to pay dat five cents in de day o' judgment!"

No mathematical explanations could make old Dinah see her comical mistake, and, giving her the extra five cents to enable her to realize a quarter on two pies at ten cents a piece, I left her in a "brown study," trying to make out how there could be anything queer about it.

We had strict orders not to forage on the surrounding country, but it was commonly understood among the boys that if these orders were disobeyed they would not be shot for a military crime. Two men in our ranks, besides Blinn and Brixy, became famous for their foraging exploits.

The boys had grown weary of their regulation fare, "salt horse," and were longing for some fresh pork. "Where to obtain it?" was a very serious question. Very few of the inhabitants were left in possession of their homes; the ground had been fought over and camped upon by both armies, and what few houses and out-buildings remained were strongly guarded by a detail from headquarters.

FORAGING

Foraging was, for several reasons, a very difficult matter, and unless one possessed a venturesome spirit that could carry him away for a long distance from camp, and brave the danger of capture by guerillas that were thick in that part of the country, all idea of "fresh pork," or even a stray chicken, had to be abandoned.

Somehow, Jim, one of the champion foragers, had learned there was a solitary pig at a farm-house some distance away, but a very strong guard was detailed, and the house was the quarters of an officer. How to get that "porker" was then in order, for Jim was bound that it should supply his company with fresh meat. After waiting for several days, and after a very careful survey of the ground, and seeking a favorable opportunity, the night was selected, a moonless one, and the party set out. It consisted of Jim and Sam, two kindred spirits. Sam, by the way, was Jim's pupil, and an apt one he was.

Jim had selected a time when the guard on the house was a comparatively new one, from a regiment but recently sent to the front, for with a "vet" he would have but little chance to work the scheme he had planned. Arrived at the house, Jim kept himself concealed from the guard.

Sam advanced boldly and was challenged by the guard.

"A friend with the countersign," was the reply to the sentry's challenge. And then, after a few introductory remarks, the question was asked, "Is there any chance for forage here? Are there not some chickens, or something a fellow could get? queried Sam.

"No, indeed," says "greeny." "Colonel so-and-so has

this house as his quarters, and he needs all the extra
poultry ; and I have seen nary a chicken about. There
is one pig that the boys, I am told, have tried several
times to capture, but he is in the pen yet, and will stay
there as long as I am about."

"Oh!" pleaded Sam, "just let me look at him."

"No, indeed," says the guard; "I am put here to guard
him, and I mean to keep you away."

So taking up the guard's attention, as was his plan,
Sam grew more urgent. Meanwhile Jim had slipped up
behind the pig-pen, slyly opened the door, found the pig,
and gently began scratching its head. More energeti-
cally Jim scratched, gently pulling piggy towards the
door of the pen. Still keeping up the scratching and
pulling, the young "porker" was slowly drawn out
towards the road, which at that point was dug out and
ran for a considerable distance lower than the grounds
surrounding the house. Finally, Sam persuaded the
guard that his intentions were honorable, and said,
"How can I steal the pig with you looking right at me?
Why, you could shoot me before I got any distance."

Thinking that Jim by this time surely had accomplished his purpose, and not hearing anything in the
neighborhood of the pen, he went over and peered in as
well as the darkness would permit, the guard standing
not far off to stop him if he should attempt to seize the
pig and run. Seeing the open door and no signs of the
pig, he decided to follow Jim.

Bidding the guard good night, and expressing his
dissatisfaction at the waste of time, and the non success
of his expedition, Sam slowly moved down the road. He

overtook Jim a few rods away, and took his turn in scratching, Jim, meanwhile, going to rear, and gently pushing piggy on, not too forcibly however, lest he should make a noise. Thus slowly, step by step, the captive was enticed a safe distance from the house, and on reaching a piece of woods he was suddenly stabbed, and foully murdered, and before morning was hanging in Jim's tent.

The boys, including the lieutenant, who was officer of the day, and had given Jim the countersign, were feasted on fresh pork. Many were the "porkers" Jim took, often under the very nose of the guard, by the "scratching" process.

The news of Jim's exploit reached our part of the division, and at once produced an effect. The enterprising Herr Blinn, and the equally enterprising Brixy, immediately put their heads together. Their looks were as wise, their utterances as confidential, and their movements as mysterious as if they had been the two greatest generals of the army, planning a campaign that would forever wind up the Confederacy.

That night both men were missing.

"Where's Blinn?" queried Sanderson at a late hour.

"What do you want of him?" asked the guard officer.

"Why, nothing much, only its rather lonesome around here with so much of the army gone."

The foragers did not get so far but that they were within the lines next morning. Brixy was looking a good deal the worse for wear, and there were sundry rents in certain parts of his clothing which appeared to give him a good deal of concern, and which were the occasion of frequent remark among the men, especially on account of their location.

"Dot vas a fine trip," ejaculated Herr Blinn.

"Did you leave anything?" inquired Sanderson.

"Oh, yes; we left der coop."

"Nothing more, I guess."

"But dot Brixy came near being defeated and losing der rear of hisself. Shentlemens, he turns his back on nopody."

"I CAN'T LET GO."

This was quite true; Brixy much preferred to be looked at from the front.

"But it vas von great success; all except der getting over der picket fence," Blinn went on to say.

"Tell us all about it!" broke in a number of interested bystanders.

"Vell, shentlemens, we put von pox by der fence, and ven dot Brixy vas holdin' der shickens, and getting over, vy, his pants pehind got cotched on der pickets, and dere he vas!"

"And what did you do?" some one asked.

"I thought I vas shust split with laughing, but I didn't drop der shickens."

Blinn roared again as he thought of the comical situation, and then continued, "Dere he hung, and shust hollered, 'I can't let go!'"

All enjoyed Blinn's narrative of the experience of his expedition, and all were ready to accept an invitation to his mess at dinner time, but Herr was more in the habit of foraging for himself than for others.

Barney Roach especially was amused at the account of Brixy's mishap, and giving a comprehensive flourish of his shillaly, he exclaimed, "Hi, mon, if I had been there I would have taken you down from the fence, Brixy, as the good Samaritan lifted the mon off from his baste."

Brixy thanked Barney for his good will, and I have always thought to this day that Barney's speech was intended to bring a compensation in the shape of a half chicken, roasted, and was successful in doing it.

Next morning there was another advance, and our large body of troops was on the move, expecting that Lee's army would soon come to a stand, and Grant would make a resolute attack.

Often on the march two lines of soldiers would be side by side, perhaps with the artillery in the road between them. On these occasions considerable chaffing would be indulged in, especially if the soldiers were from different States. There were two regiments in our corps which never met without having a "wordy battle." One day they were marching directly opposite each other with the road between them. Words and chaffing were continually passing between the two regiments, when after a silence of a few moments, a man with a very large mouth said something witty.

Immediately a comrade in the other regiment called out, "Just look at that fellow's mouth, it was put in hot and has run all over his face."

Such a shout as went up from both regiments, and ran from one end of the line to the other, can better be imagined than described.

"That mouth," remarked another, "was made especially for foraging."

When we moved to the front, where our cavalry had been more or less engaged in skirmishing with the enemy, we formed line of battle and advanced about one hundred yards beyond the cavalry line. The cavalry were then ordered to move towards the left of the line to find the correct position of the enemy.

The place was small, only a tavern, a mill and two or three houses which formed the village of Cold Harbor. We had reason to change its name by christening it Hot Harbor, for so it proved to us. We formed in line of battle and advanced about five hundred yards, occupying a position more advantageous than the one the cavalry held before our arrival.

Here it was intended we should remain until the troops were ready for the assault on our right and left. But owing to an unaccountable blunder we were forced to charge the very strongest portion of the enemy's entrenchments, without support from either the right or left wings of our army. And this blunder was caused by an intoxicated field-officer, who was riding a white horse similar to the horse our division commander rode, and our men supposed it was General Russell. This officer rode out in front of our lines, and cried out, " Forward men ; charge their entrenchments ! " and waving his sword, rode along urging the men forward, swearing he would drive the rebels to perdition or Richmond. Our brigade was formed in two lines, our regiment, with two others composing the rear. And a most determined charge of both lines was made, actually capturing the first line of the enemy's works, but as no supports were on hand to reinforce our ranks, we were compelled to fall back, for we were subjected to an enfilading fire from all directions, and our loss here was terrific. As the officer who was responsible for the blunder was killed, of course there was no official inquiry why the charge was made.

We fell back about one hundred yards, and here we made a stand and held our position, which was an advantageous one, although the enemy made a counter charge, supposing they could easily repulse us ; but this they found to their cost was a hazardous experiment, as we drove them back behind their entrenchments, and during the remaining portion of the day a constant and withering fire was sustained.

Here we lost some of the bravest men of our command. And when the shades of night settled down, the fusilade of small arms ceased, and we immediately entrenched our position, throwing out pickets, so as to be apprised of danger should a night attack be made. After our entrenchments were finished, we lay upon our arms, ready to resume the offensive at a moment's notice.

This first attack was made June 1st. The 2d of June was spent in preparing for the general assault all along the lines, and gave us an opportunity for a little rest, which we so much needed. Word was passed to all the officers along the line, that a general charge would be made at four o'clock the next morning, and a given signal was agreed upon.

True to time the charge was made the next morning about four o'clock, June 3d. In some places the charge was partly successful, and in others the reverse. It was one of the most desperate of the war. In some portions of the line our men scaled the enemy's entrenchments, and a hand to hand encounter ensued, and deeds of daring were performed by men in blue and gray. On our immediate front we were not as successful as we desired; the ground had been newly plowed, and the entrenchments were in the form of a crescent, we occupying the centre.

And what added to our disadvantage, one or two of our own batteries were stationed in our rear, firing over our heads, and owing to bad ammunition, a premature explosion of shells was frequent, and not a few of our men met their death in this way from our own guns.

Another difficulty presented itself here; the troops on our left were not able to advance as rapidly as we; and this exposed us to a flank fire, and caused terrible slaughter among our men. Out of thirty-five I led into this valley. of death, twenty-seven were killed and wounded, myself among the latter. Yet several of us remained within fifty or sixty yards of the enemy's breastworks, until in the darkness we again threw up entrenchments, so that we might not lose the ground we had secured at such an immense amount of human suffering.

The ball from which I received my wound struck the bone of my right arm, about six inches above the elbow, taking off a splinter, and then glancing away and instantly killing a poor fellow who stood by my side.

That was a terrible battle at Cold Harbor. One bleeding sufferer, lying on the field, was nearly crazed with pain, fever, and thirst, and calling to me for assistance, he gasped, " Bring me water, captain."

REMOVING THE WOUNDED.

" I would if I had it," I answered.

" Water, for God's sake, water!" he cried. " I'll give you a thousand dollars in gold for one drink of water."

If he had offered me all the gold ever dug I could not have granted his dying wish.

During those dreadful hours there " was hurrying to and fro " in order to save our army from utter defeat, and to care for the thousands who were wounded and disabled.

General Grant estimated our entire loss during the three days' fight at 7500 men.

CHAPTER XXVII.

"In wonders, fiction drops its plume,
And fact bears off the palm."

HE battle of Cold Harbor, in which the army of the North lost so heavily in its desperate and futile effort to drive the enemy from their intrenchments, was succeeded by some important strategic movements. These may be very briefly described.

The game of force was to be succeeded by the game of wits, and rapid marches to take the place of bull-dog struggles.

Just what General Grant's intention was lay buried within his own astute brain. The army of the North knew no more of it than did the army of the South. It soon became evident that another flanking movement was in the wind, though it was not easy to guess the final object of that movement.

The army indeed seemed as if it were advancing directly upon Richmond, over the old ground which had been bathed in blood in the Peninsula campaign, and, of

(320)

almost every foot of which thrilling recollections dwelt
in the minds of many of the veteran soldiers.

Lee seemed fully convinced that Richmond was the
goal of our march, and it was evident that he was making hasty movements to guard the capital of the
Confederacy from capture.

"May I be dropped by a bullet if I like this!" cried
Sanderson, discontentedly. "There's bad luck in those
marshes. If we cross that confounded Chickahominy
I'll feel like giving up the ghost. We had to turn tail
from there once, and will have to do it again."

"Don't you get into a spring fever about that,"
answered Thompson. "There's a new hand at the helm
now, my boy. You bet there'll be no runaways where
Grant holds the reins."

"I hope not, py gracious," remarked Herr Blinn. "It
was in dere dat Johnny Reb sold me mit dem pad eggs.
Dunder unt blitzen, wouldn't I like to see him shoost
once! I pet I gives him a sound egg vor his rotten
ones."

These words brought out an incident which the boys
had long since forgotten, and there was much twitting
of the fat Dutchman over his bad bargain as the march
went sturdily on.

The next day, however, the corps was withdrawn from
the front, and replaced by other troops. The line of
march now led toward the James.

Rumors of projected movements also began to circulate
through the ranks. It was reported that Sheridan had
made a cavalry raid across the James, had cut the rail-

roads running south from Richmond, and had brought in four or five hundred prisoners.

This rumor was followed by others of a yet more exciting character. The vanguard of the army was crossing the James! Boats and pontoon bridges had been called into service! The movement towards Richmond was a mere feint to amuse the enemy! The army was about to be shifted to new soil, where the foot of Northern troops had not yet trodden, and the seat of war to be transferred to the heart of the enemy's territory!

It may well be said that these tidings roused a sudden fever of enthusiasm in the army. The men had marched towards the swamps of the Chickahominy with a sinking of the heart. It was to them as if years of war had been lost, and they were to begin over again where they left off in the memorable Peninsula campaign.

But the hope of fresh fields, of the actual penetration of the territory of the Confederacy at a yet untrodden point, of carrying the war deeper into the South, blew like a cheering breeze upon their hearts, and they marched onward with cheery faces, and words of hopeful assurance.

That night, at the bivouac of the regiment in which we are specially interested, new reports gained currency. Lee had smelt the rat and was rushing his army at all speed into Richmond. Our advanced force had attacked Petersburg and been repulsed. Kautz had taken the city with his cavalry, and held it for an hour or two, but the infantry column had failed to support him, and he had been driven out.

Five days later a more determined effort to capture

this city was made. On the night of June 14th, the corps of General Smith, of which our regiment formed part, was marched south past Bermuda Hundred where General Butler had erected a remarkably strong line of fortifications, to the Appomatox, which was crossed on a pontoon bridge. The troops then encamped for the night, in front of the defences of Petersburg.

That evening a conversation took place between two of our characters which we must repeat, as it is necessary to the introduction of a strikingly interesting episode of the war.

The two men in question were Captain Knox and Sergeant Vail, now sergeant by merited promotion, who had seated themselves with the freedom of old friendship, and disregard of distinctions of rank, on a line of fence which had escaped the demands of the camp fires. From where they sat the long line of fires could be seen, with the men flitting about them like phantoms, the whole forming a curious, weird, and interesting spectacle.

"Many a one of the heedless fellows who are laughing over their rations around those fires will be supping with Pluto to-morrow night," said the captain, gravely. "Such is war. We carry our lives in our hands, and death becomes no more to a veteran soldier than the crossing of a stream."

"That is true," replied Vail, in a tone of deep earnestness. "It has often surprised me how hardened and reckless men can become. Yet to me that has never been the worst feature of this war. It is, in a certain sense, a struggle of brothers. The line between North and South often divides families as well as opinions, and one is never sure in pulling the trigger that he is not sending his bullet to the heart of a father or a brother, or of some blood kindred."

"I imagine there is no great danger of that," remarked Knox, lightly. "There may be old friends in the two armies, but I doubt if there are many such close relatives. But what is the matter, Vail? You are shuddering as if you had been struck by a chill."

"I am not speaking at random," answered Vail, gloomily. "I have never yet entered a battle without the feeling I have described."

"You? What do you mean? I don't see what you are driving at."

"I may as well let you into a secret, Captain Knox, which I have never yet revealed to a comrade in the army. I know I can trust you not to speak of it. I have a brother in the South. He went there years before the war, and I have reason to know he was deeply infected with secession sentiments. In fact I am satisfied that he is in the Confederate army. Can you wonder, then, that a battle is always more to me than a mere question of life and death? I may at any moment be guilty of fratricidal murder."

"Well, I declare!" exclaimed Knox. "I should never have dreamed of that. But suppose your brother is there. The chance of your meeting him face to face is not one in ten millions."

"Yet that one may come."

The morning of the 15th dawned clear and bright. The troops were in motion early. By noon they had reached the desired position, in front of the entrenchments that guarded the city of Petersburg.

To this point they had marched with light and cheerful hearts, in anticipation of a cheap and easy victory. This feeling was heightened by the capture of some rifle pits on the way. Into these General Hinks had charged with the negro brigade, and driven out their defenders on the run.

But the feeling of the troops somewhat changed as they now came to a halt, and found themselves in front of a strong line of defences, running far away to the north and south, while their guns were posted to sweep the ditches and ravines of the broken ground, and to pour a cross fire over the level spaces.

RIFLE PITS.

It was impossible to know that these strong earthworks were really very poorly defended, and General Smith, with a caution that proved very unfortunate in the end, deferred the assault until near sunset, so as to make the most careful preparations.

The assailing columns showed three distinct faces to the enemy. Kautz, with his brigade, was well to the left; Brooks occupied the centre, and Martindale lay on the right. The sun hung low in the heavens when the order to charge went out to the division commanders, and passed from man to man along the line.

"How do you feel, now, Vail?" asked Captain Knox,

as the regiment stood in charging column, waiting impatiently for the word. "Got any of last night's premonitions?"

"No," smiled Vail, in reply. "To-day's sun has banished them."

As he spoke the order to charge passed along the line, and with a loud cheer and a wild dash the men sprang forward.

From the entrenchments before them came a line of fire, and a shower of bullets swept the intervening space. The cannon also roared defiance and sent their plunging balls through the charging ranks.

Here and there men dropped dead and wounded. Yet the volley was really not a very heavy one, and the grim veterans did not take the trouble to reply to it as they dashed forward. The important point now was to reach the foot of those frowning walls of earth.

The volley was repeated in a dropping and desultory manner, that had no more effect than would have had a sprinkle of rain in the faces of those battle-maddened veterans.

In the next minute they had broken their way through the abatis, leaped into the dry ditch outside the works, and were scrambling with furious haste up the steep declivity.

The well-ordered lines were now broken into fragments. It was every man for himself and "the devil take the hindmost." The opposing troops sprang fiercely up with the wild Confederate yell, and fired at short range upon their climbing foes.

But all this lasted scarce a minute. At fifty points

men gained the summit of the enbankment, and engaged in a hand-to-hand fight with the enemy. Others were clambering up like a line of busy ants. The opposing Confederates showed but a thin and feeble front.

"Lend me a hand, Vail," cried Captain Knox, to the sergeant who had just gained the summit.

A quick hand-jerk from Vail and the worthy captain was drawn upwards, and stood for the moment tottering from the sudden impetus.

At this instant a stalwart Confederate rushed fiercely at him with levelled bayonet. Captain Knox took an involuntary step backward over the edge of the hill, and the next moment was rolling helplessly down the declivity.

Vail, who had gained firm footing, raised his piece and fired with a quick aim at the captain's antagonist. Simultaneously the latter turned his bayonet against him, and rushed forward with a furious oath.

He saved his life by the movement. The charging bayonet knocked up the muzzle of Vail's rifle, and sent the bullet flying astray. But the two pieces became locked, and for an interval the combatants stood glaring at each other with eyes that blazed with fury.

Suddenly a strange cry came from Vail's lips, a cry like that of one who has received a mortal wound.

The rifle fell from his nerveless hands, and he staggered a step backward, trembling like a leaf. His antagonist, too full of the rage of battle to consider the cause of this strange movement, strove with another oath to disengage his locked bayonet, and slay his helpless foe.

But short as had been the interval of this fight others of the clambering troops had gained the summit, and one of these levelled his musket at the Confederate. Fortunately for the latter the piece held fire. With a yell of rage the Federal soldier clubbed his musket and advanced furiously upon his foe, who had just then disengaged his piece.

At the same instant Vail, with a repetition of his startling cry, sprang forward, and threw his arms around the Confederate soldier in a grip of nervous energy.

"This man is my prisoner!" he shouted, in hoarse tones. "Charge! The rascals are running. I will take care of this one."

With a stare of surprise the Unionist ran on, swinging his clubbed musket in circles around his head, and leaving Vail to hold his captive.

The latter struggled violently, but he was held as in a vice.

Yet powerful as the man seemed who held him, his face was pallid and his knees trembled.

"Yield!" he cried, in a low set tone. "It is your only hope. You are a dead man if you resist. Do you not know me, Joe Vail?"

The prisoner gave one quick glance at the face of his captor, and then a groan broke from his lips, while he ceased his struggles, and yielded nervously to that powerful grip.

"Harry! Harry Vail!" he whispered. "My brother Harry! Good God, do we meet here and thus?"

"Thank the God above you that it is no worse," rejoined Vail. "It is only His mercy that has saved one of us from being the other's murderer, and a doomed man in life and death."

"I have long feared this moment," answered the prisoner, with ashen lips. "Heaven curse this fratracidal war, in which brother stands opposed to brother, and father to son!"

"Amen!" rejoined Vail, fervently. "Only last night I had a prevision of this scene and this moment. I let myself be laughed out of it. Yet my waking dream has come true."

"Good Heavens, you don't say that!" cried Captain Knox, who had just at this moment regained the parapet, and came limping forward, lamed by his fall. "Is it then to your brother that I owe my sprained foot, and came near owing worse? If that is the case I admit that 'there are more things in heaven and earth than are dreamed of in my philosophy!'"

He looked earnestly in the face of the prisoner, a stalwart, bronzed, bearded man, taller and stouter than Vail, yet with a family likeness to him in features and expression.

The two brothers stood with clasped hands, gazing with something of wistful longing into each other's faces, the war fury of their late demeanor having subsided into the softness of family affection, with something of horror yet remaining from the late moment of startling discovery.

"You may as well sit down and talk it out," said Knox, as he limped away. "The fight is over."

What he said was true. The entrenchments had proved very thinly manned, and their defenders were now in full flight, hotly pursued by the charging column.

In those few minutes a line of formidable rifle pits and entrenchments, two and a half miles long, with four strong redoubts, and other works of defence, had been captured.

Yet the pursuit was not kept up. The troops were recalled and ordered to rest on their arms in the works they had just captured.

For hours that night the two brothers, so strangly reunited, sat in long and earnest conversation. They had much to say to each other on family affairs, and on the events of their lives since their separation.

It was near midnight when they ceased talking, and when each lay down to catch a few hours' repose. The questions of the war had not failed to come up between them, and Sergeant Vail had tried earnestly to convince his new-found brother that he was pursuing a false and traitorous course, and should avail himself of this opportunity to exchange the gray for the blue, or to leave the army and seek his family and friends in the North.

But to his surprise and disappointment Joe Vail proved to be a man whom no arguments could change, and who had cast his fortunes with the South, and meant to cling to his convictions to the bitter end.

"We may as well save breath, Harry," he said, in a kindly tone. "I fancy neither of us will convert the other, and we must wait till this dreadful war is over before we can be truly brothers again. I have a wife and children in South Carolina. For them I have fought, and for them I will fight to the close."

"Against them, I think," answered Harry, bitterly. "And against your country."

"Not against you, at any rate. Further words are useless. Let us part friends and brothers. Good night and good bye." He stretched himself on the grass as he spoke.

"Good bye?" in a tone of surprise.

"Yes, to this argument," laughed the prisoner.

PICKETS ON DUTY.

Harry sighed, and followed his brother's movements. Debate was evidently useless, and within ten minutes both seemed lost in sound slumbers.

During the remainder of the night all was quiet. There were, it is true, low and incomprehensible sounds from the direction of the city. And a rifle shot from the picket line startled the camp about three o'clock in the morning. But it proved to have been fired at a supposed lurking figure, and those whom it had disturbed were soon asleep again.

Yet when Harry Vail awakened near daybreak of the next morning, it was to learn the true meaning of his brother's " Good bye."

He lay alone. His captive had vanished during the night. Only the impression of his body in the grass remained as evidence of his ever having been there. It was he then that had stolen through the picket lines, calling forth the one shot of alarm. The escaped prisoner was safely back again in the ranks of his chosen friends.

That Sergeant Vail was annoyed and vexed we need not say. He had hoped that the morning's argument would have a stronger effect on his obdurate brother than that of the night.

But there was little time for regret, or even for thought. The army was up and preparing for action. All questions of family interest must give way to those of soldierly duty.

And then to the utter dismay and anger of the troops it was discovered that the over caution of their general had robbed them of their prize. During that whole moonlight night the veterans of Lee's army had been crossing the James and streaming down in hurrying hosts towards Petersburg. The spade had been busy all night long. The meaning of the strange sounds they had heard was now evident. When morning dawned a new line of works before the city stared the astounded Union army in the face. And those works were densely filled with the veterans of the Confederate army. Ten long months were destined to pass ere Union feet should tread as victors in that city which had been at their mercy but one short night before

CHAPTER XXVIII.

IN THE JAWS OF DEATH.

" Hair breadth 'scapes."

S my wound incapacitated me from service for a time, I wish to continue my narrative in the words of a comrade of the Sixth Corps, Sergeant Ulmer, one of the color-bearers of his regiment, a gallant soldier, and a genial brother of the camp.

It is not my purpose to relate the whole history of Sergeant Ulmer but rather to give certain striking instances of the perils of a soldier's life, from his interesting experiences.

I shall continue the narrative in his own words, letting him tell his story to the reader as he told it to me in person.

"It was on the morning of May 12th, 1864, (said Sergeant Ulmer). Grant was now at the head of the army of the Potomac, and was leading it southward in that series of desperate engagements, by which the Confederate army was hurled back through the Wilderness to the entrenchments at Richmond, there to make the last stand of the terrible war.

"On the morning of the date above given, Hancock, at the head of the Second Corps, made that memorable charge in which he captured a whole Confederate division, together with a battery of artillery and several Confederate generals.

"The Sixth Corps was ordered to support him. Our regiment was on the extreme right of the line. The State flag, one of the two colors of the regiment, was in my care. I speak of this as it has an important bearing on what followed.

"The charge which our brigade made on that day was one of the most difficult, and most grandly executed, of any achieved during that terrible campaign. The ground was of the most annoying character. Before us lay a pine thicket, bordered by slashings through which we had to force our way in the face of a severe fire from the enemy. Beyond that lay an open space of about one hundred yards in width, and faced by the works of the foe.

"It seemed the act of madness to venture into that fire-swept space, over which poured a very hail storm of bullets. Yet without a second's hesitation, and with a wild yell of defiance from thousands of Union throats, the brigade dashed fiercely on, as it seemed into the very jaws of death.

"Down went men like grass blades before the scythe of the mower. Soon a thousand men lay lifeless or wounded, yet still, with the impulse of fury, the line swept on. Through the abatis of the enemy's works it dashed, mounted the breastworks, and drove out the foe with a fiery impetuosity which they strove in vain to resist.

"For a while the left of the regiment was inside the works, colors were snatched from the hands of the Confederate color-bearers, and many prisoners were captured. Lieut. Justice. of Co. "A." dropped dead on the spot, pierced by an enemy's bullet. A member of another company raised his musket and aimed at the Lieut's assassin: but in vain, the cap was wet with the rain that then fell in torrents, and it failed to explode. With a fierce oath he lowered the musket, and ran the Confederate soldier through with the bayonet, killing him instantly.

"Our part of the regiment, being the extreme right, and unsupported, failed to cross the breastwork. In a moment the order came to 'lie down,' and we dropped on the earth, in line of battle before the abatis, glad for the moment to escape the withering fire of the enemy.

"At this point began a thrilling personal adventure to myself. one of the most perilous that any soldier ever encountered in any battle. I must narrate it now in cold blood, but could I paint the situation in its living colors of fire and blood, and truly express my own feelings at the time, the reader could not but be thrilled as if he were himself in the fury and flood of war.

"Whispered orders to 'fall back' passed through the regiment, which were quietly obeyed, the only line left in front of the hostile works being that of the dead and wounded. Not hearing the order, and mistaking the line of dead and wounded for the regiment, I remained stretched at full length in front of the abatis, still grasping my flag.

"Half an hour passed by. Then a wounded man on my left asked:

"'Are you wounded?'

"'No.'

"'Then why don't you go to the rear? The regiment fell back some time ago.'

"If ever a man was startled it was I at this information. I gazed hastily round and saw that it was true. I was the only sound man left in front of the enemy's works.

"This might not have mattered so much under ordinary circumstances. But just now bullets were whistling thick about me. The wounded were frequently struck a second and a third time, some receiving a mortal wound while suffering from the first. My comrade on the left was struck twice while lying beside me. In fact not a man of the wounded was ever taken from that death-swept field alive. Those who were unable to crawl away were fairly riddled with bullets.

"My situation was a terrible one. Had I been wounded I would have lost all hope. But with all my powers remaining I could not give up. There I lay, in full view of the Confederate works, which stretched far away to the right and left before me. My flag was a conspicuous object. The least movement on my part would be sure to draw a volley, there being then none of our men in front to divert their attention.

"If I ever prayed with fervor for protection and deliverance I did at that moment, the most perilous of my life. There was but one thing to do. It was certain death to continue there. It might be certain death to make a dash for safety. Yet I nerved myself for the deperate effort.

"With the greatest caution I divested myself of my blanket. I then took off my haversack, and my belt with pistol and ammunition, retaining only my canteen, in order that I might have water in case I was wounded.

"Thus lightened, I cautiously worked myself around, so as to face the rear. I had been before facing the earthworks. As I still lay, like a tiger crouched for the spring, a bullet from the Confederate works glanced across the small of my back, and cut out a piece from my coat an inch wide and six inches long. A half inch lower, and it would have gone through my back bone. As it was I felt as if a hot iron had seared my skin.

"There was not a second to lose. It was evident that the foe, seeing no hostile line before them, were firing recklessly at the wounded. It was death to stay—death to go, perhaps. But anything was better than that horrible uncertainty. The instant I made a decided move the shots came quicker. Evidently I had drawn attention to myself.

"There was but one thing to do now. With a quick movement I sprang to my feet, still grasping the flag, and started on a quick run across the plain, taking a ziggag course so that no one could aim deliberately at me.

"Away I went, running as I had never run before, bounding over dead and wounded, desperately anxious to cross that fatal hundred yards of open space, and gain the shelter of the forest beyond.

"And never had man before such need for haste. My movement seemed the signal to draw the fire of the whole line of the enemy. Bullets flew around me like hail stones in a fierce storm. Mud was splashed on me

22

where they struck the ground at my side, showing tha*
the enemy had the range. Yet not a bullet struck me
or my clothing.

"As I ran I clung to my flag, dragging it at a trail
behind me, grasping the staff near the centre. A
very few seconds brought me to the edge of the woods.
Here trees had been felled to form a barrier, and as I

COMRADE ULMER SAVING THE FLAG
OF THE REGIMENT.

scrambled through, the flag caught in the branches.
Had I possessed my sober senses just then I should
probably have let it go, and looked to my own safety.
But to my excited fancy the flag seemed part of myself,
and I frantically jerked to tear it loose, heedless of the
storm of bullets in the air. It yielded to my fierce
effort and on I dashed, the whole line firing at me as fast
as they could load and pull trigger.

"Once again the flag fouled between two trees. A
twist and a jerk released it, and on I went in my

desperate charge for life, glad to the soul that I had gained the shelter of the trees.

"But now a new danger menaced me. A line of Union troops sud'enly sprang to their feet before me and began firing. Bullets from my friends began to accompany those which still whistled through the woods from my enemies.

"'Cease firing! Cease firing!' I yelled, in frantic excitement, at the full strength of my voice.

"In an instant, as if by magic, every musket dropped. The officers rushed to the front and cried, excitedly:

"'Who are you? Whence do you come? Are there any men or regiments in front?'

"'None,' I answered, as I sank exhausted to the ground. 'None but dead and wounded. Thank God, I have come alive through the very gates of hell, with the whole Confederate army firing at me. For God's sake, comrades, fire high! The ground in front is strewn with wounded, who are being riddled with bullets.'

"In a moment there was an excited crowd around me, listening to the story of my escape, and congratulating me on my good fortune.

"'And bless me if the brave fellow hasn't brought off his colors through all that storm of bullets!' cried an officer. 'You should get your shoulder straps for that, my man. The regiment ought to prize that flag.'

"Escaping from their warm congratulations, and inquiring the position of my regiment, I made my way slowly back, picking up a haversack here and a blanket there, and moving towards the rear, where I was told the remnant of the regiment lay.

"At some distance back I met the provost guard, which is posted in the rear at every battle to prevent straggling. They stopped me, but I had only to point to the track of the bullet across my back as passport through their lines.

" A short distance further brought me within sight of the regiment, or what was left of it, for out of that terrible half hour, from ten to half past ten of the morning of May 12th, only seventy-five men marched back —not a full company out of the shattered battalion!

" The colonel rode out to meet me, and, grasping my hand, congratulated me on my escape, and for bringing back the flag. They had given me up for lost, and felt sure that the flag was gone. In fact the regiment was wild when they heard the story of my desperate flight through the fire of the whole Confederate line, aiming at me at short range, for not a shot from our side had distracted their attention during my mad break for the woods.

" I cannot go further into the details of this terrible fight. I have told all my own experience of it. History tells the rest. I can but say that for hours the conflict continued about those deadly earthworks, and that at the end of the battle the dead were piled in heaps— literally ' in heaps,'—for I saw them four or five men deep the day after the battle. And I saw where a tree, about eighteen inches in diameter, had been actually eaten through with bullets, until it fell, crushing the living and the dead alike beneath it, as it crashed downward within the rebel works.

" It was on this field that General Grant penned that

memorable despatch, which became the watchword of the remainder of the war: 'I will fight it out upon this line if it takes all summer.'

" With one more incident I will close my narrative of the Wilderness campaign. On June first the advance of the army, fighting by day and marching by night, reached Cold Harbor. Here we relieved a line of cavalry, who had been holding the ground against odds since daybreak.

"At 3 P. M. our regiment, in company with some others, charged on the enemy. I can see the line yet in its beautiful formation, moving across the field as if on parade, the colors slightly in advance, and hesitating only for a moment as successive storms of grape and cannister from the enemy's guns swept through the ranks.

" We finally gained a position on a hillock, a few yards in front of the Confederate line. Here at sundown we began to entrench ourselves, using hands and bayonets to scrape the dirt, in lieu of entrenching tools.

" Exposed and perilous as this position was we held it stubbornly for a week or more, so close to the enemy that every man who raised his head above the line of the earthwork was sure to be hit. We were fairly forced to burrow in the ground. Trenches had to be dug to cover those who went to the rear for water, and even with this precaution many of our water-bearers were killed. It was about as ugly and hot a position as could well have been selected.

"After three or four days' fighting, with occasional charges, the surface between the works was thickly strewn with the dead of both armies. Such of the wounded as were able had crawled in during the nights. But many yet lay out unable to move, and who could not be rescued, since the least movement was sure to draw the fire of the pickets. The dead bodies, under the blaze of the June suns, began to send up a horrible stench, and the sufferings of the wounded were indescribable.

"This terrible exigency ended in a truce, to last for two or three hours, and permit each side to remove its wounded, the loss being pretty equally divided between the blue and the gray.

"I need not say that both sides took instant advantage of this truce. Men from both lines swarmed like ants over the breastworks, and the work of removing the poor and helpless sufferers was hastily begun.

"Meanwhile a striking fraternization took place between the soldiers of the two armies, who crowded the space between the lines. On every side the lately blood-thirsty foes could be seen shaking hands, with every sign of friendliness, while such remarks as these greeted the ear:

"'Well, Johnny.'

"'Hello, Yank.'

"'Don't you wish the war was over?'

"'Give us some coffee.'

"'Have you any tobacco?'

"One might have thought they had been old friends, met after a long parting.

"But promptly at the time named for the truce to end a change came over the spirit of the scene. Such a wild scamper as began towards the respective earthworks was seldom witnessed And five minutes afterwards the crack of the rifle was again heard. Such are the vicissitudes of war.

"I need but say in conclusion of this chapter, that our march through the Wilderness ended on the banks of the James, the army of the Potomac having fairly driven the foe back to his lair."

CHAPTER XXIX.

THE TRAIL OF THE BULLET.

" The whizzing shot was sent,
The ' silver cord ' to sever ;
It struck ! It's force was spent ;
It's work will last forever."

OMRADE Ulmer's story contains another highly interesting episode, relating to the shadowy side of a soldier's life, which I shall give, as in the last chapter, in his own words, letting him speak in the first person. He can tell his own exciting experience far better than I could tell it for him—

"From Washington the Sixth Corps was removed to the valley of the Shenandoah, where it took part in the brilliant victories of Opequon, Winchester and Fisher's Hill, concerning which I have nothing of interest to add to the dry details of history.

"I must hurry on to the important battle of Cedar Creek, fought on October 19th, 1864, in which I had a terrible experience, which brought my career as a soldier to a sudden, and almost to a fatal termination.

"This engagement will be remembered as that mem-

orable one in which the gallant Sheridan snatched victory
out of defeat. It has already been amply told in history
how the Eighth and 19th Corps were surprised by
Early's army about day dawn, the surprise being aided
by a dense fog, and
were driven back in
confusion for a dis-
tance of four miles.
The story of Sheri-
dan's mad ride from
Winchester, his hasty
rallying of the dis-
mayed and retreating
troops, and his turn-
ing of the triumph of
the enemy into a dis-
astrous defeat, has
been similarly told in
prose and poetry.

GEN. PHIL. SHERIDAN.

Sheridan's ride is a picturesque event that the American
people cannot soon forget.

"As for my personal share in this exciting battle I
can but say that the Sixth Corps was roused in the early
morning by the sound of musketry and cannon to the
left. We fell promptly into line, hurried to the field of
conflict, and fought as only brave men could fight.

"But being overlapped by the Confederate line on the
right, we slowly retired, keeping our line of battle
unbroken, for a distance of about two miles. Our orders
were to fall back to a piece of woods in our rear.

"We were going back, step by step, closely followed

by the enemy, when I was suddenly hurled flat on my face, with a sensation as if I had been struck a violent blow with a club on the legs from behind.

"My first feeling was one of surprise. It took me some little time to realize what had actually happened. I then knew that I had been wounded, and in the leg, as I found that I could not move my limb.

"Fearing that I might bleed to death I removed the leather strap from my canteen, and knotted it around my leg above the wound. Then with my bayonet I twisted it as hard as I could.

"Judicious as the movement was it produced such an intense pain that I found it impossible to bear it. I hastily removed the bayonet, and flung it away. The bleeding might be dangerous—perhaps fatal—but such pain as that was more than mortal man could long endure.

"While I had been doing this our line had been going back step by step, and the Confederates advancing. Immediately after I threw away the bayonet, and resigned myself to the inevitable, the line of hostile skirmishers came up, and passed over me in pursuit of the retreating corps.

"Then came their first line of battle, the officers on horseback urging their men onward, and the men occasionally firing as they advanced. It was a new experience for me, to lie there in bleeding helplessness, under the feet of the victorious foe.

"The second line of battle quickly followed, the officers, with a humanity I had hardly looked for, telling the men to be careful, and not step on the wounded.

They actually 'broke to the rear' in passing two or three of us who lay near together.

"There was another experience of army life now to follow. The line of battle had not passed far onward when it was succeeded by an irregular line of stragglers and 'bummers,' whose sole object seemed to be plunder.

"No sooner was the line at a safe distance ahead, and the eyes of the officers otherwise engaged, than these vultures of the battle field descended like a swarm of carrion birds, and at once commenced their robbery of the dead and wounded.

"Fortunately they showed no desire to injure us further than to take possession of our valuables. In fact they were rather inclined to indulge in friendly brag, their style of conversation being something of the following:

"'Say, Yank, I reckon we've got you this time!'

"'Got you on the jump, we'uns have, and you bet we won't stop till we drive you into the Potomac, at Harper's Ferry.'

"'Hello, Yank, where's Sheridan?'

"'What have you got in your pockets?'

"This was the question in which they seemed most interested, and which they proceeded to put to practical proof without waiting for the answer.

"I had a new pocket-book, with some ten dollars in notes and currency, and also a ten dollar bill in the pocket of a little diary in which I had begun to write that morning. The only words in that diary, whose record came to such a disastrous end, were the following:

"'Awake this morning early; heard heavy firing on

the left. Roll-call was ordered, and stood in line. Broke ranks and packed up.' And so broke off my final record of the war.

"The first 'bummer' who searched me descended like a shark on my pocket-book, saying he guessed as how he would take care of that.

"'Don't want to rob you, Yank, but this stuff won't be no use to you in our hospitals. Here's the 'shin-plasters' as goes there. A fair exchange ain't no robbery.'

"He handed me a dilapidated purse, which contained eight or ten dollars, perhaps more, in Confederate currency.

"I cannot say that I exactly saw the force of his proverb. It did not seem to me quite 'a fair exchange.' It was well, indeed, that I did not set much store by my new acquisition, for the next bummer that came up fell in love with the old pocket book and its 'graybacks,' and took possession of them.

"'What else you got, Yank?' he demanded, as he proceeded to search me.

"Lighting on my diary he ran hastily over the leaves, but failed to perceive the pocket that contained my remaining cash.

"'I don't want that trash,' he exclaimed, flinging it back contemptuously.

"A quiet smile passed over my face, which I took good care not to let him perceive.

"So it went on, plunderer after plunderer passing over the field, and searching the helpless and the dead.

"Piece by piece my private property was confiscated—

my pipe, my tobacco, and all my small treasures. But the diary remained uncaptured. Nearly every one ran over it, and flung it back with a contemptuous growl. Its contents remained to serve me a good turn thereafter in the hospital, and buy certain little luxuries outside the regulation provender.

"I had received my wound about eight o'clock. By ten our part of the field was deserted, except by an occasional straggler who would come along and repeat the search.

"There were several wounded and dead near me, and many others lay stretched over the field. We implored all who came to remove us from the field and take us to the hospital, with the invariable answer:

"'Can't be done yet. Our own wounded has got to be looked after first. When that's done you-uns 'll be took off.'

"The roar of cannon told us that the battle still continued. But it was growing more and more distant, showing that our army was still falling back before the victorious foe. A feeling of hopelessness came over us, and mingled with the anguish from our wounds. It seemed evident that the army of the Union had been disastrously defeated, and that we were left there to perish miserably on the field, or to languish through the living death of the Confederate prisons.

"Mingled with this was the torture of thirst, which now began to oppress us. About noon a horseman in Confederate uniform came riding by. He drew up his horse, and sat in the saddle looking down on us, with eyes of compassion.

" 'Poor fellows,' he muttered, 'I am sorry for you. Don't you want some water?'

" 'Yes,' we cried in chorus.

" 'I'll fill your canteens,' he replied.

"He sprang from his horse, gathered as many canteens as he could carry, and rode away again—a true missionary of mercy.

"He was gone so long that we almost gave him up in despair, when up he rode, with the canteens dripping with cold and sparkling water.

"The poor fellows on the ground could not resist the impulse to give him three cheers. He tipped his hat, and rode away, followed by a fervent 'God bless you! We hope your lips may never crave in vain for water.'

"Some considerable time afterwards another cavalryman rode up. He was of different callibre from the last. I had a new poncho, or rubber blanket, which I had recently drawn from the quartermaster. This I had spread over me to keep off the chill of the October air.

" 'That is just what I want,' he cried.

" 'Don't take it from me,' I pleaded. 'You don't know how cold it is here, on the damp ground.'

" 'All right. I'll fix that.'

"Away he rode. What was his object I could not imagine. It was a quarter of an hour before he returned, carrying a bundle, which he threw on the ground.

" 'We'll see if we can't fix you, my lad.'

"Springing down after his bundle, he jerked off my blanket, and laid it over his saddle. Then he spread over me a thick covering of tent cloths—portions of shelter tents which every soldier carries.

"'There, it will be queer if that don't make you warm.' Away he rode, with my last article of plunder.

"The hours of that miserable afternoon passed slowly on. Not another soul came near us. Even the sounds of the battle had long died out in the distance. We seemed utterly deserted, and left to die in misery. Some conversation was kept up between the wounded, but there was little relish for talk, except of the most gloomy character. The still, set faces of the dead, so near us, were a horrible vision, from which we could with difficulty remove our eyes.

"Here and there cries of anguish came from desperately wounded men, but many suppressed even their groans and bore their pain in silence. Some even died without a sound, with the courage of martyrs. Such a horrible situation I had never been in before, and pray God I may never be in again. The field of battle, after the conflict has passed, is one of the most terrible torture chambers that have ever been known upon the face of the earth.

"As for myself, after throwing away the bayonet the pain of my wound had not been extreme. It had bled considerably, but not dangerously. I was weakened, yet retained some of my strength.

"The day had passed and evening was approaching. Yet the field continued deserted.

"'Are we to stay here all night?' cried one of my comrades, in anguish. 'Are the Confederates going to leave us here to die? Have they no feeling or pity?'

"'Looks as if they hadn't,' muttered another, angrily. 'I know I've picked up a good many hurt Johnnies in my time, and they might return the compliment.'

" 'They will surely be here after us,' I replied. 'The hospital corps must have its hands full. But our turn will come. Hello! yonder comes a man now!'

" It had been so long since we had seen any one, that all eyes were turned toward the person I had espied—a single foot soldier, who was advancing towards us.

" 'How goes it, lads?' he cried.

" 'Kind of bad,' we groaned, in response. 'How long are you fellows going to leave us here?'

" 'What regiment do you belong to?' I asked.

" '— West Virginia,' he replied. I failed to catch the number.

" Taking it for granted that he was a member of one of the Confederate regiments from West Virginia, I demanded:

" 'Anyhow, Johnnie, it ain't square to let us bleed to death. Haven't you fellows sent out a detail to take up the wounded?'

" 'Johnny!' he cried, indignantly. 'Who are you talking to? I reckon I'm as sound Union as anybody here.'

" 'What!' I exclaimed. 'You are not a Confederate soldier? What brings you here, then? Do you want to be captured and taken prisoner to Richmond?'

" 'Not much, I reckon. Why, hang it, don't you know that we're the bosses? Haven't you heard how little Phil came up and rallied the troops, and sent the Rebs spinning back like sheep?'

" 'You don't mean to say that our side is victorious, and that we are not prisoners in the enemy's hands,' I gasped.

"'Nary time. We give them blazes, I tell you. Got fifty-four guns, and 2000 prisoners, and the field's our own.'

"The shouts of joy, and cheers from weakened throats that followed this surprising but welcome announcement, must have done good to the heart of our visitor. For the moment we felt as if we were well again, in the glad thought that we were to be cared for by our own friends, and were safe from the neglect of Southern hospitals and the misery of Southern prisons.

"The battle of the afternoon, and the Union victory, had taken place three miles to our right. Hence our ignorance of its important results. I learned that my regiment was to camp on the same ground it had left so abruptly in the morning.

"I sent word to my company that I lay on the ground wounded. I being their orderly sergeant a squad from the company soon came in search of me. To my hopeful joy I was lifted tenderly from the field, and borne carefully to the surgeon's tent, where my wound was dressed, and I was made as comfortable as possible for the night, very glad indeed that my bed was not made in a Confederate camp.

"I have narrated these events in detail, as I feel that they cannot but be of interest to the reader. After hearing so much of the life in front of the enemy's line, amid the roar of battle, and the bursting of shot and shell, some record of the scenes behind the enemy's line, in the desolate misery of the wounded's bleeding ranks, and among the sharks of the battle field, may serve as a useful foil to the story of battle and victory.

23

"The next morning, while the wounded lay waiting to be taken to the field hospital at Middletown, a scene took place which I may briefly narrate.

"General Torbert, then in command of the cavalry, rode up, accompanied by his whole staff. There was a serious and somewhat stern look upon the general's face.

"'Who is in command of the regiment?' he demanded.

"'Captain Spear,' was the reply.

"'Call Captain Spear.'

"That officer quickly presented himself, a little disturbed by the character of this visit.

"'Yesterday my men, on overtaking the enemy, captured among other trophies this flag,' said the general.

"He lifted his hand and displayed the State flag of the regiment.

"'How is this?' he demanded. 'Am I to understand that a regiment that has always borne the good record of yours has voluntarily surrendered its flag to the enemy?'

"'No, sir. By Heavens, no!' cried Captain Spear, indignantly. 'I can explain its loss to your satisfaction, general. On falling back yesterday our color-bearer was shot. A soldier took the colors from him. He in his turn was killed. But the lads, thinking he was only slightly wounded, passed on, fancying that he would quickly join them. In that way the flag fell into the hands of the foe.'

"'I am very glad to hear that,' replied the general. 'I felt sure that a regiment of the record of yours, which has never lost a flag in action, would have never voluntarily deserted its colors. I now return you your flag, and earnestly congratulate you on the manner in which you have sustained the honor of the brigade—my own old command. I am proud of your noble record—very proud.'

"With that he rode away, followed by the vigorous cheers of the regiment, who at the moment silently resolved that that flag should never again leave their hands, while there was a man left to grasp it, or a musket to defend it.

"My subsequent experience may be more briefly described. I would avoid it altogether, but that it is an important component of a soldier's life. Hospital experience has none of the busy stir and daring adventure of life in field and camp. It is the shadow side of warfare. Yet it is a side through which many thousands of our gallant soldiers passed, and the story of war cannot be made complete without a record of this, its darker phase.

"My own experience presents certain features of interest which may aid to relieve it of its somewhat monotonous aspect.

"Reaching the field hospital I was kept there for a few days, and then sent to Winchester, in an army wagon with two wounded comrades.

"Here a halt was made and the choice given us of going on to Martinsburg by the same conveyance, with the chance of dying on the road, or remaining where we were. It was explained that if we could stand the additional journey to Martinsburg, railroad communication could there be made, and we might be sent on to Baltimore or Philadelphia. Otherwise we might remain indefinitely at Winchester.

At the mention of Philadelphia my spirits revived. If that city was once reached I would be not far from my home. And a yet gladder thought was that there dwelt one whom I had left behind me with the kiss of love, who I knew was waiting eagerly and lovingly for my return.

"'Drive on,' I cried, impetuously. 'I will stand it, no matter how dangerous or painful it may be. What say you, comrades? Are you ready for the ride?'

"'Yes,' they eagerly responded. 'It is nearer home, at any rate.'

"'Even if it be nearer to the home above,' I reverently replied.

"Yet we did not well know what was before us. Laid on a little straw that was scattered over the tops of ammunition boxes in an old ammunition wagon, and driving all night long over rough roads, 'corduroy' most of the way, tossed and jolted, our wounds intensely painful from the constant shock, that long journey seemed worse than dying ten times over.

"We arrived in Martinsburg about ten o'clock in the morning, where we were taken to a private house, and laid on a mattress spread on the floor.

"I was so trussed up that I could not move any portion of my body except my head and hands. A long splint ran from under my left arm to my foot. Another clasped the opposite side of my leg, and the whole was tightly wrapped with many yards of bandage, until I was about as capable of motion as a mummy.

"The people of the house kindly cared for us, and gave us coffee and food. On the afternoon of the next

THE WOUNDED CARED FOR AND THE HUNGRY FED.

day, Sunday, we were loaded in cattle cars on the Baltimore and Ohio Railroad, and just at dusk the rattle of the rolling wheels told that we were once more in motion on our journey home.

"Late on Monday morning we reached Baltimore. While waiting here in the cars for our turn to be removed, a pleasant incident occurred which served to throw some light upon our dark journey.

"A benevolent-faced old gentleman climbed into the door of our 'palace' car, and kindly asked us our names, and if he could do anything for us. He seemed particu-larly attracted to me, asked my father's name and address, and promised to write to him.

"He said his name was Seth Reed, and that he took a great interest in the soldiers. The truth of this his actions clearly evinced. Every day before going to the bank in which he was a clerk, he would visit the hospital, and bring some one of his 'boys,' as he called them, some little delicacy. Nothing seemed a trouble to him that would add to their comfort, and I can but hope the kind-hearted friend to the soldier may yet live to read this tribute to his benevolence and sympathy.

"I was taken to Jarvis' Hospital, where I had my first good night's rest, in a clean and comfortable bed, for more than a week. Hard floors or mother earth had been my only sleeping place till then since I had received my wound.

"The surgeons thought my limb could be saved, and it was enclosed in a wire cage suspended from the ceiling of the hospital. That is, it was raised a few inches from the bed, in a frame work of wire, so that I was obliged to lie constantly on my back.

"Yet the injury proved too serious. The wound would not heal nor the bones unite. And finally a serious hemorrhage took place, which forced the surgeons to the conclusion that their efforts were in vain—the limb must come off.

"The bullet had entered the inner part of my leg about six inches above the knee, passed through flesh and bone, and come out on the outside opposite its entrance. Here its force was spent, and it was stopped by my clothing, and fell into my shoe, whence it was taken by the surgeon who first dressed the wound.

"The amputation took place in late November, I being left with just seven inches of limb. The winter was passed in the hospital. Here we received the best of treatment and the most careful attention, and despite the monotony of the situation the invalids managed to get some enjoyment out of life.

"Yet my wound did not heal to the satisfaction of the doctors. The surgeon suspected the presence of dead bone, which must be removed. So one March morning, when on his rounds, he produced his case of instruments and with the simple remark, 'It won't hurt,' he proceeded to cut open the end of the limb, with a coolness to which only a born surgeon can attain.

"It was my private opinion just then that 'some one had lied.' It certainly did hurt, and that most decidedly.

"I know that for the space of five minutes I did some very promiscuous howling.

"'That's right,' he said. 'Yell away as much as you like. It will make it feel better.'

"I fancy he was right in that. I fear I would have

burst if I had tried to keep in the yell, so I managed to give him a very good illustration of my vocal powers.

"He removed about three inches of dead bone, and then closed the wound. He ordered me plenty of milk punch, with, I fancy, a plentiful allowance of brandy. The result was rather unexpected to me. I had hardly tasted liquor in my life, and this flew to my head, so that ere long I was singing away as happily as a king, with all pain forgotten, and life seeming all sunshine. I was, in fact—drunk, for the first, last, and only time in my life.

"In short, I behaved so ridiculously before the head surgeon, who soon afterwards came into the room, that he grew angry, and sternly demanded :

"'What ails that man? What does he mean?'

"On learning what had happened, however, he changed his tone, examined my wound, and passed on.

"From that time forward my recovery was rapid. On the 29th of May, 1865, I left the hospital with my father for my home in the North. Bidding good bye to my kind friend, Mr. Reed, and his wife, I took the evening train for home.

"I should be glad if this were the end of my story. But unfortunately there were dark days yet in store— long weeks of peril and suffering.

"At Trenton we had to change cars. While waiting on the platform for the expected train, the inevitable 'small-boy,' who is never happy except when in mischief, came rushing by with an empty baggage truck which he had found upon the platform.

"I stepped backward to avoid collision. But

unluckily my crutch slipped into an auger hole in the planks, and down I came, striking my wounded leg a violent blow on the hard planks.

"Completely overwhelmed by the fall and the resulting pain, I had to be carried in anguish into the car, and my expected happy home-coming was suddenly changed to an occasion of deep sadness.

"The villagers had awaited my arrival with pleased expectation, and as the train reached the station the village band stood on the platform, prepared to strike up some stirring tune, such as 'See the Conquering Hero Comes,' or a similar warlike air.

"But when they saw me carried from the car in my father's arms, 'A change came o'er the spirit of their dream.' Sorrow took the place of joy in their faces, and the band silently disappeared.

"Months passed ere I recovered from the effects of that unlucky accident. It was after midsummer before I was myself again, and even then the healing was not complete. In December of that year, having removed to Philadelphia, while dressing my wound an artery suddenly gave way, and I was in imminent danger of bleeding to death.

"The necessary consequence was, after I had regained sufficient strength, a third amputation, this time at the hip joint. From this final operation I in time fully recovered.

"I mention the fact of this final amputation in particular, as it has more interest and importance than may appear to those who do not know the full difficulty and peril attending an amputation at the hip joint.

"I need but say here, in corroboration of this remark, that of the eighty-six operations of this character which took place during the war, only six of the patients were alive at the end of the war. Of these, only three now survive, one of this fortunate number being myself.

"And I may conclude by saying that the surgeons imputed my recovery to my sobriety and sound constitution, saying that if I had been a dissipated man I could never have survived the operation.

"It is but just, in closing this chapter of peril, and nearness to the gates of death, that I should speak of the skill and great surgical ability of the operating surgeon, Dr. Thomas G. Morton, who, assisted by Drs. Hunt and Agnew, performed this critical operation at the Pennsylvania Hospital. It was owing to their constant attention, ably seconded by the corps of house doctors and trained nurses at the hospital, together with the blessings of Divine Providence, that I am to-day enjoying perfect health, surrounded by a loving wife, children and scores of friends, while the past, with its hair-breath escapes and exciting scenes, seems but a dream.

"With these concluding words, the narrative of my war experience comes to an end."

CHAPTER XXX.

" Theirs not to reason why,
Theirs but to do and die."

URING all the summer and autumn of 1864 General Grant had his face set toward Richmond.

Vigorous operations had been carried on by the army in every part of the country where it was possible to strike a blow that would hasten the approaching conclusion of the war. Our men saw the star of hope coming out brighter and brighter, and made but little account of their hardships and sufferings.

Our sturdy commander, Sedgwick, had fallen in battle, and had left us only the memory of his valiant services. Henceforth he was to rank among the heroes who slept under the honors of the brave.

In the earlier part of the season Sherman had been operating in Georgia, and at Rocky Face Ridge and other places, had proved his own generalship and the lofty courage of the troops he led so successfully. At Rocky Ridge it was made manifest that stones and

(302)

broken pieces of rock could be used for missiles, and were formidable missiles, too, in the hands of an enemy well protected.

Whoever else tired of the march, and siege, and conflict during that long period of campaigning in the Shenandoah Valley, Barney Roach, at least, showed no signs of weakness, and flourished his stick with characteristic vigor. When Barney was given to understand that his stick was not a weapon that was approved by the highest military authorities of the land, and had better be dispensed with, he hid it under his soldier's coat, conveniently ready for any emergency. Barney considered it an unpardonable offence that no code of tactics taught the use of the shillaly. That appeared to be the only objection he had to the country of his recent adoption.

By this time he had found a crony in Brixy, and took frequent opportunities when off duty to instruct Brixy in the use of his favorite weapon.

One morning they were sparring together, and were swinging their arms in a manner suggestive of a windmill in a hurricane, and an interested group was looking on.

"You're awkward, mon," exclaimed Barney; "if ye were in a shindy ye'd be sure to hit the head ye didn't strike at."

"Don't think a feller can learn this business all at once," Brixy replied. "I want to do it scientific, and it's going to take time."

"Begorra, ye've fooled round with that ould musket till ye're about spiled; a mighty poor definder of your country ye are, sure."

Brixy kept backing away as Barney made up to him, and appeared to be trying to get out of the reach of his adversary.

"Stand up, mon!" shouted Barney. "No fear that ye'll hurt Barney Roach; ye wouldn't hurt a flea with one o' your little taps."

At that moment Brixy made a quick pass toward Barney with a "vim" that showed there was ample strength in the arm of the country boy. The blow was a vigorous one, and Barney not being quick enough to ward it off, it came down on his head and face with a force that caused him to give a sudden scream.

"Och, ye divil, what did ye do that fer?" shouted Barney. The blood was flowing from his battered nose, yet the group of men could not refrain from a burst of laughter.

"You thought he never would learn," ejaculated one; "but I guess he knows how."

Barney was equal to the occasion, and responded, "It's rare sport, byes. This is the kind of weapon that does the damage; didn't I tell ye there's nothing for foighting like a shillaly?"

When Barney was bantered on account of his battered appearance and the black mark he carried on his face, he maintained that there was nothing out of the way in having a little fun now and then, and he thoroughly enjoyed it, as sure as his name was Barney Roach.

"You handle the shillaly, Brixy, better than you do the pen."

The remark came from the comrade who had written Brixy's first letter to Jane, and who, since that memorable occasion had penned sundry other gushing effusions, some of them explanatory and aiming to effect a reconciliation, which finally took place, and others expressing in most emphatic terms the unbounded affection and devotion of Joe Brixy toward the girl who, he declared, was "jist an angel even if she did milk cows and wash dishes."

" I've got Jane's picture yet," said one of the boys.

"I know all about that," retorted Brixy. "You fooled me once; made me believe she was your girl, and the fellers laughed at me; but Jane says as how you're her cousin, and she gave you her picture when you enlisted, and that's the way you got it."

The mystery of Jane's photograph being in other hands than those of Joe Brixy was now explained.

Our division commander passed at this moment, and Barney, with awkward politeness, raised his soldier's cap, and did his best to show honor to the general.

"Barney's improving," Sanderson remarked. "Do you know what he did soon after he joined our regiment ? "

" Tell us," ejaculated several.

"Well, he was sent one day with a message to the general's tent, went in and stood there in most unsoldierly fashion, with his cap on. The general, happening to look up, said, 'Man, take off your cap!' 'Excuse me,' said Barney, 'but I can't stay.' "

Barney's face reddened at this narration, and he shouted, " I tell ye, byes, I may not know the ways of this country as some do, but if ye'll find any mon that will go into a foight with better pluck than I, then Barney Roach will take off his cap to him."

"Hurrah for Barney!" cried the bystanders.

"Anyhow," continued Barney, "I'll not get drummed out of camp for being a shirk."

The drumming out of one man took place the next day, an intimation of which we had at this time.

Limback was a well-known character. How it was that he came to enlist we never found out. Whether his home was not one of the most congenial—he had a wife and several children—or whether in a fit of patriotism he had joined the army, we knew not. It could not have been so much the money, as but a small bounty was then offered, and the pay of a private was but thirteen dollars a month. Anyway, he did enlist, and from that day forth his shirking commenced.

When the details were made to go in the woods to cut down trees, which was one of the first things the regiment was set to work at, Limback would manage to get off in order to help the company's cook, or would get detailed to do something for the captain, an easy sort of man—anything to escape work. When we were employed at fort building, I don't think Limback did a whole day's work in all the time we were thus engaged. When it came to marching, and there was the slightest possibility of meeting the enemy, he was sure to be on the sick-list and in the ambulance, either doubled up with cramp, or some other complaint.

By some hook or crook he shirked the battle of Fredericksburg, and managed to get on the opposite bank of the river. He turned up all right on the march back to camp, and in winter quarters was happy. When the spring-time came and a forward movement began,

Limback was suddenly taken very ill. On the celebrated mud march he was in the ambulance and stuck fast in the mud. When it was known for a certainty that it was impossible to go any further and the only thing to do was to get out as best they might, Limback quickly got over his illness, and did turn in and help pry out his ambulance, having an intuition that he possibly might want it to ride in again.

Well, we got back to camp, and when the army again moved, and the second battle of Fredericksburg was fought, behold Limback had shirked that, and turned up after the battle with a bad cold; in fact, had lost his voice.

From that day forth his only mode of speech was a whisper. In vain the boys would try and surprise him into speaking loud. All knew he was playing it; he wanted his discharge, and the surgeon would not give it. Only at night when suddenly awakened by a pin-thrust, would he make any audible noise. The officers and men were growing tired of this state of affairs. Notwithstanding all the remarks that were made about him, and frequent efforts to surprise him into speech, it was hard to catch him off his guard. Once, however, the lieutenant of the company did so, and that was the end of Limback's pretence, although he would frequently relapse into his whisperings.

A court-martial was ordered, he was found guilty, and the sentence was, "Limback to have his head shaved, and be drummed out of camp." The day was set and had now arrived. Having been under guard since the sentence of the court was pronounced upon him, he was brought out before the regiment, which was drawn up in line of battle, the ranks were opened, and the front rank was faced about, forming a long line of soldiers. Limback was then seated and his head shaved completely. Then with a file of soldiers behind him at a charge bayonet, a board around his neck on which was written "coward" in large letters, his hands tied behind his back, he was started up the line.

The band played "Poor Old Robinson Crusoe" just behind him. Thus he was marched up and down the line and out of the camp, the soldiers behind him quickening his pace at short intervals by the prick of the bayonet.

With no pay he was dishonorably discharged, and thus ended his term of service.

The interest manifested by our men in this proceeding is sufficient evidence of its rarity. It was very unusual to be compelled to call any man a coward. Our troops vied with one another in heroism. Even in our darkest days they held on to their purpose with grim resolution, and never lost faith in their cause. And when ordered to march, and counter-march, here in the Shenandoah Valley, and there was no explanation of their mysterious movements save as it lay in the astute brain of General Grant, they quietly accepted the situation and were ready for every demand made upon them, and every sacrifice required. In the emblazoned firmament of their hope, the stars of the North were waving their salute to the "Southern cross."

It must not be supposed that during this period, when our army was gradually drawing its lines around the central point of the Confederacy, the Federal navy was idle. The waters floated heroes as brave as any who made up the army of the Cumberland, renowned for its recent exploits, the forces operating in the southwest, or the army of the Potomac.

Several important naval successes were gained during the latter part of the year, while at the same time our war vessels met with some reverses. The blockade running steamer Nando, alias Let-her-rip, was captured off Wilmington, North Carolina, by the United States steamer Fort Jackson. Off Charleston the blockade runner Hope was captured by the gunboat Eolus, and the Confederate fleet on the James River, above Dutch Gap, was driven from its moorings by a bombardment opened by two new Union batteries. The steamer Flamingo was sunk in Charleston harbor by Federal guns, and the well-known Confederate ram Albermarle, lying at the wharf in Roanoke River, North Carolina, was blown up by a torpedo worked from a steam picket-boat, under the command of Lieutenant W. B. Cushing. The force of the explosion swamped the picket-boat, Cushing and one seaman only escaping by swimming ashore. The Confederate ram Tennessee fell a prey, with several other vessels, to the Union navy, and many of the terrors of the sea, which had frightened commerce and by their captures had inflicted untold injury, were now disabled, and their piratical raids were ended.

But the naval successes were not all on one side. Many bold and skilful commanders had entered the Confederate naval service in the early part of the war, and during the period here referred to, had been handling their vessels to some purpose.

24

The gunboat Undine. taken from the Union forces, was set on fire near Reynoldsburg Island, Tennessee, and two gunboats that tried to prevent the destruction were driven back by batteries on shore. About the same time the privateer Shenandoah captured the United States brig Susan, and the privateer Chickamauga arrived at Bermuda, having run through the blockading fleet at Wilmington; on her passage she made seven captures, including one ship and four barks.

Not all the disasters occurred in battle, nor were they due to the enemy. One of the saddest casualties of the whole war was the blowing up of the United States gunboat Tulip on the Potomac River. By the explosion of her boilers fifty-nine officers and men were killed, only ten escaping, all of these being scalded and wounded.

Surpassing even this destruction, terrible as it was, was that at Fort Fisher, North Carolina. General Ames' division and a part of the Twenty-fourth Corps, then under command of General Alfred H. Terry, carried the fort by assault. They were aided by a battalion of marines and seamen from the navy. For seven hours the desperate struggle went on, and finally ended in a Union victory. The next day a frightful explosion occurred at the fort, caused by the carelessness of Federal soldiers who were wandering through the captured works. By this calamity which produced a profound sensation throughout the land, two hundred and forty officers and men lost their lives.

One whose death was greatly lamented was Robert Gillette, of Hartford, Connecticut, a young and promising officer, connected with the navy. who, combining in himself all the elements of highest manhood, and fairest

HEROIC CONTEST ABOVE THE CLOUDS.

promises of a useful life, was borne back to his early home with demonstrations of sorrow. Thousands like him, and young Colonel Ellsworth, who fell in the beginning of the war, the very flower of the land, rendered the nation's struggle very costly. Whether lying in the old family burial ground, or among the unknown upon the fields of their heroism and sacrifice, no graves are more sacred than theirs.

> " So sleep the brave, who sink to rest
> By all their country's wishes blest."

It appeared to be the determination of General Grant to push the war to a conclusion by pushing the enemy to defeat. In the latter part of September he advanced his lines on the north side of the James River to within seven miles of Richmond.

General Kilpatrick, the dashing cavalry commander, was operating with Sherman; and Sheridan, whose name was now electric, and fired the boys with unbounded enthusiasm, could boast of his fourth victory in the immediate field where our forces were moving onward.

Near the middle of November, the army of General Sherman, being ready for a march through Georgia, left Atlanta, Rome, and other places of its rendezvous, equipped and supplied for a campaign of fifty days. Kilpatrick's cavalry took the lead, the division being commanded by General McCook. The advance was to proceed slowly toward Macon, to be followed by the Fourteenth Corps, under command of General Davis.

The army of the Tennessee, General Howard commanding, composed of the Fifteenth Corps under General Logan, the Sixteenth under General Smith, and

Seventeenth, led by General Frank Blair, left Kingston three days previously, destroying the railroads in its progress. The troops tore up railroads, burned bridges, and drew a considerable part of their supplies from the surrounding country.

General Sherman was ready for his renowned campaign; at all events, his mind was made up to march, and lead on a great aggressive movement. Before starting he bade good-bye to the North in this remarkable telegram, which has since become historic:

"Hood has crossed the Tennessee. Thomas will take care of him and Nashville, while Schofield will not let him into Chattanooga or Knoxville. Georgia and South Carolina are at my mercy, and I shall strike. Do not be anxious about me; I am all right."

When the news of the forward movement by Sherman reached us, our men were a good deal excited.

"We will meet them in Richmond," exclaimed Brown.

"Three cheers for Richmond!" shouted Barney Roach, and gave them at the top of his voice, yet all alone. "Why don't ye give the cheers?" asked Barney, with an indignant look.

"Don't you know anything?" asked Sanderson. "Richmond belongs to the Rebs; we're trying to capture it; why do you want to cheer for Richmond?"

"I mean three cheers for Richmond when we capture the place," responded Barney.

"Better throw up your cap after we get there," said Brown; "we won't count the chickens before they're hatched."

"Hi, mon," ejaculated Barney, "there's as many chickens before they're hatched as there iver is afterwards."

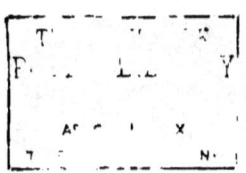

BATTLE OF SPOTSYLVANIA COURT-HOUSE

CHAPTER XXXI.

THE LAST DAYS.

"Now lulls the storm; great guns, whose brazen throats
 Spoke fire and blood, are dumb at last. Rent flags
 Shall now go back to hang in marble halls,
 The tattered trophies of the nation's strife.
 The eyes that wept shall dry their wasting tears,
 And hearts that prayed in agony and fear,
 Shall welcome back the men with scars. The graves,
 That rest the honored dead, shall now be decked
 With fairest flowers of May."

"I regard it as my duty to shift from myself the responsibility
of any further effusion of blood, by asking of you the surrender
of the army under your command."—*General Grant.*

T is with no little satisfaction that I approach the end of my narrative, and reach the point where I can describe the last scenes in the great strife.

My wound, received at Cold Harbor, was severe, yet I was determined it should not keep me out of the army so long as I had any time to serve.

Neither this, nor a previous wound, received soon after I entered the ranks, leaving a bullet which I have since carried in my body, incapacitated me long for duty. I do not regret any sacrifice made in the conflict, any blood spilled. (373)

But the reader who has turned these pages with their light and shadow—more of shadow than sunshine, as was inevitable in a record of the war—will not be averse to reaching a conclusion.

"If we had all fared as well as you have, Knox, we should say that the war had been to us a right good fortune," remarked Sanderson one day, as a few were standing together discussing the situation.

" By the way, Knox," asked Sergeant Vail; "how do you and that Southern lady get along on the secession question? Is she still loyal to the South?"

" I hope," said Knox, " she is loyal to me : that is the most I care about."

" May that come true," continued Vail, "and may we never hear that the fair Mrs. Knox has seceded from Captain Knox!"

"Shentlemens," interposed his majesty, Herr Blinn, " I'm shust von unhappy man."

" You look thin and troubled," said Sanderson ; I've thought for some time there must be something the matter with you ; is it domestic trouble?"

" Vat you means by domestic? Is it somedings about my vife? No, shentlemens, for dree year or more we has no drouble ; she vas dere und I vas here, und we has no drouble."

" An easy way to keep out of it," remarked Sanderson, "but what makes you unhappy?"

Blinn put on the most woe-begone expression ever seen in our regiment up to date, and replied, "Dis is von miscrabeel coundry ; dere's nodings left in dis valley— no pig, no shicken, nodings but empty pig-pens und hencoops. It vas time dis war vas over."

Herr appeared to be in actual suffering, and was quite as downcast as any man would be who had failed in business, and was reduced to starvation. In fact, the principal business of the fat man seemed to be that of obtaining supplies, on the sly, from the enemy's country, and now that nothing was left after the marching, counter-marching, and successive raids on the farm-houses, Blinn thought it was time to either whip or get whipped, and go home.

We knew, as the whole world knew, that the final throes of the long conflict were imminent, and soon there would be an end of battle, foraging, camp frolics, and dangers in which death might be lurking.

In December there were active operations in Tennessee. The beginning of General Sherman's march toward the seaboard was the signal for General Hood to march north with 35,000 men. It was rumored that he meant to strike a blow at Thomas, and capture Nashville. He met the Union cavalry, but continued to advance, not finding any serious obstacle until he reached Franklin. Here General Schofield made a halt, after retiring, as he had done, before Hood's troops, and quickly threw up entrenchments.

The axe, spade, and shovel, were among the best friends of our army, and their use, in which the boys had become experts, gained many battles, and freed many lives from jeopardy. Of course, if Hood could succeed in his expedition, there would be a grand Confederate success to counterbalance Sherman's bold march toward the sea, but the words of Sherman's last telegram came true. Schofield and Thomas were equal to their work.

There was a fierce engagement at Franklin. Defences of logs and earth had been thrown up by the Union troops, and behind these they awaited the onset. It came, and with fury. If valor could have given Hood a complete victory, it would have been gained. Four times he ordered his brave men to charge, and as many times they were repulsed, with terrible loss from our fire of artillery and musketry. With desperate courage they assailed the breastworks before them, until it became evident that their attempt was as hopeless as it was sanguinary. Their loss was five or six thousand men, and a number of intrepid officers, among them General Cleborne.

During the night Schofield obeyed his orders, which were peremptory, and fell back toward Nashville. Soon Hood appeared near the town, with the remnant of his shattered army, only to find their progress arrested by the strong fortifications surrounding the city.

It was thought by those who were looking on, and exhibiting a conspicuous ability in telling what ought to be done, that it was a serious breach of generalship for Thomas to delay in attacking his enemy, and beating him back. Even Grant so far shared this feeling that he was about to remove Thomas from command, but when all was ready, and a dense fog came down, which would lend secrecy to the movements of the army, Thomas ordered the attack, displayed fine generalship in the disposition of his men, made a strong demonstration on Hood's right, causing him to send re-enforcements to that point, and at this critical juncture Generals Smith and Wilson assaulted his weakest position, and literally swept the field.

The next day Thomas followed up his advantage, fought another battle, in which his colored troops displayed a bravery unsurpassed in the annals of the war, and the proud days of Hood's army were ended. He lost in this expedition 24,000 men, and retired in utter defeat.

GRANT'S HEADQUARTERS IN THE WILDERNESS.

The spirit of the North at this time was shown in the fact that on the first of December, the great Sanitary Fair, held in New York, closed its accounts, the net proceeds being $1,180,091.27. This was a voluntary contribution to the heroes who in camp, field, and hospital, were in need of supplies to add to their comfort, and relieve their sufferings.

Five days later, President Lincoln, elected for the second term, sent his annual message to Congress, asserting that the war must be pushed to its termination, and there could be no peace until the power of the Confederate government was broken, an event which was close at hand.

It only remains to sketch the operations of General Grant, and the surrender of Lee. It is not, nor has it been, my purpose to dwell upon those details of history which are so well known, and for the repetition of which there was no real occasion, but rather to depict the phases of army life as seen by one who fought and bled in the ranks. I do not wish a single line of this narrative, true to the facts and the real experiences of our army boys, to be construed as expressing any brutal exultation over a defeated and fallen foe. The Confederate soldiers fought with a valor never surpassed, and no man will pretend that our Union troops did not meet foemen who were worthy of their steel.

Grant so disposed his forces as to insure a successful advance all along the Union lines. Sheridan from Lynchburg, Virginia; Stoneman from East Tennessee; Canby from Mobile, with an army of 38,000; and other forces from Vicksburg and East Port, Mississippi, and Nashville, Tennessee.

Sheridan was the first to take the field. In the latter part of February, 1865, he set out from Winchester with 10,000 cavalry, in two divisions. Having pushed on to Waynesboro, he met General Early, his old foe, who by this time had good reason to dread the dashing Union commander, and gave battle at once. The result was a total rout of Early, with a large loss of prisoners and artillery. On to Charlottesville our enthusiastic troops went, destroying the railroad and bridges, and thence toward Lynchburg and Richmond, making havoc with the James River Canal, passing north of Richmond to join the army before Petersburg. The history of the war affords no record of any other cavalry expedition attended with equal success.

It was the intention of Lee to abandon both Richmond and Petersburg, escape with his army, and unite his forces with those of Johnston, who was retreating before the advance of Sherman, now moving northward after his celebrated march through Georgia.

Lee made a vigorous attack on Grant in order to cover his retreat, but the assault was met so bravely that General Gordon, detailed by Lee to capture one of the Union forts, lost the day and was forced to surrender with 2000 troops. General Meade at once sent into the engagement the Second and Sixth Corps, which seized and held a line of Confederate entrenchments. In the afternoon Lee made a determined effort to regain his lost ground, but was hurled back in each attempt, and suffered heavy loss. Grant's forces had decreed that Lee and Johnston should be weakened by being separated, and the brilliant tactics of the great Confederate commander should fail.

Grant despatched troops to cut off the enemy's attempted escape toward Danville, and this coming to the knowledge of Lee, he selected 17,000 of his best veterans to thwart the movement. He gained only a momentary success. Grant's forces assailed and carried the earthworks behind which Lee was entrenched, and drove him to Five Forks, by which was his only way of retreat.

This place had been strongly fortified by the Confederates, and here on the first day of April was fought one of the bloodiest battles of the war, resulting, under the skilled generalship of Sheridan, in the complete overthrow of the enemy. They fled in wild disorder, and were pursued six miles.

A vigorous bombardment along the Union lines during the following night prepared the way for a fierce assault at daybreak, and Meade on the right, and Sheridan on the left, pressed the enemy so hotly that in utter confusion they rushed westward along the Appomattox River.

This was on Sunday. That afternoon Jefferson Davis, while in church at Richmond, received a telegram announcing that Lee had been routed, that Petersburg was in the hands of Grant's army, and there was no alternative but to evacuate Richmond and leave the town to its fate. Davis was not slow to act, and under cover of night escaped, yet even then refused to believe that the Confederate cause was lost.

In Davis' house President Lincoln held a levee on the following day, and received the congratulations of many of the Union defenders. But the leading men of Richmond had fled, and General Ewell, with a madness born of defeat, had fired the town. The Twenty-fifth Corps of the Union army under General Weitzel entered, and immediately set to work to stop the wanton destruction of property.

In his flight Jefferson Davis halted at Danville long enough to issue a proclamation, declaring that Vir-

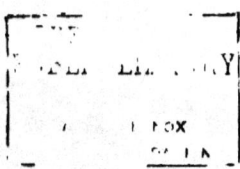

SURRENDER OF JOHNSTON TO SHERMAN.

ginia, with the help of the people, and by the blessing of Providence, should be held and defended, and no peace ever be made with the infamous invaders of her territory.

It was evident that Lee could not resist his foe, nor save his army, and when he was so completely surrounded and hemmed in that all hope was gone, Grant sent a demand for his surrender.

Several communications passed between the two opposing commanders, and at length Grant wrote, "The terms upon which peace can be had are well understood. By the South laying down their arms they will hasten that most desirable event, save thousands of human lives, and hundreds of millions of property not yet destroyed."

Lee was willing to meet Grant with the view of arranging for a general restoration of peace. This interview was politely declined. Peace could be had by surrender, and in no other way.

The same day, April 9th, Lee requested an interview with reference to Grant's first proposition.

A truce was established, the formalities were agreed upon, and the Confederate army was paroled, the men being permitted to return to their homes. Bells rang their jubilee, and millions of hearts beat with gratitude and joy. It is to the credit of the Union army that its veterans, although flushed with victory, abstained from any appearance of insult toward the vanquished.

Seventeen days afterward Johnston surrendered to Sherman, and his army of 27,500 men was disbanded.

Our boys, as may well be imagined, were not slow to accept the opportunity of returning to their homes. Long and painful separations were over.

But for all there was rejoicing among our gallant men ; they wept when the sad hour came for them to be parted. Together they had marched and fought, suffered and bled. The merry Sanderson brushed away a tear as I took him by the hand, and Vail was as speechless as I was when we parted. It was so with all who have been made familiar to the reader in this narrative, and their names need not be repeated.

Old comrades and heroes ! The years past have not effaced the memory of those days of heroism and companionship in our country's service, and years to come will only render more sacred the names spoken at rollcall, as one by one they are chiselled in marble, and hard by them a grateful people scatter memorial flowers, the emblems of the soldier's immortal honor !

I pay you tribute in these closing lines. Those last days were days of tragedy. We saw our martyred President, shot by the hands that sought to pull down the old flag, carried to his tomb. We saw the President of the Confederacy captured, and then magnanimously pardoned. And now, after the smoke has lifted from Fair Oaks, Malvern Hill, Antietam, Fredericksburg, Gettysburg, the Wilderness, and a hundred other battlefields, we see a restored Union and a saved nation offering that shelter and security which are born of a lasting peace.

Comrades ! The record of your splendid services, and the scars that many of us carry, are evidence that life has not been altogether a fruitless thing. If it has had its perils and agonies, it has also had its triumphs. Farewell !

— A —

COMPLETE CHRONOLOGY OF THE WAR

SHOWING THE NAMES AND DATES OF BATTLES AND SKIRMISHES,

THE NUMBER OF MEN ENGAGED, THE DIFFERENT

COMMANDERS, THE LOSSES ON BOTH

SIDES, AND THE RESULTS OF

THE ENGAGEMENTS.

Date.	Battles & Skirmishes.	No. of Men Engaged.		Commanders.	
		Union.	Confed.	Union.	Confederate.
1861.					
Apr. 12	Fort Sumter, S. C.	47	7,000	Maj. Anderson.	Gen Beauregard
" 18	Pennsylv's soldiers mobbed at Balt'e.	....	....	....	....
" 19	6th Mass. attacked at Baltimore.	...	....	....	....
June 1	Fairfax Ct. Hse. Va.	....		Lieut. Tompkins	....
" 3	Philippi, W. Va.	...	1,500	Col. Kelly	....
" 10	Big Bethel, Va.	2,500	2,200	Gen. Pierce	Gen. Magruder.
" 11	Romney, Mo.	......	....	Col. Wallace	J. E. Johnston.
" 17	Edwards'F'r, W Va	300	....		
" 17	Booneville, Mo.	....	....	Gen. Lyon	....
" 18	Cole Camp, Mo.	800	....	Captain Cook's Home Guards	Gov. Jackson...
July 2	Fall. Waters, W. Va.	....		Gen. Patterson	Col. Jackson....
" 3	Monroe, Mo.	600	1,600	Col. Smith	Gen. Harris....
" 5	Carthage, Mo.	1,500	10,000	Col. Sigel	Gov. Jackson....
" 11	Rich Mount., W. Va	....		Gen. Rosecrans.	Col. Pegram....
" 12	Barboursville, W. V	....	600	....	
" 13	Carrick's Fd, W. Va	....	....	Gen. Morris	Gen. Garnett...
" 17	Fulton, Mo.	600	1,000	....	Harris & McNeil
" 18	Near Harrisonville, Mo	170	500	Maj. Van Horn.	Capt. Duncan..
" 18	Blackburn's Ford	....	....	Col. Richardson	....
" 21	Bull Run, Va	18,000	30,000 to 40,000	Gen. McDowell	Gens Beaureg'rd & Johnston...
Aug. 2	Dug Springs, Mo.	...	....	Gen. Lyon	Gen. McCull'gh
" 5	Athens, Mo	500	1,200	Capt. Moore	Martin Greene.
" 10	Wilson's Creek, Mo	5,500	22,000	Gens. Lyon & Sigel	Gens. McCullough & Price
" 13	Grafton. W. Va.	55	200	Capt. Dayton	Cochran ......
" 20	Hawks Nest, W. Va.	11 Ohio	400	....	....
" 29	Forts Hatteras & Nav Sq Clark, N. C.	300	......	Com. Stringham & Gen. Butler.	Com. Barron & Col. Martin & Maj. Andrews

Union			Confederate			Notes
Killed	Wn'd	Pris. & Miss'g	Killed	Wn'd	Pris. & Miss'g	
......	......	......	......	5	......	Notwithstanding 2,200 shots and nearly 1,000 shells were fired, no lives were lost; or while saluting the flag before evacuating two of Anderson's men were killed and several wounded.
......	......	......	......	......	......	One colored man from Pottsville, Pa., struck on the head with a brick drawing the first blood from Union volunteers.
2	7	......	9	......	......	Several of the mob wounded.
2	8	......	55	......	6	
2	20	......	16	......	12	Kelly severely wounded.
15	30	......	18	......	......	Lieut. Grebble and Major Winthrop killed
......	1	......	2	......	......	
1	4	......	15 & W.	......	......	
......	......	......	......	......	......	
23	20	30	10	20	30	
2	10	......	3	27	......	
4	......	......	25	75	......	
12	30	......	500 W & M	......		
......	......	......	......	......	600	
......	......	......	15 & W.	......	......	Confederates defeated in both battles, losing 250 killed, 1,000 prisoners, 5 guns, several colors and 1,500 muskets.
20	60	......	......	......	......	
11 & W.	......	......	......	......	......	
......	......	......	14	......	......	Confederates repulsed.
150 & W.	......	......	......	......	......	Confederate loss very large.
480	1,011	1,000	600	2,000	......	Federals defeated.
9	30	......	40	81	......	
3	18	......	20	26	18	
223	721	......	265	800	31	McCullough's report, 265 killed, 900 wounded. Confederate loss, their own estimate, 421 killed, 1,817 wounded; Gen. Lyon killed.
......	......	......	21	......	......	Confederates repulsed.
......	9	......	50	......	......	
......	......	......	49	51	700	Federals captured 31 cannon, 1,000 muskets, regimental colors, etc.

Date.	Battles & Skirmishes.	No. of Men Engaged.		Commanders.	
		Union.	Confed.	Union.	Confederate.
1861.					
Sept. 1	Boone C. H., W. Va	......	500	Capt. Wheeler..	....
" 4	Shelbina, Mo......	660	3,500	....	M. E. Green...
" 10	CarnifexF'y,W. Va.	4,500	5,000	Gen.Rosecrans.	Gen. Floyd....
" 11	Lewinsville, Va...	....	....	Gen.W.F.Smith	J.E. B. Stuart...
" 12	Cheat Mt'n, W. Va.	....	9,000	Gen. Reynolds..	Gen. Lee......
" 13	Near Booneville Mo	150	600	Capt. Eppstein.	Col. Brown....
" 17	Blue Mills, Mo....	1,970	4,500	Scott..........	Gen. Atchinson,
" 17	Marratstown, Mo..	600	400	....	....
" 20	Lexington, Mo...	2,460	20,000	Col. Mulligan..	Gen. Price.....
" 21	Papinsville, Mo....	......	....	Gen. Lane.....	....
" 23	Mechanicsville Gap	875	700	....	....
" 23	Romney, W. Va...	875	1,400	....	....
" 25	Chapm'nsv'e, W.V	1,000	......	Col. Engart....	....
Oct. 3	Greenbrier, W. Va.	5,000	15,000	Gen. Reynolds..	Jackson........
" 4	Chicamacomico, NC	1,000	2,500	Col. Hawkins..	Col. Barlow....
" 6	Flem.W.Va,H.Gds	......	......	....	....
" 9	Santa Rosa Is. Fla.	365	1,500	Col. Wilson....	Gen. Anderson.
" 10	Near Hillsboro,Ky.	50	300	....	Cap. Holiday...
" 11	Big River Bdg,Mo.	50	600	....	J. Thompson...
" 15	Linn Creek Mo....	15	45	Lieut. Kirby....	....
" 19	Big Hur. Crk., Mo.	220	400	....	....
" 21	CampWild Cat,Ky..	4 Reg. & Art.	6,000	Col. Garrard....	Gen. Zollicoffer
" 21	Frederictown, Mo.	2,000	500	Col.Carlin, Ross and Baker....	Col. Lowe and Jeff Thompson..
" 21	Balls Bluff, Va....	1,900	4,000	Col. Baker......	Gen. Evans....
" 21	Saratoga, Ky......	......	100	....	....
" 25	Springfield, Mo...	150	2,000	Zagonyi........	Col. Pierce....
Nov. 7	Beaufort, S. C., & Forts, Walker & Beauregard......	15,000	....	Com. Dupont & 4 land officers	....
" 7	Belmont, Mo.	3,500	7,000	Gen. Grant & McClernand....	Gen. Polk and Cheatham......
Nov. 8	Rolla, Mo......	....	....	....	....
" 8	Piketown, Ky.....	....	....	Gen. Nelson....	Jno. S. Williams
" 9	Piketown, Ky....	....	....	Gen. Nelson....	Jno. S.Williams
" 10	Guyandotte, W. Va	....	....	....	....
" 11	Guyandotte, W. Va	....	....	Col. Zeigler....	....

Union			Confederate			Notes.
Killed.	Wn'd.	Pris. & Miss'g.	Killed.	Wn'd.	Pris. & Miss'g.	
......	6	......	35	......	5	Confederates routed.
......	......	......	......	......	......	Unionists defeated.
15	80	......	......	......	......	Federals successful.
6	7	......	......	......	......	
9	12	......	100	......	50	Withdrawal of Confederates.
40	75	......	25	3	......	Col. Brown killed. Confederates repulsed.
12	90	......	......	......	......	
2	6	......	7	......	......	
......	......	......	10	72	......	Surrender of Mulligan and about $100,000 worth of spoils.
17	39	......	......	......	......	Confederates routed.
3	10	......	35	......	......	Confederates retreated.
......	......	......	20	......	47	Confederates defeated.
4	8	......	200	K. W. & P.		Confederates routed.
8	30	50	......	......	......	Retreat of Union forces.
......	......	......	......	......	......	Confederates defeated.
15	30	......	160	K. W, & P.		Confederates repulsed.
2	3	......	......	......	......	Bridge destroyed, Union guards captured.
1	8	......	5	5	......	
......	......	......	5	13	......	
......	......	......	15	9	......	
5	20	......	about	1,000	men	Confederate lost tents and supplies.
6	41	......	190	......	......	Lowe killed.
223	266	455	over	300 K	W& P	Baker killed.
......	2	......	13	......	24	
18	26	19	80	55	27	A remarkable charge; although successful, more than one-half of Zagonyi's brave men were killed, wounded or missing.
8	25	......	......	......	......	Confederate loss heavy, with nearly all of their military supplies.
80	288	265	260	428	280	
8	20	......	400	K&W.	2,000	
4	20	......	10	15	40	
......	......	......	400	& W.	2,000	
250	......	......	......	......	......	
......	......	......	......	......	......	Confederates defeated and town destroyed in revenge for the massacre of the day before.

Date.	Battles & Skirmishes.	No. of Men Engaged.		Commanders.	
		Union.	Confed.	Union.	Confederate.
1861.					
" 17	Cyprus Bridge, Ky.	....	....	Col. Alcorn....	Hawkins.......
" 24	Lancaster, Mo.....	450	420	Col. Moore.....	Lt. Col. Blanton
" 29	B.Walnut Cr'k, Mo	......	......	Maj. R.M.Hugh	... .
Dec. 3	Salem, Mo............	......	300	Maj. Bowen....	Col. Freeman..
" 9	Freestone Point, Va	......	......	......	....
" 13	Cp.Al'gh'ney,W.V	750	2,000	Gen. Milroy....	Gen. Johnston..
" 15	Berlin, Md....	....	......	......	...
" 17	Mumfordsville, Ky	Part of 32 Ind.	several regim's	Col. Willich....	T. C. Hindman.
" 17	Osceola, Mo........	......	......	Gen. Pope....	
" 18	Milford, Mo......	......	......	Col. Davis.....	......
" 20	Drainsville, Va....	......	......	Gen E. O. C. Ord	Gen. Stuart.....
" 21	Hudson, Mo......	104	400	Maj. McKec....	......
" 28	Mount Zion, Mo...	450	900	Gen. Prentiss...	Col. Dorsey....
1862					
Jan. 1	Fort Pickens, S. C.	......	......	Gen. Stevens...	Gen. Bragg....
" 4	Huntersville, Va..	740	......	Gen. Milroy....	....
Jan. 7	Blue Gap, Va.....	......	2,000	Col. Dunning..	....
" 10	Prestonburg, Ky..	3,000	2,500	Col. Garfield...	Gen.H.Marshall
" 11	On River, Cairo, Il.	3 stmrs	4 boats	....	...
" 19	Mill Springs, Ky..	300	8,000	Gen. Thomas...	Gen. Zolicoffer..
Feb. 6	Fort Henry, Tenn.	7 Uni'n gunbts.	......	Com. Foote....	Gen. Tighlman.
" 8	Roanoke I'd., N. C.	100 v'ls 11,500	2,000	Goldsborough & Gen. Burnside	....
" 13	Blooming Gap, Va.	......	......	Gen. Grant & Com. Foote..	....
"15 16	Ft Donelson, Tenn	18,000	20,000		Gens.Floyd,Pillow & Buckn'r
" 21	Fort Craig, N. M..	1,500	2,000	Gen. Canby....	Col. Steele.....
" 26	Keitsville, Mo.....	100	800	....	...
Mar. 4	F'ts Clinch, Ferdi n'd & St.Mary,Fl	......	......	Com. Dupont..	....
" 6,7,8	Pear Ridge, Ark...	12,000 to 20,000	20,000 to 30,000	Gens. Curtis, Siegel & Davis	Van Dorn, Price & McCullou'h
" 8	Hampton Roads,Va	Fleet..	Fleet..	....	....
" 9	Hampton Roads,Va	Monitr	Mermc	Col. Worden...	Cap. Franklin & Buchanan....

Union			Confederate			Notes.
Killed.	Wn'd.	Pris. & Miss'g.	Killed.	Wn'd.	Pris. & Miss'g.	
11	14	......	......	......	25	Confederates routed.
2	2	......	13	......	......	
......	5	......	17 & W.	......	5	Maj. Hough one of the 5 wounded.
15 & W.	......	......	39 & W.	......	......	
......	......	......	......	......	......	Defeat of Confederates.
35 & W.	......	......	......	......	......	Confederate loss about 200.
......	1	2	2	0	.....	
10	17	......	60	......	......	Confederates routed.
......	......	......	......	......	350	
2	8	......	......	......	1,300	Complete victory for Union forces.
7	61	......	43	148	......	Victory for the Federals.
......	......	......	10	......	17	Stock train captured by Federals.
9	48	......	150 & W.	......	35	
2	8	......	......	......	......	Capture of the fort by Union forces.
......	......	......	......	......	......	Capture of $50,000 to $80,000 worth of army property by Federals.
......	......	......	15	......	20	Confederates routed.
3	25	......	6	......	25	Confederates routed.
......	......	......	......	......	......	Confederates retreat to their batteries, Columbus, Ky.
30	200	......	192	62	78	Confederates defeated.
few	37	......	0	10	130	On account of Grant's delay, caused by bad roads, Foote stormed and captured the fort.
33	212	.....	15	18	2,000	Capture of 6 forts, 35 to 40 guns, nearly 3,000 muskets, stores, etc.
2	......	.....	13	......	75	
445	2,776	150	231	1,000	......	Buckner captured and surrenders the fort, with guns, muskets, stores, etc. Floyd and Pillow, with part of Confederate force escaped. There were from 12,000 to 15,000 prisoners & missing.
62	162	......	......	......	......	Confederate loss not reported.
2	1	......	1	......	......	Confederates repulsed.
......	......	......	......	......	.....	Confederates defeated.
203	972	176	over 1,100	about 2,500	1500 to 1,600	Confederate loss heavy, including Gens. M'Cullough, Slack, M'Intosh.
22	62 & P..		0	......	......	Union fleet defeated with loss of Cumberland.
......	......	......	......	......	.....	Merrimac whipped and Buchanan wounded.

Date.	Battles & Skirmishes.	No. of Men Engaged.		Commanders.	
		Union.	Confed.	Union.	Confederate.
1862.					
Mar.	9 Burk's Station, Va..	14	150	Lieut. Hidden..	....
"	13 New Madrid, Mo..	......	......	Gen. Pope & Com. Foote..	Gens. McCrogan & Stuart.....
"	14 Newbern, N. C....	......	......	Gen. Burnside & Com. Goldsb'gh	Gen. Branch...
"	18 Salem, Mo.......	250	1,000	Col. Wood.....	Cols. Coleman & Woodside..
"	21 Indian Creek, Mo.	65	......	Capt. Stevens..	....
"	22 Independence, Mo.	......	......		
"	23 Winchester, Va...	8,000	13,200	Gen. Banks....	Gen. Garnet...
"	26 Warrensburg, Mo.	60	200	Maj. E. Foster.	Quantrill.......
"	26 Humansville, Mo..	350	500		
"	28 Pigeon Ranch, N.M.	30,000	1,100	Col. Hough....	Col. Scurry....
"	28 Apache Canon, N.M	1,300	2,000	Maj. Chevingt'n	....
"	28 Warrensburg. Mo..	......	......		
"	29 Middleburg, Va...	......	......	Geary	Stuart & White.
Apr.	6 Pittsburg Landing & Shiloh, Tenn....	70,000	60,000	Gens. Grant & Buell........	Gens Beaureg'rd & Johnston...
"	8 Island No. 10, Miss.	....	20,000	Gen. Pope & Com. Foote..	Gen. Wallace...
"	11 Fort Pulaski, Ga..	....	385	Gens. Gilmore & Hunter......	Gen. Olmstead..
"	11 Huntsville, Ala...	......	......	Gen. Mitchell...	....
"	11 Fort Macon, N. C.	....	150	......	....
"	12 Monterey, W. Va.	......	......	Gen. Milroy....	....
"	12 Chattanooga, Tenn	......	......	Gen. Mitchell..	....
"	16 Wilmington Is., Ga.	200	600		
"	18 Yorktown, Va....	118,000	53,000	Gen. McClellan.	J. E. Johnston.
"	19 Camden, N. C.....	2,000	1,100	Gen. Reno....	....
"	25 New Orleans, La..	......	......	Com. Farragut & Gen. Butler..	Gen. Lovell....
"	25 Fort Macon, Ga...	......	......	Gen. Park & Goldsborough	Col. White.....
May	3 Farmington, Miss.	....	4,500	Gen. Paine.....	....
"	5 Williamsburg, Va.	....	30.000	Gens. Hancock & Hooker....	Gens. Johnston & Longstreet.
"	5 Lebanon, Tenn....	......	......	Gen. Dumont..	Gen. Morgan...
"	6 Harrisonburg, Va.	....	200	Ira Harris' Cav.	Ashby's Caval'y
,,	7 West Point, Va....	30,000	larger	Gens. Franklin & Sedgwick..	Gen. Lee......

Union			Confederate			Notes.
Killed.	Wn'd.	Pris. & Miss'g.	Killed.	Wn'd.	Pris. & Miss'g.	
			3	5	11	Hidden killed.
			100	W. & M....		Stores and supplies captured to the value of $1,000,000 by Federals
91	466		50	198	200	Capture of forts, stores, cannon, muskets, etc., valued at $2,000,000, by Federals.
25	& W.		100	& W.		Col. Woodside killed.
					20	Three Confed. captains captured.
			7		11	
105	445	46	900	W. & P....		Confederates routed.
1	11		9	18		Maj. Foster wounded.
			15			Confederates repulsed.
						Union forces successful.
			151	200	95	Confederates defeated.
3			16		20	
						Confederates retreated.
1,735	7,882	3,956	1,728	8,012	959	Confederates defeated. Gen. A. S. Johnston killed.
			17		6,700	Island captured with cannon, 7,000 muskets, stores and war supplies.
1	3			5	380	Fort surrendered to Federals with over 100 cannon and mortars and general supplies.
					2,000	
	2			4		
	3				2,000	Confederates repulsed.
14	31					Confederates withdraw.
1,856	& W.	370	2,600	& W.		Evacuated by Confederates.
13	48		60	& W.		Confederates defeated.
36	120					Forts St. Philip and Jackson capitulated. Eleven gunboats, the ram Manassas and iron-clad Louisiana captured.
1	2		8	21	150	Union victory.
2	12		30			
300	700		420	800		Confederates saved their supplies.
10		26	66		183	
1		1	10		6	
294	& W.					Confederates defeated. Union loss about the same.

Date.	Battles & Skirmishes.	No. of Men Engaged.		Commanders.	
		Union.	Confed.	Union.	Confederate.
1862.					
May 8	McDowell, Va.....	....	....	Gen. Milroy....	Gen. Jackson...
" 9	Slater's Mills......	....	....		
" 9	Pensacola, Fla	3,000	....	Gen. Arnold...	Gen. Bragg....
" 9	Farmington, Tenn.	....	20,000	Gen. Paine	Gen. Bragg....
" 10	Norfolk, Va........	5,000	....	Gen. Wool......	....
" 10	Near Fort Wright on Mississippi riv	6 gunb.	8 gunb.	....	....
" 12	Natchez, Miss.....	....	....	Com. Farragut.	....
" 16	Front Royal, Va..	17	300	Geary	....
" 16	Trenton, N. C....	....	....	Maj. Fitzsim'ons	....
" 17	Chickahominy.....	....	....	Gen. McClellan.	....
" 19	Lacy, Ark........	150	600	Gen. Osterhouse	Col. Coleman...
" 18	Princeton, Va....	....	....	Gen. Cox......	H. Marshall....
" 19	Corinth, Miss....	....	....	Gen. M.L.Smith	....
" 23	Lewinsville, Va...	1,300	3,000	Col. Crook.....	Col. Heath....
" 23	Lewisburg, Va...	....	3,000	Col. Crook.....	Col. Heath.....
" 23	Front Royal, Va..	....	22,000	Col. Kenley...	Stonewl Jackson
" 24	Mechanicsville, Va.	....	....	....	....
" 24	New Bridge, Va...	....	....		
" 25	Winchester, Va....	4,000	25,000	Gen. Banks....	Gen. Jackson...
" 27	Hanover C. H. Va..	....	13,000	Fitz J. Porter..	Gen. Semmes...
" 30	Corinth, Miss.....	....	....	Halleck, Pope & W.T.Sherman	Gen. Beauregard
" 30	Front Royal, Va..	....	....	Col. Nelson....	....
" 31	Fair Oaks, Va.....	6,000	....	Gen. Casey.....	Gen. Longstreet
" 31	Fair Oaks, Va.....	....	....	Gens. McClellan & Sumner....	J. E. Johnston.
June 4	Murfreesboro, Ala.	70	....	Capt. Chilson..	Stearnes ....
" 5	Fort Pillow, Tenn.	10 g'bts	6,000	Com. Foote....	Gen. Villipigue.
" 6	Memphis, Tenn....	5 gunb. 9 rams.	8 war v	Col. Ellet......	Com Montgom'y
" 6	Harrisonburg, Va..	....	....	Col. Wyndham.	Gen. Ashby....
" 8	Cross Keys, Va....	....	5,000	Gen. Fremont..	Gen. Jackson...
" 9	Port Republic, Va..	....	....	Gen. Shields...	Stonewl Jackson
" 10	James' Island, S.C.	....	....	Gen. Benham..	Col. Lamar.....
" 16	Secessionville, S.C.	9,000	14,000	Gen. Stevens...	....
" 17	St. Charles, Ark..	....	....	Col. Fitch......	
" 22	Oak Grove, Va....	....	....	Gen. Hooker...	Gen. Lee.......
" 26	Mechanicsville, Va.	6,000	12,000	Gen. Stoneman.	Ewell & Jackson
" 27	Gaines' Mills, Va..	....	....	Gens Porter, Slocum, French, Meagher & Palmer	Jackson, Ewell, Longstreet & 2 Hills........
" 27	Cold Harbor, Va..	33,000	56,000	Gen. McClellan.	Gen. Lee.......

Union			Confederate			Notes.
Killed.	Wn'd.	Pris. & Miss'g.	Killed.	Wn'd.	Pris. & Miss'g.	
29	200	......	40	200	......	
3	14	3	14	......	......	
......	......	......	......	......	......	Evacuated by Confederates.
200	& W.	......	......	......	......	
......	......	......	......	......	......	Surrendered to Wool without a fight.
......	......	......	......	......	......	Confederates lose 2 boats.
......	......	......	......	......	......	Captured by Farragut.
1	3	13	......	......	......	
......	0	......	0	......	......	Fitzsimmons wounded.
......	......	......	......	......	......	Confederates driven across the river.
15	31	......	150	......	......	Confederates routed.
30	70	......	......	......	......	Union defeat.
12	31	......	30	large	......	
40	& W.	......	......	......	100	Confederates defeated.
14	50	......	73	......	125	
......	......	......	......	......	......	Union forces defeated with heavy loss.
10	& W.	......	50	......	50	
2	0	......	65	15	30	
......	......	......	......	......	......	Federals retreated.
53	326	& M..	110	500	500	Confederates routed, and loss of army supplies.
25	......	......	32	......	......	Over 2,000 prisoners captured by Pope, and large war supplies. Beauregard routed.
8	5	1	......	......	150	Re-captured by Federals.
......	......	......	......	......	......	Casey driven back.
891	3,629	1,222	2,800	3,897	1,325	Confederates completely routed.
6	......	64	......	......	......	
1	......	......	......	......	......	Fort evacuated by Confederates.
......	......	......	......	......	......	Memphis surrenders to Union forces
89	W&M	......	60	W&M	......	and 7 Confed. vessels destroyed.
130	500	......	500	......	......	Confederates carried off wounded.
124	292	515	unknown	......	......	Number said to be large.
85	192	128	150	W. & M.	......	Union forces defeated.
863	W&M	......	......	......	......	
......	......	......	200	& W.	......	Unionists destroyed the battery; 150 Union troops killed by a gunboat explosion.
200	......	......	......	......	......	Confederate loss much heavier.
300	K. W.	& M.	1,500	W. & M.	......	Confederates driven back.
......	......	......	......	......	......	Heavy loss of Union forces, 16 officers killed.
4,000	& W.	2,000	9,500	& W.	......	Lee's army successful.

Date.	Battles & Skirmishes.	No. of Men Engaged. Union.	Confed.	Commanders. Union.	Confederate.
1862.					
June 28	New Market, Va..				
" 29	Savage Station, Va.			Heintzleman....	McLaw & Magruder.......
" 29	Peach Orch'd, Va.			Meagher&Sedgwick........	
" 30	Luray, Va........			Gen. Crawford..	
" 30	Frazier's F'm, Va.			McCall, Hooker Kearney.....	Hill & Longstr't
July 1	Malvern Hill, Va..	90,000	60,000	McClellan......	Gen. Lee.......
" 1	Booneville, Mo....	728	4,700	Sheridan........	
" 6	St. Charles, Ark...	4,400	5,500	Col. Fitch.....	Gen. Hindman.
" 7	Bayou Cache, Ark.		6,000	Gen. Curtis	Gen. Steele....
" 8	Pleasant Hills, Mo.				Quantrill .....
" 9	Hamilton, N. C....				
July 11	New Hope, Ky....		450	Col. Moore....	Jno. Allen.....
" 13	Culpepper, Va....		100	Gen. Hatch....	
" 13	Murfreesboro, Tenn		4,000		Forrest........
" 15	Fayetteville, Ark..	600	1,600		Rains and Coffer
" 17	Newberg, N. C....				
" 19	Memphis, Tenn...				
" 25	Courtland, Ala....				Gen. Armstrong
" 28	Moore's Mills, Mo.	700	800	Col. Guitar.....	Porter and Cobb
" 29	Bol'nger's Mills, Mo	120	180	Maj. Lasear....	Maj. Tenley....
Aug. 2	Orange C. H., Va..		1,700	Gen. Crawford.	Gen. Robertson.
" 2	Ozark, Mo.......	9	125	Capt. Buck.....	Col. Lowther...
" 3	Memphis, Tenn...				Jeff. Thompson.
" 5	Baton Rouge, La..	2,500	5,000	Gen. Williams..	Gen Breckinridg
" 6	Kirksville, Mo.....	1,000	2,500	Col. Neills......	Porter.........
" 6	Tazewell, Tenn...	3,000	12,000	Col. DeCourcey	Stevenson ......
" 9	Cedar Mountain, Va	8,000	24,000	Gen. Banks	Gen. Jackson...
" 11	Kinderhook, Ky...	108	175	McGowan.......	
" 11	Independence, Mo.	250	600	Col. Buell.....	Gen. Hughes...
" 12	Gallatin, Tenn....	300	1,800	Col. Boone....	Morgan........
" 16	Warfield, Ky......	70	208	Capt. Smith....	Witchers ......
" 18	W. Oak Ridge, Mo.			Capt. Moore....	
" 19	Clarksville, Tenn..	200	600	Capt. Mason...	Johnson........
" 20	Edgefield Junc., T.	20	1,000		
" 21	Bowling Green, Ky		500	Capt. Goodwin.	Woodward.....
" 22	Richmond, Ky....	400		Col. L. Metcalf.	
" 25	Bloomfield, Mo....	130	300	Maj. Lippert...	Hicks.........
" 27	Haymarket, Va....			Gen. Hooker...	Gen. Ewell.....
" 28	Groveton & Gainsville, Va.......			Reynolds, Reno & Heintzelm'n	Stonewl Jackson
" 30	2nd Bull Run, Va..	35,000	46,000	Gen. Pope....	Lee & Longstre't
" 30	Richmond, Ky...	9,000	15,000	Gen. Manson...	Kirby Smith...
" 31	Bayou Sara, La....			Admiral Porter.	

Union			Confederate			Notes.
Killed.	Wn'd.	Pris. & Miss'g.	Killed.	Wn'd.	Pris. & Miss'g.	
400	2,029	.....	.....	.....	1,000	
700	....	......	400	.....	2,500	Union forces driven back.
150	& W.	......	1,500	W. & M	....	Confederates forced back.
1	3	......	4	.....	......	
300	1,500	325	1,700	.....	......	
375	1,800	....	900	3,500	.....	Estimated loss during the 7 days, Union, 1,582 killed, 7,709 wounded, 5,958 missing. Confederates, 3,150 killed, 15,255 wounded and 1,000 missing.
41	W. & M	...	65	.....	.....	
4	5	.....	24	30	40	
8	40	.....	110	.....	.....	
9	15	.....	6	5	.....	Unionists defeated.
.....	.....	.....	.....	.....	.....	Captured by Union army.
.....	.....	.....	.....	.....	.....	Confederates defeated.
.....	.....	.....	5	11	.....	
33	62	800	50	100	.....	Unionists defeated.
.....	.....	.....	.....	.....	.....	Confederates dispersed.
.....	.....	250	.....	.....	.....	Town captured by Confederates.
6	32	.....	.....	.....	.....	
3	157	.....	.....	.....	.....	Unionists defeated.
10	30	.....	52	100	.....	Confederates defeated.
.....	.....	.....	10	.....	.....	
3	5	.....	11	55	.....	Defeat of Confederates.
.....	.....	.....	3	7	25	
.....	.....	.....	.....	.....	.....	Confederate defeat.
56	175	& M.	600	W. & M	....	Confeds. defeated. Williams killed.
8	25	.....	128	.....	.....	Sixteen prisoners shot for violating oath of allegiance to United States.
3	15	57	250	& W.	.....	Confederates repulsed.
450	660	290	230	1,047	30	Confederates repulsed.
3	.....	.....	7	.....	27	
20	.....	230	.....	.....	.....	
.....	.....	.....	.....	.....	.....	Union forces captured.
2	4	.....	9	30	.....	
.....	2	.....	4	.....	19	
.....	.....	.....	.....	.....	.....	Union surrender.
.....	.....	.....	8	18	.....	
.....	7	.....	25	& W.	.....	
10	40	.....	25	& W.	.....	
.....	.....	.....	20	60	.....	Confederates routed.
.....	.....	.....	300	& W.	.....	Confederates vanquished.
8,000	W. & M	....	.....	.....	.....	Confed. defeat in both, loss 9,000.
800	4,000	9,000	700	3,000	.....	Confederate victory.
200	100	4,000	250	520	.....	
.....	.....	.....	.....	.....	.....	Place destroyed by Porter.

Date.	Battles & Skirmishes.	No. of Men Engaged.		Commanders.	
		Union.	Confed.	Union.	Confederate.
1862					
Sept. 1	Chantilly, Va......	...	......	Reno,McDowell	Hill, Longstreet
" 1	Midon, Tenn......	500	......	Col. Dennis....	....
" 1	Britton's Lane, Ten	......	......	Col. Dennis....	Gen. Villipique.
" 2	Plymouth, N. C...	300	1,400	Capt. Hammell.	Col. Garrett....
" 6	Washington, N. C.	500	1,200	....	....
" 7	Poolesville, Md....	......	......	Col. Farnsworth	....
" 9	Williamsburg, Va..	... ...	500	Col. Campbell..	Col. Shingles...
" 10	Cochrans, Mo.....	370	800	Col. Greerson..	....
" 14	S. Mountain, Md..	......	4,000	Hooker & Reno.	Longs't & Hill.
" 15	Harpr's Ferry, W.V	12,000	35,000	Gen. Miles.....	Gen. Jackson...
" 15	Mumfordsville, Ky.	2,500	6,000	Col. Wilder....	Gen. Duncan...
" 16-17	Antietam, Md....	85,000	65,000	McClel'n, Hooker, Sumner & Mansfield.....	Gens Lee and Jackson......
" 17	Mumfordsville, Ky.	4,500	25,000	Col. Wilder...	Gen. Chalmers.
" 19	Iuka, Miss......	12,000	16,000	Gen. Rosecrans.	Gen. S. Price...
" 20	Owensboro, Ky...	450	......	Lt. Col. Wood..	Col. Martin....
" 20	Shirley's Ford, Mo.	......	600	Col. Richie ...	....
" 27	Augusta, Ky......	120	500	....	....
" 30	Russellville, Ky...	......	......	....	....
" 30	Newtonia, Mo.....	600	7,000	....	....
Oct. 3	Blackwater riv, N.C	......	......	....	....
" 3-4	Corinth, Miss......	25,000	40,000	Gen. Rosecrans.	Gen. Vandorn..
" 7	Lavergne, Tenn...	2,600	4,000	Gen. Palmer....	....
" 8	Perryville, Ky.....	18,000	40,000	Col. McCook...	Bragg & Polk..
" 10	Chambersburg, Pa.	......	2,000	....	Gen. Stuart....
" 18	Lexington, Ky....	......	1,500	....	Morgan........
" 18	Frankfort, Ky....	2,500	......	Gen. Dumont..	....
" 19	Gallatin, Tenn....	......	......	....	Gen. Forrest...
" 20	Marshfield, Mo....	100	200	Col. Stuart.....	Col. Dersey....
" 21	Hallsboro, Ark....	......	......	Gen. Geary....	....
" 21	Lovettsville, Va...	......	......	Gen. Slocum...	....
" 22	Maysville, Ark...	10,000	7,000	Gen. Blunt.....	....
" 20-30	Florida River.....	......	......	Col. Beard.....	....
" 22	Pocotaligo, S. C....	4,450	......	Gen. Brannon..	Col. Walker....
" 23	Waverly, Tenn....	200	800	....	....
" 27	Putman's Ferry, Mo	......	1,500	Col. E. Lewis..	....
" 28	Clarkson, Mo.....	......	......	Capt. Rodgers..	Clarke........
" 28	Fayetteville, Ark..	1,000	3,000	Gen. Herron....	Col. Cravens...
Nov. 11	Lagrange, Tenn....	......	......	....	....
" 11	Garrettsburg, Ky..	......	800	Gen. Ransom...	Gen. Woodward
" 17	Kingston, N. C....	......	6,000	Gen. Foster....	Gen. Evans....
" 28	Cane Hill, Ark....	2,000	2,000	Gen. Blunt....	....
Dec. 2	Charlestown, Va...	......	......	Gen. Geary.....	....
" 7	Prairie Grove, Ark.	7,000	28,000	Gen. Heron....	Gen. Hurdman..
" 7	Hartsville, Tenn...	......	......	Col. Moore	Gen. Morgan...
" 13	Fredericksburg, Va.	32,000	25,000	Burnside, Sumner, & Hooker	Lee, Jackson & Longstreet...

Union.			Confederate.			Notes.
Killed.	Wn'd.	Pris. & Miss'g.	Killed.	Wn'd.	Pris. & Miss'g.	
1,000	W & M	......	1,000	W & M	......	Heavy loss on both sides. Gen. Kearney killed.
5	60	......	110	300	......	
5	50	......	110	260	......	
4	......	......	30	40	......	Confederates routed.
27	50	4	31	35	......	
2	7	......	7	8	6	
......	......	......	......	......	......	Unionists defeated
......	......	......	4	10	......	
443	1,806	76	500	2,030	1,500	Confederates defeated. Reno killed.
......	......	11,583	......	......	......	Union surrender. Miles killed.
8	27	......	500	& W.	4,500	
2,010	9,416	1,043	3,500	16,400	6,000	Death of Mansfield. Unionists hold the field.
500	700	4,500	500	700	......	Unionists defeated.
125	200	......	260	500	......	Confederates defeated.
......	......	......	38	20	......	Confederates routed.
......	......	......	80	......	......	Union forces defeated.
15	......	......	75	& W.	......	
......	......	......	50	& W.	16	Confederates defeated.
140	W. &	P.	......	......	......	
6	15	......	300	600	......	
315	1,812	232	2,000	7,850	4,300	Confederates repulsed.
5	10	4	......	80	175	Confederates defeated.
916	2,943	489	1,300	3,000	200	Confederates defeated.
......	......	......	......	......	......	Seized clothing and committed various depredations.
6	......	125	10	15	......	
......	......	......	......	......	......	Confederates routed.
......	......	......	......	......	......	Confederates defeated.
1	......	......	4	7	15	
1	3	......	......	......	40	
1	5	......	15	30	......	
......	......	......	......	......	......	Beard gets colored recruits.
15	106	2	20	60	......	Brannon defeated.
2	2	......	25	25	......	
......	......	......	10	40	......	
......	......	......	12	......	44	Clarke captured with supplies.
2	6	......	8	......	......	
......	12	......	16	......	134	
1	7	......	16	40	20	Confederates defeated.
200	& W.	......	......	......	400	Gen. Foster successful.
......	......	......	......	600	100	Confeds. routed, 4 steam's captured.
......	......	......	70	& W.	145	Confederates defeated.
495	500	......	2,000	& W.	......	Confederate defeat.
55	......	......	50	......	......	Federal cavalry surrenders.
1,182	9,028	2,146	580	3,870	130	Unionists defeated with great loss.

Date.	Battles & Skirmishes.	No. of Men Engaged.		Commanders.	
		Union.	Confed.	Union.	Confederate.
1862.					
Dec. 14	Baton Rouge, La..	......	......	Gen. Grover....	......
" 19	Holly Springs, Miss	......	......	......	Gen. Van Dorn.
" 21	Davis' Mills, Tenn.	250	......	Col. Morgan..	Gen. Van Dorn.
" 23	Dumfries, Va.	......	4,000	Gen. Sigel.	......
" 28	Elkford, Ky.	175	350	Maj. Foley.	......
" 29	Elizabethtown, Ky.	250	2,800	Lt. Col. Smith..	Morg. Guerillas.
" 29	Vicksburg, Miss...	......	65,000	Gen. Sherman..	Gen. Johnston..
" 30	Parker's C. R., Tn.	......	7,000	Gen. Dunham..	Gen. Forrest....
" 30	Stone River, Tenn.	43,400	62,490	Gens. Rosecrans and McCook.	Hardy & Polk..
1863					
Jan. 1	Galveston, Tex....	300	3,000	Col. Burrell....	Gen. Magruder.
" 1	Hunt's C. R., Tenn	6,000	......	Gen. Sullivan..	Forrest ....
" 3	Murfreesborough, T	43,000	62,400	Gen. Rosecrans.	Gen. Bragg....
" 7-8	Springfield, Mo....	600	5,000	Gen. Brown....	Marmaduke ....
" 11	Hartsville, Mo....	700	4,000	Maj. Collins....	Marmaduke....
" 11	Arkansas Post, Ark	......	......	Admiral Porter & McClern'd.	Gen. Churchili..
" 15	Bayou Teche, La..	......	......	......	......
" 20	Sabine City, Tex..	......	......	......	......
" 22	3d Siege of Vicksb'g	......	......	Gen McCl'rnand	......
" 30	Blackwater, Va....	......	......	Gen. Peck......	Gen. Pryor.....
" 27 to Feb. 1	Fort McAllister, Ga	3 g.bts.	......	Com. Worden..	......
" 2	Middletown, Tenn.	......	......	Stokes.	......
" 3	Ft. Donelson, Tenn	......	4,500	Col. Harding...	Gen. Wheeler..
" 15	Cainesville, Tenn..	250	500	Col. J. Monroe.	Morgan........
Mar. 1	Bradyville, Tenn..	2,300	800	Gen. Stanley...	......
" 5	Thompson's St., T.	6,000	30,000	Col. Coburn....	Gen. Van Dorn.
" 7	Unionville, Tenn..	......	......	Gen. Minty....	......
" 9	Fairfax, Va.......	......	......	Gen. Stoughton.	......
" 13	Port Hudson, La...	......	......	Com. Farragut.	......
" 17	Kelly's Ford, Va..	200	......	Gen. Averill....	Gen. Stuart.....
" 18	Milton, Tenn......	1,323	4,000	Col. Hall.......	Gen. Wheeler..
" 20	Jacksonville, Fla..	......	......	......	......
" 22	Steele's Bayou, Miss	......	4,000	Gen. Sherman..	......
" 22	Mt. Sterling, Ky...	200	......	......	Col. Clark.....
" 25	Brentwood, Tenn..	300	3,000	Green C. Smith.	Gen. Wheeler..
" 30	Somerset, Ky......	1,200	2,800	Gen. Carter....	Gen. Pegram...
Apr. 2	Woodbury, Tenn...	......	600	Gen. Hazen....	Col. Smith.....
" 3	Snow Hill, Ky....	......	......	Gen. Stanley...	Morgan........
" 7	Charleston, S. C...	9 w'r v	......	Com. Dupont...	......
" 9	Pascagonla, La....	180	300	Col. Daniels...	......
" 10	Franklin, Tenn....	......	15,000	Gen. Granger..	Gen. Van Dorn
" 13	Greenville, Miss...	......	......	......	......
" 17	Vermil. Bayou, La.	......	......	Gen. Grover....	......
" 17	Vicksburg, Miss...	......	......	Com. Porter....	......

Union			Confederate			Notes.
Killed.	Wn'd.	Pris. & Miss'g.	Killed.	Wn'd.	Pris. & Miss'g.	
						Evacuated by Confederates.
						Unionists captured.
			20	30		
						Confederates defeated.
			17		57	Confederates defeated.
600	1,500	1,000				Union army repulsed.
200	& W.		1,000	W. & P.		Confederates repulsed.
1,533	7,241	2,795	11,000	W. & M.		Confederates repulsed; heavy loss
160						Union defeat. Com. Renshaw killed.
200	W. & M.		400	300		
1,533	6,000					Confederates defeated with 9,000 killed and wounded.
17			300	W. & P.		Confederates repulsed.
30	10		150	W. & M.		
100	500		200	& W.	4,750	Confederate loss. Churchill killed.
						Confederates defeated.
						Federals defeated.
						Fruitless siege.
24	80					Confederates defeated.
						Efforts fruitless.
						Confederates evacuate.
15	60	51	130	390	150	
	4		20		8	
						Confederates routed.
100	300	1,200	175	450		Unionists defeated, surrendering the largest part of the command.
			50	78	60	Capture of Confederate supplies.
						Stoughton captured.
						Union fleet driven back.
55	& W.				80	Great heroism of boys in blue who repulsed the enemy.
18	30		40	145	12	Confederates defeated.
						City captured by Federals.
						Confederates repulsed.
						Federals repulsed
16	W. & M.				50	Town captured with supplies.
12	25		50	195	35	Confederates defeated.
			20		30	Confederates defeated.
			20		50	
1	10		2	5		Union attack unsuccessful with loss and damage to vessels.
			20	50		
100			300	& W.		Confederates repulsed.
						Confederates routed.
						Successful run past the town.

Date.	Battles & Skirmishes.	No. of Men Engaged. Union.	No. of Men Engaged. Confed.	Commanders. Union.	Commanders. Confederate.
1863.					
Apr. 18	Fayetteville, Ark..	2,000	3,000	Col. Harrison..	Gen. Cobell....
" 25	Greenl'd Gp., W. Va	75	1,500	Capt. Wallace..	Gen. Jones.....
" 26	Cape Girardeau, Mo..	....	8,000	Gen. McNeill..	Marmaduke....
" 29	Fairmount, W. Va.	330	5,000	Col. Mulligan..	Gen. Jones.....
May 1	Port Gibson, Miss..	..	......	Gen. Grant....	Gen. Brown....
" 1	Monticello, Ky....	5,000	......	Gen. Carter....	Pegram........
" 1	Boulinsburg, Miss.	....	11,000	Gen. Grant....	
" 1-5	Chancellorsville, Va	95,000	60,000	Gen. Hooker...	Gen. Lee.......
" 3	Fredericksburg, Va	......	......	Gen. Sedgwick..	......
" 10	Horse Shoe, Ky..	....	4,000	Col. Jacobs.....	Gen. Morgan...
" 12	Raymond, Miss....			Gen McPherson	Gregg & Walker
" 13	Linden, Tenn.. ...	55	110	Col Breckenr'dg	......
" 14	Jackson, Miss....	......	......	Gen. Grant.....	Gen. Johnson...
" 16	Champ'n Hills, Mis	......	......	Gen Grant.....	Gen. Pemberton
" 16	Baker's Creek, Miss	25,000	25,000	Gen. Grant....	Gen. Pemberton
" 17	Big Bl. Bridge, Miss	......	......	Gen. Grant....	Gen. Pemberton
" 22	Gum Swamp, N. C.	......	......	Col. J. R. Jones	
June 4	Slauria, Miss......	3,000	....	Col. Kimball...	Wirt Adams...
" 4	Florence, Ala....	......	......	Col. Cornyn....	......
" 5-7	Milliken's Bend, La	....	2,500	......	McCullough '...
" 11	Triune, Tenn.....	......	5,000	R. B. Mitchell..	Forrest ....
M'y27to June 14	Port Hudson, La..	......	......	......	......
" 14	Winchester, Va....	7,000	......	Milroy	......
" 17	Aldie, Va.........	cavl'ry	artil'ry	Col. Kilpatrick.	Fitzhugh Lee...
" 20	Lafourche, La.....	......	......	......	......
" 25	Hoover's Gap, Tenn	......	......	Willich	Claiborne ......
" 25	Vicksburg, Miss...	6,000	......	McPherson.....	......
" 27	Shelbyville, Tenn..	......	......	Gen. Stanley...	......
" 28	Donaldsonville, La	......	......	......	Gen. Greene....
" 28	McCon'ellsville, Pa	......	......	Pierce	Camboden .....
" 30	Hanover Junc., Pa	......	......	Gen. Pleasanton	Confed. cavalry
July 1	Carlisle, Pa......	......	......	Gen. Smith.....	
" 1-3	Gettysburg, Pa....	70,000	70,000	Gen. Meade....	Gen. Lee.......
" 4	Vicksburg, Miss..	......	......	Gen. Grant....	Gen. Pemberton
" 4	Helena, Ark......	9,000	10,000	Gen. Prentiss...	Gen. Holmes...
" 9	Port Hudson, La..	......	......	Gen. Banks....	Gen. Gardner...
" 13	Funkstown, Md...	......	......	Kilpatrick......	......
" 14	Fall. Waters, Va..	cavl'ry	......	Kilpatrick......	......
" 16	Jackson, Miss.....	......	......	Gen. Sherman..	Gen. Johnston..
" 17	Natches, Miss....	......	......	Gen. Ransom..	......
" 17	Elk Creek, Ark....	2,400	5,000	Gen. Blunt.....	Gen. Cooper....
" 18	Fort Wayne, S. C.	......	......	Gen. Gilmore...	......
" 20	Wytheville, Va....	......	......	Col. Powell....	......
" 23	Manassas Gap, Va.	800	600	Gen. Spinola...	......
Aug. 2	Culpepper, Va.....	cavl'ry	cavl'ry	Gen. Buford....	Stuart ....
" 17	Grenada, Miss.....	......	20,000	Col. Phillps...	Gen. Slemmer..
" 22	Ark. River........	4,500	11,000	Gen. Blunt.....	Gen. Cooper....
" 22	Pocahontas, Ark...	......	......	Col. Woodson..	Gen. Thompson
" 26	Brownsville, Ark...	......	30,000	Gen. Davidson.	Marmaduke....
" 27	Rocky Gap, W. Va	3,000	....	Gen. Averill....	Gen. Jones.....

Union			Confederate			Notes.
Killed.	Wn'd.	Pris. & Miss'g.	Killed.	Wn'd.	Pris. & Miss'g.	
5	17	......	......	......	......	Confederates defeated.
2	5	......	80	& W.	......	
25	& W.	......	49	200	......	
......	......	......	......	......	......	Unionists surrendered.
300	700	.....	410	740	......	Confederates repulsed.
......	......	......	66	W. & M.	....	
99	500	.....	1,000	& W.	500	Gen Tracy killed.
1,510	9,518	5,000	1,580	8,700	2,000	Hooker defeated.
......	......	......	......	......	800	Sedgwick successful.
42	......	......	90	......	......	
51	181	......	800	W. & M.	....	Union army successful.
......	......	......	43	& W.	......	
70	200	......	400	& W.	......	Johnson defeated.
426	1,840	189	2,520	& W.	1,795	Confederates defeated.
1,700	& W.	......	2,600	& W.	2,000	Confederates repulsed.
......	......	......	......	......	......	Pemberton defeated.
1	7	60	2	6	196	Col. Jones killed.
1	16	......	......	......	105	
2	3	......	......	......	95	Confederates routed.
108	202	......	121	......	......	
6	......	......	21	75	& P.	Confederate blockade runner sunk.
1,000	W. & M.	......	......	......	......	Unionists repulsed.
2,000	W. & M.	......	......	......	......	Federals defeated.
......	......	......	......	......	100	Confederates repulsed.
8	16	......	54	......	50	Confederates repulsed.
40	100	......	......	......	......	Confederates retreat in confusion
100	W. & M.	....	......	......	......	The fort held by Confederates.
6	40	......	......	......	760	Confederate fortifications captured
6	15	......	110	300	125	Confederates repulsed.
......	......	......	2	35	......	Confederates routed.
1	15	......	......	......	......	United States barracks fired.
2,834	13,710	6,643	3,490	14,520	13,600	Confederates totally defeated.
545	3,688	303	9,000	& W.	31,000	Gen. Grant's victory.
250	& W.	......	450	1,000	1,200	Confederates defeated.
500	2,500	......	100	700	6,408	Union victory.
50	& W.	......	100	& W.	50	
29	36	......	130	& W.	1,300	Confederates defeated.
100	800	100	72	500	764	
......	......	......	......	......	......	Confederates defeated.
10	25	......	60	30	100	Confederates defeated.
......	......	......	......	......	......	Unionists defeated.
65	& W.	......	75	......	120	Defeat of Confederates.
30	100	157	2,500	W. & M.	....	Confederates routed.
......	......	......	......	......	100	
......	......	......	......	......	......	Confederates routed.
......	......	......	......	......	......	Confederates retreated.
......	......	......	......	......	......	Thompson and 100 men captured
......	......	......	......	......	......	Confederates repulsed.
100	& W.	......	......	......	......	

Date.	Battles & Skirmishes.	No. of Men Engaged.		Commanders.	
		Union.	Confed.	Union.	Confederate.
1863.					
Aug. 29	Bayou Metoe, Ark.	8,000	7,000	Gen. Davidson.	....
Sept. 1	Ft. Moultrie, S. C.	Fleet..	......	Capt. Badger...	....
" 2	Morris Island, S. C.	......	......	Gen. Gilmore...	Gen Beauregard
" 3	Knoxville, Tenn...	......	......	Gen. Burnside..	Gen. Buckner..
" 9	Cumberland G., Tn	......	......	Gen. Burnside..	Gen. Frazier...
" 9	Tilford, Tenn.....	300	1,800	Col. Hays......	Jackson........
" 19	Chicamauga	55,000	50,000	Gen Roscerans..	Gen. Bragg.....
Oct. 8	Shelbyville, Tenn .	......	......	Roscerans......	Gen. Wheeler..
" 10	Madison, Va.......	Cav...	Cav...	Kilpatrick......	Stuart ....
" 10	Blue Spring, Ky...	......	......	Burnside	....
" 10	Farmington, Tenn.	......	......	Gen. Cook......	Gen. Wheeler..
" 11	Merrils' Cros., Mo.	1,600	2,000	Gen. E. Brown.	Gen. Shelby....
" 14	Bristoe, Va.......	......	......	Gen. Warren...	Gen. Hill.......
" 18	Charlestown, Va...	......	......	......	Imboden.......
" 20	Gainesville, Va...	......	......	Kilpatrick......	Gen. Stuart.....
" 25	Pine Bluff, Ark....	725	4,000	Col. Clayton....	Marmaduke....
" 28	Wauhatchie, Tenn.	......	......	Gen. Hooker....	....
Nov. 1	Louden, Tenn......	......	......	......	....
" 3	N. Lawrence, Tenn	124	395	Maj Fitzgibbons	....
" 3	Colliersville, Tenn.	......	......	......	Chalmers ......
" 3	Bay. Cokay, La.....	......	......	Burbridge.... ...	Walker ....
" 6	Droop Mount., Va.	......	4,000	Gen. Averill....	Jenkins ....
" 7	Kelly's Ford, Va..	......	......	Sedgwick	....
" 16	Campbell's, Tenn..	......	......	Gen. Burnside..	Gen. Longstreet
" 23-25	Chattanooga, Tenn	80,000	50,000	Gen. Grant.....	Gen. Bragg.....
" 62	Mine Run, Va. ...	......	......	Gen. Meade...	Gen. Lee......
" 28	Louisville, Tenn...	225	300	Maj. Beers.....	....
" 29	Fort Sanders, Tenn	......	......	......	Gen. Longstreet
Dec. 4	Wolf River, Miss..	......	4,000	Col. Hatch.....	....
" 14	Bean's Station, Tn	......	......	Gen Shackelford	Longstreet .....
" 28	Charlestown, Tenn	......	......	Laibold	Gen. Wheeler..
" 29	Mossy Creek.....	......	......	Gen. Sturgis....	Longstreet......
1864					
Jan. 3	Jonesville	300	4,000	Maj. Baens.....	Gen. S. Jones...
" 16	Dandridge........	......	......	Gen. Sturgis....	Hood, Johnston.
" 28	Fair Gardens, Tenn	......	... ...	Gen. Sturgis....	Gen. Longstreet
" 28	Scottsville, Ky....	150	500	....	Col. Hamilton..
Feb. 20	Olustee, Fla.......	4,900	10,000	Gen. Seymour..	Gen. Finnegan..
" 22	Dramesville, Va...	180	......	......	Moseby........
" 25-28	Tunnel Hill. Ga...	......	......	Gen. Palmer....	Gen. Wheeler..
Mar. 14	Fort DeRussey, La	......	......	Gen. Moore.....	Gen. D. Taylor.
" 24	Union City, Ky....	490	1,000	Col. Hawkins...	Forrest ....
" 25	Paducah, Ky......	655	6,000	Col. S. G. Hicks	Forrest ....
" 30	Mount Elba, Ark..	......	......	Col. Clayton....	Gen. Dickens...
May 5-7	Wilderness, Va....	......	......	Grant & Meade.	Gen. Lee......
Apr. 8	Sabine, La.........	......	18,000	Banks.........	Kirby Smith....
" 9	Pleasant Hills, La.	......	30,000	Banks & Smith.	Greene........
" 12	Fort Pillow, Tenn.	......	6,000	Maj. Booth.....	Forrest ....

Union			Confederate			Notes
Killed.	Wn'd.	Pris. & Miss'g.	Killed.	Wn'd.	Pris. & Miss'g.	
39	& W.	......	100	& W.	3,008	Confederates fled.
						Badger mortally wounded.
						Confederates evacuated.
						Occupied by Burnside.
					2,000	Captured by Union forces.
						Surrender of Union forces.
1,644	9,262	4,945	2,390	13,400	2,000	Withdrawal of Union army.
						Confederates defeated.
						Kilpatrick driven back.
100	& W.					Confederates defeated.
					240	Confederates defeated.
30	& W.		55	73	......	Confederates defeated.
200	& W.		500	& W.	450	Warren successful.
		434				Entire Union force captured.
190	W. & M.					Confederates defeated.
12	55		295	& W.	......	Brave repulse of Confederates.
76	339	22	305	1,200	100	Hooker successful.
475	W. & M.		705	W. & M.		Confederates routed.
			7	8	24	Confederates defeated.
			198	& W.	50	Confederates repulsed.
708	& W.		1,790	W. & M.		Union forces retreat.
102	& W.		305	& W.	100	Confederates defeated.
365	& W.				1,900	Defeat of Confederates.
350	& W.		1,000	& W.	......	
757	4,520	330	362	2,185	6,142	Confederates defeated. Missionary Ridge captured.
100	320	......	no report	...	......	Confederates defeated.
			21	10	21	
28	& W.		700	W. & P.	...	Confederate assault unsuccessful.
						Confederates defeated.
650	& W.		900	& W.	......	Union forces defeated.
	13				125	Confederates defeated.
100	W. & M.					Confederates defeated.
30	30	240				The brave Illinois troops fight eight hours before taken.
150	& W.					Unionists defeated
			65	......	110	Confederates routed.
						Unionists repulsed. Town captured.
195	1,170	450	950	W. & M.		Unionists repulsed.
16	...	70	1	4	......	Unionists defeated.
75	& W.				300	
46	& W.				320	
						Hawkins surrendered.
13	45		300	1,090	......	Confederates repulsed.
15	W. & M.		100	& W.	......	Confederates repulsed.
3,290	9,270	6,790	2,000	6,025	3,450	
195	900	1,800	300	1,205	......	
100	680	308	300	1,200	500	Confederates repulsed.
						Wholesale slaughter of Unionists after their surrender.

Date.	Battles & Skirmishes.	No. of Men Engaged. Union.	Confed.	Commanders. Union.	Confederate.
1864.					
Apr. 17	Plymouth, N. C...	......	15,000	Gen. Wessels...	Gen. R. F. Hoke
May 10	Cloyd Mount., W.V	... .	......	Gen. Crook.....	Jenkins ....
" 12	Fort Darling, Va..	... .	......	Gen. Butler....	Beauregard ....
" 15	New Market, Va..	... .	......	Gen. Sigel......	Breckenridge...
" 8-21	Spottsylvania, Ct.				
	House, Va......	... .	......	Gen. Grant.....	Lee ....
"13-16	Resaca, Ga........	......	......	Hooker........	
" 24	Wilson's Wharf,Va	......	2,000	Gen. Wild......	Fitzhugh Lee..
" 25	Dallas, Ga........	......	......	Gen. Sherman..	Gen. Johnston..
" 27	North Anna, Va...				
" 28	Hawe's Shop, Va..			Gen. Sheridan..	
" 30	Bethesda Ch., Va..	......	......	Gen. Warren...	Ewell.........
" 31 to					
June 12	Cold Harbor, Va...	125,000	50,000	Gen. Grant.....	Gen. Lee ......
" 5	Piedmont, Va.....	......	......	Gen. Hunter....	Gen. Jones.....
" 10	Guntown, Miss...	......	......	Gen. Sturgis....	Kirby Smith....
" 11	Cynthiana, Ky....	......	......	Gen. Burbridge.	John Morgan...
" 14	Pine Mountain, Ga.	......	......	Gen. Sherman..	
" 15	Petersburg, Va....	100,000	70,000	Gen. Grant.....	Gen. Lee ......
" 19	English Channel...	Kear'g	Alab'a	Capt. Winslow.	Capt. Semmes..
" 24	Lafayette, Tenn...	400	300	Col. Watkins...	Gen. Pillow....
" 25	Weldon R. R., Va.	......	......	Gen. Meade....	Gen. Lee ......
"10-27	Kenesaw Mt., Ga..	......	......	Gen. Sherman..	Johnson ......
July 9	Monocacy, Md	......	14,800	Gen. Wallace...	Gen. Early.....
" 12	Fort Stevens, D. C.	... .	......	Gen. Augur....	Gen. Early.....
" 18	Island Ford, Va...	......	......	Gen. Wright....	Gen. Early.....
" 20	Peach Tree Crk.,Ga	......	......	Gen. Sherman..	Johnston.......
" 20	Winchester, Va....	......	......	Gen. Averill....	Gen. Early......
" 22	Decatur, Ga......	......	......		
" 22	Atlanta, Ga.......	......	......	Gen. Sherman..	Gen. Hood.....
" 24	Winchester, Va...	......	......	Gen. Averill....	Gen. Early.....
" 26	Big Creek, Ark...	280	1,500	Col. Brooks....	
Aug. 4	New Creek, Va...	......	......	Brad. Johnson..	Col. Stevenson.
" 7	Moorefield, W. Va.	... .	......	Gen. Averill ...	McCausland....
" 16	Front Royal, Va...	......	......	Gen. Merrit....	Kershaw.......
" 16	Dalton, Ga........	600	5,000	Col. Siebold....	Wheeler ....
" 18	Deep Bottom, Va..	......	......		
" 22	Weldon R. R., Va.	......	......	Gen. Warren....	
" 23	Fort Morgan, Ala..	......	......	Admr. Farragut	R. L. Page.....
" 25	Reams' Station, Va	......	......	Gen. Warren...	Gen. Early.....
" 31 to					
Sept. 1	Jonesboro, Ga.....	......	......	Howard........	Hardee & Lee..
" 2	Atlanta, Ga.......	......	......	Slocum	Gen. Hood.....
" 4	Berryville, Va.....	... .	......	Crook	Gen. Early.....
" 4	Greenville, Tenn..	... .	......	A. C. Gillem ...	Gen. Morgan...
" 7	Readyville, Tenn..	230	2,000	Col. Jordan....	Dibrells........
" 19	Opequon, Va......	......	......	Gen. Sheridan..	Gen. Early.....
" 22	Fisher's Hill, Va..	......	......	Gen. Sheridan..	Gen. Early.....
" 26	Pilot Knob, Mo....	......	10,000	Gen. Ewing....	Gen. Price.....
" 30	N. Market Hghts,V	......	......		
Oct. 2	Saltville, Va......	2,500	......	Gen. Burbridge.	Breckenridge...

Union			Confederate			Notes.
Killed.	Wn'd.	Pris. & Miss'g.	Killed.	Wn'd.	Pris. & Miss'g.	
100	& W.	1,600	1,700	W. & M....		Unionists defeated.
500	W. & M....		900	W. & M....		Confederates defeated.
420	2,395	200	400	2,010	100	Federals defeated.
120	560	240	85		320	Unionists defeated.
2,140	7,960	2,577	1,000	5,000	3.000	
600	2,147		300	1,500	1,000	
2	40		250	& W.		Confederates defeated.
						Confederates repulsed.
220	1,400	300	2,050	W. & M....		
48	304	15	600	W. & M....		Confederates driven back.
			60	300	81	Confederates routed.
1,905	10,575	2,450		1,200	525	
					1,500	Union victory. Jones killed.
2,200	W. & M....		410	& W.		Sturgis rem'd for disobeying orders.
200	& W.	1,200	300	275	400	Federals defeated. Town burnt.
						Confederates defeated.
1,200	7,470	1,800				Confederate loss 9,000.
						Alabama sunk.
100	W. & M....		100	& W.		
603	2,400	2,200				
1,300	6,400	758	4,650	W. & M....		Johnson flanked.
125	200	400	300	450		Unionists defeated.
50	325		100	200	200	Confederate retreat.
320	W. & M....		500	W. & M....		
295	1,400		5,000	W. & M....		
			300	205		Confederates defeated.
1,520	W. & M....		700	4,000	M....	
495	2,150	1,000	2,480	4,000	2,000	Gen. McPherson killed.
995	W. & P....					Unionists defeated.
50	& W.		50	100		Col. Brooks killed.
20	50					Confederates retreated.
7	50		100	& W.	425	Confederates routed.
31	& W.		40	300		
						Confederates repulsed.
400	1,750		2,000	W. & M....		
3,000	W. & M....		600		1,100	
					600	Confederate commander captured.
3,000	W. & M....		1,500	W. & M....		
			400	2,000		Confederates defeated.
						Atlanta surrendered.
100	& W.		500	& W.	60	Confederates repulsed.
			50	80		Confederates rep'd. Morgan killed.
11	W. & M....				130	
4,000	W. & M....		4,000	& W.	4,200	Confederates defeated.
650	& W.		450		1,100	Confederates defeated.
9	60		1,000	& W.		Confederates repulsed.
390	2,035		1,995	W. & M....		
325	W. & M....				150	

Date.	Battles & Skirmishes.	No. of Men Engaged.		Commanders.	
		Union.	Confed.	Union.	Confederate.
1864.					
Oct. 5	Altoona, Ga.......	1,700	7,000	Gen. Corse.....	Gen. French ...
" 7	Darbytown Rd., Va			Gen. Kautz....	....
" 19	Cedar Creek, Va...			Gen. Sheridan..	Gen. Early.....
" 23	Big Blue, Mo.....			....	Gen. Price.....
" 27	Hatcher's Run, Va......			......	
" 28	Norristown, Tenn..			Gen. Gillem ...	Gen. Vaughn..
" 29	Newtonia, Mo....			Ford & Jennison	Gen. Price.....
Nov. 14	Morristown, Tenn.			Gen. Gillem....	Breckinridge...
" 24	Columbia, Tenn...			Thomas.........	Hood ....
" 30	Franklin, Tenn...			Schofield	Hood ....
Dec. 4	Overall's Crk., Ten			Milroy	Bates..........
" 7	Wilkinson, Tenn..			....	Forrest........
" 16	Nashville, Tenn..			Gen. Thomas...	Gen. Hood.....
" 21	New Market, Va...			Gen. Custer....	Payne.........
" 21	Savannah, Ga....			Gen. Sherman..	Gen. Hardee...
1865					
Jan. 15	Fort Fisher. N. C.	9,000	2,300	Terry & Porter.	Col. Lamb.....
Feb. 6-7	Hatcher's Run, Va			Grant..........	Lee...........
" 18	Charleston, S. C...			Gen. Gilmore ..	....
Mar. 2	Waynesboro, Va..			Gen. Sheridan..	Gen. Early....
" 8	Jackson's M'ls, N.C			Gen. J. D. Cox.	Hill...........
" 9	Wise's Ford, N. C.			Gen. Cox	Koke..........
" 16	Averysboro, N. C.	20,000		Gen. Sherman..	Hardee ....
" 21	Bentonville, N. C.. 1 corps	40,000		Gen. Sherman..	Gen. Johnston.
" 25	Fort Fisher, Va,...			Gen. Wright....	....
" 25	Fort Steadman, Va.			Genl's Parke & Hartranft.....	Lee...........
" 25	Hatcher's Run, Va.			Miles & Hayes..	....
" 29	Quaker Road, Va..			Gen. Warren...	....
" 31	Boydtown Road, Va			Sheridan.......	....
Apr. 1	Five Forks, Va			Sheridan and Warren......	Lee...........
" 1	Ebenezer Ch., Ala.		5,000	Wilson	Gen. Forrest & Chalmers ....
" 2	Selma, Ala........		7,000	Wilson	Forrest ....
" 3	Petersburg, Va....			Grant & Meade.	Lee...........
" 3	Richmond, Va			Grant & Weitzel	Lee...........
" 6	Sailor's Creek, Va.			Sheridan	Lee...........
" 8	Spanish Fork, Ala.			Smith & Bertam	....
" 9	Gen Lee surrenders			....	....
" 11	Forts Huger and Tracy, Ala.....			....	....
" 12	Salisbury, N. C....			Gen. Stoneman.	....
" 12	Montgomery, Ala..			Wilson	....

Union.			Confederate.			Notes.
Killed.	Wn'd.	Pris. & Miss'g.	Killed.	Wn'd.	Pris. & Miss'g.	
600	W. & P....		300	1,050	P....	Confederates repulsed.
320	W. & M....		1,000	& W.	200	Confederates defeated.
590	3,515	1,892	2,950	& W.	1,260	Union victory with heavy loss.
......	......	......	......	......	1,500	Confederates routed.
150	1,050	699	201	600	205	
......	......	......	......	......	500	Confederates defeated.
121	W. & M....		200	W. & M....		
......	......	......	......	......		Unionists defeated.
45	& W.		260	W. & M....		
189	1,033	1,104	1,750	3,800	702	Confederates repulsed.
100	W. & M....		......	......		
30	175	......	......	......	207	Confederates routed.
......	......	......	2,000	& W.	4,500	Confederates routed.
2	25	36	15	20	30	
400	& W.	......	600	& W.	800	Savannah captured by Sherman.
1,200	......	......	420	& W.	400	Unionists repulsed.
175	1,236	......	5,000	& W.	1,883	
......						Union flag again waves at Sumter, 400 pieces of artillery, ammunition, etc., captured by Union troops.
40	W. & M....		......	......	1,785	Capture of Early's whole force.
......	......	450	......	......	200	Cox held his position.
......	......	......	300	& W.	200	Confederates repulsed.
78	480	......	110	......	......	Confederates retreated.
190	1,170	280	269	1,200	1,625	Johnston driven back.
47	400	30	400	& W.	470	
70	332	500	1,800	& W.	890	
50	462	177	2,900	W. & M....		
300	W. & P....		300	& W.	100	
177	1,130	555	......	......	380	Unionists repulsed.
125	710	50	3,000	& W.	5,550	Gen. Winthrop, Union, killed. Jeff. Davis left Richmond by night.
30	& W.	......	35	& W.	300	
324	W. & M....		300	W. & M....		Confederates defeated.
300	2,560	500	......	......	3,000	Petersburg taken by Unionists.
......	......	......	......	......	......	Weitzel with his colored troops entered the city first, capturing 6,000 prisoners.
165	1,000	......	1,000	& W.	6,000	Sheridan's victory.
......	......	......	......	......	5,406	Captured by Union forces.
......	......	......	......	......	26,115	Officers and men paroled,
......	......	......	......	......	......	Evacuated.
......	......	......	......	......	1,160	Confederates defeated.
......	......	......	......	......	......	Surrendered.

Date.	Battles & Skirmishes.	No. of Men Engaged.		Commanders.	
		Union.	Confed.	Union.	Confederate.
1865.					
Apr. 13	Raleigh, N. C.....	....	....	Kilpatrick.....	....
" 14	Mobile, Ala.......	... ...	....	Grang'r, Thatc'r	....
" 14	Assassination of President		Lincoln.		
" 16	Columbus, Ga.....	....	....	Gen. Upton....	....
" 17	Berryville, Va.....	....	....	....	....
" 26	Gen. J. E. Johnston surrenders	27,500	men to Gen.	Sherman.	
" 27	Gen. Stoneman ordered to suspend all Union hostilities				
May 4	Gen. Taylor surrenders all forces west of the Mississippi River.				
" 10	Gen. Sam Jones surrenders	8,000	men to Gen. Mc	Cook.	
" 10	Capture of Jeff Davis, Irwinsville, Ga., by Col.			D. B. Pritchard,	
" 10	Boco Chico, Texas.	....	....	Col. Barret......	Gen. Slaughter.
" 26	Surrender of Kirby Smith and army of 20,000.				
" 31	Surrender of Gen. Hood and Staff.				

Union			Confederate			Notes.
Killed.	Wn'd.	Pris. & Miss'g.	Killed.	Wn'd.	Pris. & Miss'g.	
......	......	......	......	......	......	Surrenders to Kilpatrick.
......	......	......	......	......	......	Surrender of Confederates.
......	......	......	......	......	2,000	Confeds. defeated. Columbus taken.
......	......	.....	......	......	......	Moseby surrenders.
4th Michigan cav.						
......	......		......	......	......	Last engagement of the war.

STATES, ETC.	Officers killed.	Enlisted men killed	Officers died of wounds.	Men died of wounds.	Officers died of disease.	Men died of disease.	Officers deserted.	Men deserted.	Officers honorably disch'd.
Maine...........	116	1,620	66	1,069	65	5,479	1	2,840	378
N. Hampshire...	91	1,006	33	531	49	2,481	1	3,705	188
Vermont........	68	1,133	39	662	34	2,964	1	1,689	312
Massachusetts...	274	3,624	104	2,027	80	7,824	3	8,415	1,149
Rhode Island....	30	446	.....	.....	21	1,052	...	1,674	47
Connecticut.....	97	1,094	48	663	63	3,246	2	6,281	385
New York.......	427	8,605	302	5,021	222	17,185	50	35,999	2,530
New Jersey.....	106	1,231	40	317	33	2,933	6	7,183	191
Pennsylvania ...	376	6,096	137	3,675	117	10,973	15	19,032	1,500
Delaware.......	9	178	10	113	7	207	...	958	35
Maryland.......	16	359	17	326	30	824	...	2,981	83
West Virginia...	58	741	23	301	20	1,792	2	1,269	292
District of Col'a.	3	43	1	8	.....	244	...	701	3
Ohio...........	280	6,283	140	4,531	159	13,195	6	13,603	624
Indiana........	294	3,140	139	2,244	220	13,172	5	7,232	443
Illinois.........	394	5,563	126	2,925	364	19,570	12	13,034	771
Michigan	154	2,554	68	1,151	78	8,421	6	6,136	595
Wisconsin.......	121	2,297	67	1,393	101	6,885	3	3,230	424
Minnesota.......	29	381	7	191	26	1,650	...	493	146
Iowa...........	146	1,926	69	1,303	127	8,515	4	1,474	65
Missouri........	89	1,461	48	767	130	7,216	15	6,983	340
Kentucky.......	82	1,103	30	669	124	5,121	24	6,541	91
Kansas.........	34	762	12	192	26	2,080	2	1,988	88
California.......	1	34	.....	57	1	298	1	758	10
Tennessee......	27	1,264	11	920	11	2,182	5	2,658	31
Mississippi.....	.....	.....	.....	.....	.....	60	...	124	.....
Alabama.......	2	32	...	31	2	228	...	200	2
Florida.........	.....	27	.....	142	.....	102	...	173	4
Texas..........	.....	22	.....	11	....	278	...	546	7
North Carolina..	.....	34	1	19	1	248	1	299	.....
Louisiana.......	2	117	2	101	1	768	...	1,240	14
Arkansas.......	8	210	3	163	1	544	7	549	7
Nevada.........	.....	8	.....	2	.....	225	1	701	1
Oregon.........	.....	58	2	7	2	665	5	856	5
Colorado	2	61	1	44	2	205	1	237	8
Indian Territory.	2	231	.....	141	.....	416	...	247	.....
Washington Ter.	....	14	4	11	.....	107	...	397	4
Dakota Territory.	.....	.....	.....	.....	.....	10	...	12	1
Nebraska Ter. ...	1	5	.....	8	1	122	1	173	2
New Mexico Ter.	.....	7	1	15	1	159	...	332	3
Penitent Rebels.	.....	9	.....	5	....	352	...	605	5
Hancock's Corps.	.....	7	.....	2	....	406	1	2,348	1
Miss. Marine B'e.	3	136	2	107	4	181	1	219	4
Veteran Reserve.	1	43	.....	70	11	1,269	4	3,534	15
Total Volunteers.	3,345	54,056	1,549	32,095	2,141	152,018	187	170,029	10,805
Regular Army...	157	1,890	.....	.....	83	2,749	5	16,360	2
Colored Troops..	124	1,790	46	1,037	90	26,211	24	12,440	427
Grand Total...	3,626	57,736	1,595	33,132	2,314	180,973	216	198,829	11,234

NOTE.—Through the courtesy of Mr. N. A. Strait, publisher, Washington, D. C., this
compiled from the offices of the Adjutant

CASUALTIES

Divided by States and Independent Organizations, from the Commencement of the
August 1, 1865.

Men honorably discharged.	Officers discharged for disability.	Men disch'ged for disability.	Officers dishon'ably disch'ed.	Men dishonob'y discharged.	Officers dismissed.	Officers cashiered.	Officers resign.	Officers mis'g in action.	Men missing in action.	Aggregate cas. ualties.	Number men enlisted dur'g war in which the-o casualties occurred-term from 3 months to 3 years.
9,293	192	6,450	...	47	22	2	457	....		28,097	64,708
2,409	8	2,407	...	...	...	7	262	....		13,201	33,025
4,417	93	4,312	...	24	6	317	...	....		16,071	32,653
11,975	316	12,500	...	11	103	8	797	... .		49,210	126,236
342	28	2,12.	...	42	17	8	253	... .		6,085	21,301
5,451	51	4,361	...	105	58	9	481	21 389		22,805	53,594
32,509	741	24,167	176	455	292	67	2,046	7 1,407		132,298	404,748
2,609	1	6,908	...	47	80	1	599	... .		22,294	67,186
24,070	562	16,706	...	128	237	39	1,121	30 1,522		87,236	323,846
842	13	456	...	...	5	...	35	......		2,868	12,171
1,684	46	826	10	60	57	6	102	... 112		7,548	42,128
4,404	34	2,218	...	52	87	2	303	... .		11,798	32,003
350	.....	218	...	6	1	...	12	... .		1,596	15,181
15,407	335	21,545	...	105	157	16	1,824	....		78,213	307,380
1,552	70	17,115	...	17	235	26	2,664	....		48,568	193,285
1,672	67	23,864	...	223	257	13	3,334	....		72,291	255,938
12,564	210	9,614	...	104	88	5	1,015	....		42,763	87,613
10,912	94	9,219	...	7	57	3	1,093	....		35,846	90,888
1,598	15	2,859	...	...	26	...	229	....		7,050	23,999
21	11	9,031	...	55	22	7	1,304	....		24,980	75,780
7,092	22	7,827	...	182	127	12	1,230	13 588		34,142	108,756
2,047	38	4,097	...	...	63	4	903	....		20,935	74,061
999	8	1,849	1	91	43	4	281	... 35		8,498	20,097
628	6	912	...	4	2	1	43	... .		2,762	7,451
700	25	4,015	...	5	8	3	112	... .		11,970	....
5	1	21	...	...	...	...	...	... .		220	....
20	2	226	...	...	...	...	5	... .		819	....
30	3	69	...	1	...	...	10	... .		561	....
34	.....	96	...	2	4	1	3	... .		1,004	....
14	.....	27	...	7	...	1	15	... .		667	....
304	7	481	...	...	...	...	21	... .		3,058	....
197	10	596	...	2	1	...	16	... .		2,314	....
24	1	69	...	1	...	...	5	... .		1,038	....
337	2	414	...	7	1	...	9	... .		2,370	....
126	2	280	...	...	...	...	7	... .		976	1,762
20	6	263	...	...	...	...	8	... .		1,334	....
73	.....	170	...	...	1	...	4	... .		785	....
6	.....	205	...	1	1	...	2	... .		238	....
10	4	240	...	...	...	...	3	... .		570	3,157
51	2	271	...	...	1	...	9	... .		852	2,395
46	2	378	...	1	1	...	15	... .		1,419	....
209	.....	182	...	8	...	...	10	... .		3,183	....
123	5	233	...	...	...	...	13	... .		1,032	....
1,688	5	8,218	..	285	28	4	129	... .		15,304	60,508
159,764	3,058	209,102	186	2,023	2,143	252	21,090	72 4,085		828,307	....
1,201	2	5,080	...	275	122	6	390	33 1,266		29,637	67,000
2,378	166	6,889	18	191	158	16	801	18 1,275		54,009	180,017
163,343	3,226	221,080	204	2 489	2,423	274	22,281	123 6,626		912,043	....

table is taken from his "Alphabetical List of Battles," an invaluable record of the War,
and Surgeon General at Washington, D. C.

Comparative statement of the number of men furnished and of the deaths in the United States Army during the late war, with percentage of troops to population and percentage of deaths to troops furnished.

States, Territories, &c.	Men furnished.					Percentage of troops to population.	Aggregate number of deaths.	Percentage of deaths to troops furnished.
	White troops.	Sailors and marines.	Colored troops.	Indians.	Total.			
Alabama	2,576				2,576	.2	345	13.4
Arkansas	8,289				8,289	1.9	1,713	20.7
California	15,725				15,725	4.1	573	3.6
Colorado	4,903				4,903	14.3	323	6.6
Connecticut	51,937	2,163	1,764		55,864	12.1	5,354	9.6
Dakota	206				206	4.2	6	.3
Delaware	11,236		94	9 4	12,284	10.9	882	7.2
District of Columbia	11,912	1,353	3,269		16,534	22.2	290	.1
Florida	1,290				1,290	.9	215	16.6
Georgia						.0	15	
Illinois	255,057	2,224	1,811		259,092	15.0	31,831	13.5
Indiana	193,748	1,078	1,537		196,363	14.5	26,672	13.6
Iowa	75,797	5	440		76,242	11.3	13,001	17.
Kansas	18,069		2,080		20,149	18.8	2,630	13.1
Kentucky	51,743	314	23,703		75,760	6 8	10,774	14.2
Louisiana	5,224				5,224	.7	945	18.
Maine	64,973	5,030	104		70,107	11.2	9,398	13.4
Maryland	33,995	3,925	8,718		46,638	6.8	2,982	6.4
Massachusetts	122,781	19,983	3,966		146,730	11.8	13,942	9.5
Michigan	85,479	498	1,387		87,364	11.6	14,753	16.9
Minnesota	23,913	3	104		24,020	13.3	2,584	10.8
Mississippi	545				545	.0	78	14.3
Missouri	100,616	151	8,344		109,111	9.2	13,885	12.7
Nebraska	3,157				3,157	10.9	239	7.6
Nevada	1,080				1,080	15.7	33	3.
New Hampshire	32,930	882	125		33,937	10.4	4,882	14.4
New Jersey	67,500	8,129	1,185		76,814	11.4	5,754	7.5
New Mexico	6,561				6,561	7.0	277	4.2
New York	409,561	35,164	4,125		448,850	11.6	46,534	10.4
North Carolina	3,156				3,156	.8	360	11.4
Ohio	304,814	3,274	5,092		313,180	13.3	35,475	11.3
Oregon	1,810				1,810	3.4	45	2.4
Pennsylvania	315,017	14,307	8,612		337,936	11.6	33,183	9.8
Rhode Island	19,521	1,878	1,837		23,236	13.3	1,321	5.7
Tennessee	31,092				31,092	2.8	6,777	21.8
Texas	1,965				1,965	.3	141	7.2
Vermont	32,549	619	120		33,288	10.6	5,224	15.7
Virginia						.0	42	
Washington	964				964	8.3	22	2.3
West Virginia	31,872		196		32,068	8.1	4,017	12.5
Wisconsin	91,029	133	165		91,327	11.8	12,301	13.4
Indian Nations				3,530	3,530		1,018	28.8
Colored Troops			99,337		*99,337		†36,847	
Veteran Reserve Corps							1,672	
Veteran Vol's (Hancock's (")s)							106	
Vol. Engineers & Sharpsh'ters							552	
U. S. Volunteer Infantry							213	
General and gen. staff officers							239	
Miscellaneous Vols., bands, &c.							232	
Regular Army							5,798	
Grand aggregate	2,494,592	101,207	178,975	3,530	2,778,304		359,528	

* Number not credited upon the quotas of any State.
† Includes losses in all colored organizations excepting three regiments from Mass.

PURSUED BY HOUNDS.

A DIGEST OF THE PENSION LAWS

RELATING TO

THE CIVIL WAR.

Who Are Entitled to Pensions.

First. Any officer of the Army (including regulars, volunteers and militia), or any officer in the Navy or Marine Corps, or any enlisted man, however employed, in the military or naval service of the United States, or in its Marine Corps, whether regularly mustered or not, disabled by reason of any wound or injury received, or disease contracted, while in the service of the United States and in the line of duty.

Second. Any master serving on a gunboat, or any pilot, engineer, sailor, or other person not regularly mustered, serving upon any gunboat or war-vessel of the United States, disabled by any wound or injury received, or otherwise incapacitated, while in the line of duty, for procuring his subsistence by manual labor.

Third. Any acting assistant or contract surgeon disabled by any wound or injury received or disease contracted in the line of duty while actually performing the duties of assistant surgeon or acting assistant surgeon with any military force in the field, or *in transitu* or in hospital.

Fourth. Any provost-marshal, deputy provost-marshal, or enrolling-officer disabled, by reason of any wound or injury, received in the discharge of his duty, to procure a subsistence by manual labor. (413)

Pension of Soldiers and Sailors who have been Totally Disabled.

On and after the passage of this act, all soldiers and sailors who have lost either both their hands or both their feet or the sight of both eyes in the service of the United States, shall receive, in lieu of all pensions now paid them by the Government of the United States, and there shall be paid to them, in the same manner as pensions are now paid to such persons, the sum of seventy-two dollars per month. Approved, June 17, 1878.

Artificial Limbs for Disabled Soldiers, Seamen, and Others.

Every officer, soldier, seaman and marine, who in the line of duty, in the military or naval service of the United States, shall have lost a limb, or sustained bodily injuries, depriving him of the use of any of his limbs, shall receive once every five years an artificial limb or appliance, or commutation therefor, as provided and limited by existing laws, under such regulations as the Surgeon-General of the Army may prescribe; and the period of five years shall be held to commence with the filing of the first application after the seventeenth day of June, in the year eighteen hundred and seventy.

Necessary transportation to have artificial limbs fitted shall be furnished by the Quartermaster-General of the Army, the cost of which shall be refunded out of any money appropriated for the purpose of artificial limbs. This act shall not be subject to the provisions of an act entitled "An act to increase pensions," going into effect June 4, 1874.

Pension to Soldiers Who Have Lost Both an Arm and a Leg.

All persons who, while in the military or naval service of the United States, and in the line of duty, shall have lost one hand and one foot, or been totally and permanently disabled in both, shall be entitled to a pension for each of such disabilities, and at such a rate as is provided for by the provisions of the existing laws for each disability. This act shall not be so construed as to reduce pensions in any case.

An Act Equalizing Pensions of Certain Officers in the Navy.

From and after the passage of this act, the pension for total disability of passed assistant engineers, assistant engineers, and cadet engineers in the naval service, respectively, shall be the same as the pensions allowed to officers of the line in the naval service with whom they have relative rank; and all acts or parts of acts inconsistent herewith are hereby repealed. Approved, March 3, 1877.

An Act Amending the Pension Laws so as to Remove Disabilities.

The law prohibiting the payment of any money on account of pensions to any person, or to the widow, children, or heirs of any deceased person, who, in any manner, engaged in or aided or abetted the late rebellion against the authority of the United States, shall not be construed to apply to such persons as afterward voluntarily enlisted in the Army of the United States, and who, while in such service, incurred disability from a wound or injury received or disease contracted in the line of duty. Approved, March 3, 1877.

[Not held to apply to Navy cases.]

An Act Relating to Commanders in the Navy.

From and after July sixteenth, eighteen hundred and sixty-two, pensions granted to lieutenant-commanders in the Navy for disability, or on account of their death, shall be the same as theretofore provided for lieutenants-commanding.

An Act Relating to Claim Agents and Attorneys in Pension Cases.

It shall be unlawful for any attorney, agent, or other person to demand or receive for his services in a pension case a greater sum than ten dollars. No fee contract shall hereafter be filed with the Commissioner of Pensions in any case. In pending cases in which a fee contract has heretofore been filed, if the pension shall be allowed, the Commissioner of Pensions shall approve the same as to the amount of the fee to be paid at the amount specified in the contract.

An Act to Provide that all Pensions shall Commence from the Date of Death or Discharge from the Service of the United States, for the Payment of Arrears of Pensions, and other Purposes.

All pensions which have been granted under the general laws regulating pensions, or may hereafter be granted, in consequence of death from a cause which originated in the United States service during the continuance of the late war of the rebellion, or in consequence of wounds, injuries, or disease received or contracted in said service during said war of the rebellion, shall commence from the date of the death or discharge from said service of the person on whose account the claim has been or shall hereafter be granted, or from the termination of the right of the party having prior title to such pension. The rate of pension for the intervening time for which arrears of pension are hereby granted shall be the same per month for which the pension was originally granted.

The Commissioner of Pensions is hereby authorized and directed to adopt such rules and regulations for the payment of the arrears of pensions hereby granted as will be necessary to cause to be paid to such pensioner, or, if the pensioner shall have died, to the person or persons entitled to the same, all such arrears of pension as the pensioner may be, or would have been, entitled to under this act.

No claim-agent or other person shall be entitled to receive any compensation for services in making application for arrears of pension.

An Act Relating to Soldiers while in the Civil Service of the United States.

All persons who, under and by virtue of the first section of the act entitled " An act supplementary to the several acts relating to pensions," approved March third, eighteen hundred and sixty-five, were deprived of their pensions during any portion of the time from the third of March, eighteen hundred and sixty-five, to the sixth of June, eighteen hundred and sixty-six, by reason of their being in the civil service of the United States, shall be paid their said pensions, withheld by virtue of said section of the act aforesaid, for and during the said period of time from the third of March, eighteen hundred and sixty-five, to the sixth of June, eighteen hundred and sixty-six. Approved, March 1, 1879.

An Act Making Appropriations for the Payment of the Arrears of Pensions.

The rate at which the arrears of invalid pensions shall be allowed and computed in the cases which have been or shall hereafter be allowed, shall be graded according to the degree of the pensioner's disability from time to time, and the provisions of the pension laws in force over the period for which the arrears shall be computed.

Section one of the act of January twenty-fifth, eighteen hundred and seventy-nine, granting arrears of pensions, shall be construed to extend to and include pensions on account of soldiers who were enlisted or drafted for the service in the war of the rebellion, but died or incurred disability from a cause originating after the cessation of hostilities, and before being mustered out. In no case shall arrears of pensions be allowed and paid from a time prior to the date of actual disability.

27

All pensions which have been, or which may hereafter be, granted in consequence of death occurring from a cause which originated in the service since the fourth day of March, eighteen hundred and sixty-one, or in consequence of wounds or injuries received, or disease contracted since that date, shall commence from the death or discharge of the person on whose account the claim has been or is hereafter granted, if the disability occurred prior to discharge; and if such disability occurred after the discharge, then from the date of actual disability, or from the termination of the right of party having prior title to such pension: *Provided,* The application for such pension has been or is hereafter filed with the Commissioner of Pensions prior to the first day of July, eighteen hundred and eighty, otherwise the pension shall commence from the date of filing the application; but the limitation herein prescribed shall not apply to claims by or in behalf of insane persons and children under sixteen years of age. Approved, March 3, 1879.

***

An Act for the Relief of Soldiers and Sailors Becoming Totally Blind in the Service of the Country.

The act of June seventeenth, eighteen hundred and seventy eight, entitled "An act to increase the pension of certain soldiers and sailors who have lost both their hands or both their feet, or the sight of both eyes, in the service of the country," shall be so construed as to include all soldiers and sailors who have become totally blind from causes occurring in the service of the United States. Approved, March 3, 1879.

***

An Act for the Relief of Certain Pensioners.

All pensioners now on the pension-rolls, or who may hereafter be placed thereon, for amputation of either leg at the hip joint, shall receive a pension at the rate of thirty-seven dollars and fifty cents per month from the date of the approval of this act. Approved, March 3, 1879.

An Act Relating to Appropriations and Examinations.

The Commissioner of Pensions shall have the power to order special examinations, whenever, in his judgment, the same may be necessary, and to increase or reduce the pension according to right and justice; but in no case shall a pension be withdrawn or reduced except upon notice to the pensioner and a hearing upon sworn testimony, except as to the certificate of the examining surgeon. Approved, June 21, 1879.

An Act Regulating Payment of Pensions to Inmates of National Soldiers' Home.

All pensions payable, or to be paid under this act, to pensioners who are inmates of the National Home for Disabled Volunteer Soldiers, shall be paid to the treasurer or treasurers of said Home, upon security given to the satisfaction of the managers, to be disbursed for the benefit of the pensioners without deduction for fines or penalties under regulations to be established by the managers of the Home; said payment to be made by the pension agent upon a certificate of the proper officer of the Home that the pensioner is an inmate thereof and is still living. Any balance of the pension which may remain at the date of the pensioner's discharge shall be paid over to him; and in case of his death at the Home, the same shall be paid to the widow, or children, or in default of either to his legal representatives. Approved, February 26, 1881.

An Act Entailing Pensions.

If any person has died since March fourth, eighteen hundred and sixty-one, or hereafter dies, by reason of any wound, injury, or disease which under the conditions and limitations of previous sections would have entitled him to an invalid pension had he been disabled, his widow, or if there be no widow, or in the case of her death without payment to her of any part of the pension hereinafter mentioned, his child, or children under sixteen years of age, shall be entitled to receive the same pension as the husband or father would have been entitled to had he been totally disabled, to commence from the death of the husband or father, to continue to the widow during her widowhood, and to his child or children until they severally attain the age of sixteen years, and no longer; and if the widow remarry, the child or children shall be entitled from the date of remarriage, except when such widow has continued to draw the pension money after her remarriage, in the contravention of law, and such child or children have resided with and been supported by her, their pension will commence at the date to which the widow was last paid.

Marriages shall be proven in pension cases to be legal marriages according to the law of the place where the parties resided at the time of marriage or at the time when the right to pension accrued; and the open and notorious adulterous cohabitation of a widow who is a pensioner shall operate to terminate her pension from the commencement of such cohabitation.

Pensions not Transferable.

Any pledge, mortgage, sale, assignment, or transfer of any right, claim, or interest in any pension which has been, or may hereafter be, granted, shall be void and of no effect, and any person who shall pledge, or receive as a pledge, mortgage, sale, assignment or transfer of any right, claim, or interest in any pension, or pension certificate, which has been, or may hereafter be granted or issued, or who shall hold the same as collateral security for any debt, or promise, or upon any pretext of such security, or promise, shall be guilty of a misdemeanor, and upon conviction thereof shall be fined in a sum not exceeding one hundred dollars and the costs of the prosecution; and any person who shall retain the certificate of a pensioner and refuse to surrender the same upon the demand of the Commissioner of Pensions, or a United States pension agent, or any other person, authorized by the Commissioner of Pensions, or the pensioner, to receive the same shall be guilty of a misdemeanor, and upon conviction thereof shall be fined in a sum not exceeding one hundred dollars and the costs of the prosecution. Approved, February 28, 1883.

Increase of Pension of Soldiers and Sailors who have lost an Arm or Leg in Service.

From and after the passage of this act all persons on the pension-roll, and all persons hereafter granted a pension, who, while in the military or naval service of the United States, and in the line of duty, shall have lost one hand or one foot, or been totally or permanently disabled in the same, or otherwise so disabled as to render their incapacity to perform manual labor equivalent to the loss of a hand or foot, shall receive a pension of twenty-four dollars per month; all persons now on the pension-roll, and all persons hereafter granted a pension, who in like manner shall have lost either an arm at or above the elbow, or a leg at or above the knee, or shall have been otherwise so disabled as to be incapacitated for performing any manual labor, but not so much as to require regular personal aid and attendance, shall receive a pension of thirty dollars per month: *Provided*, That nothing contained in this act shall be construed to change the rate of eighteen dollars per month to be proportionately divided for any degree of disability established for which no provision is made. Approved, March 3, 1883.

An Act Relating to Intent to Defraud.

Every person who, with intent to defraud either the United States or any person, falsely assumes or pretends to be an officer or employee acting under the authority of the United

States, or any Department, or any officer of the Government thereof, and who shall take upon himself to act as such, or who shall in such pretended character demand or obtain from any person or from the United States, or any Department, or any officer of the Government thereof, any money, paper, document, or other valuable thing, shall be deemed guilty of felony, and shall, on conviction thereof, be punished by a fine of not more than one thousand dollars, or imprisonment not longer than three years, or both said punishments, in the discretion of the court. Approved, April 18, 1884.

An Act to Provide for the Muster and Pay of Certain Officers and Enlisted Men of the Volunteer Forces.

Any person who was duly appointed and commissioned, whether his commission was actually received by him or not, shall be considered as commissioned to the grade named from the date when his commission was actually issued by competent authority, and shall be entitled to all pay and emoluments as if actually mustered at such date: *Provided,* That at the date of his commission he was actually performing the duties of the grade to which he was so commissioned, or, if not so performing such duties, then from such time after the date of his commission as he may have actually entered upon such duties: *And provided further,* That any person held as a prisoner of war, or who may have been absent by reason of wounds, or in hospital by reason of disability received in the service in the line of duty, at the date of his commission, if a vacancy existed for him in the grade to which so commissioned, shall be entitled to the same pay and emoluments as if actually performing the duties of the grade to which he was commissioned and actually mustered at such date. *And provided further,* That this act and the resolution hereby amended shall be construed to apply only in those cases where the commission bears date prior to June twentieth, eighteen hundre~

and sixty three, or after that date when their commands were not below the minimum number required by existing laws and regulations: *And provided further*, That the pay and allowances actually received shall be deducted from the sums to be paid under this act.

The heirs or legal representatives of any officer whose muster into the service has been or shall be amended hereby shall be entitled to receive the arrears of pay due such officer, and the pension, if any, authorized by law for the grade into which such officer is mustered under the provisions of this act.

All claims arising under this act shall be presented to and filed in the proper department within three years from and after the passage hereof, and all such claims not so presented and filed within said three years shall be forever barred, and no allowance ever made thereon.

The pay and allowances of a rank or grade paid to and received by any military or naval officer in good faith for services actually performed by such officer in such rank or grade during the war of the rebellion shall not be charged to or recovered back from such officer because of any defect in the title of such officer to the office, rank, or grade in which such services were so actually performed. Approved, June 3, 1884.

Articles of Agreement in Obtaining Pensions.

Whereas I,——————, late a—— in company——of the——regiment of——volunteers, war of eighteen hundred and sixty-one (or, if the service be different, here state the same), having made application for pension under the laws of the United States:

Now, this agreement witnesseth, that for and in consideration of services done and to be done in the premises, I hereby agree to allow my attorney,—————— of ——, the fee of —— dollars, which shall include all amounts to be paid for

any service in furtherance of said claim ; and said fee shall not
be demanded by or payable to my said attorney (or attorneys),
in whole or in part, except in case of the granting of my pension by the Commissioner of Pensions; and then the same
shall be paid to him (or them) in accordance with the provisions of existing laws.

(Claimant's signature.)
(Two witnesses' signatures.)

STATE OF ———
    County of ——— *ss.*

Be it known that on this, the ——— day of ———Anno
Domini eighteen hundred and eighty ——, personally appeared
the above named ———————, who, after having had read
over to ——, in the hearing and presence of the two attesting
witnesses, the contents of the foregoing articles of agreement,
voluntarily signed and acknowledged the same to be———free
act and deed.

(Official signature.)

And now, to wit, this———day of———Anno Domini
eighteen hundred and eighty——, I (or we) accept the provisions contained in the foregoing articles of agreement, and will,
to the best of my (or our) ability, endeavor faithfully to repre-
sent the interest of the claimant in the premises.

Witness my (or our) hand, the day and year first above
written.

(Signature of attorney.)

STATE OF———
    County of———, *ss.*

Personally came———, whom I know to be the
person he represents himself to be, and who, having signed
above acceptance of agreement, acknowledged the same to be
——free act and deed.

(Official signature.)

And if in the adjudication of any claim for pension in which
such articles of agreement have been, or may hereafter be,

filed, it shall appear that the claimant had, prior to the execution thereof, paid to the attorney any sum for his services in such claim, and the amount so paid is not stipulated therein, then every such claim shall be adjudicated in the same manner as though no articles of agreement had been filed, deducting from the fee of ten dollars allowed by law such sum as claimant shall show that he has paid to his said attorney.

Any agent or attorney or other person instrumental in prosecuting any claim for pension or bounty land, who shall directly or indirectly contract for, demand or receive or retain any greater compensation for his services or instrumentality in prosecuting a claim for pension or bounty land than is herein provided, or for payment thereof at any other time or in any other manner than is herein provided, or who shall wrongfully withhold from a pensioner or claimant the whole or any part of the pension or claim allowed and due such pensioner or claimant, or the land warrant issued to any such claimant, shall be deemed guilty of misdemeanor, and upon conviction thereof, shall for every such offence be fined not exceeding five hundred dollars, or imprisoned at hard labor not exceeding two years, or both, in the discretion of the court.

An Act to Relieve Certain Soldiers from the Charge of Desertion.

The charge of desertion now standing on the rolls and records in the office of the Adjutant-General of the United States against any soldier who served in the late war in the volunteer service shall be removed in all cases where it shall be made to appear to the satisfaction of the Secretary of War, from such rolls and records, or from other satisfactory testimony, that any such soldier served faithfully until the expiration of his term of enlistment, or until May 1, 1865, having previously served six months or more, or was prevented from completing his term of service by reason of wounds received or disease contracted in the line of duty, but who, by reason of absence from his command at the time the same was mustered out, failed to be mustered out and to receive an honorable discharge: *Provided*, That no soldier shall be relieved under this section who, not being sick or wounded, left his command without proper authority whilst the same was in the presence of the enemy.

The Secretary of War is hereby authorized to remove the charge of desertion from the records of any soldier in the late war upon proper application therefor and satisfactory proof in the following cases:

First. That such soldier, after such charge of desertion was made, and within a reasonable time thereafter, voluntarily returned to his command and served faithfully to the end of his term of service.

Second. That such soldier absented himself without proper authority from hospital, or from furlough given from hospital, while suffering from wounds, injuries, or diseases received or contracted in the service in the line of duty, and, on recovery, voluntarily returned to his command and served faithfully until discharged, or died from such wounds, injury, or disease while so absent and before the date of the muster out of his command.

Third. That such soldier absented himself without proper authority from furlough given by proper authority, and while so absent died from wounds, injury, or disease received or contracted in the service in the line of duty before the muster out of his command.

In all cases where the charge of desertion shall be removed under the provisions of this act from the record of any soldier who has not received a certificate of discharge, it shall be the duty of the Adjutant-General of the United States to issue to such soldier, or, in case of his death, to his heirs or legal representatives, a certificate of discharge.

When the charge of desertion shall be removed under the provisions of this act from the record of any soldier, such soldier, or, in case of his death, the heirs or legal representatives of such soldier, shall receive the pay and bounty due to such soldier; *Provided, however,* That this act shall not be so construed as to give to any such soldier, or, in case of his death, to the heirs or legal representatives of any such soldier, any pay, bounty or allowance for any period of time during which such soldier was absent from his command without proper authority, nor shall it be so construed as to give any pay, bounty or allowance to any soldier, his heirs or legal representatives who served in the army a period of less than six months.

All applications for relief under this act shall be made to and filed with the Secretary of War within the period of five years from and after its passage, and all applications not so made and filed within said term of five years shall be forever barred, and shall not be received or considered. Approved, July 5, 1884.

An Act Relating to Loss of Arms.

All soldiers and sailors of the United States who have had an arm taken off at the shoulder joint, caused by injuries received in the service of their country while in the line of duty, and who are now receiving pensions, shall have their pensions increased to the same amount that the law now gives to soldiers and sailors who have lost a leg at the hip-joint; and this act shall apply to all who shall be hereafter placed on the pension roll. Approved, March 3, 1885.

LATEST ACTS OF CONGRESS GOVERNING PENSIONS.

Loss of both hands...................$72 00 per mo.   Act June 17, 1878.
  "   "   feet................... 72 00   "   "   "   "
  "   "   eyes................... 72 00   "   "   "   "
Loss of one eye, the other lost before
  enlistment...................... 72 00   "   "   "   "
Disabled to an extent requiring regu-
  lar aid and attendance........... 72 00   "   "   "   "
Total loss of use of both hands...... 72 00   "   "   "   "
Loss of one hand and one foot...... 36 00 per mo.   Act Feb. 28, 1877.
Loss of use of one hand and one foot. 36 00   "   "   "   "
Loss of hand or foot.... .... 30 00 per mo.   Act Aug. 4, 1886.
  "   arm or leg............................ 36 00   "   "   "   "
  "   arm at shoulder joint.............. 45 00   "   "   "   "
  "   leg at hip joint........................ 45 00   "   "   "   "
Inability to perform manual labor...... 50 00   "   "   "   "
Totally disabled and requiring constant
  aid and attendance......................... 72 00   "   "   "   "
Total deafness in both ears................. 30 00 per mo.   Act Aug. 27, 1888.
Loss of both hands..........................100 00 per mo.   Act Feb. 13, 1889.

The Pension of Widows, Minor Children, and Dependant Relatives, is increased from $8 to $12 per month, under Act of March 19, 1886.

Pensions are rated according to the disability of the person to perform manual labor—the rating being arrived at by means of medical examinations made by Boards of Examining Surgeons appointed by the Commissioner of Pensions.

MONTHLY RATES OF PENSION. 429

TABLE 7.—*Statement showing the different monthly rates of pension, and the number pensioned at each rate, of the army and navy invalids, and of the army and navy widows, minors and dependents (war of 1861) on the roll June 30, 1888.*

Rates	Army	Navy	Total	Army	Navy	Total
$1.00	272	11	283			
1.87	2		2			
2.00	31,392	330	31,722			
2.12½	3		3			
2.25	1		4			
2.50	2	1	3			
2.06	7		7			
2.66⅔	38		38			
3.00	1,893	12	1,935			
3.12		1	1			
3.75	337	11	318			
4.00	68,563	647	69,210			
4.25	126		426			
5.00	1,402	60	1,462			
5.25	2		2			
5.33	12	1	13			
5.33⅓	35		35			
5.66⅔	6		6			
5.75	16		16			
6.00	47,267	394	47,661			
6.25	73	3	76			
6.37	2		2			
6.37½	2		2			
6.66⅔	2		2			
6.75	2	1	3			
7.00	212	3	215			
7.25	13	1	14			
7.50	901	24	925			
7.66⅔	1		1			
7.75	19	2	21			
8.00	62,362	780	63,142	304	4	308
8.12½	1		1			
8.25	24		21			
8.50	1,133	1	1,134			
8.66	1		1			
8.75	8	2	10			
9.00	367	8	375			
9.25	22		22			
9.50	27	8	35			
9.75	10	4	14			
10.00	18,826	220	19,046	4	2	6
10.25	16	2	18			
10.50	28	9	37			
10.66	1		1			
10.75		15	15			
11.00	52	10	62			
11.25	463	20	483			
11.33	1		1			
11.33⅓	9		9			
11.50	22	3	25			
11.75	22	3	25			
12.00	21,787	291	25,078	84,132	1,498	85,630
12.12½	6		6			
12.25	15		15			
12.50	187	21	211	3	1	4
12.75	706	1	707			
13.00	311	17	328			
13.12	1		1			
13.25	8	11	19			
13.33	6		6			
13.33⅓	1		1			
13.50	35	5	40			
13.75	15	1	16			
14.00	6,504	51	6,555			
14.25	31	4	35			
14.50	8	2	10			
14.75	14		11			
14.87½	1		1			
15.00	2,261	73	2,334	1,167	96	1,263
15.25	2		2			
15.50	6	2	8			
15.75	1	8	9			
16.00	11,782	86	11,868	1	1	2
16.25	12	1	13			
16.50	16	2	18			
16.75	20	1	21			
17.00	2,637	19	2,656	1,908	3	1,911
17.25	1	2	3			
17.50	21	7	31			
17.75	7		7			
18.00	2,492	46	2,538	16		16
18.25		5	5			
18.50	14	1	15			
18.75	12	2	130			
19.00	172	2	174			
19.25	11		11			
19.50		2	2			
20.00	1,616	36	1,652	2,059	123	2,182
20.75	2	1	3			
21.00	7		7			
21.25	2		2			
21.87		1	1			
22.00	1		1			
22.50	90	2	92			
23.25	3		3			
23.50	1		1			
23.75	1	2	3			
24.00	13,331	191	13,522	2		2
24.50	2		2			
25.00	382	6	388	578	111	689
25.25	1		1			
26.25	1		1			
26.75	1	2	3			
27.50	6		6			
30.00	11,096	161	11,257	588	194	782
30.75		2	2			
31.25	88		88			
32.00		3	3			
32.50		3	3			
35.00	2	2	4	1		1
35.50		2	2			
36.00	2,888	39	2,927			
37.50		1	1			
38.50		1	1			
40.00	24		24	5	2	7
40.25		1	1			
42.00		1	1			
45.00	2,519	21	2,540	3		3
46.00	1		1			
49.00	1		1			
50.00	1,403	27	1,430	90	47	116
51.00	1		1			
60.00				1	1	2
72.00	1,024	29	1,053			
100.00	2		2	3		3
166.66⅔				4		4
416.66⅔				3		3
	323,020	3,815	326,835	90,882	2,083	92,965

AVERAGE AGE AND DEATH AGE OF PENSIONERS.

The average age of the pensioners upon the roll in 1888 was fifty years, within a few days.

The average age of invalid pensioners of the war of 1861-'65 at date of death was fifty-six years; widows of the late war, sixty-one years; fathers of the late war, seventy-nine years; mothers of the late war, seventy-five years; pensioners of wars prior to 1861, eighty-two years. The general average of all was sixty-seven years, which may be taken to establish pretty fairly the average duration of the lives of pensioners now borne upon the rolls.

AVERAGE LENGTH OF SERVICE OF PENSIONERS.

The following table shows that the average pensioner served more than two years before being disabled by disease or wounds.

Statement showing number and kind of pension granted and average length of service.

Kind.	No. of cases.	Total length of service.			Average length of service.		
		Yrs.	*mos.*	*dys.*	*Yrs.*	*mos.*	*dys.*
Late war invalids, - - - - -	21,723	50,288	5	18	2	3	11
Late war widows, - - - - -	3,718	6,391	9	26	1	8	17
Navy, - - - - - - -	513	1,240	1	22	2	2	18
Mexican war survivors, - - - -	6,712	6,830	5	18	1	0	3
Mexican war widows, - - - - -	3,583	3,612	7	20	0	11	29

(1) There survive thirty-seven revolutionary pensioners, being the widows of men who served in that war. There are no survivors of that war. Three persons have been pensioned by special act, as descendants of soldiers of the Revolutionary war.

(2) There are 11,593 pensioners of the war of 1812, 806 being survivors, and 10,787 being widows.

(3) There are 21,164 pensioners of the war with Mexico; 16,060 survivors, and 5,104 widows.

(4) There are 419,763 pensioners of the war of the Rebellion, of whom 326,835 are soldiers and sailors, and the remainder are widows and dependents.—*From Commissioner of Pension's Report*, 1888.

SUMMARY OF PAGES.

Text, ...	430
Illustrations unpaged, ...	50
Total number of pages, ...	480